Tideline

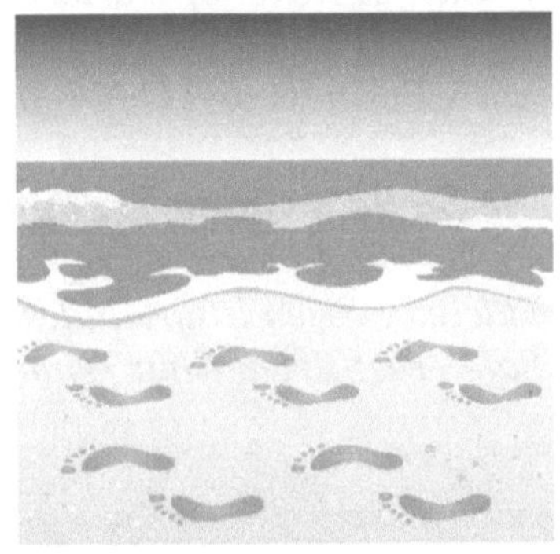

Friendship Abides

Tideline

Friendship Abides

Part Two of the
Stella's Game Trilogy

John D. Beatty

JDB COMMUNICATIONS, LLC
WEST ALLIS, WISCONSIN

First Paperback Edition ISBN 978-1-7347952-0-2
First E-Pub Edition ISBN 978-1-7347952-1-9

"Blood On/Upon the Risers"
Circa 1942

"Snowblind Friend"
Lyrics by Hoyt Axton
Performed by Steppenwolf
Copyright © 1969 Universal Music Publishing Group

"Here I Go Again"
Lyrics by David Coverdale and Bernie Marsden
Performed by Whitesnake
Copyright © 1982 Geffen/A&M

"Rangers in the Night"
Lyrics and Performance by 2nd Platoon, C Company,
3rd Battalion, 325th Infantry, 82nd Airborne Division
Copyright © 1974 Rudy Pestalozzi (unpublished)

"Lake Shore Drive"
Lyrics by Skip Haynes
Performed by Aliotta, Haynes and Jeremiah
Copyright © 1970 Bigfoot Records

"Up Where We Belong"
Lyrics by Jack Nitzsche, Buffy Saint-Marie, Will Jennings
Performed by Joe Cocker and Jennifer Warnes
Copyright © 1982 Sony/ATV Music Publishing LLC

*To every woman in uniform
and to every section/squad wife
with whom I shared
chow, classes, conversations,
desks, drinks, guard posts,
holiday meals far from home,
guarded kisses,
hugs, inspections, laughs,
long rides, marches and flights,
podiums, PT, ranges, rations,
talks, tears, tents,
walks, work,
and washers and dryers
between 1973 to 2001...
I offer my loving gratitude*

Apologia

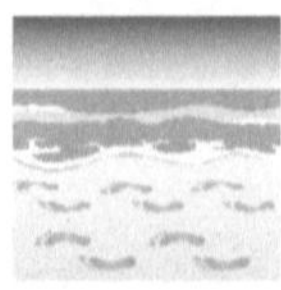

The Stella's Game Trilogy—of which this is the *second* part— is a group of interlinked stories told through four narrators; other characters come and go like wraiths. Since the *whole* story takes place over the course of nearly a quarter century and starts with young children, this is a narrative necessity.

Historical events punctuate everyone's life. The characters in this story saw remarkable history unfold. Some of those events both anchor and influence their stories.

***

To the residents of Key West, Florida and metropolitan Detroit, Michigan I offer my sincere apologies for twisting your real estate— adding and taking away some things—for story-telling purposes. The Conch Republic is a quite real marketing gimmick; Bloomfield Hills, Bloomfield and Birmingham borders were redrawn three times in the twenty-four years I lived there, so I drew the lines *my* way.

To my fellow alum and many friends of the *real* Brookfield/Greenbrier: I had to bend our stories and our *alma maters* more than a little. Thanks for the beautiful and true memories, *and* for the real DeHavens.

To my family: you know the *real* stories. Forgive my distortion of them…and the liberties I take. The truth is nobody else's business.

To Pilgrim Congregational Church at Adams and Big Beaver: We *were* members; my mother's parent's signatures *are* on the charter; my father and grandmother *were* eulogized there, and my sister *was* married there. The little church will always be meaningful to me.

To the US Army: creating JJ's, Leigh's and Mike's careers I bent *their* stories a little, too. Leigh's career as an MP predates the first women to wear the brassard by three years and the NAW program didn't exist, but it's all for the sake of the story. Thanks for the quarter-century you put up with me.

To the US Navy: Ann's story is a pastiche of internet research and a little first-hand knowledge of my sister service, maybe right and maybe wrong. A tip of the brain bucket to the intrepid *real* first mermaids, whoever you were.

And again, to the *real* Wolverine…I got *nothin.*'

Cast of Characters

The Narrators

Mike Dietz: Ranger, linguist, interrogator, counterintelligence agent
JJ Elrath: Ranger, information analyst
Ann Mueller: Diver, storekeeper, hull technician
Leigh Taylor: Military policewoman, criminal investigator

Dramatis Personae

Sam Potts—*Ann's friend*
Donna Hammerfest—*Blonde bombshell*
Debbie Ford—*Ann's friend*

Jenny Jacobs Kent—*JJ's friend*
Evan Hammerfest—*Donna's father*
Nick Paulson—*Donna's friend*
Bob Bell—*Carol Bell Mueller's brother*

Randy Newhouse IV—*Leigh's ex-husband*

Joe Dryden—*minion*
Dave Harriman—*minion*

Sid Jackwell—*Provider of services*
Eddie Evans—*JJ's friend*

Adam Block—*Provider of services*

Dave DeHaven—*JJ's former house master*

Marie DeHaven—*Dave's wife*
Karen DeHaven Watson—*JJ's friend*
Clare DeHaven Alton—*JJ's friend*

Ramdas Brahmaputra-Reynolds—*Mike and JJ's classmate*

Sarah Silverman Simonetti—*Mike and JJ's classmate*

4th Battalion, 75th Infantry (Ranger)—JJ's Unit

Tom Merrill—*boss*

Gary Semitone—*fellow NCO*

Nancy Anvers—*Spanish linguist*
Liz Devens—*Spanish linguist*
Alice Semitone—*friend*

The Mermaids—Ann's Unit

Kristin Collins—*dive buddy*

Betty Sadowski—*mermaid*
Laura Gutierrez—*mermaid*

The Dietz's—Mike's Family

Ben Dietz—*father*
Sara Dietz Halliwell—*sister*
Kiera Dietz Grun—*sister*

Monica Dietz—*mother*
Oliver Halliwell—*brother-in-law*
Norman Grun—*brother-in-law*

The Elrath/Parkinson's—JJ's Family

Stella Elrath Parkinson—*mother*
Brenda Elrath Jones—*sister*
Lois Elrath McHenry—*sister*
Charlie Parkinson Junior—*stepbrother*
Kurt Parkinson—*stepbrother*

Will Parkinson—*stepbrother*

Charlie Parkinson—*stepfather*
Roy Jones—*brother-in-law*
Simon McHenry—*brother-in-law*
Dorothy Parkinson—*sister-in-law*
Julia Parkinson Addison—*stepniece*
Mary Parkinson—*sister-in-law*
Jo—*stepniece*
Anita Parkinson—*sister-in-law*

The Mueller/Savio's—Ann's Family

Howard Mueller—*father*
George Mueller—*brother*
Jim Mueller—*brother*
Barbara Savio Mueller—*stepmother*

Claudia Mueller—*mother*
Holly Cresto Mueller—*sister-in-law*
Carol Bell Mueller—*sister-in-law*
Jenna Savio—*stepsister*
Alex Savio—*stepbrother*

The Taylor's—Leigh's Family

Ed Taylor—*father*

Cathy Taylor—*mother*

Not That Long Ago

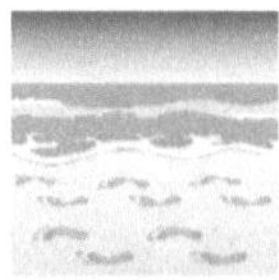

Another stop to make...

The new house on Birch Lake, where his old one had been, *looked* familiar because they had kept all that was worth keeping of the old one —the fieldstone porch, fireplace and chimney—and the geometry of the lot made them keep the same footprint. They also kept the interior layout: formal staircase leading upstairs just off the front entryway; living room to the right; dining room to the left.

Where the garage-cum-family room had been was now a great room with a vaulted ceiling. He marveled at the long island in the kitchen—*Mom would have loved it*—and at the massive limestone fireplace that stood where the back-up furnace had been, the appliance that never caught up to demand.

He walked around the place with the new owner, who asked him where the septic tank was. Right there, just in front of those flower beds, he pointed. *Spent a weekend looking for it in '67.*

An old Polaroid of the house had hung on his wall for years. He decided to give it to the current owners of the lot: no one *else* would have cared about it. Just before he gave the picture away, his wife noticed that it had people in it: in all the years that picture had hung on their wall, he had never noticed.

There's Dad and Mom and Brenda and Lois in short sleeves in the shadows on the porch.

We took those torn-up screens off it while we were moving in in '67. That picture could only have been taken in the summer of '68; the last summer Dad was alive...the only summer he spent there.

And Mom's dealing cards...

Turn the page...

1974

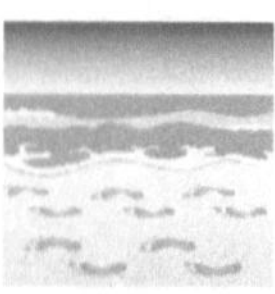

March

Mom: your deal...Hi, Clare...and Cloud! Are you playing Stella's Game too?

You're mine, Johnny.

He blinked in a quiet, softly-lit room, feeling like he was *still* falling. *There THEY were. Then I hit the ground like a skid of bricks and did my BEST landing EVER. Now HERE I am and here's...where?*

A woman in a white uniform sat on a stool nearby. He blinked at her; she smiled; said something he couldn't make out. He shook his head to get the cobwebs out—*big* mistake—because nausea hit him in a rising wave.

"Sorry," he mumbled as she wiped his face over a basin a little later.

"It's *OK*, John." She laid him back down as a tall, thin captain in a white coat softly entered.

"To be expected, Private," the captain quietly declared. "Your head's still convinced you're falling. I'm Doctor Malenkov; I'll be your primary until you're cleared for full duty. Do you know *where* you *are*?"

Private First Class (PFC) John Jacob Elrath—JJ to nearly everyone—stared at him. "Winn Army Hospital?"

"Right. Remember what happened?" The doctor flashed a light into JJ's eyes briefly, felt his pulse.

"Ah...a double-malfunction."

"That's right: *neither* parachute opened correctly. How do you *feel*?"

I hurt all over. "Not as bad as...*ugh*; can't really tell."

"Expect *that*, too. Did you see red before you hit?"

"Yessir."

"That's redout, the opposite of blackout: caused by gravity only in reverse. Just rest now. Ms. Baker will stay with you."

JJ paid more attention to Ms. Baker's uniform as the doctor left. *Chief Warrant Officer Second Class.* "Didn't mean to throw up on you, Chief."

"Just call me *April* today, John," she smiled. "Getting puked on's what I get paid for."

"You're a physician's assistant?"

"Yep." She rolled her stool closer. "I need to apologize. When we lifted off the drop zone, you started to go into shock. I provided the best warmth

I *had*: me. I, ah…" She looked away. "Unprofessional."

April was brown-eyed-pretty, buxom and hippy with dark blonde hair, maybe five years older than he. *I kinda remember…she held her chest to my head on the litter.* "*I* won't tell anybody if…"

"Two medics, the safety officer and the MP on the medevac helicopter *all* saw it."

Of all the things she had to worry about. "Pretty sure *they* won't say anything."

She smiled. "Maybe not. *You're* my first double-mal."

He *felt*, more than anything else, exhausted with a buzzing headache. An orderly brought white soda and a packet of crackers, which made him feel not *better* but *less-bad*.

Dr. Malenkov returned. "Well, Private, *good* news is you didn't break much more than your fall. Orthopedics will show you your x-rays; neurology will talk to you about the redout. Feel like sitting up?"

"How long have I been doped up, sir?" They had x-rayed every part of him…he could remember *that*, groggily.

He checked the chart. "Five milligrams of diazepam four hours ago. Ready?"

"Yessir." They put him in a wheelchair pushed by a hulking big guy who looked at JJ like he was a ghost. They pushed him into a long, tiled room with a wall covered by x-ray films.

"*Wow*," April gaped.

Yeah: wow. "All *mine*?"

"Yeah. That's *you*."

A major with thick, heavy glasses and straggly hair in a bun swept into the room and mumbled a name, followed by "orthopedics." She smiled at JJ, nodded to April, and gazed at the x-rays; her arms crossed. "Private, *I* haven't seen anything like *this* before, but others *have*. Here," she pointed. "Cracked ribs. We'll tape them. Here," she pointed to two others. "Your ankles: *twisted*, not fractured: we'll tape *them*. We *thought* your right shoulder was dislocated, but the x-ray says it *wasn't*." She shook her head. "*Every joint* in your body *moved*, young man," she sighed, "and there isn't a *damn* thing *anyone* will be able to do for you."

What the hell does THAT mean? A fair young captain with a soothing voice showed him his skull x-rays. "I don't see any hemorrhaging, and your eyes are clear. That headache and the buzzing should pass in a few days."

After the doctors left, JJ's First Sergeant and Sergeant Major came in, accompanied by a Master Sergeant he didn't recognize. After a few "you OK" and "Goddamn lucky" phrases, the First Shirt—a balding, broad-shouldered man named Soper with old Love/Hate tattoos on his hands—

smiled at April: "give us a moment, Chief?" She nodded and left.

"JJ," the Sergeant Major—a cheery-looking but taciturn man named Davis—murmured, "do you want to press charges? Those parachutes should *not* have been in the *bin*, let alone *issued*."

"If I'm not mistaken, Sergeant Major, I press *one* I have to press them *all*."

"That's right," the Master Sergeant—who had oddly uneven ears—answered. "Everyone from the jumpmaster through the riggers: everyone who *inspected* them, everyone who *touched* them."

"Top, who's *he*?" JJ glanced at Soper and nodded at the unknown NCO.

"Friend of ours with the Judge Advocate General's office."

The JAG's just doing their job. Jumpmaster's my section sergeant. He's a good guy; got me this job right out of school; got a kid on the way. "No; no charges."

"Take your time, JJ," the JAG NCO replied. "You have a month to…"

"No," JJ repeated. "No charges."

"*Your* call," Davis declared, "but *we'll* make sure *they* never screw up *that* bad again."

"Top: Sergeant Merrill had nothing to do with *me*. I went through inspection with one of the others…didn't know him." Before every jump, the jumpmaster and his assistants inspected the rigged jumpers and their gear. *Good* inspectors *might not* have allowed JJ to jump with *that* equipment; *harried* or *hurried* ones, even if *good*, *might* have anyway.

"OK," Soper answered, "just remember: responsibility can be *delegated*, but never *diminished*. Sergeant Merrill was responsible for the *jumpers*, so *he*…"

"Top, this was his first gig as a jumpmaster and his wife's pregnant. He needs *this* hassle like we *all* need a dose of the clap. Ain't it *our* job to take care of the men *and* the NCOs?"

All three sergeants smiled. "So it *is*," Soper murmured. "OK: The riggers were going to be doing every weekend and holiday requirement between now and the time they leave here anyway, but Merrill and his assistants…we'll think of something."

"Thanks, Top. Now, if you'll excuse me, the medics want to tape me up so I can get out of here."

Davis hesitated. "Want *another* jump *today*?"

I'm eighteen, and immortal…gotta get back on that horse. "Sure, Smage," JJ grunted, using the contraction for *Sergeant-Major*.

The drop zone safety officer—a company commander in the Ranger battalion—and a warrant officer/MP filled out the accident report with him while they taped his ankles and ribs with April standing by. A woman from the Veteran's Administration got his signature on a claim form; she was vague but thought that a disability pension—for reasons unclear to him—was likely. Sergeant Tom Merrill, an open-faced, bulky man with thinning but coarse black hair, brought a set of fatigues to replace those they cut off him.

JJ did a perfect landing on tiny Munsan DZ with a pathfinder class just as the sun was going down—his first solo drop from a helicopter. *Softer landing when the 'chute opens...*

Tom took JJ home with him for dinner, where he met Connie, an attractive, pleasant, and solid brunette in her fourth month of pregnancy. Connie reminded him a great deal of both his 5th Grade teacher and a high school friend—a fair-haired, curvy girl named Jenny.

But all he could *think* about was that image of two *other* brown-eyed pretty girls: his childhood friend Cloud—Claudia Mueller—and his high school friend/*not*-girlfriend/*sort-of* foster sister Clare DeHaven (*their* relationship was complicated) playing cards with his mom. The last time he saw his Cloud was in 1968, on the day of his father's funeral: he had *wanted* to see her ever since.

But it WAS her voice... I haven't heard it since '70...and Clare owes me a letter.

***

Johnny? What...?

She awoke with a start, then gazed at the window and the blinking neon sign outside, watching the curtains wafting gently in the breeze of the hotel room's air conditioner/space heater.

"Ann," the guy under the sheets mumbled. "Ann, you OK?"

Don? Don. "Fine, babe. Go back to sleep."

"You were talking in your sleep. Thought I heard my name." He touched her bare hip.

No, you didn't; sorry. "Just had a dream, babe." *Had a dream of Johnny.* She held his hand until he went back to sleep.

Seaman Second Class Claudia Ann Mueller got up from the so-so bed, pulled a shirt on, and sat in an uncomfortable chair, waiting. That's what she did these days: wait. Working as a Navy storekeeper, she was *waiting* for her next stage of training—hull technician in a couple of years...they *said*. With luck, perseverance and another enlistment contract, she'd train as a Navy diver in *about* four years...they *said*.

That's why she joined the Navy: to be one of the first *female* Navy diver ratings. She'd been diving since she was fourteen; got a C-card just after she finished 10th Grade. She *swam,* she *thought,* because she was *alive,* but she *knew* it was to escape her mother's growing madness. She *dove,* she *knew,* so she could see Johnny's face deep underwater: the image she had kept since she last saw him.

Johnny; we may never see each other again. I couldn't wait forever.

So, here was Don; a fellow storekeeper (in a different warehouse); a fellow E-2; a fellow…former virgin? *That* was hard to describe in the '70s. Sexual Revolution or not, she waited to make *that* decision just two months ago, with Don. He was a year older than she and from Minnesota, so they *also* had the Great Lakes in common. But in *Today's Navy,* there was no "dating" shipmates like civilians did. But there *was…this*: sharing a bed and some fluids in a two-star hotel room in a dark corner of Panama City on a payday weekend…or sometimes less than *this.*

Don's a good guy, Johnny: you'd like him.

"And you're a Sixty-Day Wonder," she whispered in the dark. *Sixty Day Wonder* was slang for the for-now lovers that some sailors took. *Sixty Day* because *every* duty morning might bring transfer orders effective *two months* hence. "Rather it was *you,* sweetie." She tried *not* to think like that, but she knew their separation was inevitable because she'd be in for at least eight years to get what she wanted…but at eighteen, pop culture being what *it* was and hormones what *they* were, she had *needs.*

Strictly speaking, intimate relationships like what Ann and Don had were more-or-less *verboten,* but the brass knew it was impossible to stop them because the military was becoming just another workplace in the '70s. But the policies regarding how servicemembers interacted were stuck in the '40s…and nearly everyone knew it. Women in all the services were performing more jobs every fiscal quarter that *had been* the exclusive domains of men, and were working cheek-by-jowl, day-in-and-day-out with their male counterparts. And the inevitable—like *this*—happened.

And Ann woke up in a hotel room dreaming of Johnny after having *comfortable, pleasant* sex with a guy she *liked* but barely *knew.*

Then New Year's Eve '71 came back to her. She *felt* she saw Johnny across a snow-covered field, where their Safe Tree was. *Was it him?*

She crawled back into bed with Don and drifted off, dreaming of her Johnny's beautiful blue eyes.

I NEED what Don provides, Johnny. I'm sorry. Just don't forget me.

***

"*Dietz!*" the mail clerk shouted over the chatter of people waiting to hear their name called.

"*Yo!*" PFC Mike Dietz answered, reaching for the envelope. "What's *your* problem?" The clerk was giving him a funny look as the envelope changed hands. *It's from Leigh!*

"Don't get that much from APOs is all. Family?"

"Yeah," Mike hedged, not wanting to have to explain what *mishpachah*—extended family—meant then-and-there. He had known Leigh Taylor since 7th Grade. She had joined the Army at the same time he did. He went to language school; she to the military police. Now, having learned written Russian and expanded his vocabulary (he spoke it at home), Mike was learning to be a military intelligence interrogator.

Fort Huachuca to Korea and back in…30 days? Not bad.

> *Sandy, dear*
> *…At least you're laying it on, period. Don't hesitate to tell me whatever you want—we've never pulled any punches before…*

She had given him his nickname: Sandy. He *thought* his earlier correspondence with his old junior high lab partner (and *somewhat* more later) had been a bit *too* intimate, but she…*didn't*. As he often did, he opened his reply with the Yiddish word for "treasure:"

> *Oytzer*
> *Not sure why I told you about Mary that way, but…eh, my*
> *upbringing. Jews don't confess. If we did, there wouldn't time*
> *for anything else because we always feel guilty about something.*
> *But I had to tell <u>someone</u>. Sorry I put you on the spot like that.*

There, in interrogator school, he teamed with Emily Naris—one of only three women in the class. And, one long weekend…

> *…A woman I'm partnered with here, Emily…we got too drunk*
> *and…yeah, you get the idea…Like you said, Leigh: we're going*
> *to be apart, maybe for years. We'll have lovers, but as soon as I*
> *don't <u>want</u> to tell you about mine, I'll let you know.*

Emily had wavy red hair, fair skin, soft brown eyes, and a curvy physique and was nicknamed Venus because she bore a great resemblance to Botticelli's "Birth of Venus."

Venus a Sixty-Day Jane? Probably less than that.

Sixty-Day Jane was Army *men's* slang for *their* in-service, in-uniform, for-now lovers: Army *women* called *theirs Sixty-Day Joes*, and *Sixty-Day* for the same reasons as in the Navy: orders separating them—or discharge and a trip home—were always just around the corner. *Like* the Navy, such affairs were against the rules, but impossible to prevent entirely. What with Congress and a whole lot of public pressure forcing the military to create more gender-neutral roles, women were joining men in *more* jobs, and in *more* units, *every* three months.

Mike felt awkward telling Leigh about Venus. There *had been* a certain intimacy between them, but the limits were hard to describe in '70's terms because everyone expected "intimate" friends of the opposite sex to be *doing it* and sharing everything, but Mike and Leigh weren't *doing it*…and their sharing…?

Their relationship went beyond school. The Taylors and the Dietz's had celebrated most Jewish and many Gentile holidays together for years. Exactly *why* the Dietz's took the Taylors in was hard to explain, but had a lot to do with Mike's mother's big heart and the unparalleled generosity of his father.

But, Leigh, your green eyes…I love your eyes…and the rest of you. Yeah, I do; have for a while.

***

When PFC Leigh Taylor got Mike's letter, it was after two days of night shifts—and three days of blizzard conditions along Korea's DMZ. As soon as she saw it, she tore it open, tearing up as she read.

He's right, damnit: we can't expect to save ourselves for a promise we never made. She opened her reply with the Yiddish for "sweetheart." Though she was a Gentile, she knew a little Yiddish: osmosis after seven years of knowing Mike and his family.

> *Zeeskeit*
> *As much as I treasure your friendship and want to keep*
> *corresponding, you're right. We're adults; we have adult needs.*
> *We never made any promises; it could be years before we see*
> *each other again. If I ever fall in love, I'll tell you, and we'll*
> *figure us out from there.*

Her little talk with Mike before her wedding, when he just told her to follow her heart…she kept coming back to it.

> *Sandy, for as long as we've known each other the only time you*
> *made me really angry was before my wedding. I wanted you to*
> *rescue me…to just tell me "don't." You didn't.*

She married Randy Newhouse, who turned out to be *completely* different from what anyone thought…including *her*.

> *I was mad at you because I felt trapped, and I wanted you to set*
> *me free. But you knew I had to know about Randy. So, thanks for*
> *that.*

That same day, she got a letter from her mother. Her parents had been divorced—amicably—since 1969. Her father, Ed, was a real estate developer; Cathy, her mother, a municipal attorney. They'd moved from New York to Detroit just after the riot of '67, following Cathy's hard-to-

16

pass-up job offer with Oakland County and Ed's business expansion into Michigan. Then Ed's Detroit expansion failed; he *had* to go back to New York where his main business was; Cathy had a brilliant legal mind that Oakland County was unwilling to lose, so she and Leigh stayed in Detroit.

> *Dear Leigh:*
> *Your father sends his best—I saw him last week. We hope all's well with you. Korea sounds like a magical place…glad you seem to be taking to the Army so well… I've been reading about that NAW thing <u>you're</u> in; about time the Army recognized that <u>we</u> can do anything men can…We last saw the Dietz's at New Year's…*

Leigh was in the NAW Program—New Army Woman. NAW sent 500-odd newly-enlisted and commissioned women—including Mike's Emily—into previously all-male units and jobs—and *not* into the Women's Army Corps: the WAC.

> *…I got an interrogative from the Newhouse's law firm yesterday, wanting to know about you in 1970-'71. They aren't done, honey, and we both know enough about <u>that</u> family to know they can't lose at anything.*

Leigh's ex-husband's family was the Newhouse clan of southeastern Michigan, real estate moguls extraordinaire.

＊＊＊

The next morning JJ got a standing ovation as he entered the mess hall, and, in the dark humor of Rangers, they sang the last, funereal-paced verse of "Blood Upon the Risers" to the tune of "The Battle Hymn of the Republic:"

> *There was blood upon the risers; there were brains upon the chute!*
> *Intestines were a-dangling from his paratrooper's suit!*
> *He was a mess; they picked him up and poured him from his boots!*
> *And he ain't gonna jump no more!*

But he could only *hear* his Cloud's voice; see her face.
I would give anything to be able to feel her…

＊＊＊

"We *knew* this would happen, Ann," Don smiled sincerely across their breakfast table.
And now you're going away. "Just hoping we'd…when?"

"I report to Newport News in May. I'll know what ship in a couple of weeks."

"We *could* write…"

"*That* would be weird."

"Yeah." *We never allowed ourselves to fall in real love.*

They got together at chow a few times, had dinner at a restaurant, went bowling with shipmates. They went to a motel with a heated pool on Easter—it was remarkably cold in north Florida that year. She didn't see him off when he left with his seabag; *that, too,* would have been weird. But she *had* to talk…and wrote her old friend Sam Potts:

> *Dearest Sam*
> *Don shipped out today; I feel a little empty. I knew we weren't long-term, but he was there. Sam: we were just scratching each other's itches…I don't regret Don, but was he just a stand-in for Johnny, like you were?*

June

"Specialist Taylor reporting as ordered, sir," Leigh started, whipping out a crisp salute. She just got off patrol on a hot and dry early-summer morning, sweat still staining her uniform. She was surprised that she to be called in just after her automatic promotion to E-4…like every other PFC in the Army who kept their noses clean for their first year.

"Have a seat, Taylor. Coffee?" Her company commander—Major Winslow Homer; a black, no-nonsense Vietnam veteran—returned her salute. A small woman wearing major's gold leaves sat on a small sofa on the inside wall of the cinder block room.

"Thank you, sir," she answered, helping herself to the percolator on the folding table next to the major—*Judge Advocate brass*—and smiled at the little placard that read: *Mama was an art major, and we lived in Maine: that's where my name came from.* She took a chair on the wall opposite. knowing that the offer of coffee from a superior meant that whatever *this* was about would *not* leave bite marks in her posterior.

"Taylor," Winslow started, "you handled that club brawl well. You and Specialist Armor are setting *splendid* examples for female MPs. Since you're two of the first, *that* says a lot."

"Thank you, sir." *Perp broke a guy's jaw and called me a… Yeah: mine's between my legs, jerk-weed, and yours is under your nose.*

"Major Griffin is here in an official capacity, but you are not *obliged* to comply."

"Very well, sir," Leigh replied, puzzled.

"Should *I* leave, Melody?" Winslow asked.

"You can stay if Leigh's comfortable." Melody's voice was soft, almost soothing.

Leigh shrugged. "And I won't know *that* until I know what *this* is about, so, with respect, ma'am, let's just get on with it."

"*Fair* enough," Melody replied. "Before I start—*un*officially—how have the WACs treated you two in the barracks?"

"It's a *little* strange, ma'am. Amy and I bunk with them, but we don't fall in with them. They *know* we're MPs, but when they see us in patrol kit, they kinda freak out. The WAC company First Sergeant just nods and smiles when she sees us; their officers barely recognize us." Leigh and Amy Armor were not *assigned* to the WAC company they slept with; they were *attached* for billeting. They did everything *else* with the *previously* all-male MP company they were *assigned* to.

"We'll have to live with it for now. I hear through channels that the WAC will *probably* be abolished in 1977: keep *that* to yourself.

"Now, for the *official* business, I have a request from the Federal District Court for Southern Michigan. They want you to submit to an independent medical examination to determine if you've ever given birth. The petitioners—attorneys for your ex-husband—have stipulated that the Army is independent enough."

"Um," Leigh hedged, glancing back and forth between them, "I did *that* a year ago." *I swore I was a virgin in front of a judge, for Chrissakes. How could I have given birth?*

Winslow looked as if he'd found a scorpion in a boot. "Can we back up a step, Mel?" Glancing at Leigh, he shrugged. "I've spoken to Taylor about *that* matter. I don't know if *you* know those details."

"Only what's in her records," Melody admitted. "If she wants to tell me more, she can."

"Short and sweet, Randy told me on our wedding night—a year ago Monday before last—that he had a child by another woman, and afterward became impotent." Brushing her honey hair out of her face, Leigh surprised herself with her clarity and nonchalance. "He told me we were to adopt the child after he got his law degree. I broke his jaw, dislocated his shoulder and left. *We* never consummated."

Melody grinned widely. "Did you get *dressed* before you left?"

"Frankly, ma'am; I don't recall, but I woke up next morning in my own bed and *his* underwear."

Both officers giggled. "*He* says you delivered *their* child in '71," Melody managed. "The court isn't *requiring* this exam. You *can* say no, but as a legal advisor, I know this isn't unprecedented. The results of the exam will be in a sealed envelope in your medical records, so the Army won't *officially* know…"

"I'll submit," Leigh answered.

"Again, you don't *have* to…" Winslow offered.

"It's all right, sir."

Melody smiled. "His family has some juice, don't they, Leigh?"

"In *that* part of the world, they do."

Winslow grinned at Melody, who almost laughed as he put on his glasses. "I quote the Defense Investigative Service:

The Newhouse organization controls parts of the commercial real estate market in southeastern Michigan and claims to control some government officials. However, there is no evidence that any of their influence extends so far as to affect the course of either governance or regulation."

He smiled. "I've had people under me from *Mafia* families who had *real* influence and power."

Melody smiled again. "No matter what they can do back on the block, they've run into a wall when it comes to the Army. If you want to refuse *this* request, invoke the Soldier's Relief Act, and they can't touch you for as long as you're in the Active component. If you *want*, I can contact your parents and assure them that, no matter what happens, you're immune from such civil action as the Newhouse's might wish to bring."

"My mother's an attorney, ma'am. She understands the Relief Act."

The two officers looked at each other and seemed to agree. "Leigh," Winslow murmured. "Take some time to think about this. They'll keep at it if they find a wedge anywhere. If you *don't* respond, they may give up."

Leigh inhaled deeply, sipped her coffee and shook her head. "Sir, I appreciate your concern. Knowing *that* family, they *won't* give up. Let's just do it."

Though resigned, she had to tell someone…and *that* was her old friend Donna Hammerfest, whose nickname was…

> *Blondie,*
> *Once again, I need to "prove" that I have borne no*
> *children, this time to a federal court. So, I go to another*
> *doctor, get another affidavit as to my virginity…Jesus CHRIST*
> *when will this end?*

***

Dere Clare

JJ used the odd greeting in all his letters to his family and close friends, emulating a letter written in hillbilly vernacular that appeared in his father's slim parachute training booklet from 1942. *Dere* was a code, to let those he cared most about know that it *was* him, avoiding a repeat of letter-forgery that was an amusing—though cruel to the victims—pastime at his 10th Grade school: Wolverine Military Academy.

> *Got your letter of last week here; thanks. Glad you're finishing your first year at Eastern on a high note: Dean's list! Congrats, Ware! Did Karen finally find a design school? Her art is breathtaking.*

He had spent his junior and senior year at Brookfield School, an island of peace in his turbulent life. Clare's father was one of his house masters, who took him in on long holidays. She returned *some* of his affections, but he knew better than to think he would get *all* of them—she *did* have a boyfriend, after all. Karen was her sister, a stunning beauty who was two years older, and *his* friend, too.

> *I had a hard landing a few months ago, bent myself sort of. But next Monday I'll be in Ranger school at Fort Benning— don't expect to hear from me until August. Nine weeks—if I survive—and I'll have a Ranger tab.*

He thought about mentioning seeing Clare before he hit the ground…but decided to omit *that* detail. *Most* US Army Rangers are infantry-trained, but they get more extensive training in patrolling, ambushes, and information-gathering at Ranger school. But *all* infantry battalions need non-infantrymen assigned (like JJ, who was an intelligence analyst) just to function as units, and many of *them* were Rangers. Grunts (infantrymen) go through the grueling 15-week regular Ranger school. However, most *non*-infantrymen, ROTC and West Point cadets, and some others got the *slightly* less arduous 9-week "summer" program, where JJ was headed.

And then there was…

> *Dere Jenny*
> *Glad you're doing so well at Notre Dame. I didn't know they had a business school that emphasized real estate.*

He'd known Jenny Jacobs since 2nd Grade, off-and-on. They were quasi-intimate a couple of times, but it always felt as if their mutual friend and neighbor Claudia was between them.

And there was…

> *Dere Sarah*
> *…University of Detroit was a wash? Sorry: where are you going next year, then? Any good teacher colleges closer to home in Cleveland?*

He met Sarah Silverman at Brookfield. They were *another* kind of intimate friends: nothing more than a kiss now and then, movies, and quiet talks. He wrote *her* more than she wrote to him, which he'd come to expect.

Finally…

Dere Cloud…I miss you so.

He wrote his Cloud in a composition book—he didn't have an address. He told her everything he didn't dare tell anyone else.

…The prospect of Ranger school scares the hell out of me even though they've been prepping me for a month here. I won't quit, but I <u>can</u> fail. I should do OK academically but I have trouble with the cold—you know, since Wolverine. And being on the go 18 hours a day, six days a week for nine weeks? Can I pass? Maybe. If I <u>don't</u>, can I come <u>back</u> to the 2nd Ranger Battalion? I just want you and Ma to be proud of me.

For a virgin, I sure know a lot of girls…

****

Leigh's exam confirmed the obvious. The next week, on R&R in Tokyo, at least *part* of that examination was nullified in a wild weekend with a guy she met there.

Sandy
Well, I just got back from a five-day R&R in Tokyo…I met a great guy, John, had fun all week. Yeah, it included <u>that</u> kind of fun, my friend. He has your eyes…I tried not to think of you…but we'll be apart for a long time…he also reminded me of John Elrath: have you heard from him? He said he was enlisting…

How are you settling in at Fort Campbell? You went to jump school too? Want to try that sometime…

Leigh knew JJ from their church, where they met in '69. They, too, had a different kind of intimate relationship: made out only *once*, but the *temptation…*

****

Mike got Leigh's letter at the end of a hot Kentucky day maintaining vehicles, dead on his feet and looking for some rest. He perked up, of course, just opening it.

Sure, I know that mensch. Most standup guy I could ever know. They had long talks at Brookfield while Mike tutored JJ in German (which he spoke with his father and grandfather) and JJ tutored Mike in history. JJ talked about the darkness that troubled him from his experience at Wolverine, and it *wasn't* pretty.

...I believe JJ did enlist, yes. He was looking at military intelligence—analyst, I think. If you run into him, let me know? He's probably the <u>best</u> friend I ever had...besides you, of course.

And there was something about a girl...Claudia something? Tall, leggy...went by Ann, I thought. What WAS her last name?

***

"You about ready?" The woman with Ann, a Navy lieutenant named Susan Morris who was a dead ringer for Doris Day, slipped her mask over her head. Getting ready to dive, checking the equipment and putting it on required two people: no Navy diver worked alone.

"Just about." Ann swished water into her face mask, wiping a small gob of spit onto the glass before rinsing it out. The Navy, being a hidebound and traditional organization, loathed to let *men* help *women* into wetsuits or dive gear in 1974, so Ann and Susan worked together getting ready for this dive with three civilian men the Navy hired to survey a seawall. While nearly everything they wore for the dive *was* Navy, Ann and Susan were *not* official Navy divers...but five Navy divers *were* watching. Susan would be thirty next year, so by the time the Navy got around to allowing women in diver ratings—1978, they *said* with more conviction every time—much to her regret, Susan would be past the maximum age of 31. But Susan was an undersea life-systems engineer by training—MIT, and University of South Florida—and was a part of the dive *community* anyway.

The dive was routine; the seawall was ancient and the concrete crumbling; the wall of wood pilings a hundred yards out was *barely* there. Ann's role was to log more time in the drink, and to impress the Navy observers that she knew what she was doing...*again*. It wasn't the first time she'd put on a little show...and she knew it wouldn't be the last. *As soon as I figure this dog-and-pony show out, I'll be ready to retire.*

For her, the best part of diving was that, *deep* in the water, she could see her Johnny's face again.

Dear Debbie,
...When I dive below fifty feet, I see Johnny in my mind; I wish I knew why, but I can't wait to do it again.

Other than her father and Sam, her old friend and swim teammate Debbie Ford was her most constant correspondent.

...When you embrace Bob next time, please give him an extra

23

hug for me. He has Johnny's eyes.

Debbie met Bob Bell at Ann's brother Jim's wedding, and they'd been together ever since.

July

"OK, you guys," JJ announced wearily, "I've got *three* hours of prep to do and *two* to do it in. *You* guys got the same classes *I* did. Let *me* finish my patrol plan while *you guys* make your *own* strip maps."

It was JJ's turn to lead a recon patrol that was to identify numbers on trees in a target area. "His" 11 men—four ROTC seniors, three West Point seniors, three *other* non-grunts, and Mike—nodded tiredly: they'd got maybe ten hours sleep in two days.

For the first four weeks of Ranger school, JJ and Mike were in the same platoon (that started with 40 men) but different patrols (that began with ten men). By the end of the Benning phase—three grueling weeks of seemingly endless physical training, patrolling classes and exercises, map reading and leadership drills, and tortuous road marches—their platoon was down to 21 men. *Most* had quit, some had flunked…and Mike joined JJ's patrol.

"This is a *graded* patrol, brother," Mike confided. "Sure you…"

"Brother, if they *can't* do it for their own good, *how* can they do it for someone *else*?"

Inescapable; obvious. Why don't they teach that? "Brilliant, brother. You doing OK?"

"Yeah; thanks. Never *been* so tired." JJ smiled. "Kiss Kiera and Leigh for me next chance you get." Mike's sister Kiera was two years older and had exchanged smooches with JJ one New Year's.

Much to JJ's surprise, the instructors thought the notion of empowering peer-level followers was brilliant, too, and graded him accordingly.

On his 19th birthday in mid-July JJ received a large order of fast-food French fries with a candle on it and a canteen cup of *real* coffee. Naturally, JJ shared the fries with his patrol. They also got an extra four hours of sleep since it was Friday, *and* the end of Swamp phase.

***

"Private Elrath, sir." Two days later, JJ reported to the company commander in his office—a *highly* unusual event, especially for a Sunday.

"Elrath," Captain Ned Forrest—a thin man with thinning hair and a pointed nose—returned the salute and motioned to a folding chair. "The marksmanship unit wants to know *how* you got a *perfect* rifle qualification score at Fort Bliss: you have been the only one there *ever*." The Fort Benning Marksmanship Unit was where the Army trained its champion rifle and pistol shots—a fact well-known in marksmanship circles.

"They told me that, sir." *They had me do it again a week later with a different outfit.*

"Yes." Ned blinked, grimaced. "You're the only one I've ever *heard of* do it *anywhere*. There's nothing in your record to suggest such an ability. We'd expected to see a hunter or champion target shooter do it, but…"

"I earned a rifle marksmanship merit badge in the Scouts, sir; that's where I learned to shoot. I did a lot of target shooting in school."

"Nice try, Elrath, but that don't answer it. You an NRA member?"

"Nossir. I never saw the need."

"Then…do you *have* an explanation?"

"Just one, sir. In 10th Grade, I attended a school called Wolverine Military Academy…"

"I've heard of it, and *not* in a good way."

"Yessir. It's the kind of place where, when you *leave*, you want to make a *pile* of money, *buy* the place and *burn* it to the ground. I just envision that the target's Wolverine."

"And *that* works?" JJ shrugged. "OK. I'll tell them…will you talk to them if they're interested? They, ah, want you to take NRA instructor training so you can train others, OK?"

"Sure, sir."

August

JJ graduated from Ranger school in the first week in August in the upper-middle of his class…fifteen pounds lighter and with a sore just-about-everything, but *with* his tab.

> *Dere Clare*
>
> *I know your birthday is next week, but I just got back from Benning this morning; sorry I can't get there, but know it'll be happy.*
>
> *Miracle of miracles, <u>I passed Ranger school.</u> Starting to think I can do anything…and I've been promoted to E-4; orders dated 30 July.*

JJ's promotions up to then were unassuming: after intel analyst school, he was handed orders promoting him to E-2, like the rest of his class. When he arrived at the 2nd Battalion, 75th Infantry Regiment (Ranger) after jump school, he was promoted to E-3/PFC because they didn't carry E-2s on their roster. When he came back from Benning, his First Sergeant simply handed him new eagle chevrons for his collar and orders for E-4/Specialist Fourth Class.

As soon as he got to Ft. Stewart, JJ started taking college classes. A short-haired divorcee who called herself Rusty had been a classmate in Western Civilization I before he went to Ranger school. Though the class ended in May, they *had* gotten along well enough, and he *had* her number…

> *Dere Cloud*
> *I wanted Rusty to be you. Please forgive me, but I need real loving, not just memories of what might have been.*

***

> *Dear Mama and Pops,*
> *Congratulate me profusely and heartily—please. I not only <u>survived</u> Ranger school but managed to be 2nd in the class. Got a letter from Leigh; the Newhouse's are still flogging that dead horse, apparently. Isn't there a point where it becomes harassment, Pops?*

Mike's family business was the law firm of Dietz, O'Bannon and Associates, one of the largest in southeastern Michigan.

***

> *Leigh*
> *I got your address from Mike; I hope you don't mind. He'll probably tell you about running into me in Ranger school…*

She had been on convoy route security planning training all that week…would be for another week. It was hot to the point of intolerable when she ripped JJ's letter open. *Blue-Eyes??? WOW!*

They had met in the winter of 1968-69. She liked the quiet blonde boy with the adorable blue eyes. They were, in '70s terms, a *non-couple*, but…

> *Blue-Eyes*
> *SO glad to hear from you; hope you're good because I am. Mike says you went into MI, too? In the MPs, we call <u>that</u> the oxymoron—military intelligence. But I know <u>you'll</u> improve that…if you can call my mom when you're in town, let her know about me, and vice-versa…*

1975

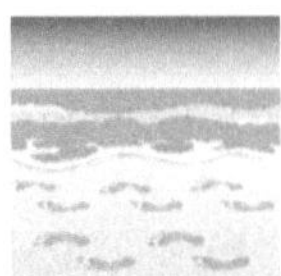

January

> *Leigh dear,*
> *Your father and I have decided to try again...*

Sure, Mom. Pull the other leg; it has bells on it.

Leigh knew that her parents still loved each other—*loudly* and *boisterously*—and knew *what* their divorce was about. That said, they never tried to hide their affections—or anything *else*—even after their divorce. Throughout her childhood Leigh heard them—and had *seen* them—in amorous throes *where*ver and *when*ever the spirit moved them.

> *Dear Leigh*
> *After many discussions with my partners in New York,*
> *colleagues in Detroit and with your mom, we've decided to give*
> *us another go in Michigan. I'm teaming with another firm, Kent*
> *Associates...*

No...FREAKING...way!

Ed Taylor was a tall and spare man with a resemblance to Michael Rennie. "How's Mom," she asked when he met her at Metro Airport's baggage claim, glad to finally be able to stop traveling: she'd been in airplanes and airports for a day and a half.

"She's fine, wants to know if you'll stand up for her."

"For...*what*?"

"The ceremony."

"You're *serious*?"

"Sure, honey."

No. Freaking. Way. When Leigh dropped her luggage on her bed, she gazed along the walls at the dozens of cardboard boxes that contained her pre-enlistment life. Cathy kept a room for her in her new townhouse that she also used as a guest room, and to store the boxes that she had packed in anticipation of her moving. *Not today; maybe not this leave.*

An intimate mother-daughter lunch the day before the ceremony was *enlightening.* "What do you hear from Mike these days?" Cathy, despite the cold Michigan weather, wore a thin silk blouse under a barely-there cashmere cardigan. Her too-short skirt made her look even colder. "He stopped by last spring."

She's 43 and looks twenty. "He's still in Kentucky; *might* get sent overseas after he reenlists in April; just got his air assault badge. For *what* I don't know, but…"

"Isn't that one of those promotion-point things?" Cathy had done a great deal of research into the Army.

"Yeah, but, between jump school and Ranger school, he's *starting* to sound more like a grunt. Heard from JJ last month; sends his best." Leigh paused. "You and Dad are *good*, then?"

"We've never been *that bad*, honey," Cathy smiled.

"Mom, I'm happy for you. I just need to update my dossier."

"Um, you've been *saying* we're divorced?"

"Yeah. Since '69?"

"Shows you what kind of investigating *they* do. Your father and I were never *really* divorced."

"But you went to court, got papers. I *SAW* them."

"Yeah, but ultimately, we just couldn't *sign* the final decree. Didn't *know* you got promoted."

"Oh," Leigh smiled, glancing at her sleeve. "Just *acting* sergeant: all the duties and responsibilities and none of the pay. Won't be able to keep 'em in my next outfit."

Other than Leigh, a couple of people from Cathy's office attended the brief re-*something* ceremony, as did Mike's parents, Ben and Monica Dietz.

> *Sandy*
> *My folks "rejoined" during my leave. Yeah, wild, right? Wilder yet, they were never really divorced…I'll tell you later. I wish you'd been here, but frankly I got so hot listening to them down the hall …maybe it was good you <u>weren't</u> here…or <u>not</u> good. Donna sends love and kisses…I should be jealous, but I'm not. I haven't found anyone else, zeeskeit.*

And, for the *first* time, she ended with…

> *All my love,*
> *Leigh*

Declarations of love in the '70s were *supposed* to be more powerful than a locomotive…that's what popular culture said. In truth, most of them were soft, pleasant, quiet and, in Leigh's case, *almost* offhand, but from that *offhand* instant on, she could imagine closing her letter no other way.

Leigh spent time with Donna, who was in nursing school and was *also*

Mike's Girl-Next-Door. For the last week and a half of her leave, Leigh and her parents spent nearly every evening together. And every night, Leigh could hear them in their bedroom just down the hall, "celebrating."

She didn't tell Mike that several times while she was home, she saw two of her ex-husband Randy's thuggish associates—Joe Dryden and Dave Harriman—watching her townhouse.

As she headed for the airport gate for Washington, she spotted a tall woman in a Navy uniform...*could that be...?* "Ann! Ann Mueller!"

She turned to look. "Leigh?" Ann smiled broadly. "My *God*...you're in the Army? What happened to...?"

"Didn't work out. I've got to catch my plane! We'll..." and they got lost in the rushing crowds.

***

Ann was glad to have had a spot of liberty at home around the holidays, but she wrote:

> *Debbie*
>
> *Just got back to Florida, ran into Leigh Taylor in an Army uniform at the airport, but that was all we had time for. She said that her marriage "didn't work out." OK, but she's wearing sergeant's stripes. That means, in the Navy anyway, she's had to have been in service since at least '73. You know anything else?*
>
> *I'll be up there again at the end of August; didn't know before I last saw you...*

April

Writing to his Cloud was JJ's best means of explaining it to himself.

> *Dere Cloud:*
>
> *All I have to prove <u>this</u> story is a copy of orders detaching us from an organization nobody ever heard of...and <u>they</u> make <u>no</u> sense without the <u>attaching</u> orders...*

"Get your *young* asses in this *truck*!" A major and two master sergeants stopped in a van below the hill and barked orders at them authoritatively. It was hard to argue; the senior men seemed *so* determined and sure.

As an E-4 with nearly two years in service—and the only Ranger—JJ had been in nominal charge of five other men picking up cigarette butts and trash on the side of a hill while they waited for their communications traffic analysis course at Fort Huachuca to start when they were— *apparently*—ordered away.

"Sir," JJ asked, "our *school*...?"

"Don't worry about *that*; we'll take care of it," the major glared, "now

29

get aboard!"

What *was* unusual about *that* afternoon was that, unlike the normal Army hurry-up-and-wait—especially on a Friday afternoon—*everything moved* with breakneck speed. They piled into the van, drove to the airfield, boarded a waiting C-130 with another score of men and took off within an hour. An hour and a half later the plane landed in California and refueled while JJ and "his" men ate soggy Air Force boxed meals on the hardstand, and were joined by even *more* men…all E-4 and below. No one knew what was going on. A grizzled Sergeant-Major handed out orders saying that the above-named individuals were *attached*—not *assigned*—to Army Provisional Command-Vietnam, Republic of. JJ stared at the paper, trying to memorize the other names. They took off in a C-141 two hours after landing.

"Hey," one PFC loudly announced after an hour. "My enlistment contract doesn't *provide* for deviation. I have the right to get off this damn airplane any time I want."

JJ sucked his teeth. "You wanna get off *now*, big-time? *Knock* yourself out."

They landed in a *sweltering,* humid place after eight hours, and an Air Force sergeant led them off the plane to a waiting line of trucks, which took them to a Quonset hut, where they were to rest up. It was the first time JJ ever *saw* a real honest-to-God half-tin-can Quonset hut.

Something's not right; even I know that.

He left the hut—which he was told *not* to do—to find some answers. A sign in front of a big container with an air conditioner in one side read US ARMY PORT NAHA LOGISTICS COMMAND. "What can I do for you, soldier," the harried staff sergeant at the desk mumbled.

Naha? That's Okinawa!!! "You can tell me what we're doing here," JJ announced, handing over his orders.

The sergeant barely looked up. "*You're* going to Saigon as soon as I get these orders cut."

WHAT! THE…!

Six hours later, they were in another C-141. By noon, they had landed at Tan So Nhat airport to the sound of distant small arms and artillery. A big, sweating Army captain named Wallace piled twenty of them into a small truck and drove—and officers didn't *legally* drive—through the crowded Saigon streets, with the sounds of fighting, the wails of sirens, and the smell of sweat, powder and fear all the way.

At the US Embassy gate, they rushed past a tumultuous crowd of refugees held back by Marines…who let *some* in. Wallace led them past more refugees to an elevator up about half-way to the top, then up a crowded stairway that stank of sweat, food and fear to the roof and left them without another word…to *anyone.*

We're just adding to the chaos.

A more orderly panic the gentle reader could *never* imagine. Marines sweating bullets in the heat ran the show—such as it was. They counted heads and gauged passenger weight by eyeball and the occasional quick heft. Every few minutes a helicopter arrived, and a herd of people moved single file to their noisy salvation. The helicopters took off after their skids barely touched the roof…and some *didn't* touch. Most of the passengers were Vietnamese, but some were Americans or French, with the odd Australian or Filipino thrown in.

In between lifts, JJ approached a skinny Marine lieutenant in a khaki shirt and blue pants. The young man looked at JJ blankly, then shouted through the din with disbelief. *"Just what the hell are you doing here?"*

"You tell us, sir," JJ shouted.

The lieutenant snatched the orders out of JJ's hand, glanced at them quickly, and shouted, *"help my Marines while I figure this out."*

For hours, JJ and "his" people—with mute smiles and nods (there was little *talking,* but a lot of *crying*)—helped the Marines keep order over the rising sense of panic as the sounds of battle grew louder and the powder-stench more intense.

Somewhere near dark, a sweaty civilian approached JJ and gave a little speech that included the phrase "a grievous error has been made." He pushed a stack of orders into JJ's hands without explanation while the lieutenant yelled, *"get out when you can"* over the roar of another helicopter.

Near midnight, Captain Wallace appeared again and drove JJ and his men back to the airport, where they *all* dashed to a far-overloaded 707. They landed back on Okinawa barely 24 hours after they had left, and in another 18 hours were back at Fort Huachuca, where they were grilled about where they'd *been* for four days. Scanning orders that *detached* them from a non-existent unit, their pop-eyed senior drill sergeant grunted, *"now I have* seen *everthang,"* and sent them off to class.

…Whenever I think about it, Cloud, I find it hard to believe it happened at all…I'm going to see Clare in a few weeks; she reminds me so much of you.

May

"Just give us your unvarnished opinion," the bosses told Specialist Mike Dietz before he sat down to listen to intercepts of voice traffic between Moscow and various Asiatic posts.

Those who grow up speaking a language in their native country are often sentimental about it, causing them to misinterpret the nuances (or *lack* thereof) of a *non*-native speaker. Mike was one of the few non-Russians in the intelligence community as fluent as a native, and, having *never* been there, was trusted by the big shots to give his opinion of what was being *said*—not *un*said—unfettered by sentimentality. And, because his childhood German was as fluent as his Russian, they also relied on Mike's views of Germans-speaking-Russian, and vice versa.

The tapes contained routine traffic about the *Mayaguez* mess off Cambodia. It was interesting, though, that *someone* in Bangkok wanted to get into the containers full of classified material evacuated from Saigon a couple weeks before, but neither Hanoi nor Moscow seemed interested. Another intercept from Phnom Penh described the Marine assault on the ship but seemed ambiguous about it. *They don't care?*

Then there was a recording from New Delhi—a voice Mike was familiar with. The voice with a Saxon accent complained, "we don't need another disaster like *Pueblo*. We just got over *that* one."

The clincher came when Mike studied the new dossier on "The Voice" in India: "The Voice" was an East German who had been in Korea while *Pueblo* was being dissected and had written a report about the examination of the spy ship's intercept gear, so badly placed and poorly installed that some Soviet experts thought it was an elaborate hoax. But "The Voice"—code-named Gregor—thought *Pueblo's* poorly-installed gear was *just* what it looked like…poor design and layout…and *he* was *right*.

The East Bloc is uninterested in legitimizing Cambodian pirates by examining the contents of the Saigon containers. "Not worth the exposure" was the key phrase…what is implied, the <u>way</u> it was said, is that the East Bloc already knows what's in the containers. They either had an asset who helped pack or inventory the containers in Saigon, or they <u>have</u> an inventory...

An After-Action report like the one Mike wrote above was supposed to be devoid of sentiment, but not so letters:

> *Oytzer*
> *You're not going to believe this, but they want me in CI.*
> *Yeah: counterintelligence; Camouflage Inspectors; spy-catchers!*
> *Wild, right?*

Then, for the *first* time, he wrote…

> *Love you,*
> *Mike*

July

They walked along the edge of Moby Pool, a blob-like concrete pond a hundred yards long by twenty wide where Brookfield families and students swam in good weather. She didn't wear shorts—she didn't *like* her legs—so her long skirt brushed the weeds along the shallow end. "Are you going to *stay* in," Clare asked.

"I *am*," JJ answered. "It's a good living; doing something to give back to the country." They walked a few paces more. "You'll write to me when I'm in Germany?"

"Uh-huh." While she *did* write, she wasn't *terribly* regular; there were silences of months sometimes.

They walked into the woods at the end of Moby; he reached for her hand; she gave it. Holding hands with her on campus was dangerous—Brookfield was a small community and her family lived there.

"Where *are* we, Ware? I mean…are we *just* two friends or…?"

"*Don't*, John." She squeezed his hand. "Please. My family wouldn't approve of…us." If her parents *thought* that they were more-or-less platonic, he could stay there for part of his leave. *That* was the complicated part of their relationship.

They stopped, listening to the kids splashing in Moby and the crickets chirping in the dark, steamy woods. "Why not?"

She turned to face him. "They look at you…different. We're friends as far as they're concerned: leave it at that."

"Should I go?" He had stayed at his home-of-record on Birch Lake—where he lived before he joined the Army—for the first two weeks of his leave. While he enjoyed being with his mom, the tensions between him and his stepfather Charlie Parkinson were palpable, so he left for his home-away-from-home at Brookfield, where Clare and her family didn't blink before laying out the guest towels.

"No." She stepped closer to him, wrapping her arms around him despite the sticky humidity. "No: *don't* go yet."

He inhaled deeply, holding her in the humid heat, feeling her heart under her peasant blouse. "Ware: I…"

"*Don't*, John; *not* before you take off for three years."

So, he *didn't* say, *I love you.*

That night, he dreamed that both Clare and his Cloud were together, laughing about…he didn't *know* what.

> *Cloud,*
> *Can I love you both?*

August

The bride, Barbara Savio *nee* Edwards, was a round-faced and slim woman with short dark hair, four inches short of—and not as muscular as—her soon-to-be stepdaughter. She wore a mild blue silk dress and only a gold wire pendant for jewelry. Ann—6-feet-1 and both maid-of-honor *and* best-whatever—wore her summer dress mess uniform with her new Petty Officer Third Class chevron on the left sleeve.

Looking like a male version of his daughter, Howard Mueller—the groom—smiled at the altar of the St. Amadeus Church in Southfield. Though *his* kids were raised in their mother's Catholic faith, Howard was a lapsed Lutheran. Barbara and her children were Catholics—the kids went to parochial schools—and the continuity was important to her.

Howard's first wife and Ann's mother—Claudia—suffered from early-onset dementia, though Alzheimer's was not ruled out. Her savage mood swings had become dangerous to herself and others; institutionalized in 1971, she divorced Howard on good terms to save the family's finances. Howard met Barbara at Claudia's second facility. Howard hired her for his general medical practice in '73. Friendship ensued; romance followed.

The attendees to the ceremony included Howard's practice partners, some friends of Barbara's, Ann's brothers George and Jim and their wives Holly and Carol, respectively, and the five children between them: George's Adriana, six; Jim's Howard, three, and Nettie (Annette), two; and Barbara's six-year-old twins, Alex and Jenna. As the Mass proceeded, Ann thought about the strange course of their lives, their mother's cruel mental illness, the utter serendipity of Barbara's warm feeling for the Mueller's.

The reception was held at the celebrated Fox and Hounds restaurant on Woodward Avenue in Bloomfield Hills. That evening, after Barbara's kids were back with their father, and the guests had all gone home, Ann and Barbara sat by the condo's pool and talked about...*things*.

"So, Ann," Barbara started, "do you *like* the Navy?"

"Love it," Ann answered. "Skilled, challenging work; I'm learning about computers and logistical management."

"Huh," Barbara said. "Found a home, eh? I *told* you I was an Army nurse for ten years: got a year in Vietnam out of it."

"Yeah. You decided not to stay?"

"Decided I was in *love*. Got out to get married and have kids."

"Didn't work out?"

"I'm here with *you*, ain't I?" Barbara grinned. "No, Nate and I didn't work out." She shrugged. "I *like* your father more than I *ever* liked Nate."

"The age difference doesn't bother you?" Howard was 56; Barbara was

39.

"Since we're *not* having more kids, it's irrelevant. I think I'll investigate office management, though; add *that* to my resume. But you're going to be training as a *what* this fall?"

"Hull technician. I start with welding and ship systems in Philadelphia in October. I go to San Francisco next spring for damage control school. I should be done with *that* by August, they say. A year after *that,* I finally get to dive school...*if* they're ready for women."

"Should I congratulate you or console you?"

"A *little* of both, maybe. Find out when we get there."

That night, Ann dreamed of her blue-eyed Johnny and another girl. *Who's she and what are we all laughing about, Johnny?*

The next day they were surprised to learn that Jimmy Hoffa, the celebrated labor boss, was last seen at the Red Fox Restaurant at Telegraph and Maple Road on the other side of Bloomfield Hills.

> *Dear Sam,*
> *...The wedding was beautiful; I like Barbara a lot. I'm suddenly*
> *a big sister to a couple of good kids... wish you were here and*
> *not in college. I miss just sleeping with a trusted friend.*

September

Detroit Metro Airport was busy almost any day of the week, but on the first Monday of the month, some concourses bordered on chaos. Ann grabbed her luggage out of Howard's trunk that morning, kissed him and her new stepmother goodbye at the American Airlines door, and waded up to the ticket counter.

Wishing he could have had the courage to ask Clare to come with him...*but she said don't*...JJ grabbed his luggage out of the DeHaven's trunk, kissed them goodbye at the Republic door, and waded into the confusion.

At 10:00 AM, Ann boarded the plane at Concourse A for Atlanta, thence to Panama City.

At 10:10 AM, JJ boarded the plane at Concourse B for Fort Dix, thence to Germany.

1977

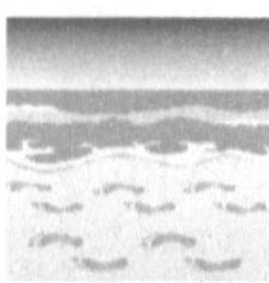

August

"Sergeant Taylor reporting, sir," Leigh snapped a salute. She had been called in while on duty, so was in full patrol kit with helmet, stick, and sidearm. Of all the times she had been called in for personal business, this was the first time she was armed. *ANOTHER meeting with ANOTHER company commander and ANOTHER JAG officer. I feel like I SHOULD shoot somebody.*

Leigh liked her company commander: a beefy Hispanic major named Jamie Donita on his third wife who commiserated with her about civilian lawyers during her in-briefing. "Have a seat, Sarge. Coffee?"

"Thank you, sir." It was boiling hot in the Georgia sun, and the sweat trickled down her back, so she was grateful for the liquids—and the reassurance as she pulled her nightstick out of its holder and laid it aside.

"OK, Leigh," Lieutenant Colonel Eve Berrigan began. "I believe you know *this* drill. Your ex-husband has *another* request."

"I *figured* as much, ma'am." On court-martial duty, Leigh saw this red-headed, skinny-as-a-rail, fiery JAG officer treat a recalcitrant in the witness chair like a piranha treated raw meat.

"Again, you *can* refuse." Jamie *could* be soothing, but she'd also heard the version of him who had patrolled Tu Do Street in Saigon back in the day. A photo on the wall showed a young Sergeant Donita with three other MPs in jungle fatigues. Another was of a freshly-minted OCS-honor-graduate Lieutenant Donita at Fort Leonard Wood.

"What would be the point of *that*, sir," she replied sardonically. *I said that?* Both officers smiled to her relief.

"OK, then," Eve chuckled. "They want a blood test to match your type against the child's type to establish—or *refute*—maternity."

"Isn't *that* already in my records, ma'am?"

"It *would* be," Jamie replied, knitting his brows. "Eve, couldn't we redact a copy of her medical records and send *that*?"

Eve shook her head. "We need to put a *sock* in this, Jamie: *six times in four years*. We'll send a redacted copy of your medical records, an invocation of the Relief Act over your signature, and a very nice legalese note from the Judge Advocate General himself *telling* them to stop."

"You *know* General Harvey?"

"I was his assistant once. He's agreed to sign a letter I drafted. That *might* get them off your back."

"We can try it, ma'am."

***

Dere Clare
Been wondering why I haven't heard from you in a
year…maybe you just don't want to. I realize that we're not <u>that</u>
kind of friends, but you can tell me anything. If you found the guy
of <u>your</u> dreams, just tell me, please?

Do I want to know the answer? They had shared intimate secrets, but their *physical* intimacy didn't go beyond lingering kisses and hugs.

"Hey, Mike," JJ called out to his roommate. They were bunked together in an 10x12 room at the 1st Battalion, 10th Special Forces Group's *Kaserne* in Bad Tölz. "You and Leigh: how's *that* going?"

"OK." Mike put his book down. "Why?"

"Clare stopped writing. I want to know what makes *it* work?"

"You mean…what makes two people *work*? There's whole libraries on *that*, brother."

"Yeah, but…what makes *you* and *Leigh* work?" *And NOT her and me…*

"Frankly…I dunno. For *us*…we started out as lab partners in 7th Grade. My family kinda took hers in; it's just the three of *them*, and *I* have more cousins than I can count. She came to my *Bar Mitzva*, but so did Donna…"

"The blonde?"

"Yeah. Donna *was* my girlfriend if I *had* one in school. We'd go out, make out, but that was it. I *never* bedded her: never *thought* about it, honestly. Second base *once* senior year, but it *felt* weird and we never did it again; we're *still* friends. But I always felt something *from* Leigh that I didn't from Donna. It just *has* to be mutual, I guess." He sat up. "I don't *know* Clare that well—Spanish classes for a couple of years—but if *I* had to tell *you* about *her*, I'd have to say she has trouble making decisions."

"Yeah. I guess you're right." *She had trouble deciding what side of a room to sit on.*

"Something they taught in interrogator school about trusting: you have to trust not only the other person but *yourself with* the other person to get them to open up. You follow?"

"Yeah." *Maybe she just doesn't trust me that much.*

Dere Cloud
Clare stopped writing a year ago now. I thought—hoped—we

37

were better friends than that. I haven't heard from you in seven years—the day before I went to Wolverine. I wish I could hear you; you're the one person I trust as much as I do Mike or Leigh or Clare, but maybe it's not mutual.

***

Let's see if time-and-uniform matters.

A week after the meeting, Leigh was told to go to the provost marshal's office after her shift—time and uniform didn't matter. She got off at midnight, changed into a barely-tolerable-or-decent, saggy-loose tank top and baggy satin shorts, took a bus across the post, and walked into the air-conditioned entry hall of the PM's office: a tile-lined bastion of power through which those accused of crimes great and small were marched to hear their charges read.

The duty sergeant at the large steel desk at the door was a whipcord-thin African-American staff sergeant named Bose who she knew slightly. Bose glanced at her ID and handed her an unsealed envelope, visibly struggling to stay focused on her eyes and *not* her immodest attire. "If you approve, just sign the buck slip," he drawled.

Worn out from a long, hot and tedious shift driving around the base, she plopped the letter on the table in front of the desk, bent over at the waist, and put her forearms down on the table. The letter was elegantly worded, wonderfully phrased, and contained just enough mumbo-jumbo to impress any legal mind. It concluded:

This is the sixth action in four years that Sergeant Taylor has felt it necessary to answer. Sergeant Taylor's and the US Army's patience is at an end. No further actions will be answered by either Sergeant Taylor or US Army without a subpoena from a federal court.

"Got a pen, Sarge," she muttered, looking up at him. *Mesmerized: SUCH a GUY.* She rolled her eyes—resisting the urge to shimmy *just* a little—grinned and murmured, "if you like what you see *now, wait* till I take a *shower.*"

Bose woke up and handed her a pen. "Sorry," he grinned.

"I've had worse," she signed the little yellow form clipped to the letter. "Guys have *no* idea how sticky a bra can get."

"That's what my wife says when she goes out in that moo-moo of hers."

She smiled, gave a *tiny* shimmy, and walked out with a *gentle, smooth* saunter. *Think two puppies in a satin bag, Sarge; it'll help you stay awake.*

 Donna,
...Surprising what we can get guys to look at on demand, to distract and get their attention at the same time. You've always

had that ability, but I should develop an allure of my own. Might come in handy when I start interrogating.

October

"What do they want…and why?" In the quiet of the intelligence (S-2) office, as they engaged in a friendly game of gin and waited for message traffic, JJ handed his section leader the letter he'd received from the Leadership Studies Institute—the publishers of *Sarge* Magazine. *Intriguing but puzzling:*

> *…the response to your article on evolution for enlisted leadership has been remarkable. We would like very much to discuss a book based on your thesis of leading-by-enabling.*

"They think your theory is worthy of a book-length treatise," Lieutenant Maynard shrugged. He was a big African-American ROTC officer; a Phys Ed major with a history minor, and a fair gin player.

"It's not really *that* remarkable," JJ replied. "Just get people to do what they're trained to do on their own."

"Considering all the leadership theories going around these days, *your* article was a breath of fresh air, Sarge." Maynard discarded the seven of hearts. "Take the initiative for your own good? Revolutionary."

"Can't imagine why," JJ frowned, picking up the seven and declaring, "gin." *They should be teaching it in Ranger school if they liked it so much.*

JJ decided to at least *sound* interested. He scratched out an outline, citing historical examples showing the evolution in the requirements for "leading" over the centuries, concluding with:

> *The requirements for enlisted leadership in the post-industrial West must shift beyond the "get up and follow me" model towards "do this for your own good," because there's just too much for enlisted leaders to <u>have</u> to do. The NCO's role should be to ensure that both the officers <u>and</u> enlisted have the internal tools—training, skills, and sense of initiative—so that the mission can be accomplished with or without their lawful leaders. Our primary task <u>must be</u> to train our replacements.*

The mail turnaround between the 'States and Germany was about three weeks *if* the writers were quick. JJ was surprised, therefore, to receive a large, fat envelope fifteen days later from the Leadership Studies Institute, containing, among other things, a contract to write a book.

The battalion intelligence officer—the S-2—was a small and astute captain named McCann, who realized that JJ's work might be a feather in *his* camouflage cover as well. He cleared JJ's schedule every Friday for the rest of the year.

While he was writing the book, he got a surprising letter from an old Wolverine schoolmate, Eddie Evans:

> *John:*
> *Trust you are well; we got this address from your mother. As soon as you get back to Detroit, call me: we have much to discuss.*

And, *finally*…

> *Dear John (no, this isn't one of <u>those</u>),*
> *SO sorry it's taken this long, but I've been sick since last spring— a bad case of mono—and as you know my family is worse at corresponding than even I am. But I'm getting caught up, my <u>dear</u> friend, and I'm writing you now. I know; it's been <u>so</u> long, but I know you write to me out of love and friendship, and I'm a poor correspondent. <u>Please</u> forgive me, my friend.*
> *I got my hair cut kinda long in back and short in front…Happy Halloween by the time you get this…I'm a semester behind in school because of this…*

> *Any time, Ware; for you, any time…*

1978

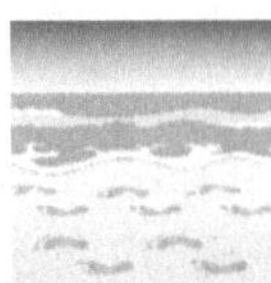

July

Took a burst of six this time, everyone: I'm in for the long haul.

As she walked down the jetway at Detroit Metro, Leigh felt an assurance she *hadn't* had for ages. Her career as an MP seemed cemented into her—she reenlisted for six years before she left Korea again, banking her re-up bonus at American Express, wishing that USAA would allow enlisted people to join.

"So, where are you headed, honey," Cathy asked on the way to the parking structure. "Georgia again?"

"Yeah. Different company, but same post. How's Dad?"

"He's in town until you leave." She smiled slightly. "You should come home more often."

"As often as my leave allows, Mom."

"You said you reenlisted?"

"Yeah: six years. The Army owns me until 1984."

"You're making it a career, then?"

"That's affirmative."

Cathy was quiet until the car was on the expressway. "There are worse things you could do." She coughed slightly. "How's school going?"

"Fine. Mostly prerequisites now. My criminal justice intro course was interesting; *not* what we got in MP school."

For the next week, Leigh got to decompress from the military for a while, spending time with Donna (who had *just* been granted her BS. N while working as an RN), and noting the vastly different ways between her distinctly military life and that of civilians. Most everyone she saw for more than a few minutes was profiled and cataloged by her MP-mode hardwired brain. Her internal clock, changing shifts every couple of weeks, was *always* on 24-hour time. She got confused when someone said "six o'clock" because, for *her*, there were *two* of them. And, when sitting down to eat, it took a great deal of will *not* to grunt the *impolite* version of "pass the *freaking* salt" like every third GI in the mess hall did.

On a Friday afternoon she drove to Beaumont Hospital at Woodward and Thirteen Mile Road to pick Donna up after her shift: Leigh often borrowed Donna's car while she was working. That afternoon, blonde-haired-and blue-eyed Donna squealed as soon as she saw her friend. "I got the NP-squared internship on Five."

"Outstanding," Leigh answered. "I'll *get* excited as soon as you translate *that* into English."

"It's a neuro-psychiatric nurse-practitioner internship on the 5th Floor. Seventeen people were competing for two slots, and I *got* one!"

"OK, fabulous," Leigh grinned. "We'll have to celebrate…shit," she suddenly changed, glancing down the hall. "Dryden, dead ahead."

Just coming out of the gift shop with a bag, Joe Dryden hadn't seen them yet. "Hope he doesn't…too late," Donna mused, as Joe looked directly at Donna first, the grinned at Leigh. "Just keep walking."

"*Mrs.* Newhouse," Joe loudly announced. "Didn't realize *you* were in town. Are you *here* to return to your husband?"

"That marriage never legally existed, Dryden," Leigh grumbled.

"Nothing that money and lawyers can't make right," Joe beamed loudly, beckoning to someone behind them. "I'm *sure* the courts will understand once…" He stepped in front of Leigh, staring at her. "Once they understand the *reality* of the situation. Hammerfest, this is private business. On your way, now."

"I go where I want, Joe," six-foot Donna smiled. "I don't think…"

"Blondie, I *said* take a *hike*," Joe growled without looking at her. "Get *your* skinny ass *out* of here." Donna's nickname came from her resemblance to the cartoon character. At about 200 pounds and 5-feet-ten, Joe had a wrestler's neck, a massive chest, and powerful arms. His small, quick eyes were that same dark, indeterminate color that Leigh was used to seeing on repeat offenders.

"*She's* with *me*, Dryden," Leigh hissed. "Now, before I scream, get *your* goat-*smelling* Neanderthal ass the *hell* out of our way."

"Go ahead and scream, bitch: I'll have you on the deck begging for it before…." Even after a decade and more of women's rights marches, a woman's scream still had the power to strike fear in most men—but Joe *wasn't* most men.

Joe's mistake was that he didn't even *look* at *taekwondo* black-belt Donna, so he barely noticed her until she seized his left thumb and swung his arm behind his back and upwards. He barely had time to grimace or reach around before *taekwondo* black-belt Leigh's swift knee flashed into his crotch.

"*Now*, Joe," Donna giggled, bending his arm up near the back of his head, "you were *saying* about my skinny ass? *Not* very nice, Joe, and we've known each other for so *very* long."

He was on his knees by now, causing mild consternation among the passers-by in the wide hallway, and drawing the attention of the security guards. Leigh squatted down to look at him eye-to-eye, smiling as sincerely as a fox to a hen. "Joe? Anything else?" He shook his head swiftly, his face a mask of pain and confusion. "Tell Randy where he can *stick* it, Joe, *if* he can get it working," she finished as Donna let go. The girls left to the sounds of Joe making excuses to his smirking associates about how he was "so surprised" to see Leigh that he was "sucker-punched."

The rest of Leigh's leave was uneventful. There was rarely a time for the rest of her leave when she didn't spot *someone*—sometimes Joe, sometimes long-headed Dave, often no one she knew—watching her every move.

> *Sandy,*
> *...Donna says hi, hugs and kisses; Mom and Dad send their best;*
> *your folks are good; your sisters seem to have serious friends*
> *who are, well, men...I'm told to expect the Fort Gordon gig to*
> *last at least two years, maybe three. They want me to go to the*
> *NCO Academy. Looks like* <u>*they*</u> *have plans for me, zeeskeit.*

***

"Diver candidates: in the water!"

Fifty-four of them walked awkwardly forward on a beach in Panama City: fins on feet; tanks on backs; masks on faces for the first time in salt water. Fifty-two of them were men; two were, for the very first time, women.

Next to Ann was Kristin Collins, a younger, powerfully muscled, five-foot-seven woman with light brown hair and quick grey eyes. They had been together since the A-phase of training at Great Lakes in Chicago—they flew to Detroit and spent Memorial Day weekend with Ann's family—and through hull tech training, as well. Ann liked Kristin's effortless sense of humor and bold, outward nature. Kristin was also willing to engage almost any male in a conversation...or *more*...except when she was working.

Though the Panama City training center was said to be "ready" to train women, the locker rooms were poorly-if-adequately partitioned between male and female; they showered in loudly-announced shifts; their ready-rooms—where they geared up—consisted of "*we're* up here, and *you're* down there: *just don't look.*"

Unlike most of the men, both women were certified divers as teenagers; they had so very little trouble with the training that the instructors soon learned to *almost* ignore them...if only their fellow students would. In a group-carry drill, Kristin was the smallest person in the class and naturally one of the first subjects to be carried by six students in full dive gear. A burly Marine balked at grabbing Kristin until she grabbed his hand and placed it on her thigh. "*There*, Jimmy. It's *just* a *leg*."

"Yeah, but it's…"

"You *never grabbed* a girl's leg before?"

"*Not* with *so* many witnesses," which got a laugh from everyone. So, they got over *that*.

> Sam,
>
> *…Glad to hear you're that close to graduation; so am I. Finally getting through dive school…like I'm finally grabbing the brass ring. But the cute guys nearly naked I must work with are strictly off-limits, and they still make me think of swimming with you and Johnny.*

August

"Petty Officer Mueller, you need to, um, secure your bust for the filming." Because women in Navy dive training was a Big Deal, the Navy squeezed as much publicity out of Ann and Kristin's presence as possible. During the last weeks of dive training, a Navy film unit was detailed to make a movie of the first women in the school. The warrant officer in charge of the film crew assigned this detail was a small, nervous man who chain-smoked Camels, and approached Ann before the filming began.

To WHAT my WHAT? "I need to *what*, Chief?"

"Tape your boobs down, Ann," Kristin grinned. "They don't want them to *move* in their movie."

That's what I thought he said. "Chief, with respect, I'd like to point out that my *breasts* don't move."

"They *do* in the water," Kristin mumbled. "Buoyancy."

"Then you should feature *Kristin*," Ann smiled. "*She's* not as *well-endowed* as I am. *Hers* don't *float*." Kristin put on her *amusingly disgusted* face.

"My orders are to get *your* image."

Tape tits, aye. "Very well, Chief."

***

By dint of good reflexes, strong swimming and more-than-fair academic ability, Ann was the honor graduate for Class 78-4, so *she* was the first female US Navy diver rating, *and* coincidentally the first woman in the *world* to *become* a naval diver rating. Master Chief Carl Brashear, the first African-American diver in the Navy, personally pinned the Second-Class Diver badge on Ann's uniform as the cameras snapped away furiously. Because it *was* a Big Deal, Ann's family came down to Florida for the ceremony. At the end, Ann took nine-year-old Jenna and Alex to meet Chief Brashear.

Ann had done what she set out to do, reached a goal that only one other woman had thus far ever achieved…but she still wanted her Johnny. She *always* saw a face she knew *had* to be his, and felt his tender touch, when she dove so deep that the light and the noise of the surface were but a memory.

> *Deb,*
> *…I was afraid, after all this time, it might feel hollow. But*
> *frankly, finally getting this rating was more fulfilling that*
> *graduating from high school…and how much I still miss*
> *Johnny…*

1979

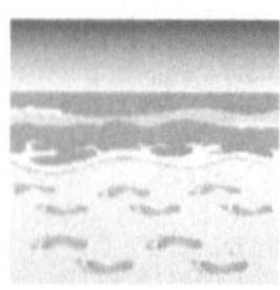

January

"Vehicles clean," JJ chattered. "*Cold* but clean." Wearing not just winter gear but rain gear and bulky insulated rubber Mickey Mouse boots—it *was* snowing—he and his dozen men washed down *their* two jeeps, one six-wheeled, articulated Gama Goat truck and two 2-1/2-ton trucks...*and* all their *trailers.*

"Close out the dispatches," the mousy-if-acerbic motor sergeant Hart Sweeny grunted to his assistant.

JJ herded his people into the big garage and out of the weather, where Mike—the second-ranking NCO (by three weeks) in the section—was checking the vehicle log books with Hart while his dozen men painted the shovels, pickaxes and other tools. For the IG inspection in two days, the logs and the gear needed to be as spotless as the vehicles.

"*Why*, pray tell us, Master Po, do vehicles need dispatching when we wash them," one of the men asked. Hart greatly resembled Keye Luke in the "Kung Fu" TV series that was then popular on American Forces TV. "Is it just a habit of mind, or is there some other, mysterious need that we miserable creatures cannot grasp?"

"Ah, Grasshopper," Hart declared, bowing his head sagely, "it is an offering we *must* make to the Preventive Maintenance Checks and Services god—PMCS by name, who can *only* be satiated with *fully*-filled-out DA Form 2404s. Whenever they're moved, they *must* be dailyed, and to be *dailyed,* they *must* be dispatched." *Dailyed* was GI slang for the pre-use inspection of *anything*, which, depending on what the thing *was,* could take anywhere from minutes to hours, and required the filling and filing of the ever-present Form 2404. However, *everyone* knew that driving a hundred meters to the wash rack didn't *need* the extra steps like checking the oil and tires and air cleaners, so it was rarely *really* done unless someone was watching...or the IG was on the way.

"Great," Mike grimaced. "Sergeant Elrath: what *other* wall buffing are *you* doing today?" *Wall buffing* was any useless chore performed either rarely or just to keep the troops busy.

"*We* have to GI the basement latrine," JJ mumbled. For the IG inspection, *his* half of the S-2 section's enlisted men got picked to do a thorough cleaning—GI-ing—of a little-used facility.

"Splendid: *we* drew the short straw on the day room," Mike mockingly replied before he grunted: "movie tonight?"

"Sure, providing I get *done* early enough. What's showing?"

"What difference does *that* make?" Before he knocked off for the day, Mike scribbled his letter:

> *Leigh*
> *...just finishing up getting ready for the IG; tired don't begin to*
> *tell it. Not surprised that even Special Forces units get IGs.*
> *Nothing surprises me anymore.*

As Mike finished his letter, JJ typed a missive to Leigh that Mike would include with his:

> *...thanks for looking in on Ma on your last leave. I wish I knew*
> *just what to say to her anymore other than 'hi' and 'bye.' Not*
> *sure I really know her...or if I've ever known her.*
> *Remember that girl I brought to church in '71? We've been*
> *writing off and on, only now; off for a year. Other girls—off too;*
> *they're married or have forgotten me now. You're my <u>last girl</u>,*
> *Green-Eyes. At risk of sounding pathetic; please don't stop.*

When he read letters from the girls in his life, he could imagine that his life wasn't as lovelessly-bleak as it *felt*. At 24, living without lasting affection and trust was *gettin'* old.

> *Dere Cloud*
> *Worn out today getting ready for the IG; truck-washing,*
> *latrine-cleaning. IG's a big thing; eyewash, mostly. I haven't*
> *heard from Clare since December '77. I wish I had an address*
> *for you, wish I could hear your voice, feel your hand; just a*
> *hand.*

February

San Diego just refuses to change.

As shipmates often do, Ann and Kristin and a half-dozen other buddies piled into a few cars and went out on Friday *after* payday. But this was two days after Valentine's, a peculiar greeting-card holiday for Today's Navy, where smiling *inappropriately* at a person of the opposite sex *can* result in charges of harassment.

Bowling is one of those activities where a participant either can *do* it or *not*...and Ann was in the latter category. People had shown her what to do and how to do it over and again, but, like dancing, she just never quite *got* it. She enjoyed the social aspects of the *activity*, but ball control was beyond her ken.

"Try keeping your wrist stiff and *behind* the ball," a voice in the next lane loudly suggested. She looked to see a weightlifter-bulky, California-surfer-guy prototype watching her.

"Tried everything else," she muttered, starting up. Her resulting bowl knocked down seven pins instead of three…or the gutter.

"Thanks," she smiled at her helper as she extended a hand, "I'm Ann."

"Welcome," he smiled back, "call me Cable."

He has eyes like Johnny. "Cable. You bowl much?"

"Naw. Just here with some friends." After a few minutes of chatting, she learned that Cable (the only name he used) was also a diver, a contractor for the Navy's many needs for underwater work, in addition to working at a surf shop. By the time they parted that evening, she felt…*maybe we'll meet again.*

> *Dear Sam,*
> *My last letter to Lansing bounced…don't know why because it's the address I've had. Sending this to your home. I met a guy here; his eyes are just like Johnny's.*

March

> *Oytzer*
> *Going to the Rangers at Stewart! Got orders this morning; I report in May…I got leave between. I'll look in on your folks, say hi to everyone I can find….*

Leigh got Mike's letter after a long and trying shift: an accident had left three people severely injured when a tank slid sideways down a hill in a remote maneuver area and smashed into a communications van. Leigh's patrol had to secure an area enclosing nearly thirty acres. She'd been on her feet for almost forty hours when she read it but lost no time at all to reply:

> *…two hours away from Ft. Gordon! This is the most exciting thing since Mom and Dad got back together!*

At the same time, she felt bad for JJ, and answered him quickly:

> *…those other girls don't know what they're missing…Blue-Eyes, I think I've fallen for Mike by mail, and he'll be a stone's throw away in May. I care for you, John, but…we'll have to see what happens…*
> *But no matter what, babe, you and I will ALWAYS be close friends.*

May

Why did I wear this? Keeps creeping up my... At least the top isn't that bad. Leigh shared a ride with a friend to meet Mike in the booming metropolis of Millen, Georgia—halfway between Forts Stewart and Gordon.

Five-nine and 170; shoulder-length brown hair and beautiful green eyes...prettier than I remember...but if that skirt was any shorter, she'd get cited for flashing. "Hi," Mike smiled as he stepped out the front doors of the lobby just as Leigh lit out of a car.

Five-eleven and 190; brown hair and oh-those-gray eyes. Sandy, you look good enough to eat. "Hi, there, stranger," she smiled. "How…" *And. We. Never. Did. THIS. Before.* They made out just outside the lobby long enough for Leigh's ride to smile, unload her bag and drive away.

"Hi, *oytzer*," he finally whispered. "Hi."

"Hi, Sandy," she smiled broadly. "You're *quite* the kisser. Had a lot of practice?"

"Not *lately*. You eat dinner?"

"No. That Dairy Queen across the street's good enough. But I've *got* to get out of this outfit first." In his room, she grabbed shorts out of her bag, then told him, "*turn* around." A few moments later, he heard "*whew! Too* small for me."

That's right... "You *borrowed* it; I'm guessing."

"*Very* perceptive. Let's go."

They got their burgers-and-fries and sat in a corner booth. "Still can barely believe you're here in front of me," she mused between fries.

"Frankly, I'm having trouble with *that* reality myself." He sucked up more of his milkshake. "I'm so used to hearing your voice in my head."

"Well, here we are. But we weren't anything but *friends* before, Sandy, despite calling each other 'sweetie' and 'treasure' in a language I don't speak. The first time we made out was an hour ago; we haven't *seen* each other since '73." She inhaled deeply, shook back her honey-brown hair, and pulled it off her neck. "I'm *not* looking for a quickie here, my dear, even if we *can*."

He looked into her emerald-green eyes. "No: not with *you*." *Want more.*

"Had *many*?"

"*Enough*."

She smiled sincerely. "*Me* too: *too* many. Let's just enjoy each other's company and be friends?" *At least for now.*

"Sure. I reserved *two* rooms."

One step at a time. "Yours *is* a double queen, so give the other up and we'll split the bill. But, Sandy: I *trust* you and I've *seen* your bare behind, but…barracks rules."

Share a room? "That boxer raid, yeah." In high school, the girls raided the boys' quarters one Chelsea morning…the stuff of legend since. "Barracks rules? Not familiar…but you and your *mom….*" *Not as inhibited as most women…* More than once, growing up, he knocked on her door to find her or Cathy *barely*-covered…and *that* sometimes poorly. *Cathy always was the sexiest mom in school.*

"Uninhibited to a *point*, pal. We stay *decent* in shared spaces; latrines are *strictly* one-person occupancy, and the *only* place we get *completely* undressed."

"OK. Drink?"

"Sure."

Jimmie-Jack's—a block from the hotel—wasn't *quite* a cowboy-country-western watering hole nor a sports-bar, but a little of both. An epic beer-can pyramid stood from floor to ceiling by the jukebox, which was right next to a small stage, which was right by the back door.

"I stopped by your folks…" Mike mumbled, watching a heavy-set guy trying to talk a tube-topped girl at the jukebox into something.

"Mom said that. She said they got together Mother's Day. How about yours? Your folks went to church with mine?"

"Yeah. Pops really likes that little church."

"I'm just glad we've got *your* family…"

"Mama welcomed *yours* into our *mishpachah* years ago. That makes *you* part of our family."

"So, if we *were* to…would it be incest?" *WHEN we finally…?*

He grinned. "No more than if we were married."

She smiled, watching another woman push off a greasy guy at the bar. "Do *you* want kids?"

"Sometimes. But I've got this *career*."

"Yeah, me too. I feel the urge, sometimes. Have to get married first."

"A single woman in my section at Fort Campbell got pregnant. She had a week to decide: adoption or discharge. She took the out." The most common reason for the early separation of unwed women was pregnancy—by five to one.

"Yeah, that changed *this* year. Now they *allow* single women abortion or adoption, but *she'd* have to pay for the former and any expenses for the latter, and she's got the first trimester to decide *and* commit. *Now* the Army's covering medical expenses before and after."

"Pretty stiff."

"Pretty realistic. How can a single mother be deployed? I know what mine went through when I was a teenager. Even with our money and your family, it was hard."

"But you were an easy kid."

"Watch it, buster. Don't be calling a girl 'easy' in a joint like this."

He smiled. "You're *not* easy."

"So, how's JJ these days?"

"He was good when I left him; he'll be back stateside by the end of the year, he thinks." He glanced at her. "You, ah…"

"We're *friends*, Sandy; we write. We went through some shit together as kids. He talked to *you* about Wolverine?"

He sighed heavily. "Yeah."

They walked back to the hotel in the steamy evening, bumping shoulders from time to time as the heat radiated from the sidewalks. Millen was a town so small the streetlights turned on at about the same time as the traffic lights changed over to blinking red or amber that time of day. There wasn't another shop, store or restaurant open after 9—even the Dairy Queen shut down, and it so quiet they could hear the traffic light relays switching off and on. "Small town doesn't *begin* to describe this place," he mumbled, reading the theater marquee. "*Days of Heaven* was like a year ago."

"You ever see it?" She brushed a bare knee.

"No. You?"

"Nope."

"It *would* give us something to do tomorrow. Not much *else* here."

"True." They reached the hotel lobby a few minutes later, stopping at the tourist literature rack. "Let's look again tomorrow. I'm beat."

She leafed through the cable TV directory in the room. "How about *Heaven Can Wait*?"

They watched most of the movie sitting on the bed *she* had claimed before she spoke up. "Can't understand the attraction of Warren Beatty."

"You don't think he's the sexiest man alive? Isn't that what *Cosmopolitan* is trying to sell?"

"Haven't read *Cosmo* since high school and barely then."

"I never asked: what's *your* position on women's liberation?"

"I never burned a bra, though I've *had* a few I *wanted* to. I appreciate the effort and sacrifices that many people have put into creating new opportunities for women." She frowned. "Why?"

"Because this is a dull shadow of the Gene Tierney film from the '40s and I want to…"

"OK." She bounded up off the bed and turned the TV off, a serious look on her face. "Just *talk*, or try to get *lucky*?" She stripped off her t-shirt angrily. "Just *talk*, *without* the TV, will take place at the table. *Get lucky* ain't gonna happen, Mike, regardless of *what* you see."

"Talk, *oytzer*. *Please*! This is *me*, OK?"

One step at a time. "OK, Sandy, sorry. A guy I was TDY with at Fort Sill…same scenario, and *he*…sorry." She pulled her t-shirt back on.

One step at a time. "I get it. You thirsty? There's a Coke machine down the way."

"I'll buy if you fly."

They sat at the little table in the sort-of comfortable chairs. They talked about feminism, anti-Semitism, the price of gas, whatever it was that was going on in Iran; movies; JJ; what happened to her marriage. It was nearly midnight before he sighed, "Leigh: I declare that *you* will not be a Sixty-Day-Jane."

"I declare that *you* will *not be* a Sixty-Day-Joe."

"Mike, before we go any further down *this* relationship road—*wherever* we're headed—you need to know that whenever I'm in Michigan, I'm a target."

"Legally?"

"Literally. I *think* Randy's family wants me dead, silenced, or back with him."

"*Why?*"

"Because he told me he can't get it up."

"He did *once*, at least."

"Yeah, but he told me he *couldn't* anymore."

"Given what he *said* you were doing *before* made everyone think…"

"Shit," she sniffed. "He *said* a lot of things that weren't true." She grabbed his hand across the table, squeezing hard. "He never *touched* me; said he was *saving himself* for the wedding night. Well, so was *I*. I'm changing the subject," she sighed, reaching into her bag. She pulled out *Profiles in Leadership: Case Studies in Command, Leadership, and Military Management.* "*This* is on my reading list for promotion."

"Uh-huh; mine, too. JJ was working on it when we were there. What do *you* think of it?"

"It's excellent. Nothing but rave reviews."

"Why am I *not* surprised?"

They smiled. She shook her head slowly; he did the same. *One step at a time.*

They changed—she in the bathroom; he in the bedroom—shut off the lights, kissed lightly and crawled into separate beds.

September

Saturday

"I've been accepted for Criminal Investigations school, Mike," she mumbled across the table. Labor Day weekend he drove up to Fort

Gordon, staying in a motel off-post so they could both catch up with homework. "I start in January. Four months at Fort Lost-in-the-Woods and I get to be a military gumshoe."

"Oh, Leonard Wood, yeah. Congratulations, babe! Really; couldn't be happier. CID's what you've *wanted*. Few women in that, are there?"

"I'm the fourth woman to get a slot, and I'll be in school with the third and fifth. Trailblazing is in my blood."

"And I'm proud of you."

She looked at him sidelong. "Mike, are you OK?" He looks…ghostly.

He sighed. "Tired, mostly. That malaria *really* kicked my ass."

"Any chance they'll put you out?"

"Not a lot. The kind of malaria I got…"

"Where'd you get it?"

He sighed. "Not supposed to say Honduras, and you *didn't* hear it…"

"Hear what?"

"Yeah. Anyway, my bugs aren't fatal." He sighed. "I'll be fine, *oytzer*. I might just be frozen as an E-5 until I can pass a PT test."

She smiled. "I'm writing to JJ when I finish *this*. Want to put something in?"

"Sure, in an hour or so. I've *got* to finish this essay."

> *Blue-Eyes,*
> *Just a short note; I'm with Mike in Georgia, thinking of you, too. Mike said you'll be back Stateside this year? Can't wait to get together again. He won't see this, honey, but Mike and I have gotten closer. You and I should have <u>before</u>, Blue-Eyes. Just wish Randy hadn't been in the way.*

"Here's my contribution," Mike handed her a single sheet, folded.

> *Hey, brother,*
> *Not going to lie: I love Leigh with all my soul. I know you two have a thing, and it's OK. I love both of you enough to know that what I feel <u>from</u> her won't be diminished by her love <u>for you</u>. But I just hope you can find who you've been looking for before too long, for the sake of your heart.*

She stuffed both in an envelope and stuck it in the mail. "Hopefully he'll get it before he comes back Stateside."

Sunday

"You look beautiful in that." Mike awoke to see a sliver of sun in the inevitable crack between the heavy curtains, and Leigh basking at the edge of the sunbeam in one of the chairs, an ivory gown covering her like a satin icing.

"Mom gave it to me for a shower present." She smiled at the window. "How'd you sleep?"

"This bed's better than my bunk, but still...*ugh*, think I got a spring stuck in my ribs. How's yours?"

One step at a time. She stood slowly and walked towards him. "Mine's not *that* bad," she muttered matter-of-factly. "I wanted to be sure *we* had a chance before I wore *this*," she purred as she pushed the gown off her shoulders and it fell to the floor, "and did *that*. Let's use *my* bed."

That's what Adam saw when he bit the apple. "Leigh, honey: are you sure?"

"Surer than I've *ever* been of making love with *anyone* else." She held out her hand. "Come on, Sandy. Let's do what we've wanted to do with each other for a decade; find out what we've been missing."

One step at a time. "I'm not...I *don't* have a *lot* of experience."

"I don't have a *lot* more, *zeeskeit*. Let's learn together."

***

"*Not* today, thanks," Leigh shouted at the door, awakened by the obtrusive knock of housekeeping. She felt him warm and sweet beside her and rolled over, gazing into his bleary, smiling eyes. "Sandy? Can I say I love you?"

"You said it before."

"*That* was passion. Now: *I love you.*"

"My father told me that the *first* thing a man feels after sex is gratitude. After *that*, if he feels warmly for the woman, it *might* be love." He smiled. "What I'm feeling *right now* I have never felt with anyone else."

She slid her hand across his chest and down his belly. "*That's* gratitude?"

"It may be in a few...*oh!* If you weren't doing *that* right now, you *might* be more convincing."

She grinned, stripped the sheet off, and straddled him. "*Now* are you convinced?"

"I'm convinced of something *wonder*ful. I've loved *you* for a very long time."

"Good." She laid down on top of him, grinding her hips. "Now, let's *really* do this."

***

"I'm *not* sorry for this weekend," she whispered in a little diner as they watched the scudding clouds across the ripening cornfields.

He sipped coffee, patted her hand. "Me neither. I love you; you love me. We make love." He shrugged. "We *want* us to be together."

She smiled but turned sad. "What are we going to do, Mike? When I go to CID school…"

"We can still write: that's how we fell in love. And we have until then."

***

A week later, when she got back to her flat from patrol, Leigh scribbled some lines to Donna:

> *Blondie*
> *I got CID school!!! I report to Fort Leonard Wood after New Year's…might see you Christmas…Spent Labor Day weekend <u>Together</u> with Mike. Don't regret it; we're fabulous, not 60-day anything. I just worry about distance.*

Then, she answered JJ's letter that was in her box:

> *…Ft. Bragg—never been there, but it's maybe a half-day's drive from Ft. Gordon: maybe we'll get together or meet someplace. I'm going to be at Leonard Wood for a few months after Thanksgiving, so maybe next spring?*
> *And you have a wedding to go to? More fun than <u>my</u> last leave in Detroit. Look in on my folks when you're there, can you?*
> *It developed, Blue-Eyes, Mike and I…I love him, but I still meant everything I said to <u>you</u> before…*
> *Love you too, Blue-Eyes,*
> *Your Green-Eyes*

October

"And what God has joined together let no man put asunder." Christchurch Brookfield was a cavernous space to have a wedding with only five guests: Dave and Marie DeHaven, Clare's sister Karen DeHaven Watson and her husband Don of two weeks, and JJ—the immediate family of the bride and their Friday's Child.

I need to be happy for her.

JJ got back from Germany with an invitation to *Karen's* wedding in hand. When he laid eyes on Clare for the first time in three years…she was expecting in January…he understood why she didn't write. That Marie would invite him to Clare's wedding *seemed* natural, but *felt* perverse.

The ceremony was brief. The pastor said the words; Jack Alton the groom kissed Clare the bride, and it was done. There was no organ, no march down the aisle, just handshakes and quick hugs. JJ looked for that flash of joy—that *glow*—he'd seen on his sisters' faces at the altar when the priest was done, *and* on Karen's a fortnight before. He saw only a hint of it on Clare, and *that* would have broken his heart if it weren't already shattered.

The reception included only members of *her* family—including Dave's widowed sister and Marie's brother and sister-in-law—*and* JJ. Jack was an *artiste*, he emphasized, who didn't *have* any family, and had little *time* for *friends* who might come to a wedding.

When the "happy" couple departed for two weeks in Ishpeming, JJ embraced Clare for what he thought might be the last time, and whispered "I love you, Ware," into her ear: it was the first time he'd ever said *that* to *any* non-family female, and it came from the very bottom of his soul.

She hugged him harder, digging her chin into his shoulder, and mewed "I *know*, John," in his ear—the closest he'd got to words of affection from a girl in years. In the quiet of the DeHaven's living room minutes later, he, Karen and Don slammed bourbon shots to keep from *thinking* about it.

JJ went to his home-of-record on Birch Lake—where his *stuff* was— and where his mother, Stella, lived with his stepfather. He sat with Stella in the big family room with the window that looked out on the dark lake. Hypnotically, she shuffled a deck and dealt ten cards. He picked up his hand absently, sliding likely plays together as she turned over the four of hearts.

"Nice party," she asked, watching him pick off the deck and discard the three of clubs.

Your game just makes everything...stop. "Clare was beautiful." He picked off the deck and discarded the jack of spades.

"I'm sure. Where are they going to live?" She picked up the jack and discarded the five of hearts.

"Clare's student-teaching in Flat Rock starting in January: she's expecting on *your* birthday." He picked up the five and discarded the three of hearts.

"The 23rd of January? I should have *kept* threes. What does *he* do?" She picked off the deck and discarded the ace of clubs.

"He's an *artiste*, he says. Hm. Nice." He picked up the ace and discarded the five of diamonds.

"Should have...*nuts*. What kind?" She picked off the deck and discarded the seven of hearts.

"*No* idea." He snapped up the seven and declared, "gin."

As JJ shuffled for another game, Charlie sat at the big table. JJ hadn't had more than a handful of civil conversations with Charlie since they'd first met ten years before. That evening, Charlie *seemed* to be sober after sundown—for *that* braggart and bully, this was known as Good Charlie. A truck dealer in Detroit, Charlie had three sons who JJ adored like they were his natural brothers, a granddaughter who was JJ's genuine buddy, and more grandchildren JJ barely knew. He dealt three hands of seven cards.

"How long are you here for, JJ," Charlie mumbled, picking off the deck and discarding the five of clubs.

"Week after Thanksgiving," JJ sighed, picking up the five and discarding the nine of hearts.

"You'll be here for the holiday," Stella replied, picking up the nine and discarding the king of spades.

"I might go see Brenda between now and then," JJ sighed. His sister Brenda was another non-fan of Charlie's.

"They'll be happy to see you," Stella muttered, watching Charlie discard the five of diamonds.

JJ stared at the five. "Yeah." He picked off the deck and discarded the three of spades.

"What do you hear from that girl from church?"

"Leigh? She's going to criminal investigations school next month."

"Oh. You had a phone call from an Eddie. He said to drop by his office any time." Stella picked up the three and discarded the ace of hearts.

"I'll go down there Monday, then."

"Who's this, now," Charlie asked, picking off the deck and discarding the king of clubs.

"Eddie Evans; friend of mine from Wolverine; office in the Penobscot Building."

The room went utterly still; Stella stopped moving; Charlie stared as if frozen in time and space; even the furnace blower and the radiators were unusually quiet.

First time I've ever seen you genuinely surprised, Ma.

And, I could knock you over with a feather, Charlie. Why?

November

"*WHAT*, exactly, do you *think* you're *doing, Johnny-cake?*"

"What...?" JJ, barely awake in his bed, blinked at Charlie standing in his doorway, bleary-eyed. *Plastered already.*

"You *heard* me: *What* do you *think* you're *doing?*" Charlie threw a large, fat envelope on JJ's bed. It had his name and the return address of Eddie's business on it. It *had* been opened, but JJ *didn't* do it.

Eddie sent that stuff HERE? Ugh. "That's *my* business, Charlie; not *yours*. I..."

"*Everything* that goes on in *this house* is *MY business. EVERYTHING* that *comes to this house* is *MY BUSINESS!* What the *HELL* business have *you* got with Evans and Towne? *Where the HELL did you get that kind of money?*"

"That's *personal*, Charlie. Now, if you'll excuse me, I'll be on my way."

"Get OUT, you little…"

JJ packed up and left, spending the rest of his leave with the DeHaven's. He left them with a last letter for Clare:

> *Dere Ware*
>
> *…No matter what or who else happens to <u>me</u> or <u>you</u>, Ware, I will always be your friend whenever you or your baby need one. Never hesitate to contact me when you need help because, wherever I am, I'll find a way.*
>
> > *Luv,*
> > *John*

* * *

"Sergeant Taylor? Excuse me."

Huh? "*Yeoboseyo*, sir. How may I help you? Excuse me, but my Korean is *very* limited." Leigh had been called to the orderly room from the reaction force room and, once again groaning over another possible something from the Newhouse's, pulled on fatigues in some haste.

The little man smiled overmuch as Koreans often did, but seemed sincerely polite. "I thank you, Sergeant Taylor: your diction is excellent. I am Mr. Kim Pok-Chin, cultural attaché of the Republic of Korea. It is my honor to ask if you would allow your painting, *Korea at Dawn*, to be exhibited in the National Gallery in Seoul for a year. Many of our officers have seen it in your headquarters and admire it greatly. I…"

Really? "I made that picture with PX paints and old pastel chalks," she smiled. "Never *thought* how good it might have been…" *First Sergeant showed it to the company commander and suddenly it was in Eighth Army HQ.*

"You underestimate your talents, Sergeant. I have seen a photograph of it—I paint a little myself—but rarely have I seen a rendering that makes me long for home as yours does." He proffered a card. "Our exhibit honors the artwork of our American allies, and my country would be *greatly* honored if we could include your *beautiful* work. We would frame it appropriately, as well. The exhibit lasts a year."

"Mr. Kim, *I* would be *honored* to be featured…"

"Not just *featured*, Sergeant: *Korea at Dawn* would be the *centerpiece* of our exhibit."

Huh. "I would be honored, sir: *dedanhi gamsahamnida*."

"You are *very* welcome, Sergeant, but the *honor* is *ours*."

Donna,
...I painted it from memory; my first view of Korea in daylight.
My art has helped to keep me sane; now it's made me famous.

December

Kamerad Oberfeldwebel: What's YOUR story?

The room was big for its purpose—10x10—paneled in particle board with a bare-beam ceiling from which hung a large and garishly bright four-tube fluorescent light. The raw brown of the interrogation cell's brown walls contrasted starkly with the white linoleum floor and incongruous green steel door. The mirror built into the wall next to the door angled slightly down. The reflection it cast was secondary to its purpose: so that observers on the other side could *see*, but not *be* seen.

The little cell contained a sturdy GSA-issue steel table, four heavy, padded GSA-issue steel chairs, and a small, gray and balding *non*-GSA-issue senior sergeant of the East German *Grenztruppen*—border guards—named Emile Gast, quietly smoking. Sixteen days before, he appeared in the headlights of a border patrol jeep just on the edge of the fence between East and West Germany, and announced that he knew about something BIG the Soviets were planning. Both Germans and Americans had been *politely* questioning Gast up to four hours a day, six days a week ever since.

In the small, steamy observation booth adjacent to the cell, Emily (whose help Mike had requested) stood next to Mike, watching the little man with professional interest. Every source has a story to tell; *their* job was to investigate Gast's story because the American powers-that-were were *sure* that Gast was lying—a dangle, in intelligence parlance; a false source meant to deceive. The politicians insisted that what Gast was saying was a *complete* fabrication. The intel wonks couldn't be sure, so they brought Mike and Emily in to get Gast's *real* story.

Between the hostage crisis in Iran and the economic shocks of the '70s that were still battering the country, another policy—and intelligence—failure would doom President Carter's bid for reelection in '80. With the Christmas holiday only ten days away, the intelligence people at Langley *had* to *know* so they could plan *something* in response, even if the White House did nothing more than protest.

In the booth with them was a nondescript man in smoked glasses—average everything in a dark suit, white shirt and narrow tie—who flashed FBI credentials, called himself Special Agent Brown and said practically nothing afterwards. He had brought the reports and files that Mike and Emily spent the past night studying. They were accustomed to the no-name, no-face "Browns" who peopled the alphabet-soup of agencies in the

EAR—Echelons Above Reality—that hovered far above *their* meager pay grades, and who did America's spying and counter-spying. Legally, military and civilian agencies couldn't work together inside the US, *but...*

"When did he eat last?" Emily asked.

"Two hours ago." Brown's voice was the most remarkable thing about him. It seemed to emanate from somewhere *near* his face...which never appeared to move behind his glasses.

"When was the last time he was dosed with painkillers?" Gast *said* he had crossed over because of bad teeth, and couldn't get better than a medic with a pair of pliers in the barracks on the other side. Dentists had extracted two teeth already; two more had abscesses that he was taking antibiotics to reduce.

"Two Darvon with his breakfast."

"What *was* breakfast?"

"Coffee, yogurt, and a banana."

"How much does he smoke?"

"About half a pack a day. He likes Chesterfields."

All of this was important, but...risk the wrath of the KGB and the *Stasi* for a *dentist? Possible*, but likely *not* the *only* reason. *People defect for less compelling reasons...but this one?*

"How much sleep did he get in the past 24 hours?"

"He slept on the plane here and in his room. Nine, ten hours total."

"How well do *you* know him, Brown?" Emily looked pointedly at him.

"I know he's been on that stretch of the fence for about year; he's a lifelong bachelor and something of a ladies' man." He shifted his stance. "His *latest* conquest was a Russian woman a month ago."

Mike smiled at Emily, then Brown. "Change of scene?" This interrogation technique was to earn the source's trust. It worked best on *non*-hostile sources, but required *time*, which was in short supply.

"How *big* a change," Brown asked flatly.

"Commissary and chapel."

Brown shrugged. "Can't hurt."

"Then...sympathy," Emily nodded. Another technique that *also* required time, and was *most* effective on sources who were just looking for *reasons* to talk.

"Yeah; *sympathy*. Venus, did *you* bring a skirt?"

Emily grinned. "*Way* ahead of you, Sandy."

"Then I need to make a phone call," Mike declared, "and *find* a rabbi..."

On a Saturday before Christmas, the Fort Meyer commissary—the base grocery store—was a busy place. Gast gazed hungrily at the abundance of fresh fruits and vegetables in the produce aisle, with *particular* interest at an end-aisle display of canned meats, and in gape-mouthed *wonder* at the cornucopia of magazines and books on the rack. It took only a few minutes for Mike to find the unleavened bread *he* needed.

The post chapel was a few minutes' walk away. Gast wore a plain suit without a tie; Mike and Emily were dressed in clean uniforms—lacking all insignia and patches other than Army and name tags, with *US* insignia instead of rank. They passed several officers in uniform on their walk, and Mike had to struggle not to salute: nothing he did could reveal his rank or status just in case Gast *wasn't* what he said he was and got back to his people. Emily walked ahead, much to Gast's distracted delight, wearing a too-short Class-A skirt.

"*Mah nishtanah?*" Mike mumbled, passing a piece of his matzoh bread to Gast as they strolled.

"Hebrew," Gast sighed as he took the bread with a small smile, hesitating before he bit off a corner and answered in German. "I haven't heard the questions since I was a boy." He gestured widely with the matzoh. "It doesn't *feel* like Passover."

Mike broke into Yiddish. "It isn't; it's the first day of Hanukah. When was the last time you observed either one?"

"My *Yiddish* is *very* rusty, my friend, but I *know* what you said," Gast answered, cocking his head and gesturing, "how's *theirs?*"

"Those *goyim?* What do *you* think?"

"Just so," Gast laughed. He looked ahead at a hastily-erected Star of David on top of the chapel sign and gasped. "A synagogue?"

"We worship with our rabbis as we please. Let's sing praises to God for the miracle of the lamp together. We'll have a Seder with Rabbi Aaron, ask the questions, and eat the bitter herbs."

Gast smiled broadly. "I've not *seen* a rabbi or observed a holy day since my father was alive: thirty years now. I've come to miss both."

***

The next morning, Emily and Mike signed their names to their after-action report on *their* interrogation of Emile Gast, Senior Sergeant of Border Guards of the Democratic Republic of Germany.

> ...Subject GAST came through a gap in the Inter-German Border (map location ATTACHMENT A) with the intent to provide attached information in exchange for dental care and religious asylum...The Soviets are stripping wheeled vehicles from everywhere to mount an exercise, crossing the border into Afghanistan on or about 25 December to rescue Kabul's pro-Moscow regime...Subject GAST'S intimate contact with MAJ OLGA VATUTIN, a USSR transportation service officer, provided him with this knowledge...routes of vehicular traffic leaving DRG marked on strip map ATTACHMENT B...Subject GAST feared for

his life because one of his superiors, CAPT BORIS BELENKOV, an anti-Semite, learned Subject GAST had on occasion invoked Hebrew-sounding prayers…Subject GAST has well-documented dental issues (ATTACHMENT C) that he wished addressed in a more medically appropriate fashion than he could get in the DRG.

They grabbed a light meal at the PX near noon, slowly drifting into sleepy oblivion. "How *did* you know?" She sucked on a straw.

"There was something about him he'd been hiding for a long time. The medical report said he had been crudely circumcised: I *guessed* that his *mohel* botched the job."

"Oh. How about a drink, Sandy?"

"Venus, *we* haven't slept in a bed in two and a half days. Rather share a nap." She smiled: They slept in their separate rooms in the visitor's quarters.

…Thought of you until I went to sleep, oytzer; dreamed of you until I woke up.

1980

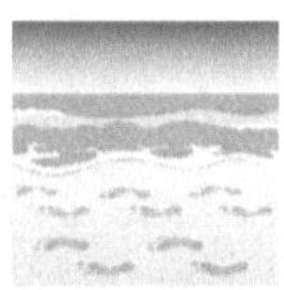

January

"Sergeant Elrath," the voice outside his barracks room door intoned. "You have a phone call from the Red Cross."

Oh, shit. "Coming." He had told his family what the Army told *him*: in case of an emergency, call the Red Cross *first*. All family emergencies *must* be verified by the Red Cross. *Mom? Charlie?* "Sergeant Elrath here."

"John Elrath," a woman's voice replied. "This is Mrs. Swann of the American Red Cross. I have a request from Stella Parkinson to check on your welfare since she hasn't heard from you in some time..."

"*Two months*, maybe," JJ replied. "My *welfare* is fine." *After Charlie read my mail before I did, I'm going to reach out? Why?* "Tell her..."

"I will, Sergeant. Just be more *reassuring* to your loved ones in the future."

"*Thank* you, ma'am; I *shall*."

> *Dere Cloud*
> *After that last goat-rope, like I'm gonna...ah, what the hell,*
> *it's for Ma's sake, I suppose. Christ, I need this like I need crabs.*

It wasn't like he didn't *want* to connect with his mom, but his stepfather came *with* her...inevitably. *And Ma needs him more than she needs me.*

> *Dere Folkes*
> *Sorry I haven't been in touch: busy with my new job at Ft.*
> *Bragg. I'm in charge of a dozen analysts here; a lot of people*
> *I've got to get to know. And I've got motor pool duties too. I'll*
> *try to connect every other week, OK?*

He struggled to just let that much be, but there was the nagging thought: *I wish I knew her better.*

February

> *Blue-Eyes*
> *...I don't have a lot of choice here, my dear.*

After graduation, newly-minted CID graduates were assigned to posts where they'd never been before, to work at jobs that they were hastily and *very* cursorily trained for—usually administration or supply—to watch, and listen, and report in support of one CID operation or another. While doing this for a year or so, they could not tell anyone but their immediate family *where* they were, and *absolutely no one what* they were doing...

> *...The only thing I can ask is that you keep in touch with Mike, or my mom. They'll just tell you I'm fine, though. I'll miss you, too, but we'll be in touch again before you know it.*

Leigh would be out of touch with Mike, *and* with JJ. Mike understood, even if he didn't *like* it. But *JJ...*

JJ read her letter with sad resignation, knowing that the requirements of the Army and Leigh's job were more important than his loneliness—relieved only by a matronly waitress in Fayetteville who smiled at him a lot. Even so...

> *Green-Eyes*
> *...The part of me that <u>understands</u> the <u>requirement</u> gets screamed at by the part that <u>doesn't</u>. My last disastrous leave with Ma...I feel like I'm running out of options to get away from it all. But, the memory of you, even though we never acted on what feelings we had and maybe <u>still</u> have, will have to sustain me...so, until we meet again, sweetheart...love ya!*

> *I have to settle for what I can get.*

June

"Congratulations, Diver *First* Class Mueller," Master Chief Bollard smiled, shaking her hand. "You *do* realize you are now *the* lead female diver rating in the Navy, yes?"

"I *do*, Chief; I *do*," Ann smiled, "but since the *four* of us aren't all assigned together, I'm not sure what that *means*."

"Well, among *other* things, *you two* are qualified to operate a hyperbaric chamber, which means we can relieve Dr. Semmes of *some* of *those* duties." Chief Bollard nodded. "*That* means we can *safely* take on *more* women in the dive program." Because even Today's Navy couldn't *imagine* a *man* being able to relate to *women*, Commander/Dr. Allison Semmes was *their* doctor—*the* gynecologist with diving medicine experience who *exclusively* treated the Navy's first female divers.

"Still can't let *men* see *women* in the tank, Chief?" Betty Sadowski's no-nonsense approach to diving came from where she learned it originally—her family's Mississippi River salvage business. "Afraid we might get pregnant or something?" First Class diver school—a grueling twelve weeks in Panama City—was the first time Ann met Betty, a tall and shapely brunette with a weak chin and flat eyes but a riotous sense of humor, who was her dive buddy throughout the program, and was on *her* way from bomb disposal school.

"Diver Sadowski," Chief Bollard replied, "the Navy believes it to be *improper*; you *know* that."

Betty glanced mischievously at Ann. "*Yeah*, Chief," she swished her skirt up suddenly. "What's *improper* about *it*?"

Chief Bollard wasn't a particularly demonstrative man, but the sudden glance at Betty's shapely thighs—that he'd seen in the water, of course—*did* raise his eyebrows. "*Great* gams, Sadowski, but you're *not* going to change two centuries of traditional respect for *your* sex by flashing your pins."

"What if…?" Betty started opening her jacket.

"Not *those*, either, Betty" Ann frowned. "Since *I'm* the lead petty officer in this outfit, you'll belay *this* evolution at once."

"Take *all* the fun out of it, Ann," Betty mock-pouted.

> *Dear Dad,*
> *…Now we're no longer an <u>experiment</u>, but a part of a <u>program</u>.*
> *As soon as we can prove our worth, women in Navy diver ratings*
> *will be <u>routine</u> members of the dive community, even if the*
> *Navy's attitudes over women is unchanged. One step at a time.*

December

"*Benign*, Sergeant," the surgeon announced as JJ was wheeled out of the operating room. "No malignancy; just sarcoidosis, as we discussed."

Great. Now will someone please get this elephant off my chest?

It was early evening before JJ was coherent enough to think, gazing out the window at the sunset over the Panama jungle. He'd been at Fort Sherman, CZ for two months of an eleven-month temporary duty before he went on sick call with a persistent, painful cough. A chest x-ray had revealed a *shadow* in his chest the doctors didn't like. A battery of tests showed not much…but there was that *shadow*…and those lymph nodes.

Then there came his mediastinoscopy, where they cut his chest open to biopsy some of those lymph nodes. Routine, including the part where they took out a chunk of a rib to do it.

And here I am.

Under normal circumstances, because it was so invasive, the Army *would* have sent him to a VA hospital close to home for six weeks of rehabilitation. But he told them…*I've got nowhere that feels like home now.* So, he spent Christmas in the visitor's quarters.

Nearly two weeks after he left the hospital, a message from his unit—

odd because of the timing—called him to Major Zoltan Perc's office. His detachment commander was a Romanian refugee who'd joined the Army in Germany after escaping his native country in 1957. An uglier yet more handsome individual was hard to imagine—his face had all the right parts but they *seemed* misplaced—with eyes like penetrating blue orbs. He *also* spoke seven languages, including fluent profanity.

"Sergeant Elrath; thank you for coming during your rehab," Zoltan returned JJ's salute. "Someone's here to see you." For someone who did not grow up with English, his speech was remarkably free of an accent.

"Hey, Mike," JJ grinned. "What brings *you*…"

"*Excuse* us, sir," Mike smiled at Zoltan. "Official *and* personal, if you get my drift." As Zoltan left, Mike and JJ sat on a small GSA sofa. "Official but *not* official, buddy," Mike declared. "What do you know of the Newhouse family?"

"Just what you and Leigh have told me and, well, his *organization* sent us a ham for Christmas in '67, and Dad was pissed about it because just before *that* he forced us to sell the place on Round Lake, then turned around and developed the property."

"OK. Do you remember Matt Dryden?"

"No: should I?"

"You threw him over a stair rail at North Hills Junior High in 1970. He hasn't walked since. Matt's *Joe* Dryden's half-brother."

"Never *knew* his name. He was…"

"Molesting Katherine Wanamaker, yeah. But do you know *Joe*?" Hard-of-hearing Kat was one of the few girls that paid any attention to JJ in junior high.

"I don't know *Joe* Dryden, either." JJ looked at Mike sidelong. "Why"

"Joe works for the Newhouse outfit and swore vengeance on you years ago. He's made extensive inquiries as to your whereabouts through unofficial channels." Mike sighed. "I'm *here* because the FBI *isn't*. Dryden's a blowhard, but he has dangerous people on his payroll. By means we're unclear on, he's had reports of *your* location since '74."

"OK," JJ shrugged. "What's…?"

"He's also been aware of *my* location, from *about* the same time."

JJ sighed, his chest suddenly aching. "That's not good?"

"*Not* good. *I'm* in law enforcement." Mike frowned. "Our question is, *why* he's interested in you *and* me?"

"Leigh's had legal trouble with the Newhouse outfit. Related?"

"Unlikely. It's like they're *watching*, but no one knows for *what*. I came down here because we want you to be aware, when you go home, that you *really* pissed someone off, someone with a *long* memory. And…" Mike smiled, "because I didn't want my friend to spend Christmas alone in the visitor's quarters."

Oh. "What do you hear from Leigh?"

"Not a *lot*; you know she's…"

"Yeah; she told me *that* much. I can still miss her, though, yeah."

"Yeah. *You've* known each other for…" Mike stopped when they heard the AUTOVON phone ring: a distinctive and loud ring. The Detachment Sergeant came in and answered; "HHC, 31st MI Detachment; Sergeant First Class Mallory speaking…*yes*, they are." He handed the phone to Mike. "Keep it short."

"Hi, Sandy," Leigh's voice was hollow over the line. The Automatic Voice Network (AUTOVON) was a Department of Defense relic from the '60s, but still was a secure way to call between stations. Ostensibly for *official* traffic, it was sometimes used *unofficially.*

"Hi, oytzer," Mike smiled, "Merry Christmas tomorrow."

"Merry Christmas to you, too, babe. How's Panama in December?"

"Hotter than Arizona, but wetter. How's it wherever *you* are?"

"I can tell you that there's snow here. Is my Blue-Eyes there?"

Mike handed JJ the phone and left, smiling. "Hi, Green-Eyes."

"Hi, JJ. Heard you were sick?"

"*Sort* of, yeah. Nothing that'll kill me, but the jury's out on whether it will see me dead. How are *you*, other than fine?"

"Never been so busy doing nothing, honey. I miss hearing from you."

"Me, too. How much longer's *this* gig?"

"Not *that* long." She paused. "Blue-Eyes, you *know* that Mike and I…"

"Yeah, but a guy can have *friends* that are *girls*, can't he?"

"Sure. I'll tell *you* a secret before I go back to Mike: *you're* a better kisser than *he* is; *I* think so, anyway. We only did it that *once*, but that was all *I* needed."

"But you don't feel the same way about *me* as you do Mike."

"Sorry, babe. Merry Christmas, Blue-Eyes. Get me back to Mike?"

"And a Merry Christmas to *you*, Green-Eyes."

He knocked on the door and Mike came back; JJ handed him the phone and left. "You good?"

"Yeah. You?"

"Yeah. *He* needed this."

"Sandy, so did *I*. I *love* you, babe."

"*Love* you too, *oytzer*."

1982

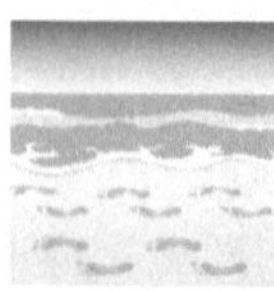

January

OK: jib crane, welding; struck the arc and I went flying. Saw the drink coming up fast and... Johnny, let me straighten that tie.

As she tried to piece together what happened, Ann stared at the ever-white desert of a ceiling and the spiderwebs on the curtains. The Coronado base hospital was, like all hospitals, sterile in places and filthy in others. She sighed loudly; Kristin suddenly appeared at her bedside. "Hey," Ann croaked, her throat dry.

"*Yeah*, hey *yourself*. How you feeling?"

"Like I flew through the air and into the drink."

Kristin made a concerned face. "You had us going for a while there."

"Going where?"

"Your attempt at levity is noted, but *my* orders are to get straight answers." She sat on the bed. "First: *who's* Johnny?"

"A friend from my old neighborhood. Why?" *Wanted to see him...DID see him working on his tie.*

"You were saying his name: a *lot*. Does Cable know about him?"

"Sort-of. Haven't *seen* Johnny in years. Anybody know what happened?"

"Power factor correction capacitors up there exploded. Don't know why."

"Happened just as I struck the arc."

"Poor ground, then. They'll ask you about it." Kristin leaned over and gently kissed Ann's forehead. "But *not* today. Just rest now."

"I'm OK," Ann complained. "Get me out of here..."

"No, you *don't*," the long-headed woman who burst through the door declared brusquely. "Not at least until tomorrow."

"Doctor Semmes," Ann began, "I'm *OK*. Really."

"Not until I *say* you are, Ann." Allison glanced at Ann's chart and glared at Kristin. "And how are *you*, Kristin? You get over that bug?"

"Yes, ma'am," Kristin answered meekly.

The doctor took Ann's pulse, looked at her eyes and ears, poked her belly, and listened to her lungs. "Bends lately?"

"No."

"Feel any tightness anywhere? Any pain?"

"Other than a little lightheaded, I'm fine."

"The lightheaded is shock, Ann. You were blown twenty feet out, rolled into a ball, and fell fifty into the harbor. Any thoughts?"

"Not…really."

> *Deb,*
> *I saw Johnny again, and NOT underwater…*

March

Alone, dead in a ditch like Marcie in that basement. And for what?

Marcie had been seventeen when she OD'd on Quaaludes and tequila in her senior year of high school. This boy had been nineteen—barely—when he smoked the hashish/opium mixture locally called *mangchi*—hammer—that had been cut with rat poison. He had been in Korea only long enough to find out where he could score. Four nights running he went out, and four mornings running he made it back in time for reveille: The fifth, he didn't. They found him in a ditch a week later.

Leigh was new to a narcotics detail. She did her undercover gig at Fort Drum, catching senior NCOs selling club liquor out the back door. In late '81 they sent her back to Korea. She already knew the slang—and mildly resented the fact that there was *still* no female equivalent of KPCOD (Korean pussy cut-off date) in general use, though FIGMO (forget it, got my orders) was still genderless.

Leigh looked at the boy's water-swollen body with sadness, distrust, and revulsion, thinking of her friend Marcie. An MP had to be present for the post-mortem just in case there was evidence to be preserved when the pathologists flayed him like a shot deer. They didn't find anything they weren't expecting: the kid drowned in his own blood when his lungs hemorrhaged. Steppenwolf played in her head…

Stoned on some new potion he found upon the wall
Of some unholy bathroom, in some ungodly hall!
He only had a dollar to live on till next Monday;
But he spent it on some comfort for his mind.
Did you say you think he's blind?

This kid was the fifth *mangchi*-related fatality in two months, and Command wanted *action*, though as usual they were light on *how* to keep bored kids from wanting to get high. CID did sweeps of their informants, put new faces into mess halls, the PX and recreation areas. Then Leigh's team got a lead on a distribution point: a container in an Ascom City salvage yard.

A month of work followed: dull nights and days of watching; taking pictures; following this guy, then that gal; working names assigned until they put a name on the face; repeat. Five guys were regulars for five weeks, alternating nights—*not* customers, but running the show. Dozens of customers showed up irregularly—a *lot* less regular than the poor kid in the ditch had, anyway.

To get into Ascom City's salvage yard with any appreciable load—they were selling at least a thousand 8-balls a night—you needed a pass; moving that much weight meant someone drove it there. So, they compared ID photos of drivers authorized to come and go in the yard to their surveillance pictures, and found *two* matches. One was an American contractor they'd dubbed Red 4. CID set up a honey trap.

A newly-arrived, fresh-faced MP, dressed in a leather halter, fishnets and ratty mini-skirt approached Red 4 at a base bowling alley and led him to an unused storeroom. She tolerated his pawing and groping *just* long enough before she announced *her* price. Red 4 growled, "I've got *this*," holding out a tinfoil wad the size of a golf ball. "Enough *mangchi* 8-balls for a *month*." As soon as he lit up behind the bowling alley, Leigh's team *sans* Leigh were all over them.

Three days later Leigh entered an overheated concrete block holding room where Red 4 impatiently waited. "OK, a few administrative matters and you can get out of here," Leigh sighed, sitting down. "Sorry about the confusion, but there's a backlog. Now," she smiled, fake glasses on her nose, fatigue shirt off and t-shirt *too* tight on a *whisper*-thin bra. "You're a maintenance contractor with the salvage yard, yes?"

"Yes, that's right. I *demand*..."

"*That's* the confusion right there," Leigh declared. "You were detained with...let's see...Morgan Cornwall. The charge is the possession of more than five grams of..."

"*Not* mine," he declared. "*She* was trying to sell it..."

"Yeah: *she* said *you* were trying to trade it for *her*, ah, *time*. The worst thing about junkies is how they all use the *same story* all the time."

"But it *wasn't* mine. Look, I..."

"Huh," she sighed as she pulled from her portfolio three photos of him *holding* the dope, and slid them across the table. "Not *yours*?"

He went pale. "That's...not..."

"Not *you*? Not what it *looks* like? Heard *those* before, too." She put the pictures back in her portfolio, inhaling *deeply* for the distracting effect. "OK, we found enough evidence at your place to turn you over to the *Korean* authorities: out of our hands. If you'll *just*..."

"You can't *do* that," he sputtered, his eyes bouncing between her chest and her face in erratic haste as he turned red, "*I'm* an American citizen..."

"*You're* involved in the manufacture and distribution of narcotics on Korean soil. They take *that* very seriously, *so* seriously they have a special prison…"

"The Slab," he grinned, staring at her eyes. "A myth." The Slab was, rumor had it, a former Japanese camp where the conditions were so brutal that death was preferable to incarceration there. Even so, the mandatory sentence for narcotics *processing* in Korea was life in prison—and no parole was *ever* granted.

"*Is* it?" She gave her shark-to-minnow smile and a *tiny* shake of her chest. "*Want* to roll *those* dice?"

He gulped, distracted again. "*What* do you…?"

"*That's* better," she smiled, removing her glasses and gently swinging her honey-brown hair…*and* her chest *ever*-so-gently. "*Much* better."

> *Sandy*
> *…It was so sad seeing that boy in the morgue. I kept*
> *remembering Marcie. I wanted to bust that asshole wide*
> *open…that story about The Slab is so convincing <u>we're</u> not even*
> *sure if it's not true.*
> *One of the guys we nailed knew JJ at Wolverine…*

That was how the *mangchi* ring in the Inchon-Seoul corridor was busted, and Leigh was promoted to Staff Sergeant without a board. It was also how *she* became acquainted with Red 4, who, coincidentally, turned out to be an alumnus of Wolverine, and one of the thieves of JJ's soul — because once they *start* talking, they *can't stop*:

> *My Dear Blue-Eyes,*
> *…I busted Jay Pardon here; he'll be locked up for a while, babe.*
> *He had quite a story to tell about you.*
> *John, my <u>dear</u> friend, if you <u>ever</u> need to talk about <u>that</u>*
> *circle of Hell, you know I'll listen.*

August

I would have killed to see her naked, but not like this.

As Clare slept beside him with her thumb in her mouth and the ancient, rusty window air conditioner finally fell silent, he reconstructed the chain of events that brought him *here*, to *her* bed as he watched the curtains in front of the sun-drenched window slowly stop moving.

On Tuesday—four days before that morning—Karen called him: Clare's daughter had died suddenly—undiagnosed heart defect. She'd stopped answering her phone; she wasn't going to work.

OK, you aren't much for letter-writing…ain't heard from you since you said that loser you married walked out before Christmas.

On Wednesday he wrangled a *fast* leave—which required a *great deal* of "sir, yes, sir" kowtowing, forelock-tugging and soul-bearing on his part—and drove all day and night Thursday in his un-air-conditioned black plain-Jane '70 Plymouth Fury III.

He pounded on her door mid-Friday-morning, then shouted from the street. She finally came to the door in a sheer green *super*-short negligée that hid *nearly* nothing…and she uncharacteristically made *no* effort to cover up. Her round face was puffy, her brown eyes listless and without her fire.

"I can't *believe* you're here," she repeated, letting him in. They shared wine and crackers—all the food she had in the house—before she crawled into bed and he held her while she wailed and screamed and cried long after sunset.

By sunrise Saturday, the top sheet was on the floor because it was *just too hot* despite the air conditioner. The male part of him wanted nothing more than to make passionate love to her; the human part wanted her to sleep away her deep, agonizing pain. She turned over and opened one shining, bleary, surprised eye. "Can't believe…"

"Happy birthday, Ware," he grinned.

She stretched stiffly, lying flat down and still before she yawned and smiled. "I *want* my *pres*ent."

"Your…?"

She ran her hand up his thigh and under his shorts. "My *present. Now.*"

We've never even made out. "Ware, are you…?"

"Shut *up*, John and *give* me my *pres*ent."

* * *

She shook her head and looked away. "*Still* can't believe you're here."

"You'd *better* believe it."

As the waitress took their plates away, Clare sounded as if she were describing some horrid dream. "I *knew* I'd made a mistake with Jack as soon as that so-called honeymoon started, but I tried to make *us* work, even if I was the only one bringing money home. One night we discussed *that*, and when I came home from work next day…the note said, 'I can't stand the *thought* of you. Your brat's with your sister.'" She glanced at him. "I wrote to *you* about it because I knew you wouldn't judge me."

"What's to judge?"

"Wish my *parents* thought that. Thanks for that letter: *some* wedding present. I take it Karen called you, or Mom?"

"Karen. But I *meant* it. Just lucky I was in-country this time."

She sighed. "I *know*." She turned sad. "Tara was playing and climbing at eight o'clock, and at ten, she was gone. Felt like Jack leaving again, only when *he* went, there was some relief. With Tara, just…*pain.*"

He reached for her hand. She took it, squeezed and let go. "Come on. This booth is uncomfortable." The afternoon was sweltering, clingy. Heat radiated off the street, the sidewalks, the utility poles and the patches of thin grass. She wore flip-flops with her long skirt and loose blouse, her thick hair bundled in a scarf. Part of him felt overdressed since he wore socks with his jungle boots, cutoffs and t-shirt. They stayed apart on their slow walk in the shadows the few blocks to her row house, sticky with sweat and struggling to breathe in the humidity.

"Feeling better?"

"Yeah," she answered, climbing the concrete steps to her door, hesitating briefly. "That's *my* phone!" They hurried into the drier-but-warm house, and she dived for the phone. She spoke briefly before handing it to him. "Mom wants a word."

Oh, great. "I slept with your grief-stricken daughter, and I plan to keep doing it as long as she's willing." "Hi, Mom." They talked for a few minutes before he followed Clare upstairs.

She stood in the bedroom in front of the air conditioning vent, untying her hair as she gazed out the window into the deep shadow of the building next door. He came up behind and wrapped his arms around her, resting his chin on her shoulder. She enveloped his arms with hers, sighing deeply. "Why *you*?"

"Why me what?"

"Why can *you* make me feel *so* peaceful? *No one* else. *You.*"

"I remind you of when you showed me the view from the hill behind Faculty Row." *Spectacular fall colors; clear blue sky; new friend.*

"I don't remember *that.*"

"Was I *that* forgettable?"

"I remember Thanksgiving when your cousin came over."

"Niece; Julia. She's twenty-six today, too."

"She brought your truck." She pulled on his arms. "I was jealous."

"Of what?"

"*Her.* She knew you better than I did."

"You had Ernie. How was *I* going to…?"

"*We* were just cuddle-buddies." Ernie, a classmate, was Clare's *official* boyfriend.

"What's *that*?"

"We'd cuddle, make out. Never went past second base…and *that* not for *long* or *often*, no matter *what* the gossips said." She turned around in his arms. "It kept everyone else away."

"On purpose?"

She stretched up to kiss him deeply. "Uh-huh."

"He got married. Newsletter says two kids now." The quarterly alumni newsletter ran announcements, profiles of illustrious alumni, news of the Brookfield community, and solicitation for donations.

"Yeah." They climbed into bed, and she put her head on his shoulder.

Oh, I'm gonna say something stupid, but I can't help it. "Come back to Bragg with me, Ware."

She sighed heavily, propping herself up on an elbow. "I *love* you for asking, but…" She put a finger on his lips and smiled sweetly before she brushed away a tear. "My family would *never* approve."

"Of *me?*"

"Of *us.*"

"Do they imagine I'm sleeping on your couch?"

"They're distracted by Karen's new baby." She laid down again and caressed him softly, absently. "Just…don't *ask* more, John. *Please.*"

As he drifted off to sleep that night, he was jolted—briefly—by a memory of his Cloud. He felt like a traitor, but he wasn't sure *who* he'd betrayed—Clare or Cloud.

Strangely, though, he could finally answer Leigh's letter:

> *Green-Eyes,*
> *Finally getting back to you. It's been a hellish spring and summer with ROTC support…*
>
> *Jay Pardon: <u>never</u> would be too soon for me to hear <u>that</u> name again. Surprised that he referred to me like that, though. They wanted me to change my story, and I wouldn't, despite what they did to me. I still get nightmares of Wolverine, and Jay, and his buddy Herman.*
>
> *If you care for me, Green-Eyes, keep what he told you to yourself. Mike knows most of it, but <u>that</u> place is just some shit that happened to me.*
>
> *…That I still have nightmares about…*

1983

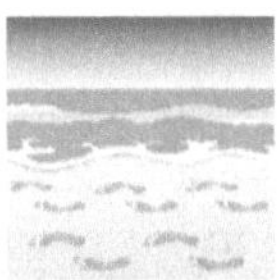

June

This walk will never be the same again.

Ann wore many hats at Coronado: storekeeper, hull technician and diver among them. But *this* hat—the lover—was being knocked off.

The little condo was just a short walk from the bus stop on Silver Strand Boulevard. She'd walked it many times, back and forth from her billets, the amphibious center, the naval air station, and the logistics center. She and Cable had had four years full of laughs, love, and adventure. They both knew that it wasn't going to be forever: they both knew he was the *third* of Ann's Sixty-Day Wonders. But after four years, *this felt different.*

She walked down Avenida Del Sol, lined with condos, co-ops and apartments basking in the sun. She waved to the sweet blue-haired grandmother who she sometimes chatted with in the lobby, and went up the elevator. His two-and-a-half room beachcomber efficiency had a bedroom barely big enough for a king bed, and a living room/kitchenette with a cupboard that *could* be used for pantry space but that Cable used as a dresser. He had added a small refrigerator, a coffeepot, a hot plate for his only saucepan, and a toaster: Ann contributed a used electric frying pan for the occasional egg and bacon breakfast. He talked about a microwave, but they were expensive.

Ann let herself in, thinking she should just leave a note and her key, saying so long: their last, loud, sort-of-not-argument left their status ambiguous, and she didn't like that. Then she got a glimpse of what cost *so* much in *that* building, on *that* floor: the spectacular view of the Pacific barely fifty yards to the southwest through the balcony's sliding glass doors. On clear summer nights, the golden-red sunset glow could last till midnight. *How could I leave this…and him…like that?*

She glanced at the clock: he wouldn't be home for a couple of hours. She thought about stripping down, getting a real bath, and waiting for him between the sheets: he liked that. She opted for the bath, *not* the seduction.

She was reading in the living room when he came in, glad to see her as ever, their earlier arguments seemingly forgotten. Cable was a typical California beach boy who reminded her of her scuba instructor when she was in high school, with sandy brown hair, a quick smile, and china-blue eyes.

They pecked each other's cheeks and shared their day. She'd run personal errands; he'd fixed a classic Dale Velzy eight-foot single-fin surfboard. "For what it cost to repair, that guy could have bought *two* new boards," he mused, sucking down a beer. "But it wouldn't be a Velzy."

"I suppose not." She tried to turn towards him on the sofa, but her bad hip objected. "Cable, do we *have* to…"

"I figured it out, Annie." He looked at her like she was a stranger. "I *knew* there could be nothing long-term for us, but I *need* more."

"Like commitment?"

"Like commitment." He gazed at the Pacific. "I'll be forty next month. I get the bends now all the time. I own this place outright, but I can't keep up the condo fees and taxes by myself if I have to stop diving."

"Cable, honey, I'm sorry," she started. "I can imagine…"

"No, Annie, *you* can't." He tried sounding disgusted but only came off as sad. "*You* have a barracks you sleep in most of the time, get three-hots-and-a-cot just for *being* there. *I* don't have Uncle Sam to fall back on."

"I have obligations, Cable. I work for them; they feed me. Works the same way."

"*You* pay the same for your room and board all the time. *My* condo fees just went up."

OK, there's your excuse. "So, you want someone to help with that?"

He seemed deflated. "Yeah, but I *need* someone who I *know* will be here next *year*, not just next *month*."

"You need a *partner*, not just a roll in the hay paying some rent."

"No, no, honey, no. I…I love being with you; I love doing *everything* with you, not *just making* love. But I *need* more."

"So, if I'm *not* in the picture…"

"Let's not…not look at it *that* way. I'm not *looking*. I *can't* as long as you're in this time zone." He gazed out the window. "I love everything *about* you, but…Annie, I can't *afford* to love *you*."

"I understand." And, incredibly, sadly, she did.

A month later, Ann got orders to report to Seventh Fleet in Yokohama in September—a 14-month tour. On their last night together, after watching the sun gloriously set over the Pacific, she dreamed of her last moments with Johnny.

> *Deb,*
> *I still miss him so much it hurts, even now…*

October

"That's not one of ours."

JJ looked at what the personnel clerk pointed to: a twin-engine cargo plane that looked like it was lining up on the Port Salines Airport runway. The unfinished Grenada airfield was one reason he and the Rangers were there.

Cuban markings. "No, it ain't. Get your weapon." He looked around at the clerks and cooks putting the headquarters together. *"Everybody,"* he shouted. *"Weapons!"*

My first taste of combat and not a grunt to be seen. "Come *on*, you guys: come *on! Hustle! Come ON!* Web gear! Helmets! *For Chrissakes, get your asses MOVING!"* Unfamiliar with the immediacy of battle, the men clumsily collected their gear and weapons. Four of them had 40 mm grenade launchers attached to their M-16s; three others manhandled a .50 caliber machine gun; two more an M-60 machine gun. *Firepower: two machine guns and four grenade launchers. Position: they'll head for cover, so...* "*This* way," JJ shouted, leading them across the hardstand.

The area was dotted with construction equipment and material. He set the .50 caliber crew down behind a stack of steel beams near the terminal. He told the M-60 crew to set up where a pair of dump trucks were parked with their dump boxes raised fifty meters to the left. He scattered the grenade launchers and the riflemen behind stacks of concrete bags along the space between the two.

Now, a clear signal...and a distraction. He rushed around and told his men: "when that gas can blows," he pointed to the back of a Russian-pattern jeep near the taxiway 100 meters away, "that fifty-caliber will open up. Then *you* start shooting at that plane. Don't stop until I tell you." At that range and angle, the gas can was a barely-visible sliver. While most shooters would balk at such a target, JJ *wasn't most* shooters.

By the time the clerks and cooks were in position, the little Russian cargo hauler—an An-26, called a Curl by NATO—had landed.

Wait till he stops...wait...wait... The plane rolled to about mid-runway before turning off towards the terminal while JJ spent precious seconds making sure that phosphorus-tipped tracer rounds were the first three out of his rifle.

The plane roared around to present its cargo door to the building. As the engines wound down, the back door/ramp began descending, and armed men started to pile out, loitering on the hardstand.

No way I get THAT lucky. He touched off three rounds quickly; the can exploded when the second shot hit it.

The hammering of the heavy machine gun was immediately joined by the rattling of the rest of the ambush as the grenade launchers *thump-thumped* away. The hardstand around the plane was alive with dust, explosions, and sparks as men started to drop and flop on the hardstand; a few fired back blindly. The ramp stopped descending, men piled back aboard as the engines roared to life again and the plane rolled away.

His scratch ambush (one of "his men" was the battalion personnel officer—a captain, no less) started cheering as their quick-thinking leader fell to his knees thanking Providence—*thank Christ there was gas in that damn can*—just as his battalion commander roared onto the hardstand.

✳✳✳

The troops passed in review—of the 7,000 Americans on the ground on Grenada, nearly 400 soldiers, sailors, airmen, and Marines paraded after the brief award ceremony for the five Silver Star winners—to include one *very*-sudden-Staff Sergeant John Jacob Elrath, Junior—and the score of others who won lesser awards. Oh, there would be more ceremonies, more awards, more speeches by the politicians once there were *enough* cameras to capture them. But *this* was for the troops, and neither cameras nor reporters were invited.

Afterward, there was a banquet for the medal-winners. Because this was the New Face of the US military *and* its emergence from the stains of Vietnam, the first American women to go into combat zones since the abolition of the gender-segregated branches—helicopter pilots, medics and MPs—joined the all-male awardees.

"*Leigh,*" JJ exclaimed when he saw her luminous green eyes from across the tent. "What in *hell* are *you* doing here?"

"*JJ,*" Leigh cried when she saw his baby-blues. "I could ask *you* the same thing. They picked *me* for *this* carnival because I'm from Michigan, so *I'm* supposed to be *your* date."

"Well, let's get some chow." The XVIII Airborne Corps headquarters cooks made the feast better than average. There were grilled-to-order steaks—not unusual but not *common*, and hard to cut with plastic knives on paper plates—*real* mashed potatoes and fresh creamed spinach that was *not* served out of big green Mermite cans that tended to continue cooking food that they were *supposed* to just keep warm—or cool, depending. There was even fresh tossed salad in big iced bowls and a fresh-baked sheet cake.

The awardees and their companions sat alone—*without* the brass or even the public information flaks—under an open-sided mess fly, a steady wind flapping the canvas. Only JJ and Leigh knew each other, which made their interaction *somewhat* weird but no weirder than the idea that the military could/would pair off strangers for social engagement. The friends concentrated on a combination of home stories and chow—and used their ever-present pocket knives to cut the steaks.

He glanced at the wings on her chest. "Did you jump in here?

"No: we air-landed two days ago."

"How'd you get jump school? I did it in '73 with the first women, but they were riggers."

She grinned. "Three years ago, we're in noon formation, and the First Sergeant *asked* for *female* volunteers while he stared at *me*. I naturally said, 'Top, I'd be *glad* to volunteer. For *what* am I *volunteering*?'"

"Filled another quota, huh?"

"Yeah. That was right *after* CID school, and I'm—*we're*—still filling quotas. Even being *here*: there were twelve airborne-qualified female MPs at Bragg. They swooped us all up in the middle of the night, put us on a plane and here we are. I just put in for warrant officer school."

"Yeah? *I've* thought of that. Seen Mike lately? Half-expected to see him *here*..."

"He's in Arizona again, training interrogators. I got a letter from him a couple of weeks ago. I last *saw* him...let's see...November '79, just before CID school."

"Mike's a great guy." he murmured, forking in the last of his dinner. *I'm genuinely glad for you, Green-Eyes, but my heart just broke a little...again.* "Like you said; we *missed* our chance."

She smiled sweetly. "Sorry, Johnny." Breaking all possible conventions, she reached for his hand on the table. He smiled, took her hand gently. *Right now, I don't care.*

Those two were *close* comrades-in-arms, a hybrid, twilight status that many service members were getting used to in the '80s: That these two knew each other before that afternoon was irrelevant. The services knew such relationships were developing, especially among the 25-35 age groups. Their problem was how to deal with them. Should they *eliminate* or *control* them? Could—or *should*—they *do either one*? Compounding the issue was the need to maintain their gender-integration mandate, meet the needs of their "go where you're sent" operational requirements—and all the while *not* risk losing those most precious and irreplaceable of military commodities: mid-career, mid-grade officers and NCOs.

As they left the tent to go back to their units, the two staff sergeants knew that, in parting, their *professional* status would be compromised if they did what they *felt* like doing. But, somewhere between her slow wink and his half-grin, they silently conspired to find out *how* to make out while wearing Kevlar helmets. When the brain-bucket rims touched, it pushed the helmets back on the neck while pulling the chin straps tight: fortunately, JJ never strapped *his* helmet on except when he was jumping, so their contact didn't restrict *their* movement. It was a *little* awkward—and amusing to *most* of their little audience, four of whom—a Marine and a helicopter pilot; another Marine and a Navy Corps-*person*—decided to *briefly* try it themselves.

> *Sandy,*
> *I now have to <u>officially</u> say that I've made out with JJ*
> *Elrath twice…it was one of the wildest, sweetest things I've ever*
> *done in a uniform…after ten years, it was time.*
> *True confession, zeeskeit: he's a <u>great</u> kisser.*

However, there *was* some brass around who were not amused because osculation between two service members in public while on duty is, perforce, bad for morale. Exactly *whose* morale *suffers* from such kissing has never been established in policy. That the kissing couples obviously didn't care *what* the brass thought distressed *them* even more.

> *Mike*
> *I can't believe Green-Eyes just…brother, you <u>know</u> she's*
> *yours, <u>not</u> mine, but can we <u>share</u> her lips from time to time, just*
> *for a few minutes?*

The American military was changing, but *not* in ways that the powers-that-were could either control or foresee…yet.

December

> *Ann,*
> *Did you see this?*

The carefully folded Detroit *Free Press* article carried a bold headline: *Bloomfield Man Wins Silver Star in Grenada* with a familiar by-line: Carol Mueller.

> *Dad,*
> *Well, I'll be damned; Johnny joined the Army, too. And he's*
> *a hero. Why am I not surprised? Doesn't say where he's*
> *stationed, or if he's married…I still need to at least say good-*
> *bye, Dad, if I have to.*

> *Deb,*
> *…My God, he's a Ranger, too! The Special Operations*
> *community's SO small…and I'm sort-of part of it…wonder what*
> *might happen…what would I DO?*

1985

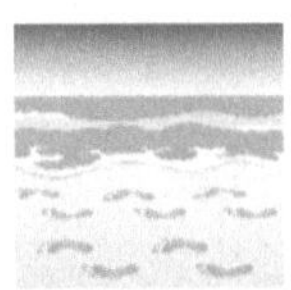

May

"Sandy: what *are* we *doing*?" They were in a shady spot on the side of the motel pool in Millen, breathing hard from a short, intense workout.

"Right now, soaking in a lukewarm pool after swimming a few laps. But you want to know…"

"Yeah."

"I could have sworn we're enjoying each other's company, *oytzer*."

I want to KNOW. "Yeah, but we'll *be*—we've *been*—separated a lot. How long can we keep this up?"

She wants to KNOW. "We've been corresponding for how long now?"

"Thirteen years, next month. But you've *had* lovers…"

"So have you." He blinked, swallowed hard. *TRUTH.* "On leave in Detroit last year I got drunk in a saloon one night and called Donna. She took me back to her place." His face became sad. "*She* got sort-of naked; *I* didn't get *quite* naked I don't *think. We* made out on her bed. I kept thinking of you."

It was all *she* could do to keep a straight face. "Mike, *she's beautiful* with or *without* clothes. And she *was* your girlfriend in high school."

"But we *never*…I just kept thinking of you." They gazed solemnly at each other. "I *couldn't*…"

Should I be jealous of my best friend—friends? "Sandy, I'm calling bullshit. You *didn't*…"

"Ask her yourself."

THIS could be fun. "OK, I *will*," she grinned and pushed out of the pool. "Right *now*."

Boychik, where is this headed? PLEASE, Blondie: DON'T BE THERE!

Back in their room, Leigh dialed Donna's number, half-hoping that she *wouldn't* be there on a Sunday morning: "Hello?"

"Donna? Hi! It's Leigh. How are *you* up there?"

"Oh, hi! I'm busy. Where *are* you?"

"Millen."

"Oh! Meeting Sandy again?"

"Hi, Blondie," Mike shouted.

"Hi, Sandy! What…"

"Blondie, tell Leigh about the last time you and I saw each other."

"Dinner the night before you left?"

"You *know* what I mean, gorgeous."

"Um…OK. Leigh, honey, you *know* we both love you…"

They DID! "OK, *you* got naked. Did *he*?" Leigh puckered at Mike while stifling a chuckle.

"We *weren't*, not *quite*… *just* underwear. I…call it a *weak* moment, but *we* were drunk…"

"And *you* thought *you* could take advantage of *my* inebriated condition." Mike nearly choked, "making out on *your* bed *nearly* in the *altogether*."

"You kept saying 'what Adam saw,' and repeating Leigh's name every time we…oh, *shit* this isn't the way I…oh, *you guys*!" They both cracked up laughing.

After several moments, Mike picked up the phone again. "Blondie, we're gonna let you go, OK? Have a good…"

"When are you guys coming home again?"

"Don't know," Leigh answered, standing in front of him. "I *might* come up Christmas: I've got a gig at Leonard Wood in February."

"*Maybe* Christmastime, Blondie," Mike added, kissing Leigh's belly.

"OK: write me with the details. See you guys! Love ya!"

She sighed, holding his head to her body, stroking his hair as he hung up the phone. "Sandy, do *you want* to stay exclusive?" In six years, they had been together a total of 31 non-consecutive days: their typical tryst was three days, but there *had* been two four-day Thanksgivings. They wrote—sometimes twice a week—and often called for birthdays and significant events…like getting orders or promotions.

"I do." *And the rest, boychik? Before you lose your nerve?* "If we ever get the chance, would you consider something more lasting? More, um, legal?"

KNEW it would FEEL different a second time. "If you're asking what I *think* you're asking," she grinned, hooking her thumbs in her Speedo shoulder straps, and *slowly* peeling her suit down, *completely*, as she stepped back. "My answer is…" she hung her face in his, "I've wanted to bear your children since we met." She kissed him deeply as his hands rested softly on her breasts. "Now I can't *imagine* making love with *anyone* but you. But, my *sweet* love," she tousled his hair, "*right* now I'm hungry. I'm buying."

"Leigh: if you're *serious*, we should make a *tsuzog*."

"A what?"

"A pledge; *tsuzog* is Yiddish. Serious thing in my world."

"Serious, like an engagement?" *Do I need to tell the Army?*

"Serious like engaged-to-be-engaged. I *have* to tell my family."

She sighed and sat on the bed opposite, smiling broadly. "We're making love *later*, Mike. But first *I* need to eat."

"And our pledge?"

"Do I need to get dressed?"

"Just…pledge yourself to me forever."

"OK: I pledge myself to you forever."

"And *I* pledge *myself* to *you* forever."

They kissed briefly. "Can we *eat* now?"

***

Perfect: South Florida in August.

JJ smiled wryly at the warning order—the orders-before-the-orders. In layman's terms, he was to be the second-straw boss to a bunch of listeners and readers, watchers and thinkers in Key West, Florida,[1] who were collecting all the information they could on the Russkies and their Latin American buddies in the Caribbean basin.

But the scratch Ranger battalion there—an overstrength headquarters company and two understrength companies with barely enough men to make *one* full Ranger company—was well-known to have *two* missions:

- To cover the Army's special operations intelligence presence,
- To provide convalescence for *very* costly special operators hurt on the job.

As always, there was a delay between duty stations—three weeks. *I could drive to Detroit, add a day for the trip down from there.* He thought about that for a while, finally deciding *what for? Nothing for me there but Ma and the old man and…well, Clare, maybe…wish she'd write.*

He tucked that away in the back of his mind, secured in a private pouch shielded from everyone except his Cloud.

> *Cloud*
> *…I need more than a few kisses and a little friction once in a while, honey. Leigh's heart belongs to Mike…we're too good friends to be rivals. And Clare…two letters in two years since she said, "I'm sorry." I wish I knew <u>how</u> to find you. Like Gunga Din; this is the life I wanted. I may deserve only what I get, but what I get for myself just ain't much.*

---

[1] He was to be the Assistant Non-Commissioned-Officer-In-Charge (ANCOIC) of the All-Source Production Center—Land Warfare (ASPC-LW) at the Southern Command Joint Intelligence Center Annex (SOCOMJIC-A), assigned to Headquarters Company (HHC), 4th Battalion of the 75th Infantry Regiment (Ranger), 4/75th in short. Ya just gotta *love* military alphabet soup.

Sometimes, when guys got orders they didn't like, they recited part of a Kipling poem as a reminder that they *have* to do what they *have* to do because it's what *they* wanted, because the last draftee reenlisted in '74.

> *Though I've belted you and flayed you*
> *By the livin' Gawd that made you*
> *You're a better man than I am, Gunga Din.*

August

Friday

Ann followed Roger into the cool, fresh-smelling Holiday Inn room, a high-profile place as opposed to where they usually got together. He brought a bag—a small gym bag but a bag nonetheless—and told her they'd be there overnight. *Is this a sign?* This guy never wanted to meet her friends, but she resisted the thought that their relationship was…

> *Deb,*
> *…Roger's a truck driver, based in Tampa. He gets here when he gets here, turns around and goes back next day. Is a Sixty-Day Joe or just a roll in the hay, Is there a difference? He's never even asked where I'm from.*
> *Have I come to this? I put it on paper and it starts to look…ugh!*

Ann and Kristin had arrived in Key West that January with two other female Navy divers—Betty and another bomb disposal expert they had worked with in Japan. Since Ann met Roger in May, she had tried to get him to meet her someplace *without* a bed, but that never worked for him. Their sex every few weeks was great, he was funny and easy to talk to, wasn't intimidated by her muscular frame, and he *wasn't* in the Navy—all things she liked. At 30, after thirteen years in the Navy, she was looking for a personal future and felt she *might* have a future with him, but *he* never seemed to want to discuss anything like a relationship deeper than…he'd leave a message at her barracks and they'd rendezvous.

They shared a quiet dinner in the hotel restaurant, talking about nothing other than her work—varied, but mostly routine—and his travels. He offered very little in the way of his personal details, and asked very little in return.

The next morning, as they parted after breakfast, she had a flash on Johnny's face, his brave half-grin, and it made her feel guilty of betrayal. But she didn't know if it was Roger or Johnny she was betraying.

***

Michael
Your sister Sara has accepted a proposal of marriage from
Oliver Halliwell...and Kiera has accepted Norman Grun...try to
make sure that you are home on the last weekend in October for
their weddings.

Mike read his mother's letter with a smile. Mike's two older sisters—Sara was a rabbi; Kiera an emergency nurse—had hemmed and hawed over boys—then *men*—for decades. After he and Leigh had made a pledge to honor Jewish traditions, now his sisters were *both* suddenly engaged: Sara to an engineer she'd known since Hebrew school; Kiera to a paramedic with the Detroit Fire Department. Now that *he* had made a commitment to Leigh...*yeah, well, a wake-up call from their "little" brother*....

He composed letters congratulating them on their upcoming nuptials, asking for formal invitations so he could get an emergency leave if he *had* to. His work schedule became somewhat tight at the end of each *calendar* year because the money came at the beginning of the *fiscal* year—1 October, when the proverbial Washington eagle shat all the money for the entire year. Though *that* reality was hard to explain to civilians, it *was* a fact of military life.

That and...*should I put in for a warrant?* That question rang louder in his head every quarter, when the acceptance lists came out...*and Leigh did*. As a warrant officer his options expanded far beyond tactical CI, as did his career path. The number of fluent German *and* Russian-speaking Army Counter-Intelligence warrant officers could be counted on the fingers of one hand—and *that* was a good thing.

Then...*yeah, then they can send me to the other side of the world...away from Leigh. Only thing that's saving me from that is this Ranger tab...I think.*

***

"This is Leigh," Leigh answered, "don't *mind them*..." Her flat-mates had passed the phone around—giggling—for some minutes.

"Leigh," a familiar voice spoke, "It's JJ. I'm on my way south, like I told you. Want to get together...?"

"WHEN? WHERE?" She shouted into the phone.

"I'm in a motel just outside your main gate right now..."

"What room?"

"122. There's a..."

"I'll be *there* in an *hour*." In 43 minutes, she was throwing her arms around him just inside his door. "Oh, wow! I didn't think I'd see *you* again for *another* ten years," she giggled, letting go: she was still in fatigues—Fort Gordon was suffering from a flu outbreak, requiring CID agents act as regular MPs for a few months—and brought a small bag.

"Glad I called. You, ah, still *working*?"

"*Just* got off shift. You're just passing through?"

You COULD have changed. "Yeah. I'll see Mike tomorrow night; St. Augustine Sunday; Homestead Monday; Key West Tuesday."

"Great! Maybe I'll bop on down and see you down there. Swimming's supposed to be *fabulous*. Just *one* thing, Blue-Eyes," she purred, stripping off her BDU shirt and opening her bag.

"What?" She whipped her t-shirt off, grinning. *Ho-boy...*

"Kiss me so I *know* it's you." She pulled another t-shirt out of her bag and reached behind for her bra clasp. "*Quick* before you have to turn around."

OH! "*Always* happy to oblige a buddy."

Moments later, she breathed, "*Oh, yeah; you're* my Blue-Eyes, all right." She smiled brightly. "Mike has my *heart*, Blue-Eyes, but *you* can share my *lips*. Now, just *turn around* so I can change…"

And tomorrow, you'll leave me alone again…and we'll still be friends.

Tuesday

Never knew water came in so many colors. Beautiful but blinding.

Boats of all descriptions dotted the varicolored sea on both sides of the ribbon of US 1/State Road A1A—the Overseas Highway—as he ventured south of Homestead on the Tuesday before Labor Day. The glare off the ocean seemed to reach up to bake everything it touched. His black Plymouth with its black vinyl upholstery absorbed every ray of the sun. *Need seat covers—tonight.*

South of the mainland the tallest structures he saw were signs and water towers. Driving ever south his first impression of the Florida Keys was…not what he expected, although he wasn't sure what he *did* expect. The clusters of buildings on each island (many were just shacks or lean-tos without much to lean *on*) seemed to be of two types: aged wood, and newer concrete block. Every one of the dozens of *inhabited* islands he drove across had a pier, and every flat, airless high spot above the water sported a roadside stand selling shrimp, shells, or lobsters—or all three. Every fifth sign hawked ice. The sun kept getting brighter, and the bridges longer (one was *seven miles* end-to-end). His Whitesnake tape blared:

> *An' here I go again on my own*
> *Goin' down the only road I've ever known,*
> *Like a drifter I was born to walk alone…*

Because friends who killed themselves at Wolverine still haunted his sleep, the safety of emotional distance always beckoned, but *that* meant staying so *darkly* alone much of the time. There was little relief for his isolation, but Leigh had happily done *that* for a night—*separate, adjoining* rooms—and a morning. In school, their *casual* friendship was easy; as *grownups*…she *said* her mother was uninhibited and so was *she*, and she *loved* to make out.

Then Mike, the *next day*, said *all that* was OK. "Her mom's a *trip*," he grinned, "and Cathy's a *beautiful* woman I saw *a lot* of back in the day, too. But *you* swam with her before *I* ever did; I trust you *both*."

And I'll never forget it, brother.

After six airless, salty, dusty, brightly-relentlessly-clingy-sticky-drippy and *HOT* hours in the car, he pulled off at the first sign of military civilization: Naval Air Station (NAS) Boca Chica. The gate guard helpfully pointed him ten miles further south to Truman Annex; *the* southernmost military base in *the* southernmost city on *the* southernmost dry land connected to the Continental United States…by a *lot* of bridges.

As he passed a sign that read "Shark Key" on a broader spread of coral and rock that sported what looked like a subdivision, he saw a square-ended vessel puttering across the turquoise water. *Powered barge? Wonder what they do?*

***

"Contact," Ann called out. The loud *PING* of the expensive magnetometer sounded when it found *something* at about the same time as a high wave appeared on the *in*expensive fish-finder/sonar screen—the two had been paired by the wiz kids in the electronics warfare shop.

"Contact, aye: Stop engine," the ensign replied. "Let go anchors fore and aft." Ann and Kristin watched the tender's shadow glide across the bottom. A thousand yards off Shark Key, their powered barge was searching for an anchor that a Coast Guard cutter had had to cut loose with a marker buoy during a big blow a couple of months before, but the buoy was gone.

Kristin reached down to feel the water from the dive platform. "Still wet," Ann smirked.

"Yup. Piss-warm too. Short suit."

"Short suit aye." Even though Diver *First* Class Ann—an E-6—outranked Diver *Second* Class Kristin—an E-5—*this* dive was Kristin's to manage: a learning experience. As they pulled on their short-legged wetsuits, Ann called to the ensign, "what's the depth, sir?"

"Two and a half fathoms." The skipper of their vessel was a young officer who was learning *his* trade under the wizened eye of the chief petty officer hovering by him.

All hands leaned slightly as the barge jerked to a halt when the anchors grabbed hold. "What does the chart say the bottom is made of here?" Ann idly thought it odd.

Kristin looked. "Sand and small elkhorn coral here. Sand inshore."

Soft bottom. That anchor might have got caught on a coral head, but this is the wrong kind of coral…breaks off too easy. "Wrong bottom."

Kristin glanced at Ann. "You thinking what I'm thinking?"

"I *am*. Sir, let's alert the Coast Guard when we get in."

"Why?" The ensign looked puzzled.

"They used the anchor for a drug drop, sir," the chief mumbled in the younger man's ear. "Guarantee it."

"Very well. Notify Coast Guard, aye." Smuggling was a way of life in the Florida Keys…always had been, even among the poorly-paid military and law enforcement. Those who ventured out on the ocean around the multitude of keys (from *cayo,* Spanish for a small island) soon learned that.

The job was routine: locate the anchor; attach the floats and the hoist cables; hit the switch and reel up the half-ton of cast iron through the barge's well. While the divers were in the water, the ensign and his crew took compass bearings on the location relative to Shark Key so law enforcement could make a note of it. Smugglers had the convenient habit of using the same spots more than once.

As she peeled off her wetsuit when the barge got underway again, Ann idly watched a black car drive over the Shark Key bridge towards Key West.

***

As JJ reached Key West, he was greeted by its enormous wooden "Welcome!" sign—dotted with shells and faded paintings of old boats and swimmers in '40s suits across the road from the Holiday Inn—and followed the signs to the main base.

At the gate, the Marines handed him a temporary pass and directed him to the Army barracks. As he drove onto the base, right next to the main gate was a two-story-high sign that read: FEMALE QUARTERS—NO MALE PERSONNEL WITHIN 10 METERS WITHOUT FEMALE ESCORT DURING HOURS OF DARKNESS.

Huh. Wonder how many women are stationed down here?

The Headquarters Company First Sergeant—an imposingly big black man named Henry Orr who greatly resembled a muscular barrel—read his orders, frowning. "You're *early*, Sergeant Elrath. You're supposed to be on leave until the middle of next month." They both waited for the other to respond until Henry looked up. "I'll get you a bunk, but it'll take a few days to clear an NCO room. Housing of *any* kind is at a premium down here." Staff sergeants were expected—in most cases—to live outside the barracks, but Key West wasn't "most cases." Down there, E-7s were living in the barracks; junior officers often waited half their tours for family housing.

Only 1300. I should get to work. "Should I report to the shop, Top?"

"Sure. Go on over there, eager-beaver. Just over...here." Henry pointed it out on the map. "Welcome to The Rock," he grinned.

"The Rock?"

"It's what we call Key West."

The Army used two of a dozen identical grey-painted new-ish three-story, flat-roofed concrete-block barracks structures on the northeastern shore of the island. Their barracks were no more than a long spit from the two joined single-story block structures that housed the Army-Navy-Marine Joint Intelligence Center Annex, which was also connected to the 4/75th headquarters. He knew Major Hugh Mercer, the commander of the Annex, from the 1st Battalion in Fort Carson, and several others from other assignments. The NCOIC—NCO In Charge—was his old boss Tom Merrill.

Another routine assignment...except... "Any idea why I'm down here, Sarge?"

"Two," Tom answered. "First, the colonel likes your book. Second, the physical pace here is slower." He grinned. "You haven't passed a PT test without a waver in four years; neither have I, but the Army doesn't want to lose us. *This* place gives us a chance to rehab."

Clear enough.

* * *

The barge tied up at the Auxiliary Pier near the Truman Annex fuel terminal. The station's gates and fence were well-maintained, but none of the sunbaked structures were less than ten years old, and many were more than fifty: the central structure of the terminal was built in 1916. The primary naval activity at Truman Annex was the oceanographic technician school—oyster trainers—whose curriculum was so highly classified and sensitive that they couldn't even take their books off the base.

The *other* naval activity was the Undersea Warfare Advanced School. The UWAS (pronounced "you-ass") was where *junior* officers and NCOs in *both* the sea service's (Navy and Coast Guard) Special Operations communities spent a month learning to become *senior* officers and NCOs. When called upon, Ann and other Navy divers—the four women called themselves the *mermaids*—acted as lifeguards during UWAS rough-and-tumble beach and off-shore exercises.

89

The rest of Ann's time was spent on routine diver duties like finding lost anchors and surveying piers and docks; hull tech jobs including repairing whatever needed repairing, and the inventory-and-issue, trade-*this*-for-*that* routines of a storekeeper.

Ann was the Lead Petty Officer/LPO—the ranking NCO—in the women's barracks. That made her responsible for the night and weekend *watch* bills—watching the barracks door during non-duty hours—and the *duty* bills—cleanup for the heads, halls and the day room, and grounds policing. These were simple lists, but they had to be maintained, posted and enforced. Ann also took her turn guarding the door once a week or so, and scouring toilets and picking up cigarette butts when her name came up.

That afternoon the air around the women's quarters stank of machine oil: someone was doing *something* in the maintenance shop on the lower deck. Twenty-four Navy women shared the drab-light-grey two-story concrete block building near the main gate with ten Marines, three Airmen, three Coast Guardsmen, the machinery storage space and maintenance shop, and soon, they were told, five *more* women.

To make room for an E-6, an E-5, and three more E-4s, Ann spent part of her evening shuffling storage and women's spaces. She supervised a detail that grudgingly put three bunks into three big four-bunk rooms (they hadn't *had* to before) to clear one for the new E-4s, and moving surplus furniture out of two small rooms on the second deck and into the lower level/bomb shelter space, opening *those* two rooms up for the NCOs. Finally, she used the last of the custom-made valve seats (that cost *her* a six-pack apiece) to repair Carmen the *Incommodious* Commode's *eternally*-malfunctioning-and-due-for-replacement-if-we-get-the-funding flush valve in the first deck head. Long before, she had stripped the *still*-installed urinals on *both* decks for compatible parts.

It was all pretty routine.

Friday

"OK: forget everything you *think* you know about women in uniform because I'm here to tell *you* that *you* don't know *shit*."

This is how the "briefing" began in the deceptively cool day room. JJ and several other Ranger NCOs were being lectured by a hard-as-nails, black Sergeant First Class drill sergeant named Greer, sent down from Ft. Jackson, *and* who was about 230 pounds of solid female muscle.

"OK: women don't have the upper body strength that men do, and they ain't *gonna* be Rangers: keep *that* in mind. And they ain't airborne-qualified yet." Greer then *conspiratorially* told her audience: "I knows y'all paratroopers calls us non-airborne soldiers 'legs,' but y'all damn-sure *better* not call *your* women that or you *will* get wrote up. And if y'all calls 'em *girls,* we'll fall on y'all like an old barracks."

When Greer said "wrote up," she meant filing an EEO action. As women made their way into the men's domains, the Equal Employment Opportunity (EEO) action was born in the early 1980s. This was/is an incredibly complex and legally-charged mechanism intended to punish non-consensual interactions between men and women in uniform.

That list of offenses originally included leers, winks, pats, wolf-whistles and other gestures. While *many* proscribed words and deeds had *always* been not just illegal but in bad taste, *some* post-feminist women began taking issue with interactions that had always been considered normal in polite society. Thus, the list ballooned to include words and actions that—in context or by interpretation—*could* be construed as harassment, such as holding doors open, offering complements based on appearance, and invitations to strictly social events. Boards and committees were flooded with EEO actions; commanders dreaded them; good servicemembers *could be* destroyed by them; letches were *sometimes* punished by them; language was curtailed by them; there were *quarterly, mandatory* classes on them for *everyone*; service members at all levels walked on eggshells because of them.

The five women—two Specialist/E-4 linguists in JJ's section, a Sergeant/E-5 and a Specialist/E-4 in personnel, and a Staff Sergeant/E-6 in supply—were *women* who were to be treated like *soldiers,* and who were *legally* just like any other members of the 4/75th.

If it were not for the fact that these were the first women assigned to *any* US Army combat arms unit, the event would have been unremarkable. As it happened, their assignment to the 4/75th meant that the gender line in the Army was about to be crossed in one of the most exclusive bastions of male privilege, though that "privilege" in the valorous-if-valetudinous 4/75th—they called themselves the *Walker Battalion* after a "Saturday Night Live" comedy sketch—was laughable. In 1985, no *women* had gone through Ranger school…and there were no *plans* to do so.

After the "briefing," JJ finished his in-processing, puzzling over the housing forms he was given. *Says "E-6, no dependents: ten months wait for sponsored government/five for on-the-economy housing." Wow…*

✻✻✻

"Come *on,* Ann," Kristin demanded. "It's *payday*; a *three-day weekend*; we're *beautiful, single* and…come *on!*"

Sighing deeply, Ann stretched her back. "So, you just want to go out and…"

"Find some *fun,*" Kristin sighed. "Let's just see what we can find."

Ann read the phone message—*Sailfish; Room 9*—wadded it up and threw it out. *Need distraction.* "OK; give me a few minutes."

"Girl," Kristin frowned later, "*you* need transfusions of estrogen."

"Why?"

"*You* want to pick up a guy wearing *that*?" Ann was in small shorts and a cropped tank top—immodest, perhaps, but *not* provocative.

"I want to go on the town with my friend wearing *this*," Ann sneered. "If I *want* to *pick up* a guy, *I* don't *need* to dress for it."

"True," Kristin sighed. "They *always* seem to be drawn to my big beautiful buddy. Just make sure your castoffs come my way, OK?"

***

JJ had money, a car, and time on his hands for the three-day long, payday/Labor Day weekend, and he was *longing* for *female* companionship, even if just for an hour's conversation.

He spent the first couple of hours just driving around. The *island* of Key West is three miles by seven. The *city* of Key West that occupies the island was an accident caused by tourism that had flagged since Castro took over Cuba. The Strip, the ten-block length of three-lane Flagler Avenue that catered to both tourists and the island's military population, was the busiest part of town. The tallest building—with the biggest saloon—was the four-story Key Wester Inn. The place—*they* said—had been around in Hemmingway's time: photos of Papa graced every wall. It was whispered that he had bedded a woman in every room of the Key Wester. Smarter heads knew that Hemmingway *left* the island for the last time before the place was even built.

The many topless joints on Key West were good for finding hookers (so was about every third street corner on payday weekend) which JJ *didn't* want, but not for *other* girls. He was about to give up on his quest when he saw the beckoning lights of—and a gaggle of girls entering—a country-western saloon near the lobster trawler docks. The incongruity of a country-western-themed bar surrounded by lobster traps and draped with old fishing nets struck him, but he ignored it.

Normally, anyplace where he could hear the inside from the outside would have just turned him off: loud music and anonymous crowds rattled his nerves. But, *now…why the hell not.*

***

Cruising downtown in Kristin's Gremlin, Ann watched the usual payday crowds. "It's *always* the *same*," she sighed.

"What is?"

"Payday. A zillion sailors we *can't* touch and a million civilians we don't *want* to. Ever do any cruising when *you* were in school, when we

92

were *supposed* to do it?"

"Some. We'd go over to Texas City: Galveston Island is pretty restrictive about that kind of thing. When the gas prices went up in '74 a lot of *that* ended."

"You were…fourteen? You were cruising *then*?"

"With my sisters sometimes. They'd use cute-little me as bait."

I'll bet. "We called it 'Woodwarding' because it was up and down Woodward Avenue. After about the third pass it got pretty lame."

"Same here. Hey, look at *that* guy there…"

***

It was crowded and coldly humid inside the saloon. The band was loud and a little out of tune, but the dance floor was lively. JJ got a beer at the crowded bar and started sucking it down when a grey-eyed blonde in a bare-midriff halter and short skirt got his attention with a smile and a wink. He smiled back.

"I'm Grace," she declared, her mouth inches from his ear.

"JJ," he answered, close enough to smell her hair.

"Let's go outside," she smiled, adjusting her top.

"OK." He followed her out to a broad swath of asphalt behind the saloon. A long wall of traps taller than he could reach stood by the seawall, stinking in the night air.

"*Christ*, that place is loud," she complained, lighting a cigarette, "getting on my last nerve."

"That's affirm," he agreed, shivering slightly. Because the air is so wet and there's little soil to hold heat, Key West *feels* cold most nights.

Grace acted like she was waiting for something, pacing slowly in odd-colored cowboy boots. "You a Marine?"

"Army. You?"

"Waitress at Danny's."

"Sorry, never been. I only got here Tuesday."

"Oh." She tossed her butt into the oily harbor. "You want coffee or something?"

Or something? "OK."

She smiled. "You got a car?"

Dimples. Cute. "Yeah. Where to?"

"Let's just get to your car."

The Fury wasn't far away. He opened the passenger side door; she smiled again and got in.

Am I missing something? He got in himself and barely closed the door, saying, "how about…" when he was abruptly cut off as she swooped in—literally—to kiss him, hard.

"There," she sighed. "*That's* out of the way. There's a donut shop on 3rd off Flagler." She adjusted her top habitually as if it didn't fit. She had no purse, just a pouch on her skirt belt.

You're a waitress like I'm a fisherman.

***

"I'm gonna try that country-western bar down by the lobster docks," Kristin mumbled. "I can *always* find a guy…"

"Just *any* guy?" Ann squinted at her friend.

"Not just *any* guy: cute ones."

"*Sober* ones, you mean. Better hurry up before it gets too late and none of 'em *are* sober." As they approached the saloon a few minutes later, they passed a black Plymouth on the way out on the ground coral driveway.

***

The donut joint was frequented by cops, strippers, cab drivers, tarpon fishermen, ladies-of-negotiable-virtue and others who lived by night and slept by day. They sat in a booth and ordered coffee and a side of fries to meet the joint's table minimum.

"So, what do you do for the Army, JJ," she asked casually.

"I'm a guided missile in-flight mechanic. Got my first flight tomorrow."

She broke into a wide grin. "Uh-huh. And *I'm* a waitress." She reached under her halter swiftly, like she was going to flash him. *This ain't Denmark, chickee,* remembering a weekend in Copenhagen where hookers displayed themselves brazenly in shop windows. Instead, she flashed a badge. "Monroe County vice."

I picked up a vice cop. Great. "Good thing I said separate checks."

She smiled. "*You* were *supposed* to be my bust for the night." She stuffed the badge back into its hiding place uncomfortably. "But when you didn't say anything outside the bar I just figured 'to hell with this: he's safe,' and decided to punch out. So, I kissed you."

I'm safe? That tattooed on my forehead? "Sorry to disappoint you."

"Don't worry about it." She slugged back her coffee, signaled for more. "Cops need nights off, too." She gave him her card in case he might need it, scribbling her private number on the back if he had some time to spare.

He was back at the barracks just before midnight.

***

"Well, *that* was a complete bust," Kristin grimaced as they walked into their building around midnight. "I don't know *how* I let you talk me into wasting my gas like that that all the time."

Ann smiled mildly. "Yeah, I just talk *your* ear off, don't I?"

"Well, that guy *you* were talking to…"

"The *first* one or the *second* one?"

"You *always* get more guys than I do. The second. *He* was a keeper."

I didn't like the look of him. "*He said* he was an Air Force lieutenant flying a C-130. He'd have had a wife and kids at home if he *was*; lived in the barracks if he wasn't."

"And *you* didn't ask him to dance…why?"

"Girl, have you *ever* seen me ask *anybody* to dance?"

"True. Never saw anyone who couldn't even *line-dance*…but *you* can't."

Saturday

Still serving, Dad. Just hope you can be proud of me.

That morning JJ tried to plot his weekend in the spartan 8x7 NCO room he'd moved into Thursday. He didn't owe Stella a letter for another week; she was out of town, so a call would be neither expected nor required. He fanned through his desk calendar, finding the faded and spotted photo of his father taped to the inside cover. *This is your thirteenth calendar. Gotta find another way to keep you around. Address book, maybe? But it's too small.* The yearbook photo of Clare was still in his wallet; pictures of other girls were in the metal box with his other papers.

A unit of social psychology due…Tuesday…essay for English composition due…Tuesday. One's got to wait unless I'm on it all weekend. Eh, I've got three days. What <u>else</u> I gotta do?

He also had to start getting ready for the E-7 board when it met February, the first time he was eligible. And he was developing the germ of an idea for another book.

Find a photographer, spit-shine the Corcorans, brush up on the manuals, finish the outline for the next book—Hiroshima Reconsidered.

And make time for a girl? Yeah, right.

***

School, promotion, and skills. Do I really have time for a guy?

In her 8x7 room Saturday morning, Ann cracked the books again. A history unit, an accounting unit, another chapter of a dive manual, more leadership, logistics, engineering and personnel management material…and a *watch* Sunday morning. She would sit for her oral board for E-7 when it convened in February. There was also a selection board for master diver candidates later in the year. *And…I'm still alone. Maybe I should have met Roger…*

She scanned the new hundred-entry reading list for Navy NCOs; books that they were to be reading, have read or at least be familiar with, numbered in order of importance. Number 56 caught her eye: *Profiles in Leadership: Case Studies in Command, Leadership and Military Management.* The title was much like many others, but the author: *Elrath, John J.*

Johnny wrote a book, too?

***

"And just what *is* this today," the short, grey-eyed girl in t-shirt and short skirt next to JJ in the chow line that evening wondered.

"Poultry…something," JJ answered. "Didn't see any buzzards overhead on the way here, did you?"

"Um," she grinned brightly, "didn't think to *look*. Next time, maybe."

Yeah, maybe. She went one way, he another.

Not long after that, he caught a glimpse of a woman in a white uniform leaving the dining hall that he *thought* looked familiar from the back…but shook his head in denial.

Can't be.

***

Who IS that chatting with Kristin?

Dressed in service dress whites for Saturday night Mass, Ann *thought* she might have seen a *familiar*-looking guy on her way out of the dining hall. She put him out of her mind.

Just because…don't torture yourself.

September

Thursday

Who IS that guy? Was HE talking to Kristin Saturday night? Army E-6…Where's he going?

JJ got his noon chow—a well-worn piece of mystery-meat-labeled-beef slathered in something that resembled both gravy and clean axle grease—and looked for a seat. He found a spot, turned…and there, three feet away… "Holy *shit*!" he cried, then sighed, "*Cloud!?*"

She stopped, frozen. "*OHMYGOD!*" she shouted, then whispered. "*Johnny!?*"

Normally, the dining facility at noon during the week was a pretty noisy place, but for some reason…that day…just then…it was…nearly silent.

They glanced around, trays shaking; beverages threatening to spill. *Everybody's looking at us?* He nodded toward the table he'd picked; she nodded slowly, sitting opposite him.

"You joined the *Navy*?" *I don't see a ring…*

"Yeah. I *saw* you in the paper…say *something else*, Johnny." *No ring…*

"I *never* stopped looking for you."

She swallowed hard, her bright eyes fixed on his, her breathing shallow before she smiled, "*I* never stopped looking for *you. Dad* sent me…"

Then it hit him: "of *all* the mess halls, on *all* the bases, in *all* the world, I find *you* in *mine*." He started to giggle; then so did she. In a few moments, they stopped, smiling.

Still, the dining facility was *so…quiet*.

A pair of Navy chiefs who Ann knew vaguely two tables away looked on with professional interest; an ensign seated behind Ann stared in disdain; an Army captain who JJ didn't know at the next table regarded them with slight alarm; two Army E-4s farther away looked on with fascination.

He tried *not* to be distracted by her body, concentrating on her eyes. "Claudia, I…"

"I haven't *used* Claudia since junior high: I go by Ann. But *you* can call me anything." Her words were quiet, barely above the silence.

One of the chiefs noisily cleared his throat and asked, "you two *know* each other, I take it," with his best authoritative-but-amicable tone.

"Old neighbors, Chief Pence," she managed, still smiling at his baby-blues. "We grew up in the same neighborhood, but Johnny's family moved. Haven't seen each other in—*how* long?"

"Since 21 November '68."

"Mm." Chief Pence went back to his coffee, muttered *sotto voce* to his companion. "*Different* services; same rating. Not an issue."

"Ma's been calling me *JJ* since Dad died," he murmured. "That's what I *usually* use."

"Oh," she said, a little louder. She stretched a hand across the table. "I went to Birch Lake before I reported," she mumbled. "A man at the door said he didn't know you, Jo…JJ."

He touched her surprisingly-rough hand, thrilling to the feel of it. "Charlie: wish he never *did* know me. *I* went to *your* place after graduation: house was knocked down. Am I, um, awake, Ann?"

She looked vaguely resigned. "Well, *somebody's got* to diagnose that damn fire manifold this afternoon, so I'd *better* be awake." She smiled. "We moved that spring. Thought I'd never *see* you again. Then Dad sent me that article about you in Grenada; *I* was in Japan when I saw it. My sister-in-law interviewed you for it."

"I talked to reporters, but your *sister-in-law*?"

"Yeah: *Jim's* wife. She was working for the Detroit *News*."

"Ah." *I remember talking to a woman…These fitters-and-turners ain't much better than Ma; I've no stomach for this crud today.* He took a bite and recalled his mother's pot roasts, often boiled into what the family called *rot post* and inevitably served with overcooked frozen peas. "I've got to finish in-processing those two Spec Fours over there today." He nodded at the two women four tables away in the rest-of-the-people section who had been staring and grinning, with an occasional giggle.

She turned to look. "The blonde's Liz; the black woman's Nancy."

"I know them as Devin and Anvers. They're mine until next week."

"Oh. Linguists, I think? What happens next week?"

"We get a new NCO for *their* section." He forked in a piece of whatever-it-was.

She ate a forkful of salad. "We can't do *this* here and now, Johnny."

"No: the whole world's watching *us*. We *have* to meet later." He looked up at her. "I've lost what appetite I had. After work?"

"Sure. I'm in the women's building, S-501. Know where *that* is? Oh, *hell*," she glanced at the clock, "now *I gotta* go." She forked a very unladylike glob of salad in and chased it with two gulps of milk, chewing and swallowing quickly.

"Yeah. Say 1800?"

"Building S-501, 1800, aye." She stood up, and before *either* of them knew it was happening, she stepped around the table, grabbed his chin and…

SMACK, right on the kisser.

Once again, two service members kissing while in uniform on duty in public spaces is well-known by policy as being bad for *someone's* morale and is somehow unprofessional. But exactly what "professional" military conduct *should* look like when two friends are reunited after a decade and a half apart has *never* been made clear. Besides, one could hardly call Ann's sleeveless top and shorts a "uniform," emblazoned with *Navy* or not.

But the reader must understand that *this* kiss was different. *This* was *their* promise-kiss—a barely-puckered touch-of-the-lips as *committed* as an air-kiss—that Claudia and Johnny had been exchanging since they were eight years old.

But *it* meant more to *them* than an hour of making out.

Chief Pence murmured, "When ya *gotta* smooch, ya *gotta* smooch," barely suppressing a grin. The other chuckled and smiled.

And the dining facility…*suddenly*…went on as if nothing extraordinary had happened.

The Army captain smiled, nodded at JJ. "Good friend, Sergeant?"

"My very *best* friend, sir."

"A relationship with someone in another service *does* make for complications."

You're right, sir. Book says so, sir. "I appreciate your concern, sir. I'm just a little stunned." *You nosy SOB. Sir.*

Anvers and Devin giggled.

Clearly, *no one* understood what *that* kiss meant…and consciously perhaps even *they* forgot…but…they *really* didn't.

Ann hurried away, her mind screaming: *Yea O God I have dreamed of Johnny Elrath for half my life and I JUST KISSED HIM in the dining facility in front of two chiefs and an ensign and I'm wide awake!*

JJ got up, gathering his tray slowly, glancing at Liz and Nancy, who suddenly looked away. But *his* mind was buzzing: *Holy HELL. Is Cloud HERE? DID she KISS me? I believe she did. HO-boy…*

***

JJ flapped his bulky and baggy battle dress utility shirt for air in his dull, stuffy, 6x8 baby-puke-green-steel-and-fiberglass cubicle, *again* wishing there was a lightweight BDU. "Devin; Anvers," he called, "you *ready*?"

"Yeah," Devin's high voice called. Apple-cheeked and petite 20-year-old Specialist Elizabeth "Liz" Devin came out of her cube, purse under arm.

"Coming," Specialist Nancy Anvers called, edging her angular face around the cubicle wall.

"Where to, Sarge," Liz asked.

"All you've got left is your field equipment issue." He sighed. "The hard stuff's done. You registered your car?"

"Yesterday, yeah."

Nancy finally emerged from her cube. "Let's get going," JJ cocked his head. *What are they smiling at, like I need to ask?* They went out in the moderately breezy air—it was a cool 85 degrees at 80% humidity—and he stopped in the bare shade of a palm tree. "Devin," he asked—he *thought*—casually, "do you *know* Petty Officer Mueller?"

"*We* don't socialize, Sarge," Liz gulped. These were the first words—higher *pitched* than she'd heard before—that Staff Sergeant Elrath had ever uttered to her that were *not* in the line of duty. Blinking hard, she dared add, "looks like *you* know her, though."

"Uh-huh." He stared up at the un-spectacular banana palm. As if Mount Rushmore were moving, he looked at Liz with a small smile. "Haven't seen *her* in *years*."

Liz and Nancy had been in Key West for one whole day and an evening. This tiny bit of information that he *just* shared with *that* smile, was, for single girls far from home, a gold mine: suddenly, they learned that their previously aloof boss was *just another guy*. But Liz *was* a military professional, which meant she *should* stay at a barely personal level. "I don't…"

"She's on latrine duty this week," Nancy interjected. "She doesn't seem to *mind* doing it. Does an E-6 *have* to?"

Have I ever talked to these ~~girls~~ women outside the line of duty? I know where they're from; I know their names; but that's it. It's sergeant's business, and I'm not doing it! As *their* NCO he *had* to answer Nancy's question. "Um," he glanced at Nancy, an attractive African-American bigger than Liz. "We do what we *have* to do. Look, I'm…" He stalled, then lost his chain of thought as the memory of his Cloud's face—*kissing close*—from less than an hour ago floated across his mind. *Christ, she DID…*

Liz grinned; Nancy smiled.

"I'm *supposed* to have inspected your room," he croaked. "*Not* a shakedown; *not* an IG. I just need to see that you've got what you need. Tomorrow." *No* such thing was *required*—but making it up forced him to concentrate.

"Sarge," Nancy replied, "Sergeant Corey looks at our room in the morning." SSG Wendy Corey reported on the same day as the rest of the women; the senior of all five of them.

OK, Wendy's stepped up. "Sergeant Corey isn't *your* first-line supervisor: that's *me*. So, after work formation tomorrow." He looked at both in turn as his mind raced. "And, ah, I need to schedule your personal interviews." He blinked. *What are they for?* "They're to get to know you more *personally*. Sorry I haven't done those yet. Been busy." *Busy, hell. You've been scared of saying something that they could complain about.* "I'll check the training schedule."

"OK," Nancy replied. "And, ah, there's something *else*: the watch?"

"Watch?"

"Yeah. The Navy has four-hour door guard shifts that change in the middle of the night. Hard to be chipper after five hours sleep…or *less*."

"Um…yeah. I'll…ah, look into that. OK: that gear's clumsy until it's put together, so I'll drive you over there…"

***

The sun was brutal on the pier as Ann gingerly adjusted the feed valve—the manifold was plumbed to compressed air for testing—with the same result as before: pegged-out pressure on all but one of the five outputs. She decided to dismantle and reconfigure the plumber's nightmare when Lieutenant-*Commander* Susan Morris nudged Ann from behind with a hard-shoed foot. "Petty Officer Mueller. With *me. Now.*"

"Yes, ma'am," Ann answered. "What'd I do *now*?"

"Just come along." Ann was led to the pier shed, a 20x20 wood-frame-

100

and-sheet-steel structure used as a guard/break shack and for informal storage. The air inside the air-conditioned hut was *dry* and stuffy but not especially cool. Susan discarded her baseball cap casually, stripped off her khaki shirt and hung it on a steel post coat tree, her t-shirt clinging to her skin. "Uncover and have a seat, Ann. Coffee?"

OK, not an ass-chewing. "Sure. Thanks." Susan was not just the chief undersea systems officer in Key West; she was also the *un*official mentor to all the Navy women there.

Susan brought coffee in foam cups as Ann snatched off her baseball cap, shrugged out of the top of her coveralls and sat as Susan brought the coffee and sat on the same wobbly bench. "As you know, Congress says 'gender-integrate,' and we say 'aye, aye.' Accordingly, my job is to ensure that the women around here don't damage their careers *or* reputations while we fulfill this mandate. You're too recognizable to have a private life in public spaces on base."

"I thought I'd cut myself off at the ankles."

"Mm, might help. Who's the GI you kissed in the dining facility?"

"Oh, an old friend." Ann tried to sound casual. "Haven't seen him in years."

Susan squinted. "Since *when?*"

"1968; 8th Grade."

"Huh. You kiss childhood acquaintances often?"

"Wasn't *that* kind of a *kiss*; he's *more* than an acquaintance." Ann slipped back into military mode. "Do I have a problem, ma'am?"

"Kissing isn't *verboten*, just discouraged—you *know* that. Waving your *tuchus* in non-regulation too-small shorts at an impressionable young ensign *while* you did it *did* raise *his* eyebrows…and probably something else." Susan smiled. "He brought the matter to *my* attention to see if there's a need for EEO action. Neither party was forced or coerced?"

"If I know *him*, *he* was as surprised as *I* that it even happened." Ann smiled wryly. "However, kisser and kissed agreed upon the performance of the spontaneous action."

Susan winked. "He's a good guy?"

"*Great* guy. *Best* guy I *ever knew. Sue*, let's be clear: Johnny's…"

"*That's* his name? *I* just heard Army E-6, *Type* Male, *Mark* Tall-Blonde-and-Blue; one each."

"John Elrath. Anyway, we were *kids*…"

"That was *then*." Susan sipped her coffee. "Now?"

Ann sighed, "I *need someone*, Sue."

"I *get* it, Annie. You know I *had* a *someone*." Ann's former dive buddy's engagement had ended abruptly that summer; her face changed briefly. "What makes me think *your* Johnny's no Sixty-Day Wonder?"

"I—I'll say *we*—wouldn't *want* that. Anything between *us* would be…" *I could lose him again any time!* "No; we've been looking for each other for *half our lives*, Sue: *we* won't do *that*."

"*Annie*, honey," Susan put a hand on Ann's shoulder and smiled, buddy-to-buddy. "I *believe* you *won't*."

***

It was close to close-of-business by the time JJ ambled back to his cube, exhausted by the dank, stuffy heat of the Central Issue Facility. He was still trying to process his encounter with his Cloud when Tom came around. "So, what *are* we looking at today?" JJ's *job*—chiefly—was information analysis and report-writing: two reports a week, more if warranted. That and whatever *else* someone dreamed up.

"Anvers and Devin are checked in; I *just* got back from CIF. You got a minute to take the stripes off in the smoking lounge?"

Tom unbuttoned his green fatigue shirt, draping it over a side chair, cocking his head. The *smoking lounge* was a small semi-enclosed courtyard between the two joined buildings where smoking was authorized and headgear and shirts—and thus *rank*—were not required. If you wanted to talk about anything personal, you *didn't* do it in the fiberglass-and-steel rabbit warren inside the building. "So, shoot."

"Until '67 I had a neighbor I palled around with. She…"

"That *looker* in the mess hall?" Tom grinned. "*Heard* about her."

SHIT! "Yeah. I hadn't seen her since '68 or heard her voice since '70, but here she *is*."

"I *heard* she's something else. *Corey* mentioned your, um, meeting."

Oh?! "*Corey* did? Huh. I haven't *seen* Claudia—Ann, now—since we were *thirteen*, and *she* looked at *me* like…"

"Were you?"

"What?"

"Her lover?"

"At *thirteen*?"

Like any good NCO, Tom could wax philosophical at the drop of a hat, and always had a story—true or not—for situations like this. "As a kid I spent summers on a ranch, bailing hay and shoveling shit with my cousin Ellen who's a year or so older. I was 14 when we had to move hay up to the top of the silo that first time. Backbreaking, hot and dusty work, even with the hoists. We went to a little spring on the other side of the firebreak behind the silo. She kicked off her boots and jumped in—clothes and all—then took 'em off and threw 'em at me, laughing all the time. I just stood at the edge until she dragged me in. We wrung out *all* our clothes, then laid out in the sun buck naked. Sometimes wondered if *she* wanted to…."

He cocked his head. "Kinda like that?"

"Yeah, a *lot* like that. We're getting together at her billets at 1800. Don't know *what* to expect."

"What do you *want*?"

What DO I want from her? "I *need that* friend who just *happens* to be a woman." *Desperately.*

"OK." Tom grinned widely. "Want me to…"

"Just casually come around the women's billets, maybe 1815, 1820 or so. But listen, I'm doing a wellness inspection in Devin and Anvers's room tomorrow morning."

"A *what*?"

"Wellness inspection. The men's rooms we see every day: *theirs* we've *never* seen. We should *talk* to Top about it. And Anvers brought up how *they* do door guard."

***

Henry Orr knitted his brows as JJ explained: "We've never *seen* their quarters. We're *guessing* they're adequate, but…"

"Well," Henry declared, "no *male* from *here* has seen it that *I'm* aware of. A step towards gender integration…"

"But should we look at all *their* billets," Tom asked. "*Those two* are *our* girls…"

"Women," JJ mumbled. "But we need to leave that to *their* sections."

"Corey *is* the senior NCO in supply," Henry said. "*I'll* talk to her. OK, Sergeant Elrath, just look around and make sure their space is clean and safe; paint especially. The IG is *death* on flaking paint these days."

"And there's their door watch…" JJ added.

"Their *what*," Henry replied, surprised.

JJ explained quickly; Tom and Henry shook their heads. "We *should* have asked," Henry sighed. "*I* just thought it was an all-night duty like *we* do, and Corey hasn't *said* anything about it." He side-glanced at JJ. "That's *sergeant's business.* Since *you're friendly* with the senior NCO in *that* building, see what *you* can work out between *her* and Corey."

***

The sun was low when JJ parked the Fury on the packed coral lot. A score or so of women—including *all five* Army women—were hanging out on picnic benches near the front door; more were in chairs and steps on the building-wide stoop/porch. *Do we HAVE to do this with witnesses?*

As he came up the walk, Ann, on the porch, saw him with his half-grin. She gave him her warm smile just as Kristin declared, "*I* saw him first."

JJ glanced at Kristin: *she was in the chow line Sunday.*

The whole of Key West was silent as Ann dashed down the walk and gathered him up in her arms.

Don't ever let go. "How I've missed you," he whispered, meeting her powerful embrace with his.

"Oh, I've missed you, too," she answered, feeling his tortured back. *What did you DO to yourself, Johnny?* It seemed an infinity before she remembered *where* she was. "John, we *have* to talk," she murmured.

But you feel SO good. "Uh-huh," he rasped.

She let go, turning around and shouting, "*guys*: a *little privacy?*" In a torrent of waves and smiles, the porch and picnic benches cleared…except for Kristin *and* Wendy, sitting *discretely* on the porch, *supposedly* reading.

"Fancy meeting *you* here," he grinned. Her pretty face and bright brown eyes were the only features that he could place. Her high-cropped and short blue-black hair, long and firm body in a tank top and mid-thigh skirt, and muscular arms and legs impressed the bit of warrior in him.

"Yeah, real fancy." She looked him up and down as they walked to the picnic benches. He was an inch taller than her six-one, maybe 230 pounds and change, with long arms, wide shoulders and broad chest: a *bigger* Johnny, with the same *unbelievably* adorable blue eyes. "We've got a *lot* of catching up to do. When did you join up?" Someone *accidentally* left a cooler on one bench, *incidentally* filled with cold beer. She passed him a can with a knowing grin, popping another. "I have *many* friends."

CHRIST is she built…just don't look below her chin. "I can *see* that. I enlisted just after I turned 18. When did *you?*"

First guy I've talked to in months who didn't talk to my chest. "Same time. We must have missed each other at the entry station by days since our birthdays are…"

"Eight days apart. The last time we celebrated *that* together was *your* twelfth birthday."

"Uh-huh." She looked around curiously as curtains moved in the barracks. "What do you *do* in the Army?"

"I'm an intel analyst. Don't ask *exactly* what I do, because if I told you, I'd have to cut off your head and put it in the safe. What do *you* do in the Navy?"

"Diver, among other things."

"Huh. Didn't know the Navy *had* WAVE divers."

"I was the first, but the WAVEs went away in '48. There are fourteen women in the rating now; four are down here; I'm the *lead* rating in the program. Is your mom still in Michigan?"

"Yeah; she got remarried. That was *him* you met."

"You told me about your mom, yeah. You told me about your sister Lois too. You have *two* sisters."

"Brenda got married in '71. How're *your* folks?"

"Dad's fine. Mom moved out in '71; Dad remarried in '75."

"Your mom *moved out?*"

"Yeah. Mom's not *well*: early onset dementia, they call it."

"Oh: sorry. How about your brothers? Did George join the Marines?"

"*Jim* wanted the Marines, but they turned him down. George became a doctor, went into the Air Force Reserves to pay for med school."

Jim taught me how to throw a Frisbee, gave me my first puff on a cigarette. "So, Jim..."

"Became an electrician. Brenda wanted to be a nurse?"

"Got her degree just before she got married. Lois got a degree in psychology and went into accounting." *Add THAT one up.* "So, want your wingman to join us?" He had a curious tilt of his head, and his brave half-grin, "or should I say 'wing-person?'"

She grinned, turned and waved to Kristin. "She's only *here* because..."

"We're not kids anymore." He glanced at Ann's face in profile and her long lashes. *Don't remember those.* He waved to Wendy, who waved back; he gestured, she came.

"She's insurance, Johnny," she murmured as Kristin approached.

Kristin shook JJ's offered hand with a powerful grip; much stronger than he was used to from women. "...my dive buddy, Kristin Collins, meet John Elrath, who goes by JJ these days."

"Dive buddy," Kristin sniffed, sitting down. "Fellow lab rat."

"And poster girl, don't forget." Ann sipped her beer and leaned back against the table; legs crossed in front of her. "We are stars in the Navy's constellation of gender diversity."

"Now, Ann, don't be bitter," Kristin chided. "You *know* we're doing important, pioneering work. But *I* saw *him first...*"

"*You* saw him first? *We* grew up together," Ann grinned.

"*I* saw him in the dining hall Sunday. Would have grabbed him *then* but I had a watch in a half-hour." Kristin smiled. "Before I forget, JJ—John, *whatever*—on behalf of the women's barracks, I want to thank the Army for adding five more names to our watch and detail bills. Now we get a watch only every *other* week—maybe."

"Oh, well, you're welcome. Speaking of which, *we* need to chat about the watch."

"Yeah," Wendy sighed, taking a proffered beer. She was a well-endowed, tall woman in a short, flared skirt and a sleeveless shell, with light-colored eyes and hair but a surprisingly deep voice. "One *more* thing *I* didn't *get to* yet."

"What about it?" Ann slipped rapidly into NCO-mode.

"We don't have a problem with the *requirement*, but the Army has door guards twenty-four-on, twenty-four-off. We don't split shifts except in special circumstances."

"Wasn't aware of that," Ann murmured. "Required?"

"Our work and training schedules are *partly* based on it," Wendy offered. "What we *could* do is have Army personnel stand an overnight watch, give *the rest* of you a break: we'd get the next day off."

"*You're* subject to staff duty nights, Wendy," JJ added.

"Yeah, I *know*, JJ," she grimaced. "Don't *you* act as CQ sometimes?"

"I might *have* to," JJ sighed. "Not enough *able-bodied* E-5's to…"

"Well," Kristin sighed. "We can *combine* the night watches. We do *that* weekends and holidays, Ann."

"Yeah. I'll get back to you."

"Stick *me* in if you need to, Ann," Wendy declared.

"OK; just to balance the week?"

JJ waved at Tom in the parking lot. "*My* wingman can join us." Tom got out of his car as Kristin smiled—a *man-killing* look on a pretty girl. She didn't seem a bit put off by his slight limp or his age: he had five years on JJ, Wendy and Ann, and thus ten on Kristin.

"So, let's talk about…" Kristin started, and soon they were chatting about gender expectations; the hazy, moving-target definitions for *harassment*; and the rising price of gas. As the sun went down and the street lights came up, Kristin stood. "I need to change for the Evening Watch, and the bugs will be out in a few minutes."

"Watch what?" Tom didn't have to act mystified. "Change *what*?"

"Evening Watch is eight to midnight," Ann answered. "We stand watches in uniform. I've got the *Morning* Watch."

"Which is…?"

"0400 to 0800," Kristin grinned, touching Tom's shoulder as she passed. "I want *all* the details, Ann."

"You good?" Tom grinned, standing up.

Ann smiled as Kristin *sashayed* away…and the men—of course—watched…every…movement. "She's a *great* dive buddy. We look out for each other…and…*guys*?"

"Huh?" JJ and Tom both snapped back to Ann; Wendy shook her head.

"She *has* her *ways*," Ann grinned.

"She *has* a *way* of *walking*," JJ agreed. "Walks *better* than…" *Lauren Bacall in* Have and Have Not.

"*Yeah*," Tom breathed. "I'll, ah, be off. In the AM."

"Me, too," Wendy grinned, taking the empty beer cans. "Wish I had *her* legs."

"Nothing wrong with yours, Wendy," JJ sighed, "if *that's* not harassment."

"It ain't if *I say* it *ain't*, JJ," she grinned, *sashaying* away herself.

Ann and JJ watched them go. "They're...*something*."

"*He's* easy on the eyes, too. E-7, yeah?"

"Yeah." JJ turned serious. "This afternoon, I realized I wasn't doing my job right by *our* women." He reached for her hand. "*You* made me see that. And I went through jump school with the first three women. They had their own TACs, did their own PT. But we only *had* male TACs then."

"What's a TAC to the Army? Ours are tactical instructors—people pushers and teachers."

"Same thing: drill sergeants without the Smokey Bear hats. But at one point, you know, it's 'spread 'em' with the parachute harness between the legs. I've rigged women for rappelling—ROTC support—and at a certain point, you're running your hands down the Swiss seat ropes between their legs. *Most* just grin and bear it; *some* think it's funny; others *want* to object but without women instructors there's no remedy for complaints, and there just ain't enough women doing it yet."

A little creepy. "Yeah. We're coddled while we expect everything...ya know," her voice changed completely. "I'm...." At that very moment his stomach growled loudly. She cocked an eyebrow and smiled. "So are you."

"I haven't *really* eaten since breakfast. That kosher deli?"

"On 5th, yeah. Let's go."

She was quiet for the ten-minute drive, but he *knew* what she was thinking. "OK, *I'll* say it," he began as they pulled into the wide parking lot, the sand-and-coral fill crunching like gravel under the wheels. "You don't *want* a 'relationship.'" He added a finger-quote flourish.

"No pop-psych, Johnny." She gazed out the side window, then turned towards him, cocking her leg up on the wide bench seat. "I *have* a relationship with you, but we can't *just* pick up where we left off...not where *we* were headed...*not* right away. I don't want *you* to be a Sixty-Day-Wonder: I've been looking for you for too long."

"I don't want *you* for a Sixty-Day Jane, either. But, honey, it's *still there*. Separation-by-orders any time."

"Yeah." She sighed. "Losing you again would break my heart."

"But we're *found*, Cloud. We *know* where we *are*; we can always write or call. If we *did* pick up from where we left off, we might..."

"Get *there*? And *then what*? One of us gets *orders*...I don't want to feel *that* alone again." *Already did that...*

"But we *won't* be. The mystery's solved: we'll *know* we still care."

"I've known *that...felt* it an hour ago, like I felt it in the lake..."

"You felt *that* in the lake?" *I was embarrassed to get out of the water with IT. And I thought A LOT about THAT for a long time. Vividly.* Their passionate embrace hip-deep in warm water on her twelfth birthday *was* memorable…*and* sensual. And *an hour ago*…self-explanatory.

"I was *just* tall enough that your *thing* under your Speedo was in *just* the right-and-wrong place, but I barely knew what it *was*." She grinned. "I didn't even know how to *confess* it." She closed her eyes. "And you were a *damn* good first-kisser."

"Was I? Who was *next?*"

"Kisses are like heroin: after that *first* one, you keep *trying* for the same thrill." She leaned into his face quickly, kissing him softly on the mouth. He held her chin, responding gently before she pulled back. "*Still* my best," she whispered, her bright eyes glowing as she leaned back against the door.

He grabbed a lungful of air. "Mine too." He stared through the windshield and side-glanced at her muscled leg before gently placing his hand on her knee: she didn't move.

"We *can't* go back *there*, babe."

"Not like *that*." He watched her, barely able to see her eyes in the lengthening shadows. "Not as *innocent* as that."

Don't move your hand. Please. Ever. "John, I'm under a microscope all the time. Next year I'm up for chief. I *don't* want to…"

"Confuse things," he finished. "Yeah, I'm up for SFC myself come February. And I have college to finish." *And a PT test to pass.*

"Me too," she spouted, relieved to change the subject. "What's *your* major?"

"History," he answered, also with relief. "I'll finish next year."

"Mine's business." She stared at the deli's sign, suddenly weary in the growing dark. She reached for his hand, holding it warm in hers. He squeezed gently. "I've got a long and boring storekeeping day tomorrow, Johnny," she squeezed back. "Let's get something to go."

"OK." He raised her hand to his lips. "Let's be buddies—like we were before…"

"Puberty?" *We had SO much uncomplicated fun before hormones got in the way.*

He chuckled. "We can't go back *that* far."

"We don't *have* to *be* anything but buddies." They leaned towards each other. "For *now*: until we get to know each other better…again. But, maybe…"

"We *can* share a *little*…"

"Chaste but affectionate…"

"Moment. A movie or a meal or a drink or a walk…a kiss 'hi or 'bye." The silence roared over the buzz of the neon sign. "But we're adults, Dee. We have *needs*." Their foreheads touched gently.

She sighed, pulled away. "*Needs*, yeah." She cleared her throat theatrically. "I *had* someone…" *Until this evening. UGH!* "Do *you*…?"

She is—or was—taken? He swallowed hard. "No."

"Huh," she clucked, rolling his hand on her thigh. "*Cute* guy like you? Funny, smart. How come?"

"I'm not as *charming* as I once was." *Brilliant, Elrath. You just nailed it.* "Besides, I've only *been* here since last week."

Can you be my naked-friend, Johnny? "You *seem* to have charmed Kristin." She squeezed his hand and felt a powerful grip back. *ASK. NOW.* "Would you rather sleep with me or make love to me?"

He swallowed hard again, his throat a desert. "Right *now*, honey, I'd rather sleep than screw. But, *RIGHT NOW*, I gotta eat."

You say the sweetest things.

They ordered one full beef-pastrami-swiss-onion sub cut into fours, two chips and two Sprites.

As they drove back to the base, Ann cleared her throat. "Johnny, let's agree on…do you know what a tideline is?"

"The level on a beach where the normal high tide stops."

"Right. Let's *both* agree, right here and now while we're both sober, and *not* hot-and-bothered, that, for *us*, there's a *tideline*, where…"

"We don't rise above…"

"*Check: no…sex…yet…babe.*" She spaced out the words for the sake of her resolve. "We *have* to have more than sex between us or *we* simply won't work."

Tired of just scratching an itch. "I need *affection*, Cloud, not just…*that*." The Fury rolled up to the women's barracks, its large sign dimly lit. "We *did* have more than sex before we grew up," he murmured. "I want—I *need*—*much more than the just sex.*"

"We *do*, and we *will,* John." They got out of the Fury and walked slowly to the building.

"Got an inspection here tomorrow morning in Anvers's and Devin's room. I'll bring Corey over here with them. See you in the morning?"

"We'll kiss on it…so *they* can see." As Kristin and a half-dozen other women—*and* Tom—watched from the porch, they gently touched slightly-wet, barely puckered lips—their promise-kiss—as they first did when hormones and all their confusing complications were unknown, far-away, unexplored mysteries.

Friday

By reveille, there wasn't a corner of The Rock that wasn't abuzz with lurid rumors. Ann could barely sleep for the five hours before her watch, and was slightly groggy when her Johnny and three Army women came up the walk. But she was a military professional ready for anything.

And her mind went completely blank.

Inspection. "J…" she began but caught herself quickly. "Morning, Sergeant Elrath."

"Morning, Petty Officer Mueller."

There followed an awkward moment, the kind—seemingly endless, however brief—where two people have too much to say to each other but don't know how to start. This pregnant pause was cut short by Wendy who simply muttered, "Ann, we're here to look at *their* room."

"Oh, *yeah*; very well." Ann turned around and opened the door again. "Attention all hands! Male on the first deck!"

A woman with no more than a small towel caught between the head and her room *eeked* and giggled. He barely saw a swish of white from the porch. "Sorry," he called.

"OK now," a voice replied.

Ann led them to their room. "Male entering," she called, knocking on the door as Liz used her key in the padlock. Ann was about to enter when…*Wait: I have no function here…and calling into a locked room? Wake up, kid.* "I'll be out here."

"Thanks, Cl…Petty Officer Mueller," JJ smiled. "Close your wall lockers, please," he began. "This isn't *that* kind of inspection." *No guidance on inspecting their lockers, anyway.* He looked around the 18x20 room, scratching down notes. *Three bunks in corners. One small table on a common wall with lamp…could use ceiling paint; walls optional—how-to?*

He gazed at a poster taped over Nancy's bunk. "My sister's in Downers Grove. Where in Chicagoland are *you* from?"

"Arlington Heights."

Not sure where either one is. He nodded appreciatively. "Passed through Chi-town a couple of times. Always wanted to stay a while, see the submarine in the museum."

"I saw it in 6th Grade. It's smaller than you'd think."

"I imagine. I saw *Das Boot*. Thirty-odd guys for three months in a space not quite ten feet wide and you can't dig a foxhole."

A map of Mexico adorned the space over Liz' desk. "You know Mexico well?"

"*Si. Conozco bien a México*," she answered with a grin.

"I'll take that as a *yes*. What *part* of Arizona are you from?"

"Nogales."

"Got down there from Huachuca once. I frankly liked the American side better."

"Cleaner. I'm really from Kino Springs."

"Just east, yeah? Studied the area *a lot* in analyst school."

"Yeah."

"How are you three fitting in? I *should* have done this earlier."

"*Hot* and *wet*," Liz mumbled.

"And *combat* units…*so* many guys…," Nancy added.

"*Deep* end of the testosterone pool," Wendy grinned. "Not used to *needing* that sign on the latrine." The building where Wendy worked had only one toilet with a sign—FEMALE—she had to hang on the door when she went: where the other four women worked had two newly-segregated bathrooms. "Gonna put a *bolt* on that door until you guys get used to *looking*…or *knocking,* or they put a *stall* in."

"Good idea." He caught Ann in the corner of his eye, standing at parade rest just outside the room. *Let's put the pin back in this grenade.* "Petty Officer Mueller, can you come in here please?"

Oh-kay. "Yeah, Sarge?"

"How would we go about painting? Does the Navy have some paperwork we'd need?"

"We have paint and other materials in general stores, but no permission's required."

"Good. Thought much about your watch bill?"

"I *have,* as it happens. We *can* put *you* in as consolidated watches…stretch out the *weekday* watches a great deal. The Air Force may have the same issue; I'll talk to them, make it work."

"OK, thanks. Stripes off for a minute, Cl—Ann." He turned to Liz, Nancy and Wendy. "Is there anything *you'd* like to know about *us?*"

They all looked surprised. "OK," Nancy sighed carefully, glancing at Ann, "what's your deal?"

"We've been friends since childhood," Ann began. "Just that. We hadn't *seen* each other since 1968. Last we *spoke* was '70. I was so surprised to see him yesterday that I forgot myself." She smiled. "I'm sure you can get *that*: I apologize."

"Nothing to be *sorry* for," Nancy went on, "but, yesterday, after chow, the Sarge acted, um, different."

"I *was* surprised—*stunned*—to see Ann again. And I apologize if I was inappropriate."

"Not *inappropriate*," Nancy grinned, "*normal* for *most* people."

Liz added, "Much like a regular guy."

Wendy mumbled, "don't get *too* personal, ladies."

"Wendy, it's OK… right *here*, for *now*." JJ smiled. "Seeing Ann again has…"

"I've reminded him that women in uniform are just that: women in uniform. He *is* a *guy*, after all." Ann arched an eyebrow, smiling slightly.

"Thanks, Ann," he interrupted. "I've been neglecting my duties towards you as soldiers. But the *sad* truth is—and don't breathe a word of this outside this room—that the Army is unsure exactly how to, um, accommodate women in combat units." He looked bleak. "*I* don't even have an SOP for *your* wall lockers: *our* SOP doesn't account for…"

"Oh, *SHIT! ONE MORE* thing I…" Wendy breathed. "Greer left us *nothing* like that. Ann, what do you guys…?"

"I have one *we* use," Ann nodded. "But we have *way* more uniforms than *you* guys do."

"True, but…*we'll* figure it out." Wendy looked back at JJ. "Want to look at *my* room, too?"

"I'm *supposed* to," he mumbled. "You have a year in-grade on me, Wendy; you saw what *I* did, so just do it yourself. Inspections in this building are new for *us*," he added. "We're taking our cues from the Navy as to just *how*…"

I've been here since January, and I've seen men in this building for duty purposes exactly once. "Ah, yeah," Ann mumbled. "*Men* have to be announced, and one of us has to watch the decks while they're inside. You *should* have been told about staying decent in common spaces during duty hours—Jill was in violation—but if you *weren't*, spread the word." *Just keep making it up as you go along, kid.* As they left the building, Ann stepped into her room and fetched the drawing for her locker display, which had scribbled notes for female garments on it.

JJ sent Liz and Nancy off to work, drawing Wendy aside. "I'll cover for you with Top…"

"*I* know you will, Sarge; thanks. *We'll* figure the SOP out." She smiled; a small, knowing smile. "She's a *beautiful* person, JJ. Good luck," she waved, walking away.

✳✳✳

Henry was surprised when Ann and JJ reported on the inspection and told him about the men-entering SOP she dreamed up on-the-spot. He perused her locker drawing: it was a *men's* SOP sketch with genderless socks and t-shirts, trousers and coats, but hers had *feminine* items stuck in with balloons and arrows. "Petty Officer Mueller," he mused, "I see the Navy hasn't got used to women in *its* ranks, either."

"No. I—*we* made *this* up out of desperation. Wendy and I haven't finished one for *your* women yet."

"Yeah. Greer wasn't a lot of *practical* help; wasn't a lot of *anything*, frankly."

"Chief…" she began.

"Top," JJ corrected her, "or First Sergeant."

"Top. In my thirteen years in the Navy, the only places really *ready* for women was boot camp and storekeeper school."

"Huh," Henry grunted. "Well, thanks for helping us on this. Sergeant Elrath, close the door. Have a seat, both of you."

Uh, oh. "What's up, Top?"

"You *know* what's up." Henry looked at each of them in turn—seriously, but not sternly. "OK: I understand from Tom Merrill that you two grew up together. Fine, but in the mess hall yesterday: *bad* juju. I'm *supposed* to *formally* counsel you." *That* meant an official counseling form would be placed in JJ's 201-file—a promotion board would see it. Those forms *stayed* there and could end his career as inevitably as an EEO complaint.

Oh shit, Johnny, I'm sorry. "Would it *help*, First Sergeant, if *I* was to accept full responsibility?"

"For a *kiss*?" Henry grinned. "Nice try, but...*what's* your first name?"

"I go by Ann."

"Ann. Very noble, Ann, but there'd have to be an EEO complaint from him for *that* to work, and none of us wants *that*." Henry grimaced. "I'm *not* going to write up *anyone* for *kissing* when *no one* was harassed or intimidated—*your* bosses say as much, Ann." He stopped, smiled slightly. "Good luck, but *please try* to keep your smooching more private."

Their meeting a few minutes later with Ann's Senior Chief Petty Officer—a round-headed, dark man named Wallace Ford with a huge mustache and biceps like baseballs—was similarly both enlightening and chastising. "Diver Mueller: great idea to announce men in that building, or persons of the opposite sex in *any* billets. *We'd* have to add: during normal duty hours except in emergencies. Sergeant Elrath?"

"Sir?"

"*Chief*, Sarge. Thanks for bringing this need for an SOP to our attention." Wallace sighed, "had to happen eventually, I suppose..."

"What's that, Chief," Ann asked.

"One of my women getting involved...sit, both of you. For *Chrissakes*, Ann: kissing in the *mess*? With *officers* and *chiefs* sitting around?"

"Lieutenant-Commander Morris..."

"Had a chat with the skipper; and *he* had one with *me* last night. Would have been *less* uncomfortable if I'd *known* about it earlier." Wallace stood up from behind his desk, coming around to sit on it, looking more like a big brother than a boss. "OK. You *know* this drill. Romantic relationships with uniform personnel are discouraged, *but*, you two being the same rate in different services makes it *far* more acceptable. *No*: for the love of all that's holy *I'm not* going to *discourage this one*. You two *knew* each other earlier?"

"We did, sir" JJ offered.

Ann elbowed him, muttering "We did, *Chief.* We were neighbors until we were twelve, but we moved apart."

"OK. I'm going to give you *my* version of what the Navy *tells* me to say: don't expect anything permanent. I…" He stopped. "Hell, you *know* all that. My oldest daughter just turned fourteen. When she brought her first boy home last month, I realized there wasn't much more *I* could do but trust what Eve and I had already taught her. So, I'll extend *that* to *you*: you *know* what's at stake; *what* this could do."

"We do, Chief," JJ answered.

"*Most* important: Be more aware of your surroundings. *Professionalism* in uniform, remember. And, JJ?"

"Yeah?"

"Break her heart, and I'll tear *you* in half. And Ann?"

"Yo!"

"Don't be *too* hard on *him*. He *seems* like a nice guy."

As they left her headquarters building, there was much left unsaid; unsayable, but Ann broke their awkward silence. "I've *got* to get to work."

"Me, too," JJ added, "I'm overdue for my introduction to our motor pool. About the paint?"

"Yeah, general stores, building E-290. Have your storekeepers tell Chief Winters *I* sent you. *He'll* square you away."

"Thanks." They stared at each other with small smiles, as if they were teenagers ending their first date. "Maybe chow tonight," JJ grinned.

"Ah…check: 1700 or thereabouts?"

"OK."

And they *quickly* kissed on it.

✳✳✳

Mike read her letter with amusement, interest and pride that afternoon:

…I had a crush on JJ while I was with Randy in school. He's a <u>different</u>-better kisser than you—he IS good—but making out with him is different than with you. I love you both in different ways, but I <u>only</u> want to <u>make</u> love with you.

He loved both friends. He also understood JJ's reluctance, however unreasonable, to *make* friends for fear that liking *him* might get them killed. He also knew Leigh was a *very* sensual and demonstrative woman, not unlike her *almost*-nudist mother: a sophomore-year incident came readily to mind. He trusted his friends enough not to be jealous over a few hours making out in a hotel room…*if* they didn't try to *hide* it—and JJ told him about it when he stopped by…but…*I wonder if all women grade kissing ability?*

114

***

In a classic example of serendipity, the reuniting of Johnny and his Cloud spawned many far-reaching events of lasting import:

- The joint Army/Navy Standard Operating Procedure—SOP—for gender-segregated living quarters pioneered in Key West was emulated throughout the Department of Defense. Duty-hours decency SOPs were posted in barracks for *all* the uniform services.
- Casual-but-official inspections of quarters throughout the US military would be forever called *wellness inspections*, meant to make sure that the areas were clean, safe, and as comfortable as any barracks might be.
- Locker SOPs suitable for *both* genders became required by both the Army and Navy.

There would soon be others.

***

The Key West dining facility crowd was thin, but *every* dining facility, mess hall, and galley in the Department of Defense serves fish on Friday. JJ brought Gary Semitone, a Ranger-qualified E-5 linguist with a bad back who arrived that day (a week early) to take over management of the 5-person linguist section. Ann brought Kristin, both in civilian clothes.

"Passable fish," JJ mumbled, gang-cutting two fish sticks.

"The package *might* be better," Kristin sighed.

"Better than MREs," Gary added.

"Never *had* them," Ann replied. "We see the SEALs with them, but *I* never…"

"Not all *that* bad. A *little* better than C-rations or Mom's cooking," JJ answered.

"Your mom's *spectacularly* bad cooking," Ann smiled. "Remember it well."

"Tell me again *why* we're eating *here*," Kristin asked. "I *have* a car; we *all* likely have enough money for…better than *this*."

"I didn't have a way to contact JJ," Ann replied. "So, we're *here*."

Kristin made a face. "OK, fine. So, Gary, tell us about *you*. What do you do for the Army? We *see* you're married; is your wife down here?"

"I'm senior linguist in the S-2 shop as of this morning. Alice and I are moving into housing on Shark Key Monday: we're expecting next month."

The conversation went on in a similar vein while they ate what they could of Fish Fry Friday. JJ was startled when Ann spoke softly as they parted. "John, what are you *up* to this weekend?"

"Laundry; homework; the usual. What've *you* got in mind?"

"Pretty much the same…*but…*"

There was a message waiting for her: *Jerry's at 8.* She sighed to the door watch, "lend me your *lighter*, Joan," and it went up in smoke.

Saturday

"We're *clear* on *what* we're *doing* here, Johnny?"

The Fury pulled up to the little frame-built, clapboarded bungalow with a corrugated-fiberglass-sheet-covered front porch and carport, screens on the windows, and air-conditioners in the walls like the rest of the places on 9th Street. The cheap tourist digs were meant to accommodate those who were only in Key West for what was either in, on, or around the water.

"We *are* clear, Cloud: we will bring each other up to speed—fill in seventeen years of life…" Ann knew the quiet place, surrounded by retirees—she and her buddies used it to do laundry and get uninterrupted showers. Available for fifty bucks a day between May and October, it was ideal for her—their—purposes.

"And…?"

"We have to *like* what we're hearing…or at least *accept* it…"

"…*before* we go *any* further." The flimsy front door behind the well-patched screen door had only a deadbolt. Inside was a 12x12 front room with a plastic '60s ball chair, two battered mismatched side tables, and a well-worn sofa. Ann dropped her laundry bag on the floor and her books in the chair. "Right. So: Laundry, talk, study, talk more, eat, talk more, if-all-goes-well-sleep-eyes-closed-snoring-hands-to-yourself-sleep, shower, leave. *That's* the schedule. Affirmative?"

"Roger that."

"*DON'T* 'roger' anything," she scowled.

"Why?"

"Just…*don't.*"

"*O-kay*," he sighed with some confusion. "That's affirm."

And they kissed on it.

She started a load of her laundry in the bathroom, where the tub had been replaced by a clumsily plumbed washer and dryer, with a vent duct-taped into the small window. In the kitchen was an electric stove with two burners removed and an old-fashioned, lock-handle refrigerator with a frosted-over freezer box, where she loaded her six-pack of soda pop.

He was on the sofa when she got back to the front room, reading and scribbling notes, reading glasses perched on his nose. "When did you get the glasses?"

"Same time you did, I'm guessing," he nodded to her books, glass case on top. "Just readers; maybe a year ago."

"This spring for me; we *are* aging, I suppose." She looked at him with a mixture of concern and curiosity. "What *happened* to you?"

"When?"

"When you got hurt. Badly."

Which time? "How did *you* know?"

"We're always looking for injuries in each other. You favor your right side, drag your right leg a little. Your neck has an odd bend, and I could feel your back is messed up. So, what happened?"

Truth. "I fell out of an airplane."

"What?" She turned pale with a mix of curiosity and surprise.

Whole truth. "Yeah. Double-parachute-malfunction from 1,300 feet."

"Um, what all did you break?"

"Other than my fall, nothing." He gave her the list of everything that got twisted, bent, cracked or otherwise rendered *not right*.

"How long were you in the hospital?"

Nothing but the truth. "Most of a day." He stretched his neck, broke off briefly for a coughing fit. "Long-term effects are one reason they sent me down here. I saw *you*."

"When?"

"Just before I hit the ground, before I went into redout: I saw your face." He smiled. "I saw you, and Ma was dealing us cards. You said, 'you're mine, buddy.'"

A friend will help you move; a buddy will help you move a body. "You *are*, buddy. Your mom was dealing *her* game?"

A friend will help dig a ditch; a buddy will help dig a grave. "Just dealing." Everyone old enough to count cards played a version of progressive rummy—Stella's Game— at his mother's house, at one time or another. "What did *you* do to *yourself*? Your hip: you keep flexing it."

"Fifteen years of diving is hard on *everything*." She smiled. "I saw *you* once. An explosion blew me off a crane I was working on. There *you* were just before I cannonballed into the drink."

"Glad I was with you."

"Me too. You want a *real* chair? Here; come on up." She offered both her hands, pulling him up easily. "I'll give you the Cook's tour. Here's the hall with a card table and *non*-matching chairs; bathroom's over *there*; this is the *back* bedroom—queen bed; here's the *front* bedroom—*king* bed, side table, dresser and what we're *after*: that old wing chair. Try *that*."

He settled into the chair that, despite its age and worn covering, was surprisingly comfortable. "This'll work." She grabbed the chair by the arms, stood up straight with it and marched back to the front room, setting it opposite the ball chair.

She flexed her hip before she sat in the ball chair. "So, let's start with the shark in the water: girls. Did that neighbor of yours at Birch Lake *ever* talk to you?"

"No, *she* never did. Waited for the school bus with her for…wait: she said 'sorry about your dad' after Dad died. So…four words in three years."

"She didn't know what she was missing."

"Oh *yeah*, she did. In 9th Grade, I was five feet eight and 135 pounds. Any idea what *that* looks like on a guy in 9th Grade?"

A tall, gangly kid who hadn't caught up with himself yet. "Yeah. I was five feet ten and 165 pounds in 9th Grade. Needed a 34C. Any idea what *that* looks like on a girl in 9th Grade? *Now*," she winked, "six feet one and 38-28-36 with a D-cup."

"What's…oh."

When was the last time I told ANY guy that? Hell, when was the FIRST time? "As of July. *We* get measured annually. OK. North Hills?"

"When Dad died, it was like I wasn't even *there*: I told you that. There was *one* girl I hung out with, but she went away."

"Kat?" *I felt a little jealous when you talked about her on the phone.*

"Yeah. Something bad happened, and I never saw her again. There was a girl in my church group: Leigh, with pretty green eyes…"

"Not…*not* Leigh *Taylor*?"

"Yeah. We…"

"You KNOW Leigh Taylor? She was on the relay squad with me; we hung out, did some skin diving. Wow! I saw her in an Army uniform at the airport a few years ago, said her marriage didn't work out, didn't have time for more. Know anything more about that?"

"I don't pry; don't think it's any of *my* business unless she brings it up. She never mentioned me?" *Or you…?*

"No! Oh, wow!"

"She's an MP: I saw her at Fort Gordon on the way down here. Got her *address* if you want…"

"Absolutely! If she'd only…huh: Small world. I *have* to write her."

"Yeah, OK. She's *sort*-of engaged to Mike Dietz, guy I went to Brookfield with…"

"Mike *Dietz*? Oh, *yeah*, I remember *him* from South Hills." She looked curious. "I probably exchanged a half-dozen words with him in junior high."

"*He* enlisted, too. He's in counterintelligence now; saw him at Fort Stewart after I saw Leigh."

"*Nice* guy, as I remember. Anyway: high school girls. Speak."

Truth. "I spent 10th Grade at Wolverine; you *knew* that."

"Last time we talked on the phone, yeah. Your stepdad wanted to travel. Must have been expensive."

"There was a scholarship fund for our educations." He knitted his brows. "More like Charlie didn't want me around. But Wolverine: more like a prison camp than a school—*no* girls there. Then there was Brookfield. Jenny Jacobs went to Greenbrier. Remember *her*?"

"I went to a museum a Brookfield once. Jenny moved the same time you did."

"Yeah: moved in across the lake. I had a couple dates with her. *Your* turn. Boys at South Hills and Central. Go."

"I didn't *do* much dating; too busy with Mom and swimming. After Mom left…I wanted to concentrate on just *living, and* diving. Bill Nyquist was my junior prom date; Steve Hole for senior prom. The rest of the parties I went with Debbie aid Leigh."

"Debbie Ford?"

"Yeah. *Then* there was Sam. Anytime Sam."

Good-natured roly-poly buddy Sam Potts? "Potts?"

"Yeah. We could make out and cuddle but we *both* knew he was just a stand-in for you."

"Cuddle-buddy."

"Nice turn of phrase."

"Not mine. So, your *first*?"

"Sam."

"Really?"

"We *did* get naked more than once but we…not *really*."

He grinned. "New Year's Eve '71: *Sam* was with you in the window." That evening, JJ had driven to see his old home, and happened to see someone in her house just across the empty lot between their houses.

"That WAS you on the other side of our Safe Tree. Who was with *you* in the truck?"

"Clare DeHaven. So, you *didn't*…with Potts?"

"No, not with Sam." *I started this.* "Panama City; a guy named Don. But who's Clare?"

"*You're* on a roll. Panama City."

"Don and I were as 'together' as sailors can get until *he* got orders for a ship. He was sweet: we were *each other's* first. There was *Rick*, a Marine I went with before I got orders for hull tech school; Rick was nice, but impermanent. Then there was Cable in Coronado, a civilian—over four *years* with him, but *he* wanted permanence that *I* couldn't give him. Then there was Roger—here—until recently."

Answers that. "I'm your rebound, then?"

No matter who I'm with, you're there, somewhere. "No." She smiled. "Absolutely *not*. You're my ever-buddy."

"So…Roger."

She gazed out the window. "Not much to tell. Every few weeks—*sex*, *not* social—since May; a *lot* like Cable, really, but *Cable* and I went out. Never formally *anything* but…yeah, just sex. But he's gone up in smoke." She gazed at him solemnly. "Now you know the names of all the guys I ever slept with. I've gone *out*, but not…What about you? Who was *your* first?"

"Jenny and I went skinny-dipping on my 17th birthday."

That was the first time Sam and I…oh, wow! "She was cute."

"She *was*: I'd say still *is*, though I haven't seen her since '73. We came *very* close on my 18th, just before I enlisted. She told me once: 'Claudia trusts you, so *I* trust you.' That make sense?"

"Yeah. A girl thing. Tell me about Clare."

"She's the daughter of a teacher at Brookfield whose family took me in because Charlie didn't want me around on long holidays. She and I were close like *we* were a *little* close, but we weren't…"

"Naked friends?"

"Eh, yeah. We wrote; she wasn't much of a correspondent. Her family was—*is*—kind to me. She and I didn't…*connect* until '82. I asked her to come with me then; she said 'sorry;' her family wouldn't approve. There's been others—Rusty at Stewart—*my* first; Tina in Germany couple of times; Lily at Bragg, but *they* didn't *feel* like anything but…"

"Heat and friction." *But Clare was different.*

"Exactly. And Leigh…we made out, but we *couldn't* go too far because of Mike; his family took me in, too. Now you know *my* entire sexual history. I just wish some relationship *I* have might last long enough for me to get used to it. And I wish I knew what I was doing *wrong* except that I'm *not* charming."

"You've charmed enough girls." *Clare, Johnny. Later.* She got up and stood by the window, looking at the sea in the distance between houses. "And I *love* the Navy, John."

"And I love the *Army*." He came up behind her. "But I'm *tired* of *alone*, Claudia."

"So am I, John. *I need* us to be friends no matter what…" *…we DO in the next few minutes.*

He wrapped his arms around her from behind, rested his chin on her shoulder. "We *said* we would be, at our Safe Tree."

"*Can* we, my *sweet* Johnny? Would *you* get frustrated if *we*…don't?"

"Honey, I need a good and lasting friend a *lot* more than I *need* sex." *Can do that myself if…* She pressed herself against him. "I told you: I'd rather sleep with you than make love to you."

"Hard to believe with THAT sticking in my butt, buddy. We've *seen* each other naked: that 4th Grade sleepover in your basement."

"And through three feet of muddy lake water when we were 12."

Trust him now or trust him never. She turned around in his arms, smiling. "Want *another* look?"

"We're *not* nine anymore."

"Nor twelve." She smiled broadly, stretched her back and flexed her hip before she took his hand and led him into the back bedroom as she pulled her tie blouse off, and in moments…they were staring at each other, a couple feet apart.

"You're beautiful," he breathed. *Incredible.*

"You're pretty OK yourself." *Breathtaking…scar on your chest.* "Johnny: can we do *US* chastely; like we did at eight…and *nine…and twelve*? We'd have to forget about making out, and the rest of the bases. If *not*…there's a bed." *I WILL gladly, but I'd rather wait until WE'RE ready…and I feel better about Clare.*

Oh, GOD what I wouldn't give…but SHE doesn't really want to… "Claudia, *OUR* first lovemaking should *not* be *just because* we can't resist." He turned away and picked up his shorts and her skirt. "WE *need* to do what we promised here," he grinned, handing her the skirt, standing inches away. "We need to *know* each other again."

WE win, Johnny. "You're right, but I need my panties *first*, babe."

And they kissed on it…trembling; naked; eyes-barely-open.

***

They studied at the table in the hall, touching hands from time to time. She finished her microeconomics module at nearly five that afternoon, just before he finished his social psychology unit. "Hungry?"

"Sure am." They walked along dusty, sunbaked 9th Street's narrow, crumbling sidewalk. Lawns on Key West suffered from benign neglect and lack of water. Though it rained on some part of the Lower Keys every third day or so—often for a few minutes and sometimes on one side of a road and not the other—it often boiled off in the sun just as fast. There were no watering restrictions most of the time, but *fresh* water was expensive. Some owners spread a load of gravel in their yards every so often, but most just let their little patches of earth go to weed and dust.

A hot dog stand on the beach had a Romaine salad cone on their menu. They ate on a bench on the beach.

"When's sunset?" He munched on a hot dog, swigging beer.

"Another hour and a half. This salad cone…ugh." She grabbed a few of his fries. "Ever see it here?"

"No. You?" He broke off half his hot dog. "Here."

"Thanks. There's a ceremony down at Land's End, that way a mile or so. Banging drums and passing pipes around. We went down there once. Not *that* spectacular."

"Huh. I called you when I got back from Wolverine; the number had changed."

"*Dad* did that. I was the second-fastest 400-meter freestyle swimmer in the world for about five weeks in '70. We got tired of the calls in the middle of the night."

"*Really?* Congratulations." He kissed her temple.

"I thought about you a *lot* then; wanted *you* to be around."

"I'd rather have been *there* than Wolverine, I'll tell ya." He shook his head quickly. "*Anywhere* but there."

"Rough?"

"You got *that* right."

"Want to talk about it?"

"*Not* today, Cloud."

They talked about what had happened to their families: JJ, his trials with his stepfather Charlie and his friendship with Charlie's sons, his sisters he barely knew and a niece and nephew he didn't either; Ann, the cruel madness of her mother, the joy of her brother's marriages, her two nieces and one nephew, stepbrother and stepsister. Their second beers were warm by the time the gold-red sliver of the sun dipped below the azure-black ocean, and they strolled back to the bungalow. They played gin at the little table, keeping score in their heads until the numbers got too big. "Let's hit it, Ann."

"OK." She stared at him seriously. "We're *not* going to…"

"Honey, I haven't slept more than eight hours in two days."

"Me neither. Just think of it like a sleepover, but no peek-a-boo."

He grinned. "*No* peek-a-boo."

Ann wore a long shirt; JJ PT shorts. They smiled as they made the bed before Ann frowned slightly. "John, is *this* fair? I *can* sleep in the queen."

He shook his head with a grin. "Fair? What *would* be fair, honey? I've been making love to you in my imagination since I knew what *it* was. Every girl I've ever *been with* gets compared to *you*." He sighed deeply. "*Fair?* Too abstract a concept. We said *not now* and *not now* it shall be."

They lay on the bed, not touching before he murmured, "did our *mothers* keep us apart?" There was a year and a half—before he went to Wolverine—when they kept *promising* to get together on the phone, but somehow their *moms* could never *quite* make it happen.

Would make sense. They lay together for several moments, neither speaking nor moving before she sighed, sleepily, "I wondered about that myself. Maybe. Sleep now, babe," she whispered. "Shh."

Sunday

She woke with the sun, luxuriating in the joy of *his* just being there. "Morning, Johnny. Sleep OK?"

Watching the rays of light trace down the wall, he had been wondering at the last four days. "Morning, Cloud. Yeah, OK; not used to sharing a bed." *Is she just humoring me?* He looked away. "I don't want you to hang out with me just out of habit."

"You're not a *habit,* babe; you're my *best buddy.* I *love* your company: always have. Don't you *get* that?" *No matter who else I'm with, you're always there.*

"I *feel* it, but I don't *understand* it. Can you get *that?*"

No, I can't imagine. "Just…*feel,* babe." *YOU are the part of ME I thought was lost.*

"I'll try. Just don't let me bore you."

"I won't." She looked deep into his eyes, her nose nearly touching his. "Don't *ever* think I don't care deeply for you, *sex* or *not.*" She pecked his nose and sat up. "Ready to hit the shower?"

"Together?"

"Ah, no. Not that the shower isn't *big,* it's just that I don't get a lot of *real* privacy."

"OK. *You* first."

"I'll start the coffee; you start the sheets in the wash."

"Sure." He grabbed her wrist quickly. "Know how *many* women I've woken up with?"

"No."

"You and Clare."

"Makes *us* special?"

You have no idea. "Very."

She held his hand on hers. "*How* special *is* Clare, Johnny?"

He sighed; deeply, sadly. "Clare was the first girl I ever loved—*besides* you—who loved me back, but I haven't *heard* from her in two years. As much as *I* wanted it, *she and I* could never work." Tears welled in his eyes. "*God's truth,* Cloud. She and I could *never* be together. I saw *you* with *her* once—you were both *laughing.* And when I was with *her,* I saw *you.*"

That's good enough, kid. She wiped his tears with her thumb. "Thanks, babe," She pecked his nose. "*Now* start the sheets."

Wonder if this isn't just a long dream that's not wet yet…except I'm awake. Get with it, Elrath. After starting the washer, he gazed out the living room window at the placid, aquamarine sea visible between the buildings across the street. *A week ago, could I have imagined?* Hearing her start the shower, remembering the image of naked and grown-up Ann from mere hours ago, gesturing to the bed and saying "*there.*" *Waited half my life to hear that for real…*

Clare's a ghost-he-loves. She smiled and gloried in the warm water as it blasted down from overhead. The 6x8, two-sided shower enclosure with its three shower heads (and separate water heater) built into a corner of the bungalow was accessed through a corner of the kitchen where a small pantry had been, the kitchen's back door having been augmented with a shower curtain. The house side was wavy glass block from foundation to roof, the two outer sides of the box were green corrugated fiberglass sheets on a rusting metal frame that extended from the roof eve to just off the ground. Its concrete floor was sloped so that the runoff went to a drain on the back patio. Heavy iron hooks revealed the big shower's true purpose: to clean the salt water from dive gear.

To him, an hour later, the shower was noisy, the water warm and the stall large and blessedly solitary. *At least it won't pool around my ankles because some wise guy dropped TP in the drain.*

Cloud. My Cloud. There was a part of him that still couldn't quite believe it. He felt both refreshed *and* happy; it had been *a long time* since he was both at the same time…even after his evening with Leigh.

When he dropped her off at her building just after noon, they kissed 'bye—*not exactly* a promise-kiss—in front of several grinning witnesses. She merely smiled wryly, announced "show's over, guys," and went inside, laundry bag over her shoulder.

She glanced at a phone message without a name, wadded it up and flushed it.

***

 Dad,
 You're not going to believe this: Johnny Elrath is
 STATIONED here. We met by chance at chow on Thursday.

On paper it's too simple. She wrote those words at the beginning of her letter and stopped, staring at the concrete block walls and little casement window. She tried to organize the swirl of exhilaration and joy of the past four days, tempered with caution, that passed for thoughts and feelings, making an origami dragon and horse while she thought: *I've been a Navy professional since '73. Will be for at least another eight years. Now, here's Johnny: didn't know how much I missed him. Known him since 1955. Missed him since 1970.* She added what she knew of his family.

 …His mother's fine, but his stepfather doesn't like him, and it's
 mutual. Tell Jim Lois's married and lives in Chicago. Tell
 George Brenda's married and lives in Midland; has two kids.

Your old Girls-Next-Door. A glance at her desk diary showed that she owed another letter:

> *Deb!*
> *Johnny Elrath is stationed down here in Florida. I <u>never</u> expected to see him again as much as I wanted to…he goes by JJ these days…we're chaste, for now. Think of your relationship with Bob: you two waited until after high school, yeah? Until you were ready? Johnny and I have to wait, too—yeah, at thirty—until we feel right.*

Does this make sense? Bob Bell—Jim's brother-in-law—and Debbie had been seeing each other since Jim's wedding in '71. *They* were chaste until college. Sam *would* understand a chaste relationship, but she's lost touch with him. *Who else might…?*

> *Dear Barbara,*
> *We haven't corresponded, but I need to talk. Dad will tell you about Johnny and me…Is intimacy <u>without</u> sex reasonable between adults? I know—it depends.*

She didn't think anyone around her—even Kristin—would understand what their tideline meant to her—and to *him. Can't explain to them what I can't explain to myself other than…I DON'T want Johnny for a Sixty-Day Wonder, but holding his hand…irresistible eyes…that grin…ho-boy. But he DID give me Mike's address.*

> *Dear Mike*
> *Remember me from South Hills? I met John Elrath here a few days ago: you knew him at Brookfield. <u>We</u> were friends as kids. How've you been? I'm writing Leigh, too…*
> *Anyway, JJ mentioned Wolverine, that school he went to for 10th Grade, but he won't talk about it. Any idea why Wolverine's such a sore subject?*

And then there was…

> *Leigh!*
> *I got your address from Johnny Elrath! Wild that you two knew each other! I joined the Navy same time you joined the Army, apparently…You said you and Randy didn't work out, but there's not-work-out and there's run-away. If you want to tell me or not, it's OK…I wrote to Mike today, too, asked him about Wolverine. Didn't know how much you knew about it…*

***

I just want to shout: 'I found my Cloud, Mommy! I found her!' But she's not "Mommy" anymore. I wish I knew who—or <u>what</u>—she was.

His heart was finally slowing down by the time he started his Sunday afternoon correspondence. Every other week, no matter *where* his mother was, he sent a letter to Birch Lake. Non-letter weeks he called when he was in the country and knew she would be home. Even though it was a "call" week, he knew they were out of town, so, no five-minute Sunday-rate call on his phone card. *That* had become the sum of their relationship.

> *Dere Folkes:*
> *I ran into Claudia Mueller down here. She joined the Navy*
> *as a diver in '73. She goes by Ann these days...*

Those stark words on the typed page *had* to be enough. *Charlie the asshole denied knowing me when she came to the house. She WASN'T avoiding me: her dad changed their number for a good reason.* He elaborated on his earlier, bland description of fun-filled Key West, and once again answered her most persistent question: *when will we see you again?*

> *...Can't say when I might get up there again. Might be easier—and*
> *more entertaining—if you came <u>here</u>. But I might take leave at the*
> *end of the year.*

After closing that one, he felt obliged to write another:

> *Dere Clare:*
> *I found her down here in Florida, the girl in the window, the*
> *one you said I saw when I looked at you. She joined the Navy.*

He wasn't sure he would get an answer—but he wanted her to know. He wrote a similar letter to Karen, who he hadn't heard from either. He had to tell *somebody* he *might* hear from again, but...*how do I explain grown-up love-without-sex?*

> *Jules:*
> *I told you about Claudia Mueller, how we got separated.*
> *Well, I found her...*

He and his stepniece Julia had shared intimate, bonding experiences that never got as far as sex—or even making out. *She's as close to a forever-completely chaste naked-buddy as I've got...*

> *...Remember skinny-dipping in the lake? I felt <u>safe</u> with you—*
> *that's how I feel with Ann...We need to get together sometime.*

He smiled as he sealed Julia's letter, imagining how she might recall the night that *they* never talked about afterwards, despite several more outings. Of course, with tongue *firmly* in cheek…

> *Green-Eyes*
> *Guess who I ran into here in Key West, who <u>you</u> <u>knew</u> in school and you <u>didn't tell ME</u>? Yes! Claudia Ann Mueller! Some friend YOU ~~were~~ are! …still love ya, Green-Eyes. She says hi, said she'd write…*

Finally, …

> *Cloud*
> *I found you at last, but I can't decide if I should give you <u>these</u> letters or not: two composition books will be a lot to take in. Give us time, honey.*

***

As they left the dining facility, Kristin hooked an arm around Ann's elbow. "Those *eyes*! Mind if I borrow your Johnny sometime, just for a night or three? I *did* see him first."

Ann rolled her eyes, patted Kristin's hand. *Kristin, you shameless…* "He's a free agent: ask *him* if you want. We're the best kind of friends that two people can be: *buddies*, like you and me."

"Buddies my *ass*. That lip-lock this morning…"

"*Lip-lock?* We barely brushed lips."

"Brushed? You were in a passion-lock for *two* seconds at least." She kicked a rock out of her path with a flip-flop and brushed a bare knee. "Ask me, and…"

"Not *asking* you, Yenta. Neither of us *wants* *that* kind of a relationship." *Yet.*

"*Yenta? Who* you call Yenta?" Kristin gathered her scoop-neck shirt up like she might a shawl, flashing her muscled belly at two men walking by. She wrinkled her nose at one and winked at another. "Wrong word, anyway: you're looking for *shadchan:* matchmaker. But *this* matchmaker *knows* when a man is in the market."

"Well, John's looking in the wrong place if he wants *that* from *me*." *Yet.* Ann looked sideways at her friend. "Maybe *Tom's* in the market for *you*."

Kristin put on a creditable ignorant look. "Tom…Tom…Oh, *Tom*. Well, he's a *perfect* gentleman, damnit. Polite conversation but no down-shirt glare or anything even *remotely* like that despite *my* best bra. He didn't even stare at my chest! Or *yours*, or *Wendy's: hope* he isn't *gay. You* need boyfriends who know a lower class of people."

You're a good dive buddy and a better-than-average diver, but your shameless flirting hides a very broken heart. "He's *not* my *boyfriend*, girl. Get *that* through your head. And Tom *has* a wedding ring."

"True." Kristin sighed. "I'll have to ask him about *that* because he *feels* better than *he* did."

That guy you joined the Navy to get away from: the one you don't talk about? "Maybe that's a good thing, buddy."

***

JJ was ready for some fresh air. *The best* place to get a breeze without a boat around there was a manmade mole of pounded coral fill and sand between steel pilings adjacent to the Army barracks parking lot. The slightly-tapered-and-curved mole shot twenty yards out into the Florida Straits, three yards wide at the end and four at the base. Wood pilings at the end supported weathered planks that passed for seats. He sauntered to the end, plopped himself down on a board, and thought, briefly, about nothing at all.

"How'd it go with your pretty friend?" Tom had snuck up behind him.

"Fine. We've been friends as long as we can remember."

"Huh." Tom squatted on an adjacent board. "More than *that* from what I *hear*."

"You hear good *sometimes*; not *this* time. We're pals; buddies. We *don't* want to screw *that* up with sex."

Tom nodded as if he had to agree with himself. "Maybe if Connie and I had been better friends…ah, maybe."

"What happened?"

Tom shrugged. "When we lost the baby in '74, we slowly slid downhill. When I got orders for *here* last November, she flat-out said 'no' and filed on me."

"Sorry, Tom." He meant it, but there was nothing else to say. Divorce was so common in Special Operations they were numb to it. "What's next?"

"I sign the papers when I get 'em, and we're done." Tom's voice was flat. "Nothing else for it."

"You talked to a lawyer?"

"Yeah. A JAG guy came down from Homestead. I signed the Relief declaration so I wouldn't have to go to court in Colorado." He heaved a sigh. "Congress made this easy."

He needs a distraction. "You as tired of the barracks as I am?"

"I'm looking; *hard,* but it ain't that easy here. Might have a line on something end of the year. Interested in splitting something?"

"Maybe. Tell me again why *you're* down here."

"First my bum knee, then nephritis and a tumor on my right adrenal gland a couple years back; haven't been *quite* right since. I've got another year to pass a PT test, they tell me."

"Oh. How did you get on with Kristin? Or *Wendy*, for that matter?"

Tom shot up straight. "Wendy's a *beautiful* woman, but I *won't* shit where I eat. Kristin's a *cute* girl; got a grip on her."

"They hit the weight room more than most women do."

"Makes sense." He was quiet again. "I *know* where she lives. Maybe I could go over there."

"Sure."

"Walk on the beach; drink maybe. Nothing *has* to come of it."

"Nope."

"She's single. I'm gonna be soon enough."

"There ya go. Knock yourself out."

"How about a double-date? Me and her, you and, um…"

"Ann."

"Yeah. What'd ya think?"

I think you're ready to jump on any female that'll hold still. And—God forgive me—I'll help.

Monday

They can't get it together in Afghanistan, and they want Guatemala?

JJ was parsing another report on Soviet Bloc advisor activity in Central America just after noon chow when Captain Mercer walked a guest around the shop. "As I live and breathe," JJ mumbled, shaking Mike's hand. "What cat dragged *your* ass down here?"

Mike smiled broadly. "Uncle Sam, *that's* which one. They sent me *here* to straighten *your* ass out."

"Needs it. Here long?"

"Couple, three weeks. Helping your Russian linguists out."

"We'll get together later. Where are you billeted?"

"Top'll talk to you about that," the captain mumbled. "*Tarpon* season just started: not a *room* in the Keys for love or money. He'll have to bunk with *you*."

They spent the afternoon shifting his room around to accommodate another bunk, desk and wall locker. They were walking to the dining facility when Ann called to JJ from behind. "Yo, Johnny: wait up." When Mike turned around, she was as startled to see him as JJ had been. *Those deadly grey eyes!* "You *have to* be Mike Dietz."

Those legs! Even in dungarees! "I am, and *you must be* Ann Mueller! Got your letter; haven't answered yet, sorry…"

"That's OK," she smiled, reaching for a hug. "*Leigh* did. Haven't seen you since you came to a dance in 10th Grade."

"Yeah," Mike agreed. "You joined the Navy."

"*That* explains all my blue clothes," she smiled as she hooked both men's arms. "I'm hungry."

Three childhood friends who met by chance a thousand miles from home shared an indifferent ham and au gratin potato dinner, but the *one* thing on JJ's mind was… "What do you hear from Leigh these days?"

"Saw her Labor Day weekend; she's got a field exercise."

"I haven't seen *her* since that time in the airport," Ann grinned. "But what happened with Randy?"

Mike shrugged. "It didn't work out. Complicated, so…I *remember* now. *You're* that leggy *Claudia* JJ asked me about."

"Yeah. *You* forgot all about it," JJ grinned.

"Forgot *what*," Ann wondered, adding, "and *when* did *I* get 'leggy'?"

"Mike and I met in a hotel lobby in the summer of '69, and he said he knew *of* you, would pass a message. He for-*got*."

"Yeah, sorry." Mike smiled. "Listen, I'll be busy most of the time I'm down here, but I'll *make* some time to get together. Leigh's got a CID thing at Leonard Wood early next year, but we should all of us get together sometime."

"We need to make a point of it," Ann answered. "Sooner than later." She put on her mock-cross face. "And when did *I* get *leggy*?"

"Um," Mike sputtered, "I always thought you had great legs: you, Leigh, Donna…."

"Donna? The Blonde Bombshell of Central High?"

"Yeah, my Girl-Next-Door and Leigh's best friend since 7th Grade."

"I was *your* girl next door," she murmured, winking at JJ.

"*You* were my girl in the suburb across the street," JJ corrected. "But, Mike, you can't call her *that* in Today's Army."

"Not unless I want to spend the rest of my career fighting the EEO complaint," Mike agreed. "But Ann, can I say *just once*—off-line—that I think you *probably* still have great legs?"

Off-line: Unofficially? This COULD be fun. "No complaints, Sergeant Dietz," she smiled. "*Just* because I'm wearing shorts. Don't *try* it when I'm wearing dungarees."

"Um, Ann," JJ sputtered, "you *are* in dungarees."

"And what's *under* them, Sergeant Elrath," she replied tartly.

"We'd better shut up, JJ," Mike sighed.

"What's the fun in *that*, Mike," she grinned.

Oytzer
…JJ looks more at peace with the world than I think I've EVER

seen him. Can't decide if it's because of Ann or you, or maybe both. He needs both of you, I think. But, I'm not sure I mind.

Wednesday

"Hi, Mike," Ann smiled, sitting down across from him. The dining facility breakfast crowd was thinning by the time she got there. *Most beautiful grey eyes I ever saw.*

"Hey, Ann," Mike grinned, gulping his eggs. "You swimming today?" She was in knee-length sweatpants and a sweatshirt; an outfit that the UWAS people often sported *very* early in the morning. *Prettiest brown eyes on the best figure I ever laid eyes on.*

She sighed, "all-*night* UWAS exercise; *my* turn for lifeguarding. How's your week been?"

"Busy. Lifeguard often?"

"*Not* overnight, but we get the next day off when we *do*." She cut a peach with a spoon. "*Different* subject, Mike: what do *you* know of Wolverine? Johnny mentions it, then clams up; Leigh won't say much." She cleared her throat. "Something there *won't let up*."

He stared at his eggs. "It *would*," he mumbled at length, picking up a slice of toast. "We *talked* about it; through other sources I know a *little* more." He sighed and looked up at her; she had two inches on him. "Trying to think of the *best* way to…how much do you *want* to know?"

"As much as I *can*. I've *seen* some shit, Mike," she declared, shifting her weight off her crampy hip. "Don't sugar-coat it." *Please tell me what's in that dark hole.*

"Knowing *what* I know, I sometimes wonder *how* he stays sane, *how* he follows orders, *how* he still laughs, or even *smiles*." She didn't flinch. "Imagine being *fifteen* in a place where there's *no* affection at all; *no* fellow feeling; *no* love. Imagine being surrounded by guys getting beat up for just *talking* to you, and *killing* themselves because *they* were punished for *wanting* to be your friend."

She blinked; he went on. "Our friend *told* the authorities that he saw someone do something *horrible*, something *unspeakable* to someone *else*, and because he told them *what he saw,* a bunch of guys pitched him out a second-story window."

She seemed startled. *You're NOT shitting me, are you Mike?*

"*Every week* after that, he was *ordered* to *say* he *lied*. When he *wouldn't, every* Saturday and most Sundays, while nearly everyone *else* was watching movies, he had to march around in big circles." He wiped away a tear quickly; she did the same. "Nearly every night, he got walloped in his sleep with a rolled-up towel."

Who could make that up? "My *God*."

"And *this* went on for *eight months* without *respite*, without *holidays*, without family or friends; just constant repetition of punishment and isolation within four walls from October to June. And, neither his *parents*, nor the *faculty*, nor the *staff* at this institution *seemed* to give *two shits* about *any* of it. Then, when he *finally* escaped back home at the end of the school year, *Charlie* wanted to send him *right* back."

They sat quiet, staring at each other. "Sandy," she whispered at length, "I've lost my appetite. Let's get outta here."

They walked quietly to Ann's barracks—even their footfalls seemed hushed. It was nearly a mile, but they uttered not a word. She led him to the picnic bench where she and JJ had talked that first evening and sat down heavily before she declared "1970-'71, yeah? *I* was winning swimming trophies and *he* was...*shit*." She started to shiver violently before Mike stretched an arm across her shoulders; she held him as if she were drowning and he were a life preserver.

It was some minutes before she let him go, wiping her face with her hand. "Holy *hell*," she complained. "I *never* thought..."

"*No one* could, Ann," he cleared his throat. "Yet, that school still exists."

"How? *Someone* should have complained by now."

"Apparently *not* to the right people. I know some *other* things about it—my father's firm was in some litigation that involved the school and JJ. But, even for *you*, I *can't*..."

"No, *don't*, Mike," she sighed. "*This* conversation stays between *us*." She leaned over and pecked his cheek. "Just us, Sandy."

"OK. Where'd you hear *my* nickname, Legs?"

Legs? "School," she smiled wryly. "*That* and those *eyes* of yours."

"I remember *you* always got away with *shorter* skirts than other girls." He grinned, sadly. "My Grandfather, Rabbi Mordechai Dietz, had a *unique* interrogation technique: he just asked JJ what *burdened* him on a Passover Saturday and all *this* shit spilled out and God help me I couldn't *not* listen to him for hour after *hour* before Grandfather told him that God is in the hearts of the righteous whether they believe it or not so that believing in one's self is *still* believing in God." He inhaled deeply. "Whatever fate put me outside the library that day also put us *here* together this morning, Legs. I don't know *why*..."

"It doesn't *matter why*, Sandy," she smiled unevenly. "I *asked* and you *answered*. Forewarned is fore-armed." She pecked his cheek again. "*Legs...just* between *us*. You probably should get to work."

He smiled, whispered "*you* are the *best* thing that's *ever* happened to him," pecked her forehead, and walked away.

Oh, Christ, babe...

Friday

"This is the *best* kind of baseball," Tom declared. "Amateurs playing for bragging rights." The evening's entertainment was the Monroe County Fast-Pitch Softball Championship Consolation Game between the Key West Conchs and the Islamorada Pelicans at Marathon's Municipal Field, an hour up US 1.

"Better than what the majors do for money," JJ agreed. "Ain't been the same since the '81 strike." They used two cars on what was *not* a double-date (Ann had a watch the next morning; Tom and Kristin were going out for drinks), just four friends hanging out in the same place. Mike begged off: press of work, he claimed.

The ladies were suitably attired: shorts and tank tops, with sweatshirts tied around shoulders. The gentlemen were somewhat more genteel in t-shirts and jeans. After all, they were sitting on wooden bleachers in the open air behind rusty chain link fences, not upholstered seats in a clubhouse.

Everyone stood for the playing of the National Anthem, and, as local tradition required, stayed standing for the first pitch. As they sat down, Ann asked, "did you tell your mom that you ran into me down here?"

Odd reaction, too. "Yeah. Did you tell your dad?"

He was surprised. "Sure. I've been thinking about it, Johnny."

"*It* what?"

"Your lack of luck with the ladies. From a *woman's* perspective, buddy, you're a *little* intense. You don't just *care* about things; you *obsess* over them. Can be off-putting." *Especially on a first date.* "Just think about it." *It's surprising that you even HAD first dates, babe.*

The play-by-play announcer was a local high school gym teacher, with some color commentary between innings by a familiar voice. "The guy doing color…I think I know him," JJ muttered.

"Yeah?" Ann was staring at some*one* or some*thing* on the other side of the field.

JJ watched Ann as he caught sight of Tom and Kristin two bleachers down out of the corner of his eye, laughing at the clown show along the third base fence. "He cut my head off and sewed it back on."

"Huh? What?" Ann wiped a tear quickly. "*What* did you say?" *Don't ever let them see you cry.*

"I said 'what are you looking at over there?'"

She inhaled deeply. "See the 3rd Base coach for the Pelicans? That's Roger. See that *woman* behind him—the black-haired one in the jersey—and the two girls that came in with her? *That's* his *family*. I didn't even *know* about them until now. But that's not what you said. You said something about the color announcer."

"I *did*, but…"

"Johnny, just *leave it*." She swallowed hard, blinked hard. "*Please*, babe." She wiped another tear and squeezed his knee. "Leave it."

Oh, my God: of course, she didn't know. "Want to go?"

"*No*," she answered too quickly. "No, I'm OK. Let's…just…watch the game. And, what about the color announcer?"

"He sounds like Al Kaline, played for the Tigers. I *tried* to play baseball with his son."

"Uh, your Little League…"

"Continental League. I was so bad even Dad didn't want me to play more than two seasons."

"You *were* pretty bad, weren't you?"

He bumped her shoulder. "*Please*, no more reminders."

The 3rd Inning was more eventful than the scoreless first two: two runs each. In the 4th, JJ caught a glimpse of Roger staring at Ann from the Pelican's bench. He *didn't* see, just moments before, that their eyes met—briefly—before she looked away.

How could I have been so stupid? Explains why he didn't want to be seen with me. Asshole. She's my color, my age, smaller. Have a beautiful life, jerk. Protect yourself, pretty wife. He WILL stray again.

By the 6th Inning, the Conchs were up by one run. Kristin and Tom…he *hadn't* done anything rash, but she *acted* like she wanted him to.

Waiting in line for two-for-one hot dogs along the 1st Base fence during the 7th Inning stretch-and-mutt-races, JJ mumbled, "Is Kristin always this…?"

"Flirty? With non-Navy guys, yeah." Ann watched Tom laughing at something Kristin whispered in his ear. "I don't think she's done anything dumb." *Like I have.* "One guy at a time. Should I slow her down?"

"Tom can do that himself. It takes two to tango, but I'm not sure Tom's ready to dance." Tom broke off a lip-lock to Kristin's disappointment.

The score was tied by the end of the 9th when a pop-fly to the catcher ended the inning. "How late do you want to stay?"

Ann glanced at her watch. "Let's see." She squeezed his knee. "I don't mind how late it is when I'm with you."

"Thanks."

"Any time, Johnny. For you, any time."

Extra innings ended when the first homer was hit off a pitching machine: Islamorada's lead-off batter—their shortstop/3rd Base coach/Ann's ex Roger, who already had three hits that night—put one over the right-field fence.

JJ took Ann back to her billets, walking her up to the porch. She reached out for a hug and pecked him on the lips. "Thanks, Johnny. I needed that. And I need *you*."

"Any time, Cloud. For you, any time."

***

There's at least one Dinky's Tavern in every big town—by different names, of course—that crooks and cops alike take advantage of because of their dark anonymity. Dated and seedy inside with a TV over the bar; blind, deaf and dumb regulars glued to half the stools from after-work to last call; dilapidated booths—where non-regulars furtively plan what to do elsewhere—covered with beat-up, patched and taped vinyl of red or black or both. Some feature dancers in stages of undress who would just as soon do something else if *this* didn't pay as well. If the Dinky's of this world were a franchise chain, *their* sign would read *"trillions* and *trillions* served."

Dinky's was just a block from Fort Zachary Taylor on the western edge of Key West. Mike came in the squeaky front door while a bored brunette gyrated her G-stringed hips to "I Will Survive" on the little stage. He grabbed a beer at the bar and quickly found the always-dark corner by the back door. As expected, Adam Block was waiting for him.

Mike had known round-headed Adam since he came to work for the family law firm. At first, Adam was the family chauffeur. As Mike grew older, he realized that Adam had more than one job. Dressed in a t-shirt and khaki pants, Adam nodded at Mike as he sat, smiling slightly. "Mr. Mike: good to see you." Adam had called Mike that since childhood.

"Adam," Mike grinned. "Welcome to The Rock."

Adam nodded. "Miss Mueller and Mr. Elrath: are they read-on?" "Read-on" in *their* world meant "given enough information to know what's going on."

"I haven't had the opportunity for a *full* briefing." Mike sipped his beer. "Find anything down here?"

"Newhouse is *aware* of Mr. Elrath's presence here, *and* Miss Mueller has suddenly appeared in their chatter. Anything on your end?"

"No. If they *have* any sources in the Army, I'll find them. My NCIS counterparts don't know of any in the Navy." He sipped his beer. "Still, they *also* know where Leigh and I are?"

Adam nodded. *"And* that *you're* down *here.*"

"Jackwell's *that* well informed?" Sid Jackwell, a former minion of the Newhouse organization, had contacts in the Byzantine Newhouse world.

Adam nodded. "He sees Joe Dryden calling the shots. Miss Leigh's torments are not from *Randy.*"

Mike grimaced. "I don't see Dryden backing those lawsuits on his own: it's too expensive."

135

"I don't either," Adam agreed. "Though for *who* and just *why* we don't know. We *know* he holds a grudge against Mr. Elrath; can't explain *his* interest in Miss Leigh, or *you*."

Huh. "*Her* I get: *she* whipped his ass more than once. But JJ?"

"Old family feud; *that* we know."

"Are you still looking into Wolverine?"

"That place has become a puzzle I need to solve so I can sleep better at night." Adam sighed. "What Mr. Elrath *endured* there…Grown men have broken under less."

"I told Ann about it; broad outlines. She…took it well."

Adam nodded. "*That* poor guy needs all the help he can get."

> *Oytzer*
> *I told Ann something more of Wolverine than <u>you</u> probably know; she asked. Can't say what she'll do with it.*

October

Tuesday

"Your arthritic nodules haven't changed, Sergeant," JJ's new orthopedist—a young Navy lieutenant with bony hands—mumbled, scanning his x-rays. "Concentrate on strengthening and mobility." Most of the members of the 4/75th had standing appointments at the Navy base hospital. "Much pain?"

"Mostly stiff."

"Just *keep moving*."

Back at work by two that afternoon, he was trying to finish his training plan for the battalion's field exercise when Ann sat heavily in his side chair. "OK, what's up?"

"Wendy has a family emergency and needs to go home but can't afford it, finance-wise. Know any sugar-daddies?" As the only two E-6s in the women's barracks—and the only two from Michigan—they had discussed a *lot*, including finding an apartment together…if they could *find* one.

He opened a desk drawer and pulled out a business card. "She needs to have the Red Cross call *this* outfit to verify the emergency. Give *my* name as the referral."

CloudWays…toll-free number. Not a cheap card, either; thick, slick, three colors. "What's this?"

"They help service members in trouble. Where does she need to go?" *Never asked where she was from; probably should have.*

"Someplace in Nebraska I never heard of; her father's taken ill where *he* came from. Where did *you* hear about these guys?"

"Germany."

Too cagey by half, buddy; usually I can't shut you up. "I'll pass it on. You ready to quit?"

"I'll see you at chow, maybe."

She encountered Nancy in the aisle. "Sarge, checking out." Then to Ann, "Chow?"

"I'll meet you."

Ann passed the card to Wendy, who frowned at it but muttered, "nothing ventured, nothing gained."

Ann met Nancy halfway through her poultry potpourri—the cooks *called* it chicken chop suey; she didn't see buzzards overhead on her way to the dining facility.

Back in her room, she cracked open her biology textbook and studied until Wendy knocked on her door. "Ann, I'm flying out tonight. I called JJ for a chat and he offered me a ride to the airport; he's on his way."

They waited in the tropical chill until JJ arrived. "When Ann gave me the card I wasn't expecting much, but, *geez*, did it get *results*. I fly out at one—stops in Tampa and St. Louis before Sioux City—and ground transportation to Niobrara will be waiting. I'll be at Grampa's place by nine tomorrow morning. All for a hundred fifty bucks round trip. And they'll bill me! What *is* this outfit?"

He shrugged. "Like I told Ann, they help people in need."

"*How* did *you* find out about them?" Ann glared at JJ uncomfortably.

"Ma got sick when I was in Germany." JJ smiled at Wendy. "*When you're ready…*"

"Give me one-five more mikes."

Fifteen minutes; not a problem if Cloud would just…let…it…go. He avoided her glare. "Please just leave it, Cloud. The important thing is we're helping a buddy."

Your casualness is odd, buddy. "OK, John." *For now.*

Friday

"Don't know if I *can* ask *you* to look at it." They sat in the day room just off JJ's barracks entrance while he was Charge of Quarters.

He squinted. "Wouldn't it be classified?"

"Official use only. We figured out *how: now* we need to say *why* our *how's* better than the civilian surveyor's. Not much more to it." Ann was trying to edit her demolition justification notes into a report she could turn in, but it was resisting her charms.

"Huh. Didn't know you guys *did* that."

"We do second-opinion surveys cheap. We don't *always* do the demolition." She shrugged and handed him the folder. "You might as well. Just make sure it makes sense."

"OK." He perused the three pages. "Looks like Brenda's handwriting." *And she owes me a couple letters.* "Coffee? I've got to make a round."

The day room was no more than 20x20, with a mixture of stacking and straight-back chairs, a couple of battered tables, a small TV, a ping-pong table, and a bookshelf with well-worn paperbacks and old magazines that included *Nugget* soft-core skin mags. *Wonder what would happen if...*

Two men came in, saw her and stopped as she looked up. "Don't mind me: I'm just visiting Sergeant Elrath."

"*Oh,*" the shorter one exclaimed, visibly brightening. "You're *her.*"

She got up, extending her hand. "If Ann Mueller is *her,* then that's *me.*" They were Rick Wynne and Mickey Harris: Rick was a tall redhead; Mickey a shorter, stockier, blonde, both with the swagger of military athletes. Rick walked with a cane, and Mickey wore a back brace. "What do you guys do for the Army?"

"We're Rangers, um…how do we address you? Petty officer or what? They don't *tell* us that." Rick seemed genuinely confused. "I know you're not a 'ma'am,' but…"

"Since *you're* not in uniform, Ann is OK. But my *rating* is Diver or Petty Officer First Class; my *grade* is E-6." She pointed to the chevrons on her dungaree sleeves. "'Petty officer' is proper; 'diver' is optional. There's no one word for *petty officer,* like your "sarge.'" She smiled. "Gossip aside, we're *just* good friends; clear?" The small-town Key West milieu leaned towards the salacious, though she *had* put the matter to rest in the women's barracks.

"Fine by me, um, Ann. We're going to *try* to play ping-pong." Rick seemed unsure but determined. "You can play the winner?"

Equal parts charming, distracted, and curious. "OK." *Hope Johnny gets back soon.*

JJ returned bearing coffee and a red pencil. "You met Wynne and Harris?"

"Yeah, Sarge," Mickey said, missing the ball clumsily. "We've met." He served badly. "Got a class on courtesy."

"I get to play the winner, providing there *is* one," Ann muttered.

"Mm," JJ mused, studying Ann's essay. "Might take a while." *OK, bits and pieces here, there, and everywhere. Need...* "Bullets. Make *this, this,* and *this* bullet points. Take all *this…*" he underlined several phrases, "into your closing. Turn *this,*" he circled three lines as a block, "into your first paragraph." He handed it back to Ann. "Follow me?"

Should be OK. She sipped her coffee before grabbing his hand. "I think this'll work. Thanks." The ping-pong game ended after a few noisy minutes—neither of them was especially good, given their physical issues. "Who won," Ann asked.

"Not sure," Rick replied. "Hard to keep score when you're *this* bad. Rain check, Ann?"

"Sure. Name the time and place."

The door guard—a PFC from the personnel section—appeared. "Sarge, there's someone here for you."

"Well, let him…"

"Not a *him*; a *her*. FBI?"

What? "I'll come."

"I'll see you later."

"Or visit me in jail."

They headed for the door, hooking fingers gently until he saw a familiar face, and he gave Ann an odd, puzzled look. "*Jules*? You're about the last…"

"Hi, JJ," she suddenly embraced him. "I needed to pop down and ask some questions."

Beautiful girl. Am I jealous? Ann watched with slight alarm. "I'll see you…"

"No-no, don't go," he grinned. "Julia, this is Ann Mueller. Ann, my niece, Julia Addison."

"His *first date*," Julia grinned as she shook Ann's hand. Her hair was light red, her eyes the same adorable shade of blue as JJ's, and with a figure fit for a magazine spread. "If JJ wants, come on along." She grinned at Ann mischievously. "*You're* his Cloud."

I AM, am I?

JJ looked skeptical. "What brings you down to The Rock?"

"What 'rock?'"

"Key West."

Julia looked to Ann as if for sympathy. "Can't he *just* be happy to see somebody?"

And she knows about ME? "Nope. *You* should know that."

"I need to ask my *favorite* uncle some questions: his name came up." Julia took off her jacket and unhitched her gun holster before she sat down. "Is the door closed?"

"Yeah."

"We fairly secure here?"

What the…? "I believe so."

Julia gazed around, finally lighting on the skin magazines. "In *this* investigation, I can't *be* too careful." She looked at JJ business-like. "Do you remember a Leigh Elizabeth Taylor? She was…"

"Sure. Are we formal? Remember, I've *seen* you…"

"Yes, you *have*, but *try*, Sergeant."

"Yes, ma'am. Yes, I do."

"*I* know her," Ann interrupted. "Went to school with her; swim team."

"Well," Julia beamed. "Glad I *caught* you. Can either of you give me *any* details on her in fall of 1970 to spring of '71?"

Ann sighed. "State finals November '70: we won the medley. We swam about every day all winter. She hung out with Randy Newhouse and his bunch. Why?"

"JJ: anything?"

"I was at Wolverine that year—you *knew* that. From June '70 I didn't see her again until Christmas '71."

"OK, Ann, I need you to think: her *physical* appearance. What did she *look* like in the spring?"

Ann scrunched her nose. "She looked *normal*. What...?"

"JJ: same question."

He inhaled deeply. "Only if you tell me why."

"OK," Julia smiled. "You said Newhouse? Know anything about *them*?"

"Um," Ann started, "Leigh *married* Randy Newhouse, yeah? What I remember of Randy Newhouse was that he was a combination of ladies' man and asshole. I was caught in a brawl when he and his little mob tried to beat up Mike Dietz..."

"Yes, Mike Dietz," Julia mused. "I need to talk to *him*, too."

"I'll see if he's here."

Julia was surprised. "He's *here*?"

"Held over for another week."

JJ left Ann and Julia alone. "What is this *about*, anyway," Ann asked quietly. "Seems far afield..."

"I'll explain when he gets back." Julia grinned brightly. "He missed *you* terribly." She looked away. "Even when we were skinny-dipping, he didn't see *me*."

"Do *that* much?"

"Just once; we're pals," Julia answered softly. "He's indestructible."

"He's...*something*."

JJ came back with Mike in tow. Julia showed him her credentials—and as required, Mike showed *his*—and Julia started again. "Mike: in the timeframe of late '70 and early '71, what do you know of Leigh Elizabeth Taylor?"

"When the Newhouse's say she was pregnant? I was..."

"*WHAT?*" Ann cried. "*Impossible*! I saw her in the *shower* that winter!"

"Mike?"

"I started Brookfield that September, but we got together with her family for Thanksgiving, Christmas, Passover. We were *certainly* together

Mother's Day '71: I remember her father turned 41 that day. *Someone* would have noticed if she was pregnant."

"OK. JJ: anything *else* on Leigh?"

"I talked to her a week before her wedding. She didn't seem sold on the idea, but seemed...trapped."

"OK," Julia sighed. "Mike, you probably know much of this, but for the benefit of JJ and Ann: the Newhouse organization has been claiming that Leigh gave birth to Randy's son on 15 May 1971 and that she abandoned the child after deserting Randy shortly after their wedding."

"*She* told *me* they never consummated, before *or* after the wedding." Mike glanced at JJ and Ann. "She left him *literally* on their wedding night when he told her about his son; expected her to adopt him."

"Shit," Ann blurted. "*She* wouldn't abandon a child."

JJ took Ann's hand. "I don't know her *well*, but I know *that* much."

"Anyway," Julia continued. "The Newhouse organization has had some troubles that interests federal law enforcement—shady dealings with shady people. The maternity matter has come up during the investigation, and it seems that *your* name, *Unka* John, came up."

"Why?"

"We're not *sure*, but someone in the Newhouse organization wants you dead."

"Why," JJ interrupted. "I've had NO dealings with them."

Julia stared. "Joe Dryden?"

JJ stared at Mike. "That's who *you* told me about back in '80 and I still never heard of the SOB. You're down here because..."

"Yeah," Mike murmured, "a *little*. I *am* a Russian linguist—*that's* why I came down here—and I *am* in CI. External threats to military personnel's my job...part of it, anyway. Just...didn't expect to run into the Bureau down here."

>*Leigh*
>*Just got your letter of last week: SO good to hear from you. You enlisted a week after you annulled Randy? Wow.*
>*Mike mentioned your troubles with Randy's family, so did Johnny's FBI agent/niece we talked to...Mike's explanation of Wolverine chilled my blood...*

Tuesday

JJ stared at the illogical equation taped to the wall above his desk, his back still smarting from taking down and stowing the tents from their latest field exercise at the old missile base. He was using the formula as the "hook" for a book he was planning:

Japan started a war it knew it couldn't win

+

Japan invented the suicide bomber

=

Japan was ready to surrender before Hiroshima because it rationally knew it couldn't win.

Why would anyone think THIS adds up? A knock on his door shook him out of his reverie. "Sarge, you have a visitor."

"Send him down."

"It's a girl, Sarge: Petty Officer Collins?"

"*A woman*, Hodges," JJ answered, mildly irritated. "I'm coming." He checked his watch: nearly 2200. *What could SHE want at this hour of the night?*

Kristin, in disheveled dungarees, paced anxiously by the CQ desk. Incongruously, he couldn't remember *seeing* Kristin in dungarees before. "Ann's in the hospital." On the way there, Kristin filled him in. "She's felt bad for days, but this afternoon she doubled up, bleeding." Between the Ranger's field exercise and Ann being swamped by the sudden arrival of several thousand requisitions of back-ordered parts and supplies, they hadn't seen much of each other much for two weeks.

"Bleeding, as in…"

"Yeah, *that* kind." She craned her head around. "Hospital's…"

"I've been here often enough." They went through the front door together, but she stopped in the lobby.

"In the emergency," she pointed, "down there. Good luck."

With outer calm and inner turmoil, he marched down a long hall to a nurse's station. "Petty Officer Mueller?"

"Room 4." A matronly nurse at the counter looked sad, but with her face it was hard to tell if she didn't *always* look like that. A prune-like nurse sat in a chair by the door of the small, darkened Room 4.

Ann dozed on a gurney, pale. He took her hand, cool in his. "Hi, Dee." Somehow, his childhood name for her *felt* right.

She looked up, bleary-eyed. "Johnny…hi. How…?" *Of everyone I could see now, you're top of the list.*

"Kristin."

"Good buddy."

"Yup. What's going on?"

"Not sure. Awful cramps. Started…*ugh*. Doped me up; can't think straight." Just then a Navy commander swept into the room, glanced at the monitors, then grabbed her chart as Ann struggled against wooziness. "Allison, can…?"

"In a minute, Ann." The doctor finished with the chart, then glanced at JJ in a way he wasn't used to. "Who's *this*?"

"Commander Semmes, Staff Sergeant Elrath. JJ; Allison." JJ shook hands with the severe-looking woman who he thought bore a strong resemblance to Lucille Ball.

"We'll keep you here tonight," Allison sighed. "We're not sure yet just *what's* happened. Sergeant, if you could step out for a moment."

"*He* stays," Ann grunted, gripping his hand with surprising strength.

Allison shot him a look, then Ann before she shrugged. There was a fluffle of the sheet before the doctor raised Ann's gown: he looked away, blushing. After a few minutes, Allison announced, "OK. You're not *actively* hemorrhaging; nothing we have to fix." She stripped off her gloves. "I'm scheduling a D&C for tomorrow."

"Ugh, *must* we? My cycle has *never* been regular; you know that."

He blushed again, gritting his teeth. *I know what cycle means and what a D&C is, barely. Maybe I should have left…*

"Yes," Allison smiled, "that's one reason for it. Some material we need to evacuate." She glanced back and forth as if talking to a couple. "Sleep well tonight, both of you."

"Yes, ma'am, and thank you," he answered. "What can I tell Petty Officer Collins?"

Allison smiled. "Just tell Kristin that *I* said there's nothing to worry about." She took Ann's hand, glancing at him. "*He's* a keeper, Ann." Both Allison and the nurse glanced at them as they left.

"They think…"

She squeezed his hand. "Let 'em think what they want. Take Kristin home."

Before he left the hospital, he stopped off to see Gary and his wife Alice, who had delivered their daughter Gabrielle that afternoon.

Wednesday

"Oh, *God*," she sobbed in the bright moonlight. She had stripped off her shift at the car, and stood in a bandana bra and cutoffs at the water's edge of the tiny, unnamed Shark Key beach…and cried.

Half our lifetime brought us here. "Just cry, honey." He stood a few feet away, listening over the lapping surf.

"Not fair to *you*," she sniffed, shifting her weight off her crampy hip, stretching her arms wide, muscles rippling across her back, soft breezes ruffling through the brush of her hair. "But, I…"

Hell, Cloud. What do I say? "Don't worry about *me*, honey. You said you needed…"

"*AIR*. And it's sweet of you to indulge me." She signed deeply. "I didn't *know* I was pregnant. I just thought…I've never *been* regular…"

Miscarriage. "I *know*, Cloud."

"Didn't even think it was *possible.* Then Allison says my uterus isn't…." She looked out on the water trying to calm the tempest of her mind, watching the dark surges of deep turquoise move like shapeless monsters in the ocean. *Ten to twelve weeks, she said. Our weekend at the Holiday Inn—so twelve weeks—only possible time. We made a baby, you JERK Roger, and I lost it.* She sighed again, a heart-rending sound against the surf. "Babe, I'm sorry. If *you* ever want children, look elsewhere."

"I *never* thought about it, honey." *True fact.*

She turned as they stepped towards each other until they were inches apart and she pecked his lips. "Tag, you're it."

"I saw our Safe Tree three years ago." A gnarled old apple tree in a vacant lot between their childhood homes had endured harsh Michigan winters for at least half a century.

"Yeah?" She wrapped her arms around him gently, water lapping around her bare feet. He held her as she started to sob again, shuddering. The tide rose wave by wave, rising to his boot-tops before receding again as she cried, her cheek against his, their hearts beating as one, her tears trickling into his shirt, his starting to flow. The breeze chilled her skin, making her shiver and grip him tighter. "*Never* let go, babe."

"Never, my love."

"Great song, isn't it?" She relaxed her grip, wiped her face with her hand. "We'd better…"

"Not *yet*, honey," he whispered. "Not before *you're* done."

She wept in his arms for several more minutes, finally letting go. "Babe, I *need* to get back."

"You sure?"

"Uh-huh." She kissed his cheek and turned towards the car. "Are you working this weekend?"

"No, finally: we're done with the field for now. What do you have in mind?"

"Just laundry and homework."

Saturday

"Hey," JJ called as he opened the screen door of the 9th Street bungalow. Kristin's green Gremlin was already parked in the carport; JJ had pulled his Plymouth in behind it.

"Hi, guys," Ann looked up from her book. "You brought beer."

"Yeah; thought four people could put a dent in a case," Tom grunted. He and JJ lugged their laundry bags and a case of beer between them. Ann was in jeans and a t-shirt in the ball chair when they came in; Kristin could be heard cursing and banging in the bathroom; the big wing chair was where they had left it.

"Fine," Ann replied. "Kristin's fixing plumbing in the bathroom. Ten bucks in parts and some elbow grease got us the place for two nights."

"Does she *know* anything about plumbing," Tom wondered.

"We're hull techs, Tom. We know *something* about plumbing."

"Hull means *plumbing*?"

"Hull *includes* every ship system. You need it, we build it or fix it."

"Hull techs? Thought you were *divers*."

"Divers have to do *something* in the water to support the fleet. We're underwater overachievers."

"Good one." Tom looked wistfully at the doorway.

"Go on in there, Tom. She'd be disappointed if you didn't."

"Guess they hit it off," JJ muttered.

"She *says* so. I'm reading my American history unit on the Gilded Age. Know anything about that?"

"The Sunday between wars? A little." They chatted about the time in American history between the end of the Civil War and the beginning of WWI as he settled in the chair.

After a while, the washer was noisily operational again, and Tom came back to the living room for the beer. "Fridge big enough for all of it?"

"Oh, yeah," Ann replied. "The hot dog stand on the beach has beer, too. Stay away from the salad cone." Tom went back out to the car for his own books, setting them on the little table in the hall as Kristin went into the shower.

All was quiet until… "Ahoy the house," a woman's loud voice called. "Prepare for boarders!"

"Betty! You made it back," Ann grinned, looking up. JJ looked up to see a woman in short overalls in the doorway. "Did *Laura*…?"

"That's affirmative," another voice called. "EOD mermaid's all present."

"Betty Sadowski, Laura Gutierrez: introduce yourselves to the guys," Ann announced. "So, how did it go?"

"Well, the damn thing didn't go BOOM, and we removed it," Betty replied. "*That* was the object of the evolution."

"What…evolution?" JJ stood up, but didn't have to feign being mystified.

"They've been at Guantanamo for the past week," Ann explained. "Something stuck to a ship?"

"Yep," Betty answered. "A Chinese copy of a Russian version of a British pattern magnetic mine stuck to a guided missile frigate. Damn thing was a leftover from the Korean War: they *had* to have picked it up in Flying Fish Channel outside Inchon a couple weeks ago. The *evolution* was the coordinated actions that resulted in rendering the damn thing safe and removed. You Army guys *don't* use that term, huh? The *Navy* uses it all the time."

"You guys are EOD?" Tom asked from the doorway.

"Really? Nerves of steel and all that?" JJ was surprised.

"Shocking, ain't it? We can *vote*, too." Laura gazed benignly at JJ. She was a little shorter than Betty's five-feet-ten, in a short tank top and capris, with long blonde braids and light skin, and more muscle than JJ had ever seen on *any* woman…or many *men*.

"That's not…" JJ mumbled.

Laura laughed. "*Yeah*, I know. *You* must be JJ."

"They sent *us* down there because we've got more time with the robots than *their* guys do." Betty tried to sound matter-of-fact.

"You disarmed it?" Ann was slightly curious.

"Naw," Laura answered, "the best way to disarm a '50s-era Chinese *anything* is to wait for it to rust to pieces or blow itself up. Their guts are both too robust and too delicate."

"Yeah," Betty agreed. "But *this* one was never armed. So, where are *we* in laundry order?"

"Kristin should be in the dryer soon," Ann mused. "I'm next, then JJ, then *Tom*, then *you* two." She watched the two divers size up the men, *somewhat* theatrically.

"*We* could be doing laundry *long* after dark, Hutch," Laura muttered, arms across her chest.

"*Yeah*, Starski. I'll take the dark one in the doorway." Betty—half a head taller—glared at Tom like a barracuda might a goldfish, hands on hips. "So: two falls out of three?"

"We can…sure," Tom stuttered. "I don't *have* much—I use quartermaster laundry for my uniforms. We can do ours together."

Betty feigned surprise. "*We* just *met*, and *now* you want to *mix* our *unmentionables*? In-*deed*, sir!"

"Don't call me 'sir.' lady; *I* work for a living." Tom growled. "I'd never tarnish your virtue…"

"*That* so?" She brushed his chin with a finger, putting on a vampish grin as she expanded her chest: in a tight white tube top *sans* brassiere, *her* chest *was* a sight. "I ain't a 'ma'am' neither, sarge, and leave my *virtue* out of it. But it's a *washing machine*, not a bed. Just don't think you can *try* anything just because you *might* manhandle my *bloomers, buster*."

"That leaves you and me, pal," Laura smiled at JJ a little *too* brightly. "Arm wrestling or pistols: you choose."

"Oh, pistols: I ain't that strong." *And I'm probably a better shot.*

She laughed. "I *like* this guy, Ann." She smiled. "Don't worry about it, cutie: I've been up for twenty hours. I can *sleep* until it's my turn."

JJ was curious. "How many EOD types are down here?"

Laura smiled enigmatically, sashaying towards him and affecting a Slavic accent. "If I didn't know better, *bubeleh,* I'd think you were a Russian spy."

"You know *bubeleh* is Yiddish, right," Kristin called. "Bubee Batsheva used to call us kids that."

"Spy in next *dacha,*" JJ grinned, with some sort of Slavic accent.

"OK, Natasha Fatale," Ann mumbled. "We *get* it. Only he *ain't* Boris Badenov."

Laura giggled. "There's twelve EOD techs down here. More old ordnance around than you'd think." She stretched, her muscled belly rippling. "Listen: get me up when *those* love birds go into the dryer, OK? I *really* need some sleep."

Betty and Tom had consolidated their laundry by the time Kristin emerged in a dorm shirt—hair dripping—and slung her laundry bag into a corner of the front room as Tom and Betty went to the backyard (through the back bedroom) where a volleyball net was erected.

"*My* turn." Ann glanced at JJ. "*I* don't have a lot either; don't need to be doing it all day. Gimme *yours*, Johnny."

He slid his half-full bag across the floor. "Briefs, t-shirts and socks, pair of jeans, shorts."

Kristin, in front of the window, dried her short hair briskly and regarded JJ with a small smile before turning to look at the sea while he went back to reading. "JJ: keep your nose in your book for a minute."

"OK." He could barely see her rummaging in her laundry bag.

"*Don't* look." She stood in the corner of the room as she changed into *too*-short pleated skirt and tie-blouse. "OK now." She gazed out the window again. "Surf's not too high, JJ. Might go shell hunting later. You game?"

"Don't know what I'd do with shells."

"Exotics you can sell for a penny a pound. Mostly it gets me closer to the sea." She paused to flap her towel. "I just wish…"

"Where *are* you from?"

"Galveston." She looked pensive, hanging her towel on a rack over the side window: all the windows were so equipped. "Wish I still enjoyed the water as much as I used to."

"How's that?"

"Before I joined the Navy, I swam all the time, fresh water and salt. Every chance I got I was in the water. Got my first C-card when I was fifteen. But now…" She heaved a deep, resonant sigh.

"Busman's holiday," he declared.

"What?"

"Means you do the same thing for recreation as you do for work. When you make a hobby a profession, that's what you're doing. Analyzing information is what *I* do. Just happens now I…"

"Wow," she laughed, "Ann *said* you were kinda nerdy!" She smiled seriously. "She also says you're sweet and indulgent. I've been with her for the last eight years, and I've *never* seen her as happy as she's been since last month. *You're* about to get a tampon test."

"A *what*?"

"We like to know how comfortable guys are dealing with *our* needs so we send you out for tampons. Guy balks: he's not *ready* to be serious. He goes, he *is*. He asks what *kind* before we *tell* him, the test was unneeded." She laughed: "*You'll* pass."

"Yeah? What do *you* do for amusement if swimming ain't it anymore?"

"I study, I hang out, I shop, and I'm a sucker for romance novels: trashier the better. You?"

"I read, I write, I study, I go to movies."

"Huh. *One* of us hurt you, didn't she?"

"No one specific: I'm just…"

"Gynophobic, unlucky or afraid of rejection?"

Pretty smart. "Two and three. My timing's usually bad, and no guy likes to get laughed or sneered at by anyone. How about *you*? One of *us* did a job on *you*, too."

"Yep," she sighed. "Why I joined the Navy. And *we've* done a great deal of damage to a *lot* of *you*." She grinned. "I've *had* guy friends—got a *Navy* full of 'em now—but the *guy* codebook is so much different from *ours*."

"Codebook?"

"The signals we send each other." She made a face. "OK, look at me: just…look."

"OK, you're attractive. Now what?"

"What *else* do you see? Not because you know what I *do* and who I *know*, but *see* as in…what do you *visualize*?"

"You're fashionably dressed…"

"*This* outfit is rummage-sale-discards, *not* fashionable." She pulled her skirt up—it didn't have *that* far to go—revealing a bare hip. "Now?"

"Not sure what you're getting at."

She rolled her eyes. "You *don't* see yourself ravishing me?"

"Am I supposed to?"

"*YES!* You're a *guy*, for the love of *chocolate!* I'm eligible, attractive, and *smiling at you*!"

"So, the way you're dressed—or *not*—and the way you *look* at me has some bearing on what I'm supposed to *think* of you? Then, I'm supposed to throw a switch that turns all that off when we're in uniform?"

She looked at him sidelong. "*YOU* have a very different codebook, buddy. That switch; *I* don't have one, but *most* women I know do. Love-of-my-buddy, guys *are* supposed to: the species *requires* it. I dress…"

"Women dress for each other; Van Morrison was *right* about that," Betty announced, coming in the room. "Clothing is wearable wealth. Wearing designer clothes is more important now than ever. Sociology and psychology, double major. Working on a paper on the degradation of Anglo-Saxon mores and social…*what?*"

Kristin was giggling. "I was just…I just told JJ he was nerdy but in a good way, and then we got…Oh, *wow!*"

"Nerds of the world, unite, JJ," Betty declared, "power to the typewriter," offering a palm.

"Power to the word processor," JJ answered, slapping it.

"I need to get one of *those*," Betty admitted. "You *got* one?"

"I'm watching," JJ sighed. "Need the technology to settle down."

"Wait…*Elrath*…*You* wrote a book, didn't you?" Betty looked at him suspiciously.

"*Tell* her, Staff Sergeant Famous," Tom muttered from the doorway.

JJ grimaced. "I wrote *most of* that book, and the staff of the Leadership Studies Institute wrote the rest."

"*Profiles in Leadership: Case Studies in Command, Leadership and Military Management,*" Ann called from the kitchen. "Number 56 on our reading list."

Reading list? "Huh. Didn't know that," JJ muttered.

"So, what's it about?" Betty sat on the sofa; Kristin and Tom joined her.

"The fundamental concept of leadership at *our* level is backward in post-Industrial Revolution warfare: war has gotten too technical for the old model. The supposed *art* of leadership needs to be driven towards *preparing* the led to *participate*—to take care of themselves in their *own* best interests. The profiles are little vignettes of leaders, the most *successful* of which, without 'leading' in the flag-waving sense of 'get up and follow me,' *enabled* followers who succeeded. I say give the troops the tools to take care of themselves, while *we* make sure they know how to use them. What *we* do is *management* called *leadership* because *management* is less heroic. We need…*what?*"

Betty looked surprised. "*Not* what they teach *us*."

"It's not *fashionable* for *us* yet, either. What we do would be *micro*managing if the officers did it, but that's why they have *us*." *The*

Navy thinks it's good, huh? Wish the Institute would tell ME that.

Tom grinned. "Our boss thinks his is the best treatise on leadership theory in a generation. One reason he's down here."

As the day went on there was beer and cold cuts, conversation and laughter, studying and book sales. JJ woke Laura up as Tom and Betty's laundry went into the dryer. Everyone went to the beach for dinner and to watch a corner of the sunset. As they walked back, JJ and Ann lingered behind. "How're you feeling, honey?"

"Tired, mostly, babe. Sad. Empty. Would have sunk my career." She crossed her arms. "I wasn't even *thinking* about kids; now it's *all* I think about."

"Do *they* know?"

"They know something *female* happened, that I'm on light duty for two weeks, and I'm off dive status for a while. They don't *ask* more." She paused. "*You* don't drink much. Two beer's your limit?"

"More's irritating. But I need to ask *you* something: Do I *bore* you?"

"Frankly, a little." She bumped his shoulder. "Our tastes are pretty much the same, but I like art for its own sake, and you don't."

He furrowed his brow. "You said I'm intense. I'm working on that." *Here goes.* "Tom might have a line on a place first of the year."

"*I'm* tired of the billets." *WHAT did you just say, kid?*

"I'll keep you posted."

"OK." She paused. "Mike's gone now?"

"Last week, yeah." He pecked her cheek and sighed. "*That's* from *him.* I *wrote* to you...sort of. I wrote you letters in a couple of composition books; turned into a kind of diary. I want you to read them sometime."

"OK."

That evening there was Stella's Game (there was a drawer full of playing cards in the kitchen), and JJ won not a single deal. For no obvious reason, the men also sang "Rangers in the Night," to the tune of "Strangers in the Night:"

Rangers in the night, exchanging passwords;
Wandering in the night, who said the last word?
Looking for a fight; we're Rangers in the night!

Biting snakes in two; oh, how tasty,
Eat the earthworms too; let's not be wastey;
Ambush on the right, for Rangers in the night!

They sounded *not at all* like Sinatra...and *no* scooby-doobie-doo, either.

Ann and Kristin were staying overnight, but Kristin and Tom weren't *there* yet. "They do this a lot," JJ told Tom on the drive back.

"That's what Kristin said," Tom replied. "How's Ann doing? Kristin said she was under the weather. She's worried about her...."

"Better, she says. It's Kristin's job to worry about her buddy."

"Yours too, pal."

"True that. You and Kristin...?"

"Awkward. I'm *ten years* older, but *that* ain't it. I get on with Betty; she's 33, but again, the E-7/E-6 thing. *That both* services object to."

"Not if they're *not* in your chain of command. Unless..."

"Unless they need an excuse, yeah. But I *just* signed Connie's papers."

You've got a problem I could only dream of: a choice between two women.

***

Oytzer
In Michigan with our families makes me remember how much
I miss you...

"I proclaim you husband and wife together in accordance with God's laws! *Mazel tov!*" Nathan's right heel smashed his lightbulb just before Kiera smashed hers. Their wedding was colorful, with extensive floral arrangements not usual even for uber-liberal Temple Emmanuel. The groom and his family were "off the *derech*"—not particularly observant of Jewish customs—not that Kiera ever *had* been *that* observant, though her family observed holy days. Despite this, the Grun's and the Dietz's preferred a religious ceremony to a few minutes at the courthouse.

...What you said about JJ being aloof except with a few people;
yeah, I see that.

Compared to Kiera's, Sara's more pious ceremony with Oliver Halliwell—a shirtsleeve relative of the O'Bannon's, the Dietz's law partners—that afternoon was downright austere. The reason for the unusual timing was to accommodate Mike, who could squeeze in just two day's leave around that last weekend of the month.

Mike was best man for both grooms though he barely knew them. It was good that his sisters were friends (and each other's maids), else blood might have been spilled at their combined reception.

A huge number of Dietz and O'Bannon uncles, aunts and cousins— many of whom Mike didn't know well—attended the Baroque Circle mansion reception. Catering for over two hundred guests was no easy task—and a tent big enough for a *hora* was erected—but Adam's job of keeping the family safe was harder still. His attention was caught by a

151

hulking-big Hispanic in a white busboy's coat—in the wrong pattern. He had a streak of gray hair rising from his forehead, and his ID *said* his name was Herman Jimenez.

One day, oytzer, you and I will find a way to satisfy both the Army and ourselves so we can be together.

November

Friday

"JJ," Wendy began, "we hear *you* know how to weld."

In the 4/75th, Friday afternoons were often spent performing vehicle maintenance. The twenty-two enlisted people in the S-2 shop had direct responsibility for eight diesel-powered Chevy Blazers without trailer hitches, four small Jeep trailers (for Jeeps they no longer *had*), and a 2-1/2-ton truck and its trailer left over from the Korean War. "Maintenance" for operators almost universally meant *cleaning* or painting. JJ and about half of the section were out doing their due diligence when Major Fred Batten, the battalion supply officer, came out with Wendy. Fred had silver hair, a bad foot and the demeanor of a genial soda jerk.

"One of my *rustier* talents," JJ replied. "Haven't lit a torch for a dog's age. What do you need?" He hadn't done *any* welding since the summer he enlisted, and even *before* then, not a lot.

"The Cowling is busted and there's a party on Veteran's Day. We can't replace it and can't use it in its current condition." The Cowling—said to be a war trophy— was a trough about seven feet long and three feet wide, with angle-iron legs bolted on at each end so it could be used as a barbecue. When JJ first saw it, it stood in the warehouse, one end on its legs and the other resting on a jack stand. The material on one end had failed badly, threatening to tear off.

JJ knocked on it with a knuckle. "Aluminum. *I* can't help you, but I know who *might*."

"There's a case of beer in it for the repair," Ed intoned.

"See what we can do."

The Navy's main welding shop was five blocks across the base. Ann wasn't there; a sailor pointed to Kristin tacking some steel together. *She looks like a gnome in welding gear.* He hammered a steel table for attention and she looked up and lifted her shield. "Hey, guys; sir. Visiting working sailors?"

"Petty Officer Collins, we need someone who can weld aluminum," JJ stated officiously.

She lifted her helmet off and shook her short hair out of her little welder's cap. "Weld *what*, Sergeant Elrath?" Wendy described the problem.

"Let me change out of this Nomex corset and I'll take a look." Like everyone else on the Rock, Kristin knew that the Rangers had no assigned mechanics for their vehicles, let alone welders.

In a few minutes they were in the Ranger's wooden supply building adjacent to their motor pool. Kristin fingered the ragged tear; knocked on the trough a couple of times. "Sound metal. It got too hot and some idiot poured water into it." She sighed. "I *could*; but *our* weld shop would need a work order."

"That could take *weeks*," Ed mumbled, "and we need it by next *Monday*."

Kristin put on a thoughtful face. "If you could *get it* to Popeye's..."

"What's that?"

"Welding shop on the north shore. He's got a TIG rig I could use, but his is *not* portable." She glanced first at Ed, then JJ before she winked at Wendy. "*Cost* ya."

"How much?"

"*Less* than a lap dance, but *more* than a case of beer." She smiled. "If you can *get* it there, *I'll* work it out: I'm knocking off for the day, anyway. Meet you there in an hour. Bring enough labor to get it off and on again. Wendy: if you can help with *my* gear..."

"Sergeant Elrath," Ed declared, "I'll get the deuce-and-a-half dispatched while you get The Cowling loaded." The thing was clumsy, not heavy. They used a long cargo strap lengthwise to hold the two ends together, and piled four more people on the truck.

When the truck arrived at the old boathouse, they saw Kristin and Wendy talking with the owner and understood why Kristin called him "Popeye:" the raw-boned man affected a permanent squint and smoked a corn-cob pipe. Kristin wore bib-overall cutoffs with a shirt wrapped around her waist, with what looked like a (not very) wide rubber band for a top. Both she and Wendy—in shorts and a *way-too-tight* tank top—stood *very* close to Popeye. When they finished negotiating, Kristin pulled her shirt on hastily and came smiling to the truck as Wendy pulled on a windbreaker. "Two cases of Heineken and a half-gallon of Jack Daniels." Wendy shrugged. "*Best we* could do."

What did it cost YOU, girls? "Sir?"

"We can live with that," Ed announced. "*Where* do you want the thing?"

"One more thing, sir," Kristin smiled a deadly come-hither smile, "it's going to cost someone *else* a night out."

"Someone...*who*," JJ narrowed his eyes.

"*Two* nights," Wendy smiled—altogether, a beautiful woman.

"*Don't* play dumb, Sergeant," Ed growled. "It's the unit's *honor* we're talking about here."

***

"Reporting" to the women's billets just before 7 that night, Ann met JJ with her mock-cross face. "*Two*-timing me, are you?"

"It's payment-in-kind, Cloud. You *know* how this works."

All too well. "You kids behave," Ann grinned as they left. "Don't keep her out *too* late, young man."

They had dinner at an Italian place that only the locals knew about—and they *kept* the tourists ignorant—on Upper Sugarloaf Key. After dinner, they went to a well-lit but quiet lounge on Big Pine Key, where they chatted about a lot of things…including the project just completed. "Where'd that thing come from?" She sipped her wine.

"It was the cowling off a Chinese MIG that some Ranger brought back from Korea—no one ever *asked* how."

"*Aircraft* aluminum? Not *that* stuff. And, it's the wrong grain pattern. That structure's *centrifugally cast*; *probably* a pipe." He stared at her, surprised. "What? Gotta *know* the stuff to work with it."

"I know enough about welding to know *that* much."

She was suddenly serious. "Johnny: Ann loves you. And *you*, my friend, love *her. You* need to tell *each other*."

"I only ever said *that* to *one* girl."

"How did *she* work out?"

"We just…petered out."

"Buddy, you and Ann will *not* just peter out."

Saturday

The night was quiet, as it often was that time of year in the Keys: insect activity was practically nil between Halloween and Easter. A group of women laughed about something as they walked to the barracks door just after one in the morning. Ann, on watch, sat on the porch next to the barrack's mascot, Penelope the Potted Palm. "Ladies," she smiled. A small cacophony of replies came back as all but one of them went inside. Wendy sat down on the steps.

"Nice night," Ann sighed.

"Fine night. You should know, Ann: He's *haunted*." They glanced at each other. "JJ's haunted."

"You think so?"

"I saw him out on the perimeter one night last month; wide-eyed. I have a cousin, 'Nam vet. Once, after a backfire, he looked like JJ did that night." She stood up. "*Something haunts* him, too."

And I know what it is. "And he owes you dinner, I hear…"

"Sunday breakfast and I'll call *us* even. It was for *my* outfit, too."

"For *what*? Showing your…?"

"*Don't* tell me *you've* never given a *little* peek for an off-line favor."

"I *won't*."

***

"Did you *have* to show *so* much to *that* guy?" They sat at the end of the mole, sucking beer. She reached for his hand: he took it.

"Popeye? Nothing comes from women in *his* world without *giving* something, even if it's just a peek-a-boob." She sighed, *slowly* shifting her top with a side-to-side movement. "Do *you* want…?"

"She's *our* best friend."

"*You're* not *chaste*, are you? Come on: come clean."

"I should kiss and tell?"

She reached for his chin. "*Just* a kiss, Johnny?" He smiled and leaned into her face, lingering on her lips *just* long enough. "Like…*that*." She smiled. "Cop a feel?"

"I *respect* you too much for that."

She pecked his cheek. "Thanks for dinner. Maybe noon chow Sunday?"

Is it me, or this place? Had more luck in three months here than I have in two years anywhere else.

Tuesday

The order from the Department of the Army—the day after Veteran's Day, yet—wasn't a *bit* apologetic:

Memoranda for Record:

1. *All members of US Army Active Component combat arms units shall be qualified as Marksman (minimum) with their primary weapon to be considered eligible for promotion in FY 86.*
2. *No wavers shall be allowed for 1. above.*

Debbie Beibl (up for E-6 that year) in the personnel shop and Wendy (up for E-7) had not *been able* to qualify when they enlisted in the WAC. *Now* that the WAC was gone and they were in the 4/75th, they *had* to qualify with the M-16 to be promoted, and no one wanted to deny them that. The nearest rifle range was the Marine's 100-meter range out on Sand Key; the *next* closest was in Georgia.

Thus, a marksmanship class was needed. Because most of the enlisted women on Key West lived in the same building, this need soon became widely known. The Marines *originally* claimed to have the best shooter on the Rock, and the Navy had a SEAL who was *said* to be handy with a gun.

155

But there was *only one* NRA-certified rifle marksmanship instructor *in* Key West...and JJ was in the *Army*, and his credentials—*perfect* rifle scores—*were* hard to argue with.

Nonetheless, the Ranger's Headquarters Company commander, the Marine's company commander, and the Navy's dive activity commander made an officer's club wager (according to witnesses, after *at least* three rounds of tequila shots): a shootout between the three shooters for bragging rights, if nothing else.

Thursday

The bleachers were half-full in the base gymnasium, with five Army, twenty Navy, five Marine, two Air Force and three Coast Guard women attending: the marksmen from the other services and a host of others decided to see what was *so* special about *this* guy...so did scores of others.

After formal opening remarks and safety announcements, JJ started with... "A company of Russians goes into a valley in Afghanistan and gets *all* shot up. One of the survivors says there's a sniper in there. 'One sniper,' the division commander sniffs. 'We'll take care of *that*.' He sends his whole division into the valley. Well, there's this big firefight that lasts a couple of days, and the division commander manages to escape with a handful of his men and radios *his* boss: 'there's two of 'em!'"

He let that old joke slide—*some* people hadn't heard it. "Soldiers; sailors; Marines; and the *rest*; are here on Gilligan's...never mind. Much of what you're about to see isn't in *any* books. I've been working with women using shoulder arms for a while, and I've concluded that the fair sex just ain't *made* for rifle marksmanship the way it's taught for men. If my demonstrator, Petty Officer Mueller, will come out here..."

Ann, in dungaree trousers and a t-shirt, stood up in front of the class. "Now: the female neck is generally longer *in proportion* to the head and shoulders, and the body *usually* shorter, even if my demonstrator's not the best example of *that. Sergeant* Corey, can *you*...just for a minute?" Wendy came down and stood next to Ann. "OK: Sergeant Corey's five foot eight..."

"Five-*ten*," Wendy loudly announced, frowning.

"OK, five-*ten*. Petty Officer Mueller's six-*one*. Much of *her* height is...as you can see...between her hips and her shoulders. Wendy's height's in her *legs*." Both women—as rehearsed—stared at him, *archly* annoyed. "OK, OK, you're *both* high in our regard because of your roles in Today's Military." Soft chuckles followed. "Rifle marksmanship's *dry* as *dust*, folks: bear with me. Thanks, Sergeant Corey; take your seat, please.

"Now, women's shoulders are generally wider *in proportion* to body size but usually *sloped* differently than a man's." JJ gestured vaguely; *Ann* was *much* more specific with her hands, much to everyone's amusement. "These factors combine with the musculature of the female upper body…" she turned sideways with a flourish; "and wider hips…" she faced front again…with a *ba-boom* swivel, which got another nervous laugh; "to make comfort behind a shoulder weapon in the prone supported position difficult *without* additional support for the upper body—we'll get a laugh outta you guys yet. *Now*," he gestured to his stack of sandbags, "we'll *try* to show the way women *should,* in *my* humble opinion, handle a shoulder arm in the prone supported position."

As rehearsed, Ann started by doing everything wrong that she *possibly* could, including lying on her back with sandbags as pillows. JJ carefully positioned her shoulders, arms, back, and hips, shoving a rolled-up sleeping pad under her diaphragm.

Standing between Ann and the crowd, JJ explained the alignment. "Note the straight line from the muzzle of the weapon to the firing side heel. Note, too, that it's not her *hip* that's aligned as with men, but her *leg.* The female hip is wider than the male's: thank God for evolution. *Theirs* won't quite…line…up…like…"

Ann rolled onto her side, scissoring her legs. He waited for the giggles to subside, making well-rehearsed puzzled faces. By the time he looked again, she was back more-or-less where she was supposed to be.

"Petty Officer Mueller," JJ announced theatrically, "you *moved.*"

"I'm not a crash dummy, Sarge."

"You're no dummy at *all*, Ann, but I'm not *supposed* to call you a doll."

"Thanks, JJ. Barbie's got *nothing* on me."

The class ended with a Q&A session. The first question was from Wendy. "What foundations would *you* recommend for this, Ann?"

"*No* bra of mine could be comfortable in the prone supported position. I haven't tried those new sports bras yet. Navy regulations say 'as needed' for foundations." She scanned the crowd for Emily Toliver, the senior female Navy NCO on base. "Chief Tolliver, can we make uniform exceptions 'as needed' for marksmanship training?"

Emily didn't hesitate. "For the limited purpose of rifle qualification and practice, exceptions *should* be made. I can't speak for the sister services."

"The Marine regs say, 'as needed *for decorum,*'" Corporal Amy Tanner added, "but such exceptions *should* be allowed, even if *un-decorous.*"

"*In*decorous, I think," JJ mused.

"As long as it means 'to keep from flopping,'" Wendy added. "*Our* regs read 'as needed,' too, but I wouldn't go braless in front of Top if I'm *not* on the range. His ideas of *decorum* are pretty 19th century."

"Specialists Anvers and Dustin *had* to qualify in Basic: ask *them*," JJ pointed.

Liz, a small woman, shook her head and declared, "none, Sarge."

Nancy, a *full-figured* gal, sighed, "*looser* the better; *front* closure's easier to handle. *You* should try one, Sarge." *That* got a chuckle.

"I suppose I deserve *that* for putting you on the spot," JJ admitted, "but good to know. Remember," he added in closing. "Firearms accuracy is a great deal about upper-body strength. The more…" Ann theatrically compared her biceps to his, making a face. "Well?"

She couldn't help but grin. "Eh, *you* need to pump more iron."

"Let's *not* talk about pumping, iron or anything else." *That* got a big, if *guarded*, laugh out of everyone.

Zeroing and qualification that afternoon was smooth as silk. Maria Emanuel, a large woman in the 4/75th personnel shop who did some weight lifting, scored Expert; the rest were all Sharpshooters. The handful of Navy women who participated theoretically qualified: Ann and Betty were top scorers. On the same day, JJ, the best Marine marksman and the very best SEAL had it out. The score: Army 299; Navy 270; Marines 259.

> *Mike*
> *I'm slippin' in my old age; missed <u>one bull</u> the other day;*
> *first time since junior high. I think I can get an eye exam here…*

Tuesday

"Cold but *not* cold this morning?" While JJ was hanging around the coffee urn with other early-bird NCOs waiting for the chow line to open, Laura came in wearing the UWAS outfit. The temperature was hovering in the low '70s, but in the tropical damp, it *felt* colder.

"Lifeguard duty today," she smiled. "You?" In the weeks since they met, *they* had seen each other more than JJ had seen Ann…just the nature of their service.

"Late night. Here's the headcount."

They got their breakfast and sat towards the back of the dining hall. "Got a question for ya, JJ," Laura asked. "I see GIs with name tapes over the back pockets of their pants. What's *that* about?"

"Has to do with how laundry's done in Korea. Got one for *you*: I see you guys with baseball caps, but I *expect* to see those *sailor* hats."

"*Way* too hard to keep those Dixie cups clean. I only wear mine with my service dress uniform, which means nearly never. Why?"

"Just curious." He paused. "On a different tack, do you find *me* to be…?"

"Intense?" She grinned and picked up a strip of bacon. "Ann says you're hard to distract." She inhaled deeply. "JJ: The Navy puts women in EOD ratings through a bunch of psychological tests—*lots* more than the guys. Three of us were put out of our class because of them." She inhaled deeply. "Because of *that, we* recognize deep shit like Ann's *thing* last month."

"Last month?" *HO-boy...!*

"Uh-huh." She shrugged. "Knowing *Ann*, Betty and I thought miscarriage, yeah? *She'll* work through it. But *you* act as if nothing happened to *you*. News flash, cutie: It happened to *both* of you. You *should* acknowledge it; mourn if *just* a little." She smiled genuinely. "Because you're Ann's *very special* friend, you're *our* buddy, too. If there's anything *we* can do, *you* let *us* know. Just *try* to *feel* for the child you *both* lost, OK?"

She—they—all on their own. "Just...keep it to yourselves, can ya?" *But they...we...she...? Ho-boy.*

Monday

JJ carefully read the Thanksgiving duty rosters—*and* the mess memo— on the bulletin board:

Appropriate attire <u>will be required</u> for holiday meals, <u>except</u> for those on duty.

"Appropriate attire" was defined by mess stewards (it *wasn't* unusual) as either dress uniform or civilian coat and tie, or equivalent for women. But, in the last half-hour—when the turkey roll was cold, the gravy glutinous, the mashed potatoes rock-hard, and everything else thoroughly picked over—those requirements would be *generously* lifted.

Gary groused, "*nuts!* CQ day after Thanksgiving."

"I'll take it," JJ offered. "Stay home with your family."

"OK, thanks. I'm to ask where *you're* gonna spend Thanksgiving."

"I dunno."

"Come by us."

"You sure The Boss won't mind?"

"Alice doesn't mind being the section wife. I'm also required by She-Who-Must-Be-Obeyed to invite Anvers and Devin. That'll be a new one for me: never *had* to socialize with subordinate women, but I never *had* subordinate women before."

Section wife: The wife in the outfit willing to provide a bit of home to those far from their own. "Only if you're sure."

"Sure, I'm sure. I'm also under orders to inquire about Ann: she and Alice hit it off God-*knows* where."

"Ah, well," Ann muttered when they met at noon chow. *When was the last time I had a meal from another woman's kitchen? If it's been that long, it's been too long.* "I'll think..."

"Go, Ann," Betty at the next table told her. "Real food with a family or toothpick chow and football with us at Dirty Mike's: you *know* I don't cook in that little back room I've got. Not a real hard choice. Trade your watch Thursday night with mine Saturday morning."

Thanksgiving Day

The drive from the base to Shark Key took maybe ten minutes, even dodging the Conch Republic's Thanksgiving Day Parade: a street party that occupied most of Flaegler Avenue. The Conch Republic was a quasi-serious thing that hawked t-shirts and hats with their logo from souvenir stands all over the Lower Keys. In 1982, some Lower Keys people who'd had too many margaritas decided that they were going to secede from the United States in protest over their isolation at the end of a long ribbon of vulnerable highway. They declared their independence *from*—and then war *on*—the US. Whereupon, the Conch Republic surrendered to the US, ratified the Constitution and applied for foreign aid—all on the same cocktail napkin, which was proudly displayed at Key West's City Hall. The whole imbroglio pointed out the serious nature of the Lower Key's vulnerability to physical isolation, but couldn't help but draw attention to the pernicious effects of excess sun and rum.

Shark Key sported a military family housing suburb of bleached-out row and single-family detached houses in orderly clusters along concrete-and-packed-coral streets. The development was dotted with parking pads, playgrounds, and community buildings. Navy-grey steel containers with firefighting equipment and salt-water pumps (absent fire plugs) were nestled between the palm trees scattered around the community.

"What can *we* do," Nancy blurted as soon as Gary let them in. "We're not going to just sit around and watch *you* work."

Alice was a slight, nervously bubbly woman with red hair. "If you *could*," handing the baby to Nancy, "give Gabby a bath. She *just* ate, so she'll be ready for bed." Soon both Nancy and Liz were on the job, cooing over the six-week-old.

Ann handed her wine over to Alice, grinning widely. "Now tell me what *I* can do."

"Help me make sense of my kitchen before I scream."

"Show me." The small kitchen had painted cabinets, hardwood counters crowded with food and cookware, and was stuffy-warm from cooking. "Let me start at the sink." Soon Ann was washing, consolidating, and stacking. "One of those side tables in the living room…might…help." Alice fetched a side table into the kitchen as Ann dimly heard Liz and Nancy with the baby.

"Gary, *get* with the *program*," Alice called. "Go get the card table and the appetizers. If *we* do all the work, *we'll* eat all the food."

The men went out to a row of gray storage containers. Gary hauled out a large card table and led JJ—burdened with an armful of stacked trays— back inside. "Put *that* stuff on *this*," Gary unfolded the table legs in the living room, with its gathering of mismatched furniture typical of family housing, "and I'll go back for the rest."

"I barely saw women in Army uniforms before jump school," JJ mused later. "Still not *that* many, but more all the time."

"Yeah. I was thinking the same thing. Never had a single female in any of my units before September. Pretty soon, *we* could be outnumbered in admin slots."

"It's not a bad thing, though," JJ replied. "I don't know that *complete* gender integration would weaken the force structure like *some* say it would, except..."

"Combat arms. That'll happen eventually." JJ heard Ann and Alice chuckle about something in the kitchen.

"Yeah? When?" Nancy was at JJ's elbow, drying her hands. "How is it that women are always expected...?"

"Because *men* are," Gary said. "There's blame enough to go around about 'women's work' and 'men's work.'"

"Before we go too much further," JJ interjected, "today, here, now: I'm JJ, he's Gary, you're Nancy, *etcetera*. As soon as we get back to work..."
"Sure."

"OK," Liz joined in, bouncing Gabby on her hip.

Ann listened as she stacked plates and chimed in from the kitchen. "But you're not in women's roles *now*, are you, Nancy? I'm certainly not."

"Not what I meant," Nancy said, cracking open a beer. "No offense, Alice, but you *expected* us to be able to care for children..."

"No, I didn't," Alice called back. "I answered your question with my most urgent need at *that* instant. I'm glad you knew what you were doing."

"Three little brothers." Nancy traded Liz the beer for the baby and walked the drowsy infant into the kitchen. "Sorry, but my *point*..."

"Not lost on any of us," Alice smiled, thumbing Gabby's cheek. "I'll take her, get me out of this kitchen. Thanks *so* much, ladies."

"Your point's not lost in the *least*," Ann agreed.

Nancy replied, "no, I *meant* social expectations are skewed." For several minutes they talked seriously about women in uniform in general and the nature of military service until Gary shrugged. "And there's another thing: some will join up just to prove a point—that women *can* fight with the grunts. Not a *sustaining* motivation to suffer *that* kind of misery. In time, *some* volunteers will suddenly say 'Enough! I'm a girl! I don't *have* to be here! Get me out!'"

"Or worse," Liz blurted, "'Enough! I'm pregnant!'"

JJ shot a look at Ann. *I was worried about how you'd react to the baby, but...*

She smiled: *I'm OK, buddy; you're here,* before she announced; "dinner's in about half an hour. Let's have some of this toothpick chow."

"I saw an article about you," Liz nudged Ann, who was a head and change taller than she. "*Navy Times.* My mom's in the Navy Reserves. I was inspired…"

"Really," Ann grinned. "You were so *inspired* by me in the *Navy* that you joined the *Army*?"

"Well, yeah, *that* was a different thing. I had a boyfriend who joined the Army…"

"And *that* didn't work out," JJ interjected. "What happened to him?"

"He dropped out after a month. I didn't find out until I got home after language school."

"You don't *know* guys…*really* know them…until they do something like, well, join the Army." Gary muttered. "As my *lovely* Alice knows all too well."

Alice shot a look at Gary and made a face. "What my *charming* husband is referring to is, well." She became theatrically, hands-on-hips annoyed after carrying food to the table. "Since *you* brought it up: *I* did a stint in the Navy. Medical equipment technician, 1968 to '72; Japan and San Diego. This *friend* of mine says he's joining the Navy just to be in Japan with me, only the Navy won't *have* him, so he joins the Marines. Well, off he goes to Parris Island and gets sent to Vietnam.

"Well, you think he'd at least *write*?" She shot a look at Liz and Nancy in between trips. "*Once?* No, *not* a *chance.* But I see a *wedding announcement* in the newspaper when I get back!" She feigned indignity while she spread out the serving spoons. "I was turning down *adorable* guys left and right for *four years* because I expected that *loser* to…Then *Gary* knocked on my door and, well.…"

"All worked out in the end," JJ grinned, admiring the gradually-growing spread. "You guys get married, and we get a great dinner, eventually."

Gary sighed, hunching his shoulders. "Not quite *that* simple. I had a malaria attack just after we met, and…"

"*I* didn't want a patient." Alice crossed her arms after placing the roll basket.

"But she got over *that.*"

"And he *got* better, and he *looked* better, and he reenlisted in '77, and I wanted to *brain* him."

"And we got married in '78, anyway."

"How romantic," Ann murmured, hooking an arm around Gary. "JJ and

I joined in '73." She bussed Gary on the cheek. "*I* might have snagged him."

Alice grinned, doing the same to JJ. "Yeah, well, next time he starts snoring like a chainsaw. I'll trade you."

During dinner, conversation shifted to childhoods (Liz's mother was of Mexican descent—she spent summers there; Nancy's mom was Puerto Rican—she spent her last three school years there); to hometowns (Alice and Gary were from Hartford, Connecticut); to the dwindling number of topless bars in Key West (Liz liked them because the guys usually ignored her, which surprised the other women but not the men); to school (Ann and JJ complained about finding time and energy for homework; Gary complained that he couldn't find an accounting program that he could do while on Active duty).

Liz managed to buttonhole Ann again. "What I wanted to say was I was inspired to do things that women hadn't done before. When they asked for volunteers for the 4/75th, I jumped on it."

"Glad I did someone some good. But being a pioneer also means getting all those arrows in your back, and your breasts taped down for their movies."

"But it's important, isn't it?" Nancy joined in. "I mean, we're setting an example."

"Oh, yes, indeed. My shipmates and I are under close watch most of the time. Mostly, they tell us, because diving for a living is very hard on the body. But, too, our conduct…"

"Yeah, conduct." Liz mumbled. "You and the Sarge have been spending *some* time together."

"Not what it *looks* like," Ann replied quietly. "We're buddies *and* friends; *not* more." *Yet.* "I can only *hope you* can *ever* get *lucky* enough to trust someone like *he* and *I* trust each other."

"Do you know if there's a plan to get them to jump school?" Gary opened another beer.

"Anvers and Devin? Top says they're waiting for slots."

"What 'slots?'" Liz asked.

"Jump school," Gary answered.

"Top said 'next year' two weeks ago," Nancy added, "how often does 'next year' happen?"

"Every *year*, dear," Ann replied. "Every year."

The dishes were cleared and the kitchen cleaned up; a version of Stella's Game was played that added a deal of two sets of three and a run of five before the last deal of a run of seven and set of four; Gary talked about his Italian father and Russian mother who insisted he learn and use *both* languages; the aperitifs drunk and the guests bundled off into the night.

As the Fury pulled up to the women's billets, there was a whispered discussion in the back seat, where all three women had piled in. There was some giggling followed by two hands holding his head. "We drew lots, *Sergeant Blue-Eyes*," Ann whispered in his ear, "over who would do *this first*." There followed by *three* soft and *sweet* kisses in succession—each a *little* different—on the back of his head as they piled out.

I'm gonna be in so…much…trouble. Aw, hell: don't care; nobody saw it so it don't matter.

***

"So, Sandy: you're for Korea, you think?" They were eating at a restaurant buffet outside the Ft. Stewart main gate, Mike having flown there from Arizona for the holiday.

"I believe so, come spring," he sighed, holding her hand on the table. "An asset of mine might be there. You?"

"I'm overdue for overseas orders, but I'm *not* sure about Korea again." She squeezed his hand. "It's the life we chose."

"Yup. Want to call home tonight." He frowned slightly before he brightened. "I worry about JJ being separated from Ann."

"I think he's a *lot* tougher than that, Sandy." She shook her hair back. "Now that they *know;* now they have someone to *write* to, they'll be fine."

"Ann knew my nickname; she *likes* my eyes."

"I *love* your eyes…and the *rest* of you. She's a good friend."

"Love you, too." He sighed heavily. "Still feel like you're being watched?"

"Sometimes; not now." She gazed out the window. "Feel like I ate too much and I need a nap."

"Let's call home before you do *that*." In their room, they chatted with their parents at the annual Dietz Thanksgiving feast, a catered affair with hundreds of guests. At length, they managed a few minutes with Donna. "Hey Blondie: no annual family gathering at your uncle's this year?"

"Uncle Albert's under the weather. How about you guys? How *you* doing?"

"Good," Mike answered. "Saw JJ Elrath a few weeks ago; says 'hi.'"

"Leigh's Blue-Eyes? *Oh*, that *guy*; I could eat him *up*."

"Well, you'd have to fight Ann Mueller for him," Leigh interjected. "They connected in Florida. Childhood sweethearts. Wild, huh?"

"Ya know: that *doesn't* surprise me. Both of 'em seemed to me to be looking for *someone* in school." She paused. "When are you guys coming home again?"

"I'm *planning* on Christmas," Leigh answered.

164

"*I'm* not sure," Mike said. "Our training cycle ends on 18 December, but *I* have to prepare for the *next* cycle that starts in mid-January: I'm the junior guy in the school so *I* get to do most of the scutwork. I'll see what I can wrangle."

"OK," Donna answered. "Let me know. One more thing: Have *you* got *addresses* for JJ and Ann?"

December

Friday

> *Dearest Cutie-Pie;*
> *I got your address from Mike Dietz; hope you don't mind me writing…*

He read Donna's letter with curiosity, wondering what was going on in *her* life that she suddenly felt compelled to write *him*.

> *I'm writing because <u>you</u> have a target on your back from a long time ago, but don't sweat it much. Joe Dryden's vindictive and he's crafty, but he's not brave. Anything he does to you he'll hire done, and he's not that good at it. This I know because of Sid Jackwell…*

I was in 5th Grade with Sid Jackwell. Still don't know this Dryden.

> *My dad's a binge drunk I've been caring for since 5th Grade, but <u>you</u> endured Wolverine. I know people who <u>know</u> <u>people</u>, my dear; us survivors have to stick together. Something haunts <u>you</u>; I saw it that Passover.*

He first met Donna while he was staying at the Dietz's over spring break in '72. It was during that stay that Mike's grandfather, a wise and kindly gentleman, spoke *so* gently to persuade JJ to talk about Wolverine—and JJ started to be able to *live* with it by *sharing* it.

***

> *Hey, Ann!*
> *Leigh Taylor gave me your address… You like the Navy, I take it. I <u>thought</u> about the Air Force—yeah, I did—briefly…*
> *I understand you've been sweet on JJ Elrath for a long time. His blue eyes are unforgettable…*

She was mystified by Donna's letter, unclear as to why a schoolmate she barely knew would want to write after a dozen years, then…

Your friend Sid Jackwell left Joe Dryden's bunch years ago. I see him around town; chat sometimes. He'll try to get in touch with you sooner than later; he's got stuff to say.

Sid had been in Randy's "crew" in school. She'd known Sid almost as long she had JJ; they did their Catechism, Confirmation and First Communion together. *And*, there was…

I want to ask, woman-to-woman, about turning a guy you've known <u>platonically</u> into <u>more</u>. A guy I've known since junior high is always there when I need him. If <u>we</u> were to <u>go for it</u>, how bad <u>could</u> it get if it <u>doesn't</u> work? He seems interested, and I just got dumped again (Thanksgiving weekend, in fact). At 31 I don't want to end up alone…

How am I supposed to…?

Saturday

He couldn't *not* reply to *anyone's* letter, but he had to read Donna's over several times before he could think of a *way* to answer:

Donna,
Surprised to hear from you; write all you want, whatever you want…
Yeah, Wolverine. As easy to forget as a busted kneecap. Didn't know about your dad; I know a little about drunks myself—lived with one for a few years. Funny that you should know that it haunts me still, but I'm curious as to what else <u>you</u> might know about it…Say what you want back…

***

She felt enough kinship/sisterhood to answer Donna as best *she* knew how:

Hey Donna!
Surprised to hear from you…thanks for the info on Sid. I haven't heard from him since I enlisted. You thought about the Air Force? Really? My brother's an Air Force officer now…
As for your doormat(?), going from a friend <u>to</u> a lover is TOO easy; going <u>back</u> is TOO HARD and doesn't always work. My advice is to be clear and upfront about what you want <u>from</u> each other before you cross that bridge, because the platonic part burns as soon as you're across…

Curiously, she put her answer in an envelope and slid it back into her portfolio.

Yeah, kid: pay attention.

Friday

"Hi, JJ!" Kristin, on the other side of the shoe store, held a shoebox to her chest and waved. "Day off?"

"Hi. Worked last night. You?" He'd pulled staff duty with a newly-minted captain in Operations who made good coffee, was a history major in college (so they had *something* to talk about), and played gin like he knew what he was doing. The store clerk—a young native of the Keys with old-leather creases starting around her eyes—held out his change. He smiled, returned her "have a nice day," and turned to go.

"Me too." Kristin called after him. "Coffee?"

"Sure." The end-of-year holiday period *felt* transitional for JJ. He was at Fort Benning in '73 for Thanksgiving, and after jump school, he had three weeks' leave around Christmas before he had to report to Fort Stewart. He debated *not* taking that leave: Benning and Stewart are about 200 miles apart, and he wasn't sure he wanted to have to deal with Charlie. But he wanted his truck at Fort Stewart, so he flew home two days before Christmas and saw his mother for the holiday for the first time since 9th Grade. It was also the *last* time he'd been in Detroit for Christmas.

The Lower Keys was entering its annual cold period when the night temperature dipped as low as 68. Those who lived there weren't used to it being below 75, so it *felt* colder. The high humidity made the air feel clammy as the daytime temperature stubbornly held at around 80.

They met under the store awning out of the tepid winter sun, she in a long-sleeve sweater and shorts; he in jeans and t-shirt and jean jacket. "I think Ann's, I dunno, tired," she began. "Let's go over to the café." Sitting in a faux French wrought-metal chair, she sighed. "She's been talking about taking a liberty."

He sat across the faux French wrought-metal table. "We call it leave."

"Same thing. She might *not* come back to dive status."

"She can *do* that?"

"Yeah. You can go off jump status if you want, can't you?"

"Yeah. What's so bad about taking some time off? If she's got the *time*…?"

"But she's up for chief next year," she shot back, "and for master diver consideration. If she takes what she *wants* to take she'll lose *all* of it."

"What does she *want* to take?"

"She *said* she could take as much as six months. She *said* she might want to go home." She looked at him slyly. "*You* could go *with* her, keep an eye on her?" Smiling coquettishly, she purred "I'll *buy lunch*," stretching her arms and flexing her belly…and other parts, "or we *can*…?"

"Are you *seducing* or *bribing*?" *Never knew a girl could DO <u>that</u>.*

"Would you *mind* either one?" She winked slowly, puckered teasingly. *Girl, I…ugh…* "Just…checking."

Saturday

"Want to see *The Breakfast Club* this afternoon?" Ann knew comedies weren't JJ's thing, but it had *finally* gotten to a theater near *her.*

He shrugged. "Did you *answer* Donna?"

"Not yet." She paused, puzzled, waiting. "So; movie?"

"Want to do Christmas in Detroit? I haven't seen Ma since '79."

She narrowed her eyes. "OK: *you* have new shoes; *Kristin* has new shoes; so, you ran into each other at a shoe store? Then, *lunch;* then she *offered* more? That *vixen!* One shake of *that* tail-and-everything-else and *you guys*…" *Bless you, Kristin, and your way with men.*

"Don't blame *her*. We're *both* worried about you. You're worn out."

"What do you *mean* 'worn out?' I can knock you on your keister any time, buster."

"Yeah, I know. Ranger school told me I was a lousy hand-to-hand fighter. Fortunately, *that* wasn't a requirement." He picked up a strip of bacon as she contemplated her breakfast eggs. "Well?"

"Let's eat up and go to the movie."

***

"Affecting," Ann smiled and sighed, Simple Minds' theme song played in her head as they left the theater. *For sixteen years: Don't you forget about me.* "I *have* to tell Dad," she added with a slight quiver, "and I've been *dreading* it because…" She crossed her arms against a chill breeze.

"His little girl grew up?"

"*No,*" she snapped. Softer, "no: Because he'll want to know about the father, and I don't want to *look* like the idiot I *really was*. When *could* you go?"

"Well, Christmas is a Wednesday. Two or three days to drive. Battalion SOP says five…"

"*Drive*?" She looked surprised. "A *thousand miles?* Eh, I *have* been thinking about flying up and bringing the Rambler down here."

"Rambler? Your dad's old car?"

"Yup, the gas-guzzling Rebel beast. Dad gave it to me, but George has it at his place. It stopped running in September, so I'd have to get it fixed. I want to either sell it or drive *that* old *tank* down…what?"

He giggled. "You want to fly Air Sometimes?" Air Sunshine, the only scheduled airline serving the Lower Keys, was called Air Sometimes because the DC-3s they flew were *thought* to be dangerous. JJ knew better: those old birds were some of the safest in the world, and Air Sunshine rarely missed a scheduled flight, but it was *not* known for its amenities.

"Mm. *Three days* drive, you say? When?" *LOTS of together time.*

"My unit wants five business days' notice, so *next* Friday night at earliest. I'll call Ma tomorrow, see if I can stay there. I'll *pay* Charlie's room and board for a *few* days anyway."

"Room and board?"

"Yeah. Brenda and I had to *pay* to stay at the house: Charlie's pretty mercenary. I just think he *really* doesn't want us around. But I won't stay *there* more than a few days."

WOW. "I *think* Jenna's with her father over Christmas, but I'll call and find out. Where would *you* go after...?"

"I'll find a place. How long would you go *for*? Kristin said you can take six *months*."

"She needs to listen better," she grinned. "I can take *as much as three* months combined medical and personal leave."

"So...?"

"*Four* weeks. I'm off dive status until at *least* January. How much can *you* take?"

"*I* can take four weeks. If you *want*, I can ask Kurt to look at the Rambler."

"Your stepbrother Kurt? Yeah, sure."

"My brother Will winters in Pompano. We *might* be able to stay *there* Friday night."

"*Another* stepbrother?" He nodded. "OK. How much do you think it will cost to get there and back? Would a grand cover my end?"

"Well...Let's divide this up. How about *I* cover lodging and incidentals, and *you* cover food and gas? A grand should be plenty." They locked eyes. "Are *we* ready for *this*?"

I could never resist those eyes. "I *think we* are. But let's get this straight *right* here, *right* now, John Jacob. Tideline; *separate* beds if practical; and at least *something* modest to sleep in regardless. I'll wear my long shirt."

"*Shorts* for me: night sweats. And *tideline*, Claudia Ann."

Until we're BOTH sure.

Sunday

It wasn't a call week, but... "Hi, Ma...yeah, I know. Listen: Ann and I are gonna drive up to Detroit for the holidays...yeah...we *should* be in town 22 December...Sunday before Christmas, yeah. Can I stay *there* for a while? I... OK, Thanks, Ma. ...yeah. See you *then*, Ma...love you too..."

This was followed by... "Hey, Will: JJ. Mind if I stop by with a friend next Friday? …On our way to Detroit…Leave here about 4:30, so no later than 11 at night…OK, see you then."

That's all it took.

***

She was *somewhat* more verbal.

> *Leigh,*
> *Going home for the holidays with Johnny. Might be an interesting development. We'll be up there by the 22rd, let you know how we shake out…*

And…

> *Dear Dad,*
> *…We should be at Birch Lake Sunday afternoon; he's closer and on the way to Southfield…*

Wednesday

Suddenly, I can't think of anything but getting the hell out of Dodge.

"Sergeant Elrath: you're wanted in the colonel's office." He had been cleaning up the message logbooks when he was summoned. *Now what?*

He knocked on the door—he knew the big boss was on leave—to see… "Ram! How the *hell* are ya?"

Major Ramdas Brahmaputra-Reynolds shook JJ's hand. "My bosses are so impressed with your work down here I thought I might look you up." Ram's curly hair was shorn close to his scalp, and although he was shorter than JJ, he looked tall in tailored BDUs and fashionably thick-soled jump boots.

"So, you went OCS?" They were accustomed to *some* familiarity between officers and NCOs. (JJ encountered one of his sister's old boyfriends who had graduated from West Point: JJ addressed him by his first name when *they* met…while saluting.)

"Yeah. They tapped me for it when I finished flash school. How about you? *You* could do better than E-6."

"Don't want to have to pay for everything." JJ decided early that his role in the Army would be in the NCO corps. *But Special Forces majors don't make pleasure junkets.* "What *really* brings you down here?"

Ram checked his watch. "I hear the Officer's Club here serves a decent lunch. Let's have at it."

"Give me ten minutes." He finished with the logs, grabbed his beret and they headed out. Ann, coming up the walk as they left, saluted Ram as courtesy required.

"Petty Officer Mueller, Major Reynolds. Ann; Ram." JJ winked at

Ann. "We were at Brookfield together, Ann."

"Pleasure, sir."

Ram stopped and stared. "Mueller. Diver. I've *heard* of you. We were just headed to chow, but I don't think the Club allows dungarees."

"I can pass, sir. I'll catch JJ later."

"Consolidated dining facility it *is*," Ram declared breezily. Officers at grade O-4 and above did not partake of the cuisine at the consolidated dining facility very often. The sea didn't part, but there were suddenly dining room orderlies that weren't there before; the mess steward offered table service for Ram and his guests, politely declined.

"So, Ram: I was born in the morning, but not *this* morning. What *really* brings you to the Rock? And, by the way, where have they put you?"

"Defense Intelligence Agency."

"*Really?*" Ram was intellectually head-and-shoulders above everyone JJ knew. It surprised him that Ram joined the Army at all.

"Don't get to break bread with the Pentagon very often," Ann muttered.

"Me neither: I'm at Anacostia. I came to offer JJ a job."

"DIA wants an E-6?"

"No, an E-7. Or a GS-7, or even a WO-1. Your book made quite the sensation."

"Huh. How's your mom? Ann and I are going up on leave next week. I could look in…"

"Mom's fine; I'll see her when I go to the reunion in the spring." Ram shrugged. "Next year, you get another rocker or put in for a warrant, we'll talk again." He glanced at Ann. "Out of special operations, out of the field. Three-year gig with a promotion track. Think about it. How else you been?"

"Fair to middlin.' You? I run into Mike Dietz once in a while…"

When JJ got back to his barracks that evening, Ann was waiting for him. "Ram has a mind like a steel trap. That he'd heard of you didn't surprise me."

"Well, I *was* the first woman naval diver in the world."

"Yeah. That job would get me out of the field." *But away from you.*

"Yeah." *And away from me.*

Friday

"Delay's going to cost us," JJ mumbled. Emergency work on the Key's US 1 lifeline had started the day before they started up the Keys, but—from *his* perspective—was *lousy* timing. The traffic backup they ran into started at Marathon barely an hour north of Key West.

"Easy, tiger. Don't get ahead of yourself," Ann soothed. At one level, the Conch Republic's "declaration of *de*pendence" in their plea for "foreign" aid made sense. The four-lane US 1 is the only roadway linking the Keys to each other and the mainland, crossing more salt water than any other single road in the Continental US. The roadway is also the sole conduit for the Keys' access to power, natural gas, fresh water and phone lines—and *they* sometimes fail…hence the delay.

"Late night means a late start."

"Says *who*?"

"Well, *that* or we lose some sleep."

"Maybe, maybe not. Let's see." The traffic jam eased gradually and was entirely gone by the time they reached Tavernier. They stopped at a fried chicken shop (among a forest of seafood joints) on Key Largo for a quick bite.

"I *still* say we're an hour behind schedule."

"If you say 'schedule' again in the next four weeks I'll smack you upside the head. We're on *vacation*, babe; we *don't* have to rendezvous with the fleet twenty leagues northwest-by-southeast of Cape Whatchamacallit at zero-dark-thirty on D-plus-or-minus-one. Concentrate on getting home in one piece."

"What, ah, *destination* is…*that*?"

"Boot camp chiefs make up stuff like that: part nautical, part nonsense. Boots have to figure out which is which by studying their Bluejackets' Manuals; Cape Whatchamacallit was pretty common."

"Huh. They still teach the 32-point compass?"

"*Very* impressive that a landsman would know *that*, babe. No: they *officially* dropped that *and* the 128-point when Nimitz was a midshipman…but the boatswains still *teach* it."

"*I* only know about *them* from sea stories."

"Eh; I'll make a marlinspike sailor out of you yet."

The I-95 link to US 1 outside Homestead had just been completed, allowing them to reach Pompano faster than he remembered. Pompano, like most towns in southeast Florida, caters to that vast class of snowbirds—the long-stay tourists who head south at the first frost and stay until the trees start to bud back wherever "home" is. Like half a hundred other burgs on the Gold Coast (named for the jingle in the property owner's pockets), it consisted of older, sprawling stucco-and-tile structures with rounded edges crowded by newer steel-and-glass, square-edge towers stealing their older neighbor's sunshine.

The Parkinson's condo was a newer-looking four-story steel-and-block structure with ten single-level units, each with an outside entrance and covered parking. JJ knocked on Will and Anita's third-floor door just after 10:30.

"*Will*," JJ grinned, "*good* to see you sober."

"On *occasion*, JJ," Will—known as the "Sober Parkinson" who barely drank at all—smiled. He was tall and spare, bordering on thin, sporting a thin brown-touched-with-grey mustache easily mistaken for a shaving oversight. "And *this* is…"

"Ann Mueller," Ann smiled, offering her hand. "Sharing a ride."

"*Oh*," a pleasant and urbane brownette as tall as Ann, with a prominent chin and cheekbones answered. "Wasn't *expecting*…"

"JJ, *you've* never met Anita," Will interrupted. "Honey, *this* is my baby brother."

"Hi: never *heard* of *you* before you married Will," JJ sighed, extending a hand.

"Heard a lot about *you*," Anita answered, scanning back and forth between JJ and Ann. "The famous author-brother-war-hero."

"Don't believe everything you hear," JJ mumbled as Will herded them into the living/dining room. A small, round Victorian table and chairs, and a big silk brocade sofa with matching wing chairs in front of a mirrored wall filled most of the space.

They exchanged how's-the-trip pleasantries before JJ murmured "don't want to take *too* much advantage, but we want to try to make Chattanooga tomorrow. We can talk more in the morning. Can *we* just…?"

"Sure," Anita pointed, staring at Ann. "Right through there. Let us know if…"

In the spare bedroom was a lone standard bed.

"*This'll* do fine," Ann answered with a smile. "Tight fit," she mused when the door closed. "Bathroom."

"OK." JJ stripped to his briefs and laid down on the bed. *God, I'm beat.*

There was just enough light through the curtains for Ann not to trip over anything coming to bed. She slid in, pecked him softly on the ear, and quickly drifted off.

He awoke, aware that something had touched his ear, felt her pull the covers and drifted off again.

Saturday

He woke in the morning twilight to see her pulling shoes on at the foot of the bed. "Hi, Cloud."

"Hi, Johnny. Sleep well?"

"Woke up a couple times."

"Me too. Not used to such a little bed with someone else."

"Yeah. You been up long?"

"Long enough to get a shower. I *think* someone's out there."

"Tonight, I'll stay awake long enough to say goodnight."

She smiled broadly. "I'll count on it. Gives a girl the wrong idea when a guy falls asleep *before* she joins him."

Anita—sitting at the table, coffee in one hand and Danish in the other—smiled warmly. "Coffee? Danish?"

"Coffee, sure. Straight black, thanks." Ann sat opposite at the table, taking the proffered mug. "Danish? Sure."

"I'm sorry about last night," Anita offered as Ann bit into her pastry. "Will said he was bringing a *friend*, but they say he never brought a *girl* home. Then I couldn't tell if, well, if *you* were…"

"It was fine. I didn't mean to just drop in on you." *He never brought a girl home?*

"Oh, I'm glad to finally meet the brother that everyone talks about."

"Yeah, I guess." Ann took another bite, looking around the airy room. They chatted about south Florida weather and the price of gas until Ann asked: "Have you got a copy of his book? Mine hasn't come yet."

Anita reached behind her and pulled a small volume off a shelf. "Kurt bought copies for everyone."

Will came in. "You two plotting…oh, you found his book: thought *you'd* know all about it. I'm in that bed now and then, when I snore too loud."

"I *know* about it, but I've never seen it." Ann marveled at the tightly bound volume. *Probably unread.* Then she saw the dedication: *For Claudia, wherever you are.* She shed a tear. "Sorry: I didn't…"

"Yeah, Cloud," JJ said from the doorway. "I meant to tell you about that *before* you saw it."

"It's OK, Johnny. I'm honored." Ann explained: "We knew each other in grade school. I haven't used *Claudia* for years, but *he* didn't know that. We ran into each other in Key West for the first time since 8th Grade."

"How *romantic*," Anita smiled. "Long lost love?"

"Too young then; too busy with careers now. He's Army, I'm Navy. We're buddies."

"*Oh!*" Anita tensely met Ann's eyes: Ann nodded; Anita relaxed.

They shared pastries and coffee and conversation. Anita was in nursing school when Will came into her hospital. Ann shared how she made the transition from storekeeper to hull technician to diver at the breakneck pace of 29 months. JJ talked about his first glimpse of the Army in the 100-degree summer heat of Texas.

"We'd best be going," JJ declared, standing up. "Thanks again for…"

"Hang on, we have something *for* you guys," Will announced, going into the front door closet. "*We* won't need these, but you sure as *hell* will," as he held out two heavy winter parkas. While it was in the high 60s in Pompano that morning—typical for late December—everyone knew it was *much* colder a day's drive north.

Anita brought sweaters and a dress out of the bedroom. "For *both* of you...*and*..." she held the dress up to Ann. "It's a *sack* on me. Keep it."

"Well, I..." The dress—basic blue/black round neck sleeveless—was a *little* high-waisted for her, but she was used to settling on clothes that *almost* fit. "It's hard for me to find clothes."

"I *believe* it: size sixteen tall just *ain't* common." Anita handed her a business card that read: *Milady's Closet, Anita Rowe-Parkinson, Proprietress.* "We specialize in hard-to-fit ladies. Ask for Hillary; she and I started the place when we realized we couldn't *stay* ahead in nursing."

Will handed JJ a bundle of sweaters and long-sleeve shirts. "Just bring 'em back. Four weeks? Fine; *we'll* be here."

Anita shoved bags of sandwiches into their hands. "*Keep* the dress, Ann, really. It never fit me right anyway."

***

"I want to make Atlanta at least tonight, maybe Chattanooga," JJ declared an hour later, when they were finally headed north on I-95. Even though Saturday traffic wasn't heavy, the out-of-state plates jammed the roads with their ignorance of road courtesy. "So," he muttered, "first night. Thoughts?"

"We slept, yes?"

"I didn't bite, and neither did you. Is *this* going to work, then?"

"*I'm* not going to overthink it, babe; *you* shouldn't either."

They were quiet, tuning the radio to ever-fading stations one by one until she gave up. She fingered through the first cassette tape box she could reach in the back seat and chose "Lake Shore Drive." The lyrics to the lead song, so familiar, so syncopated, let her think of nothing but her liberty: who she wanted to see, what she wanted to do...

There ain't no finer place to be,
Than running on Lake Shore Drive.
And there's no peace of mind or place you see
Than riding on Lake Shore Drive.

She remembered the song from high school, briefly popular around the Great Lakes. Like "Louie-Louie" and "Whiter Shade of Pale," the *true meaning* of the lyrics that included "Just slippin' on by on LSD/Friday night, trouble bound," was a matter of intense debate among knowledgeable and worldly teenagers, and was almost as important as knowing enough about *Lord of the Rings* to hold an intelligent discussion on the *real* reasons for Frodo's retirement with Gandalf.

Central Florida, where hills sometimes are taller than bridges, was a welcome green contrast to the dusty and flat Keys. In some places real soil could be seen, not just sand, gravel, clay and coral dust.

"So, what do you see for yourself in the next ten years?" he asked. "Finish school, chief petty officer, and master diver. Then what?" *Do we have a future, Cloud?*

You and I need the REAL answer, don't we, Johnny? "Frankly, I'm not sure. Yes, promotion; yes, finish school; yes, even master diver, but *that* may have to wait. Diving is a lot harder on the body than almost anything else. My back hurts most of the time; my hips…*ugh!*

"Less than ten percent of Navy divers retire on dive status. Most of 'em are done after ten years; only a few last more than fifteen. We stay in the community, but our work-diving days are usually over in a decade. I've been at it full-time for seven." She felt a chill, pulling her old green field jacket closer to her. "Cold all the time; wrestling the equipment is hard work. Even in Florida, the water's not as warm as it looks. And there's the bends…"

"Bends?"

"Yeah. Pain *deep* in the body. No matter *how* careful we are, we can't avoid them completely."

"So, you may not, what, do twenty?"

"Probably *not* on dive status, but I plan to go the distance." *I actually said that out loud? Been thinking about it for—what—a year?* "No, and Kristin's right: I may *not* go back to dive status for long. I might for a *while*, but…no; master diver's out for *next* year." *Decision made.* "As much as *Kristin* wants to see *me* make it, I don't think it'll happen. She's going to C-school in January…about time, too; at least she'll only be *one* grade under Tom by April. What about you? What's *your* ten-year plan?" *Does it include me?*

"E-7, I hope, next year, if I can pass a PT test. Finish school next year. I *may* take Ram up on his job offer if I get promoted, but I'm overdue for an *overseas* tour. And there's my next book." *And you. How?*

"On what, again?"

"Japan in World War Two. See, my idea…" They drove north on I-95 before cutting west on I-10 to heading north on I-75 at Lake City, finding talk radio programs of interest, talking about books and listening to tapes in between. Their mutual favorites were Springsteen and Billy Joel, Dylan and the Who. They debated whose version of "Blinded by the Light" was better—The Boss's original or Manfred Mann's cover, though Mann's "Spirits in the Night" was *absolutely* superior. They agreed that Cher was overrated and over-played; that the Beatles were OK but over-sentimentalized; it was too bad about the Moody Blues, Jim Croce, and Harry Chapin.

The landscape changed as the hills grew bigger and the forests included scrub oaks and the occasional ash or poplar with the tall pines. The soil was more fertile, the road had more curves, and the roadway bumpier as the air grew chilly and dry. And everything—from trees to fences to telephone and power poles—was *covered* with kudzu.

At the back counter of a Valdosta truck stop, they ate some of Anita's sandwiches with the rest of the brown-baggers and washed them down with *really* decent coffee. Ann had a ham-and-cheese on rye; JJ picked a roast beef with horseradish on whole wheat. Though he usually ate quickly (that she *frowningly* drew his attention to more than once), he deliberately paced her. Eating as a social device confused him. Though he knew that eating with others *could* be pleasant, at Wolverine predators often stole food—especially desserts—or spilled it for amusement. That and the premature death of his taste buds because of his mother's execrable culinary skills made food more chore than joy. *I eat to live; I don't live to eat.*

"How are we doing on time?" She watched a truck pull away from a gas pump as they got ready to go. "And *gas?*"

"Time's OK, I think; we *need* gas. What worries *me* is *that.*" He pointed at a wall-mounted TV showing a weather report. A big snowstorm was building in south-central Canada, moving down and across the Great Lakes and the Midwestern plains. "Could *cost* us a day or so. Shouldn't be a problem until tomorrow."

"How far do you think we can get today?" She pulled her field jacket tighter around her as they walked to the car. *Damn, I should've brought my liner.*

"Chattanooga, probably."

"*I* can drive," she announced as he gassed up the car.

He tossed her the keys. "She tends to stall cold, so go easy on the gas for the first few minutes. The cruise-control should be self-explanatory, and remember: the double-nickel is *still* the law, though no one gets a ticket for 60. And, at *60* it's easier to calculate time-and-distance."

They were on the road again soon, wispy clouds scudding quickly away towards the southeast. When he could, he did his calculations. *184 miles at 60 comes to three hours and change to Atlanta—another two or three to Chattanooga. Maybe 7 or 8 tonight.* They were quiet for an hour before JJ cleared his throat. "So, you're sleeping in Jenna's room while she's with her father?"

"It's *our* room, but yeah. I *might* get to see the kids; I haven't since '78. Why?"

"I kinda like waking up with you."

Wondered when we were going to get to that. "Me too."

"Thought I'd mention it."

Glad you did. She felt a chill. "I need heavier pants. Maybe a truck stop."

"I'm a 36 waist. I've got a pair that should fit you."

Now we're sharing clothes? "Yeah, OK."

He sighed. "Do you want to get married," *OOPS!* "*That* came out wrong. Maybe? Someday, to somebody? I didn't…"

Yes, you did. "Ask me again later." *You're the first to actually ask: I need to savor it.*

"Sorry." *MORON!*

"It's OK, babe," she patted him on the leg. "I *know* what you *meant*. Anita said you never brought a girl home. Never?"

His back ached; his neck was stiff; he stretched out as much as he could and sat up again. "They knew about Julia and Leigh; couldn't *hide* them. I never *mentioned* Jenny or Clare 'cause I was never *quite* sure about *Charlie's* reaction, or *Ma's,* for that matter. I've never *had* a normal relationship with a girl, so I don't know what it might feel like."

"'Normal' being…?"

"Everything *we* have plus what we don't."

"I did with Cable, but we never co-habited for more than a few days."

"But you've had sex with the same guy more than say twice, yeah?"

"Yeah. What's *that* got to do with anything?"

"You got used to him and he to you?"

"I see what you mean. You got *used* to Jenny and Clare, didn't you?"

"Jenny: only *almost* happened once. Clare only because she needed *something* and I took advantage of her."

"You took advantage of *each other* the way you described it; *trust* me, babe."

"I suppose." He looked for Atlanta radio stations before he caught a snippet of Aerosmith and settled there, shifting in the seat. "Tom said he heard from that guy again: the one with the apartments. He'll decide soon. How about you?"

"*Not* yet. Betty's getting claustrophobic her little cube in that back room. Wendy and I talked about it, too."

"Wendy *Corey*? You tight with her?"

"We could tolerate each other as roomies. But, as of last week I think she has *other* plans: she met a *guy*."

"That happens." As they kept moving north the hills got even bigger, the roadway rougher, the traffic somewhat denser and he decided… "Just for background, *you* should know. The week before I went to Wolverine, I put a big model ship in the lake: Dad had given me the kit for my 13th birthday; took me *two years* to build. I was sailing her around remote-control and Charlie took pictures; I figured I *finally* did *something* he approved of. That same afternoon he gets a few belts in him and he tells me I *must* find a place for her, and for everything else I was building in the basement. Well, Labor Day Saturday I have her in the drink one last time before I was to take her to the model shop and he gets plastered and zooms out on the lake in the power boat; sinks her. He called her a 'Goddam bullshit waste of time' when he got back." He sighed. "Good Charlie is sober and reasonably pleasant: Bad Charlie is a mean drunk. That's why I avoid staying *there*. And Ma…I wish I knew *her* better, or *liked* her more."

Jesus! "What are you planning for your liberty, Johnny?" *It ain't hangin' with the folks; that's for damn sure.*

"For as long as I can remember, there haven't been more than a few moments that weren't carefully thought out, evaluated and studied." His voice was barely more than a whisper. "It became a survival skill for me on Birch Lake…and Wolverine."

"Sounds exhausting. I know you read a *lot*." *Obsessively, almost.*

"You…have…*no*…Goddamn…idea, Cloud. I'm going to try to *decrease* that for a while." He sighed again. "Since I no longer need to look for you everywhere, that *might* be easier. I…"

"Everywhere?"

"Nearly; every time I thought of you. I…"

"Should I be creeped out?"

"No: as time went on…no, wasn't like *that*. But *you* looked for *me*, too, you said."

"True."

"I'll get a room before New Year's." He squeezed her hand. "Join me?"

"Maybe." *Almost certainly…*

"I also want to look in on Leigh's and Mike's folks while I'm up there."

"Me, too. I never *met* Leigh's father. Do you *know* Mike's family?"

"I *stayed* with them for a while. Lovely people, magnificent home."

It was nearly 4 in the afternoon when she saw a sign for a truck stop just short of Atlanta. "I'm pulling over. I need coffee."

"Me too. Need to *seriously* stretch."

The Fury rolled to a stop far from the truck stop, out with the travel trailers and the employees' cars. As he got out and stretched in the chilly air, she stiff-legged through a mud puddle. "Gas?"

"Let's get coffee and walk around, *then* get gas."

***

It was 8 that night when they saw the sign for the Holiday Inn just north of Chattanooga, where the dark hills of Georgia gave way to the even darker mountains of Tennessee. They had been comparing Harry Nilsson's pleasant-but-dark-themed music to Warren Zevon's rough-edged but often thematically bright melodies. Since Atlanta they had speculated as to where John Stuart's "Bombs Away Dream Babies" title came from, and about the war raging between Iran and Iraq after listening to a radio talk show about it.

A steakhouse across the parking lot was more appealing than the hotel restaurant. They ordered beers while they perused the menu. "So, can we make Detroit tomorrow?" She rolled her ankles stiffly under the table.

"As long as the weather holds; but by the radio, it won't. *If* we make Cincinnati before noon and have *half*-decent weather, we *could* make Detroit before *too* late." He stretched his back stiffly.

They ordered a couple of T-bones and another couple of beers. "Wakeup call for 0600?" She poked at the overcooked beans on her plate.

"Not even. On leave, I don't do first call for anybody but airlines." He munched on a last fry. "Let's get."

In their double-queen plain-vanilla room, they watched the local weather before they switched to a "Hill Street Blues" rerun and got ready for bed while he looked in the cable directory. "Let's watch a movie; *Footloose*, if you're interested."

"Sure. Thought you didn't like comedies."

"Well, I have a confession to make."

"Another one?"

"Another kind. I'm a sucker for teen angst."

"Buddy, you're *THE poster child* for teen angst."

As the dancers raised dust in the old feed mill, he glanced at the clock. 10:30. "We should…"

"Yeah," she yawned. She rolled off the bed and stood up, pushing her sweats off as he killed the TV. They gazed into each other's eyes before she remembered. "Wait: where *are* those pants?"

He reached into his bag and handed them over. She held them out; *might work;* she slipped them on; *hah! Whadya know?* She slid out of them without another thought. "OK: they'll work." *Wait: How good a look did he just get…like it matters? The no-underwear, though…*

"Good. *Glad* I could help." They gazed again into each other's eyes. Their kiss was tender, closed-eyes and brief. "'Night, Cloud."

"'Night, Johnny." They turned off the lights and climbed into their separate beds.

Sunday

"Morning, Cloud." He could see her at the window looking up at a dull-gray sky, back-lit by the parking lot lights. He could see she *didn't* have her long shirt on, but couldn't make out what she *did* have on.

"Morning, Johnny." She switched on the valence light over the window, filling the room with soft light that revealed her flouncy, diaphanous, blood-red crop top and *very* short skirt, neither of which hid what *real* clothes *usually* hide.

"Ah, *why* that, um, *outfit?*"

"*This* old thing?" She twirled. "*Like* it?"

"I like what's *in* it. But...*why?*"

"It covers, but it's light."

Covers what? GOD, what a bod. "Where did you get *it?*"

"Porn shop in Coronado."

"Why?"

"Sometimes I like to be alluring."

"*That* you are."

AND COLD! "Scoot over," she urged, stepping to his bed and lifting the covers as she crawled in, clearing her throat. "We're *about* to..."

"Get dressed in the same room at the same time." They were quiet, facing each other. "*This* is nice. *Dangerous...*"

"Uh-huh." *I'm cold and you're the safest, warmest place I know.*

"ROTC units have barracks rules; we used them in the tents. *Covered* at least in common spaces; *naked* only in the latrine or showers." *And Devins has gorgeous legs.*

"Mighty wet in *this* little bathroom. I don't think the fan works."

"Price we pay."

"Do we *have* to? I mean, we've *seen* each other *au naturel* more than once."

"*Before puberty* doesn't count. Maybe *routine* naked...?"

She smiled and put a hand on his chest; he put his hand on hers—*above* her top. "You're nice and warm. *How* far to Detroit from here?" *This IS dangerous, kid...*

Your hand's cold, Cloud, but your body isn't. "Ten, twelve hours in good weather, which we *ain't* gonna have I don't think. But..." He pressed; she pressed. "*This* is *very* nice." *And you're very CLOSE...*

Not yet, kid. "Uh-huh. You were *saying* about *routine* naked?" *Oh, DON'T move, kid; might be an accident...*

"I *was?* Oh, yeah. We both need to perform *some* activities while in stages of undress when we're sharing a room. *So...*" he gulped. *THAT's ... HOOH!*

She shifted her hips back an *inch.* "Better?"

Whew! "Uh-huh; thanks."

"Welcome. Maybe a *little* naked is..."

"*Some*times OK."

"So, a little hair, some butt, a bare boob...?"

"Maybe we just *don't look.*"

"So, when the lights go out…?"

"*You* can strip because you like to sleep raw. OK?"

"So do *you*. But, first chance I get I want something warm to sleep in: raw's OK in the tropics, but *not* up here. Deal?"

And they kissed on it.

****

Glad I had the sense to get another snow broom.

Later that morning, the blue-grey Smokie Mountains of Tennessee gave way to the steep and rolling hills of Kentucky. The Fury was almost at the last I-75 North exit to Frankfort, Kentucky when *it* started. There was no gentle buildup of flakes, no warning—just sudden, biting, blinding snow and ice driven horizontally by a screaming zephyr. The Fury, like the rest of the traffic, went from 60 to 40 miles an hour in a headwind, then 20, then barely moving at all. The radio reported blizzard conditions from Chicago to Albany to Charlotte to St. Louis. The theme was "if you don't *have* to be on the road, *don't be*."

He gripped the steering wheel tighter, barely able to see the lights of the thick-and-getting-thicker traffic ten yards—then ten *feet*—in front of them.

"Ranger weather," he mumbled just loud enough that she could hear.

"How's that?"

"Weather so bad only *Rangers* go out in it."

"*And* the Coast Guard. Those poor guys: their book says they gotta go *out*; *doesn't* say they gotta come *back*."

It would be three hours later, as they approached Florence and the Ohio River, before either of them made another sound. "Cloud?"

"Yeah?"

He held the Fury against the wind as a double-bottom semi ahead rocked and swayed across the lanes. "Before we meet our maker on this road I just gotta know: do you shave—down there? I, um…saw…"

"Well," she answered, "it's cleaner to have *less* hair when you're wet all the time. I *sometimes* shave, but there *are* other means. Why?"

"Just wanted to know."

"OK. No problem."

A sudden shrieking wind shook and rattled them; he thought two side-by-side trucks ahead would side-swipe each other. She pulled her legs up to her chest despite her crampy hip, watching the storm, the traffic, and his white-knuckle driving. The buffeting got worse as they crossed the bridge into Ohio at a crawl.

"John," she croaked, her throat dry, "if we *were* to stop someplace and let this blow out, how long is it to Detroit in good weather?" Much as she tried, she could not *help* but sound terrified.

"Four hours or so." *Right about now I'd settle for a truck stop.*

"Let's pull off when we can." For a few minutes in Cincinnati, the wind seemed to slacken, but picked up with even more power north of St. Bernard.

They pulled off on an exit that they almost missed because of the near-blinding snow. There was a half-dozen vehicles on the ramp shoulder; some moving, some not. Others had slid down the long slope to the ditch below. Down on the road, she could barely make out a sign. "Right two miles."

The parking lot of the Ramada was full, but they rolled up to the door anyway. "Take what you can get," she shouted as they trotted to the door, parkas flailing in the battering wind. They heard more cars approaching.

"*Anything* available," JJ sighed to the older gentleman at the desk who tapped on a keyboard.

He glanced up at them. "*Only* room left is the President's Suite: *emperor*-size bed, sleeper sofa, jacuzzi, kitchenette, sitting area. $490 a night."

"We'll *take* it." JJ put his ID and credit card on the counter.

"I *thought* you were military. Let's see," the agent muttered, tapping some more. "Only fools like *us* would be out on a day like this…uh-huh: $190 a night. Sorry folks," he called to a couple and two kids just coming in. "Full up. Hyatt down the street east has rooms yet: I'll have them hold one for you." He reached for the phone.

"Really?" *Haven't had that big a discount, like, ever.*

The clerk finished his Hyatt call and hung up as JJ filled out the paperwork, "*And*…vouchers for two cocktails at the bar and an appetizer in the restaurant."

"Semper fi, Gunny," Ann smiled, seeing the clerk's tie clasp.

"Have a good evening, buddies."

Once in the spacious suite, JJ dropped his bag and gazed longingly at the recliner. "Need ice."

He came back from the ice machine just as Ann was picking up the phone. "We need to call: They're expecting us today. *And* we need to sign out."

"Yeah; just a *few* minutes, honey."

She perused the sitting area of the suite with its recliner, love seat, desk and chair, large TV and galley-like kitchenette while the phone rang and rang. *Wonder how many presidents stay here?* The road was in *her* head, too: the swerving trucks, the snow and the buffeting. *Hard to shake off. OK, the best way I know how.* "Nobody answering. I'm going to swim some laps."

I haven't seen her swim since '67. "I'll join you in a few minutes."

In the big gilt-festooned bedroom that boasted its own armless chairs and small table in a corner, she adjusted the thermostat. *I'm going to get warm for the first time all day.*

He sat in the recliner; ice wrapped in towels on his neck. The road in his head would *not* stop moving. "Ugh, I am *not* used to this." *Stop stalling.* "So, I'll call" He dialed the phone and, "hi, Charlie: JJ...*yeah*, we ran into it...stuck just north of Cincinnati...yeah, *she's* here. Cloud: it's... for *you*."

Thanks for the warning, pal. She dashed out of the bedroom naked, grabbing a towel as she passed the bathroom, clutching it to her chest. *Oh, great. What do I say to his mother? "We're sleeping together, ma'am, but we're not having sex."* "Hello?"

"Hi, honey," her father's voice answered. "Hear you're stuck in Cincinnati."

With my butt bare... "Oh, hi, Dad. Yeah, what's...why are *you there*? I just *called...*" JJ wrapped the towel around her, hugging to hold it tight.

"Stella invited us over to meet you both when you got in. We've been here all afternoon playing cards and catching up. You'll get here tomorrow, yeah?"

"Late morning or early afternoon. Can't tell what's ahead."

"I understand. We'll be here; just drive safe. See you when you get here, honey! Bye!"

That was...surprising.

Minutes later, she emerged from the bedroom wearing a two-piece swimsuit that covered her from neck to knees to elbows in heavy blue/black Spandex, leaving a small gap at her middle. It was as figure-flattering as a thick coat of paint, but unlike *most* suits, it didn't threaten to split her in half by the crotch.

He stared. "*What*, Johnny?"

On her, perfect. "Never *saw* a suit like that."

"The Navy made them for us." She smiled, but he still stared. "That's *enough*, Johnny. Leave something *on* me, or I'll catch a cold. I'll call and sign out."

"Sorry. I just..."

Yeah. As she turned to leave a few moments later, she indulged herself with a small, private smile. "Come down after *you've* signed out."

***

That'll do.

There were kids at the shallow end, but the deep end of the pool was wide enough to work out a little. She ignored the "no diving" sign and plunged in.

She started swimming slowly, luxuriating in the work, the water, the buoyancy, the unwinding. *Stroke-stroke-breathe-stroke-stroke-stroke-turn. Glorious, just glorious.* She was alone, in the water, warm, weightless.

Let me have THIS. Let me enjoy THIS. She did another slow-flip turn, realizing how much she missed the pure joy of swimming for the sake of it, not to weld a hull or find a pipe leak or survey a tangle of flotsam lodged in a pier. She didn't know how long she swam or how many turns she'd made before she realized someone was watching her. She stopped and hung on the wall.

"Hi," Her audience was a 40-ish woman with a swim cap on washed-out hair. "I was just admiring your suit."

"Thanks," Ann told her about it.

"Are you here alone? I'm Margaret."

"Ann; sharing a ride." *Just sharing a ride with a friend, and a bed for warmth, some contextual nudity and an almost-chaste kiss goodnight.... Really!* She let go of the pool wall, finding the bottom reachable.

"My husband and I are here unexpectedly."

"Yeah, us too." *Until we decide we CAN make love and not be shattered when we're sent to the opposite ends of the world...or even after that.*

"Join us for dinner?"

Am I socially available without Johnny? "Can—*here* he is," Ann waved to JJ as he approached. "I've been invited to dinner."

"Oh, bring *him* with," Margaret smiled, walking up the steps at the end of the pool. "Come down about six: we'll meet you in the bar."

JJ tested the pool with his hand. *Water's warm. Couldn't make out what was going on...didn't have time—or wit—to respond.* He slid in the water as Ann pushed herself out. He went under and pushed off the wall, glided almost halfway across without stroking, and breast-stroked the rest of the way, turning, pushing off.

Are you just showing off or is this drowning practice, Elrath? While physical training—PT—was routine for all military members, for elites like them it was imperative—even if JJ's outfit didn't require the same PT for *all* members *every* day. But if they didn't do *something* physical at least every *other* day, they tended to get stiff. For his part, his arthritis in every heavy joint would start to protest. For her, it wasn't much different.

She watched him swim. *Your heels break, honey. What...*He stopped beside her, gasping for breath, his little cough catching her attention. "I counted five laps," she smiled. "You'll have to do *another* ten to catch up. And your heels break the water in your breaststroke: can't *do* that in competition."

Dash off a few laps and be done with it. "Yeah, I know; *I* was a backstroker." He pushed off and started a backstroke, executing a passable flip-turn on the far wall. *All she wants is what you can.*

Eh, not bad. She slid back into the pool, hanging backwards on the wall. *I can leave by myself. Do I MIND if we look like...?*

You can't impress her with your swimming. "Go on in if you want," he sputtered a moment later. "I'll be along directly."

How do I explain us NOW, even to myself? She submerged and did a handstand on the bottom, scissoring then bicycling her legs before coming up again. "I'll start getting ready," she smiled as she left. *DO we look like...?*

Not quite 5. Got time. He did another two laps just to prove to himself that he *could*, and pushed out of the pool.

***

Christ, what a bod. Tonight, king bed. Naked. With Cloud. He grinned as he passed the bathroom door, glancing in, catching a glimpse of her in the mirror *sans anything. Ho-boy...*

"Johnny," she called an instant later, "be a dear and hand me my Dopp kit from my overnight." He handed it over.

She stepped out again, clutching a towel. "Stay covered tonight?"

"Just thinking that, actually." *Thinking something else, too.*

As he got dressed and she brushed her hair, she started chatting. "You *know*, we *do* think a lot alike."

Don't screw this up, Elrath. "Yeah." He gave her his brave half-grin, smiling with his face in the mirror but with frightened eyes. "*I* want what *you* want: career, then everything else. But know *this*, Cloud." He sat on the bed slowly, breathed deep.

She slowed down. "Say what's on your mind, John. Won't hurt." *I hope.*

No matter what I say, it won't sound right. He looked at her warmly, grinned, then turned solemn. "I don't know when I stopped *expecting* anything from *anyone*, even though I've craved *something* from *someone* for a very long time—sometimes settling for *anything*. But *I want THIS*."

Brush down; turn around. "This, *what*?"

Just the truth. He looked around, then back at her. "*I want to see someone every day who gives a damn whether I live or die*." He laid back on the oversized, luxurious bed, staring at the textured ceiling; she laid next to him, propped on an elbow. *Can't stop now.* "I want to matter to *them* as much as *they* matter to *me*." *That evening with Leigh...oh!*

He grabbed her arm gently, like a firm caress. "I want *you* in any way, shape, or form I can *have* you—whatever *you'll* give. I don't care how much or how little—if it's a smile and a wink once a week or a day of passionate lovemaking: I *want* it."

"OK."

He inhaled deeply. "I *love* you, Claudia Ann Mueller. I can't *remember* a time when I didn't. But I can wait until *you* are ready for *us*."

"And *I* love *you*, John Jacob Elrath." *THAT was easier than I thought it would be.* "I've waited *this* long, so *I* can wait until there can *be* an *us*. And," she swallowed a gulp of air, "I'm *tired* of feeling lonely even after *good* sex. As for the *rest*," she shrugged, smiled sweetly and winked, "*between* the extremes." *Nothing to lose but your heart, kid.*

Elrath, nobody owes you anything. "*No* high tide tonight, honey."
Not until WE KNOW... "*No* high tide tonight, babe."
And they kissed on it: lingering, loving...*more* than a promise-kiss.

***

"Two beers, a quarter bottle of wine. *Lot* more than I'm used to," he mumbled when they got back to the room.

"*And* your shots of schnapps," she sighed. "You knocked *that* stuff back pretty hard."

"Had to trade *something* with our host's Bushmills. I'll pass blood for a few days."

Why? Not now. He started to stretch and massage his back. "Let me help," she mumbled, finding his ribs under the jumble of twisted muscle. She worked it for a while before he reached for her hand.

"Better. Thanks." *Too curt.* "Not a lot of that kind of thing helps. Too much damage."

"What does the Army say about it?" She turned to get ready for bed.

"I get 10% disability now; I'll get *more* after I leave the Active component."

"What does *that* mean; 10% disability on active duty?"

"It means 10% of my pay is tax-free and comes as a separate check until next year when they switch us over to electronic payments."

In moments, they laid next to each other with the lights off, warming under the covers. He looked over at her, coughed and smiled.

"Spill it. What's *with* the cough?"

He looked away. *Truth.* "Sarcoidosis. It's a..."

"...Immune and metabolic disorder. That's the scar on your chest?"

"Yeah."

"When?"

"Five years ago. How did *you*...?"

"One of the long-term hazards of diving because we're wet so much.

How did *you* get it?"

"Nobody knows. I had this *nagging* cough for like a year before I went on sick call and blew hot on a tine test: I never got full-blown TB. *That* they could at least treat."

No treatment and a shit-load of life-long complications, including night sweats. "Sorry, babe." She put her hand on his arm.

I know. He covered her hand with his, ever-so-gently. "Nothin' for it now: it's what we suffer in the service of the republic."

"Uh-huh. 'Night, Johnny."

"'Night, Cloud."

Monday

He had stripped off his briefs while half-asleep before *something*—he wasn't sure *what*—woke him.

They hadn't turned the thermostat down—the room was *very* warm.

She smiled in the brilliant light filtering through the sheer curtains. He could see her hauntingly naked in the snow-enhanced parking-lot light glare behind her, covers around their feet. She slid over and kissed him deeply as they languidly, oh-*so*-gently and *un*chastely embraced for a *long* instant, her warm and firm breasts crushing against his chest *so* softly.

"Back to sleep, babe" she whispered, pulling away; "it's only 3."

Go back to sleep before we can't stop ourselves.

✳✳✳

He was fully dressed, looking out the window at a glaringly bright morning when she awoke. "Clear as a bell," he sighed. "And about a foot and a half of snow here. They're working on the parking lot."

"Morning, Johnny," she managed.

"Morning, Cloud," he murmured, crossing the room to kiss her cheek. "Sleep well?"

I slept fine until your wrestling woke me up. "OK. You been up long?"

"I got coffee. Yours is there."

She sat up, pulling the sheet up with her. "We made out last night."

It felt like a dream. "Regrets?"

"For *making out?* No. *Naked-in-bed-making-out* felt…dangerous."

"Sensuous; no more than yesterday morning," he grinned, patting her thigh. "Let's get going. 8:30 already."

Sensuous: THAT'S the word. "John," she smiled, letting the sheet drop to her waist. "Is naked in bed together without—*you* know—OK?"

"It WAS, honey." *OOH it was.* He smiled and kissed her. "Because I love you and we said 'no.'"

And we keep saying it.

***

"I haven't seen a snow pile *that* big since Germany," he mumbled, watching a front loader lift snow onto a mountain that was already twenty feet high by a hundred yards long.

"Can't remember *ever* seeing one *that* big," she added. At the truck stop where they got gas, a cement truck that had sideswiped a Honda was being inspected by state troopers. On the road again, they passed through a winter wasteland; everything was covered with a layer of snow gleaming and twinkling in the brilliant sun. Cars and trucks dotted the shoulders and median. A double-boom wrecker pulled a smashed Cadillac out of a drift on the northbound side while a flatbed pulled a wrecked pickup out of another on the southbound; on the frontage road, the charred remains of a double-bottom tanker was being separated from the Pacer that it collided with.

She found a Toledo radio station playing Joe Cocker's "Up Where We Belong."

Love, lift us up where we belong
Where the eagles cry
On a mountain high!

"You *see* that movie," he asked.

"Yeah. Lou Gossett was *great*."

"What I liked was where Gere's character says 'I can't quit; I've got no place else to go!' And Gossett just says 'yeah, OK.'" He sighed. "Now, *I have* a place to go: wherever *you* are."

"Johnny: *I've* got the *same* place to go."

Near the Michigan border, JJ did the math when he saw a sign for Detroit. *90 and change; at 60...*

"Johnny," she interrupted his calculations, "there's people I want to see that you *don't* know...."

"I'm with ya there."

"And I don't want us to *look* like..."

"We're *not* what we look like? Too late for *that*, honey."

"Huh?"

"Everyone sees us as *just* that. Your *doctor* does; *Laura* and *Betty* do..."

"*LAURA and...?*"

"They guessed about your miscarriage; thought it was *mine*. Laura told me. They kept it to themselves."

"They *did* that." *Damnit, I practically TOLD Allison to think that.*

"No matter *what* you tell your dad, he'll think *your* baby was *mine* because that's what he *expects*. Just *don't* say it *wasn't*."

"Dad will *hate* you!"

"*We're* not teenagers. He'll *probably* think that *we* lost *our* baby through no fault of our own, just like everyone *else* has. Your dad might offer me his condolences. Laura *already* did; said I should mourn like *you* did. Don't *offer* any *other* explanations, just don't *deny*."

"But the math is *completely* wrong!"

"Yeah, but only your doctor, *you* and *I know that*. And in 1985, honey, *they expect us* to be *doing it*, especially since we've known each other so long *and* shared not just *quarters* but *beds*. In your whole life have you ever *heard*, even in the movies, of two *very*-close-lifelong-friends sharing a bed naked and *not* having sex? Could you even make one up?"

"But we could *explain…*"

"Our tideline? Who'd *understand our need for* it outside the military, and most of *them* can't because *ours is* a unique situation? I observe our rules because I love you and I want to be *with* you." He was quiet as she looked for another radio station. "OK, look *this* up in your Funk and Wagnall's: Imagine explaining to Kristin in the back seat there *right now* exactly *why we did not* make love this morning. We *could* have; we *wanted* to; but we *didn't*. Go ahead."

Yeah, kid: you BOTH wanted it. She stared at him, then at the road ahead, the intense sun off the snow blinding. "So, we *should just…?*" *You haven't even tried to feel me up and you say we make love in your head all the time.*

"*No!* I'm *saying* that we *appear* to be the regular kind of couple that society *expects us to be*. But our *circumstances*—and our rules—make us *not* regular, military or not. We *made* those rules and we *follow* them because *WE* need them. And *I* am willing to do whatever *you* need, to stay in that twilight zone we've crossed into if that's what *you* want."

"*You'd live a lie to save my reputation?* You'd *really* offer yourself?"

"I already *have*, for *you, and* for *us*, and I will *again* if need be."

Oh… "I *love* you, John."

"I love *you*, Claudia."

***

"That 'for sale' sign in your yard," Ann remarked, "did you know?"

Newhouse Properties, no less. "Ma *said* they listed it." JJ had trouble driving on Birch Lake Road that afternoon—he was *not* accustomed to its huge crown in the middle. The neighborhood still *looked* familiar, with palatial estate-like residences, fenced-in fortress-mansions, and small cottages on huge lots. The street names were the same, but somehow it all *looked* different: there were different house colors, newer cars, pristine landscaping, added porches, new roofs on one side; ice-bound lake on the other.

"What are they asking for the place?"

"Well, four and a half acres on a twenty-five-yard lakefront; four bedrooms, three-and-a-half baths, steam heat with forced air booster/heat exchangers and central air; heated four-car garage and residential outbuilding in one of the wealthiest suburbs in the world. A million? Just a guess."

He slowed as he pulled into the driveway and rolled up the hill, around the family room to the back of the house and the garage. There were already *two* cars in front of one of the two massive doors. By the time they got out of the Fury, JJ's mother and Ann's father were outside.

"You *made* it," Dr. Mueller shouted. "The weather cooperated."

"Yessir," JJ answered, shaking his hand while he hugged his mother. Ann, taller than her father, clung to him.

"*Claudia*," JJ's mom cried, "*my*, how you've *grown!*"

"Keep feeding 'em, and that's what happens," Dr. Mueller beamed. "Please, Johnny; time *you* called *me* Howard." He had dark if aging hair, light skin, and heart-shaped face like Ann, and shared her warm eyes.

"I'm *Stella* now, Claudia," she smiled, leading them—shivering—back into the house.

"*So* good to see you, Mrs., um, Stella. Please call *me* Ann." Stella's eyes were *exactly* the same adorable blue as JJ's and shared his fair skin, but not his height. *Hope Mom looks as good as she does.* She was Ann's mother's age—sixty-two.

The family room, just inside the back door, was always cold in winter because the main system's one pathetic radiator under the big picture window overlooking the driveway and the lake just wasn't enough. The badly-positioned back-furnace thermostat was right under a duct, leaving both JJ's room *and* the family room (where Stella's plants went to die in their legions) cool.

Barbara Mueller reminded JJ a great deal of the mom in the *Family Circus* cartoon: round all over with a helmet of dark hair, a warm smile, long and slim body, and a cheery demeanor. "JJ," she mumbled, "*we're* gonna be pals."

When Ann shook his hand, she saw that Charlie Parkinson was well into his seventies, heavy-set and a couple of inches shorter than she, with blotchy skin and short, light-gray hair. His grey eyes reminded her of Kristin's, but the pungent reek of alcohol and coffee sweat he exuded didn't. She remembered the moment in '73 when he denied knowing *anyone* named Elrath, but he showed no signs of recognition and only smiled broadly.

To Ann's surprise, Jenna and Alex were there. The twins were sixteen:

Jenna a tall, blonde beauty in a turtleneck; Alex a slightly taller, lanky, darkly handsome young man in a tie and cardigan and nearly up to JJ's nose, with his mother's face and hair. "*Apparently*," Howard explained, "their father's friend…"

"…surprised *him* with a romantic getaway for two on a tropical beach that was prepaid and *of course* non-refundable," Barbara finished. "Not the first time he surprised *me*, that's for sure."

"…and they dumped *us* on Mom and Howard *yesterday* on their way *out* of *town*," Jenna added unhappily, "so…"

"I'll find a room," Ann muttered. *A week in a motel alone? Goodbye January paychecks…*

"Nonsense," Stella announced, "You can sleep in Brenda's room. *We* arranged it yesterday."

"You're *sure* it's no trouble?"

"No trouble at *all*," Charlie joined in. "But we *don't* take credit cards." Grinning, he ribbed JJ not-so-subtly. "We'll just tack it on your *bill*." Everyone but JJ and Ann had a good time with the joke.

Dinner preparations were already underway, JJ learned: there was a pork roast in the oven that Barbara had brought over. *I hope I won't have too much of Ma's cooking: she can ruin more groceries than a plague of locusts.*

Ann ventured into the small kitchen to see if she could lend a hand, but Stella and Barbara politely declined. Wandering around downstairs, she gazed at stock prints and lithographs, framed samplers, posters and rugs on the walls. There were galleries of photos of Charlie and Stella in various places and seasons: all over Europe, Australia, Japan, even Korea. One corner displayed wedding photos of Brenda and Lois—she barely recognized JJ's sisters. But there were *no* individual photos of either Stella's kids or of Charlie's. Packed boxes lined the walls in the dining room and the living room: the glass-front china cabinets were empty. *Getting ready to move, looks like.*

She found Jenna in a small hall just off the kitchen; arms folded as if waiting to be called. Assuming a similar posture, Ann muttered. "Your mom's a good cook as I remember."

"The best. JJ's mom…"

"*Less* than stellar: I remember *that* too. You were *here* last night?"

"Yeah."

"Sorry."

"Learned to play Stella's Game. But now we need a ride New Year's. We *were* going with *Chrissy*…"

While Ann wandered and chatted, JJ took Alex up to his room above the family room: he recognized a stepchild when he saw one. Showing the young man some of his treasured books, he grinned, "you get dropped off a lot?"

"Well," Alex started, "*Chrissy*—Dad's friend—is only a little older than *we* are. She wants *Dad* to go places, and she *doesn't* want…"

"…to be saddled with *you*. Been in *that* neighborhood, son."

Alex had Ann's expressive eyes and her conspiratorial grin. "Not *me*, anyway. She *likes* Jenna, does stuff with *her*." He smiled. "Are you and *Ann*, like, *friends*?"

"We've known each other since *before* we can *remember*. Like you and Jenna are *friends*, but…" *OOH! BAD analogy…*

"More like me and Brianna."

"Who's Brianna?"

"A girl at school. We, *you* know, fool around. I asked her to the New Year's party, but now I can't get there."

"OK, where's the party?"

"Wixom."

Half an hour away? "*I* can make Wixom happen easily enough."

Alex grinned widely and went to find to Jenna; Ann found JJ in his room. *Last time I found him here…when his dad died.* "There's some party…"

"New Year's in Wixom."

"Alex told you?"

"Yup. *Your* source was Jenna?"

"That's affirm. They need transportation."

"It just so happens I *might* be free."

"Buddy, we *do* read each other's minds."

"Yeah? What does 'fool around' mean to sixteen-year-olds around here?"

She inhaled deeply, grimacing. "I'll get back to you." *I need to interpret their love lives?*

After dinner, JJ was reminded how, when his mother dealt cards, she seemed to…just…calm…*everything*…down. Howard was dealing a second hand when Stella suddenly brightened. "*OH!* Ann, dear, *now* I remember: I have a message for *you* from Leigh Taylor; her mother gave it to me at church yesterday. *She'll* be in town tomorrow evening. Here's her home number. And, Johnny, a young woman delivered *this*…" she held out a Hudson's bag, "yesterday."

He looked in the bag. *OK, should work,* and handed it to Ann. "Early Christmas present."

She looked, frowned, and pulled out a flannel nightie. "Oh," she sighed, checking the label. "How…?"

"You *gave* me your size, honey. I just figured…"

So I did. "But *how*? I didn't even *mention* it until yesterday."

"I figured you'd need *something* more than a dorm shirt up here so I called Donna before we left."

Stella only smiled when he kissed Ann goodnight later. *The only girl you've ever seen me kiss, Ma.*

He made some phone calls before he climbed the stairs to his cold back bedroom, isolated from the world.

Christmas Eve

I love this…

Ann woke with the bright sun streaming into the windows. She lay quiet, warm and content in a remarkably comfortable Victorian high bed and her new nightie. When she *finally* got up, the hardwood floors, though covered with big rag rugs, were cold. She grabbed a book and her glasses, bundled up in her sweats and field jacket and went down the back stairs to the family room, sitting at the big round table by the picture window.

After a few minutes, Stella appeared in the kitchen doorway wearing a baggy polyester cross between a leisure suit and a sweat suit. "Good *morning*, Ann. Do you take coffee in the morning?"

"Morning, Stella. Yes, thanks. Straight black." Ann stretched stiffly.

"How *is* that bed? It *was* Will's bed."

"It's fine. The banging all night didn't help, though."

"Oh, sorry; the steam heat. They need to bleed it again, whatever *that* means."

"As long as the place won't blow up." *I KNOW what it means, and I can DO it, but I'm not about to on vacation.*

Stella looked away. "Your mother…how *is* she?"

"I'm going to see her this weekend. Would *you*…?"

"No, thanks." She set her coffee down, wiped a sudden tear away. "I'm sorry, Ann. We—your mother and I—thought you were getting *too* close." She stopped. "No, that was *her* excuse. *I* didn't want to watch my oldest friend fall apart, much to my shame. Keeping *you* apart…we *shouldn't* have—not like *that*. He *never* forgot *you*."

WE know. "I never forgot *him*, either, Stella, but that's in the past. We survived."

"He *nearly* didn't. Wolverine…"

"*He* won't talk about it."

"No, and I *can't* blame him. He looked *horrible* when he got back. Now he looks happier than I've seen him for a very long time."

"He *loves* his job. He can read and write and talk about history all day."

"Don't kid a *kidder*, Claudia: we've known each other *much* too long. It's *you*."

I know. "We love each other, Stella."

They were quiet for several moments before Stella murmured, "what are your plans, you and he?" Stella put her hand on Ann's. "*Neither* of you slept on Will's sofa. It's *OK.* You are *adults,* Claudia, and he's loved *you* forever: *that* may be the *only* thing I know for sure about my son. So, plans?"

"You mean, as a *couple?*" Stella waited with a faint smile. "We can't really *plan* much. We're subject to separation-by-service: They'll send us where we're needed..."

"If you truly love each other, you need to make a commitment."

She looks like Johnny sometimes—or is it the other way around? "Won't *change* anything unless one of us gets out. By the time *my* current obligations are met in '91, I'll have eighteen years' service; he'll have fourteen in '87 when he can re-up again. We *could* call it quits *then* but on the downhill side of twenty...why give up the benefits?"

Stella crossed her arms and smiled broadly. "There are more options than an altar."

"Like what?"

"A promise." Stella poured coffee. "It's an engagement-to-be-engaged; a symbol of a developing relationship. Isn't *that* where you two are? Developing?"

"Some friends of ours did that." *Mike and Leigh; their pledge...*

"Please help *me* make *my* life easier and make a *promise.*"

YOUR life? "But, anything we..."

Stella leaned back for a moment, cocking her head as if listening for something. "With a promise comes a ring on the right hand. With a *ring,* your relationship is more..."

"Socially acceptable?"

"Yes, *and* you *show* that you're unavailable. And *Charlie...*"

Just then JJ came in wearing a sweat suit and clutching his field jacket around him. He bussed both on a cheek, vaguely puzzled about a dream. *Bathtub? All that red...what was it?* "What's unavailable?"

"*You,*" Ann offered, "*or* me. Your mom thinks we should make a promise like Leigh and Mike did."

"Promise *what?*" Ann glared mildly. "Oh. We *did* that when we were eight. At the Safe Tree."

Our promise to be friends no matter what. "Yeah, but *this* one needs a ring *and* a kiss."

"A *ring?* Then it needs to be more *formal.*" He knelt at Ann's side as she grinned with a flash of both surprise and fury. "Claudia Ann Mueller: Will you *promise* to *love* me *forever?*"

She sniffed, wiped away a sudden tear, and answered: "John Jacob

Elrath: I *promise* that I will *love* you *forever*."

Stella excused herself while they exchanged embraces and soon returned and handed him his father's wedding band. "We *may* have to get it sized," he smiled as he slipped it on; it fit well enough. Just then Charlie came in and, to JJ's grateful surprise, offered *his* congratulations to them both, even bussing Ann on a cheek.

Well, Elrath what have you done now? Is this what SHE wants, or just Ma?

Stella's pancakes were ready perhaps a half-hour later. Charlie merely chopped them into tiny pieces and slathered them with syrup. JJ, finding the flapjacks to be gritty *and* chewy, tried doing the same with butter. Ann bravely choked one down and politely said "no" to seconds.

"I outgrew my twin beds, Ma," JJ sighed while they cleaned up. "Can I sleep in the old master?" That was the room where his parents slept until Charlie moved in; it had a standard bed and was *just* a few steps from where Ann was sleeping.

"Don't see why *not*," Charlie declared; Stella smiled benignly, glancing conspiratorially between Ann and JJ.

"And, ah, *three more* for dinner at River Hills tomorrow?"

"Who, JJ," Charlie asked, more curious than anything else.

"The Taylor's: Ma knows them from church."

"Oh, *yes*," Stella declared. "Cathy makes the *best kuchen*."

***

"Have you ever seen part-raw and part-burned bacon like that?" JJ dodged a kid running in the mall.

"Never," Ann smiled, her half-digested meal sitting like a rock in her belly. "As long as I'm at *your* house I'll either *cook* or *fetch* breakfast." They were overwhelmed by the rush of shoppers and the pushy, loud hawkers of wares at the kiosks who all but blocked traffic around them.

"Sounds good to me." At midday, they were browsing the crowded, trashy, understocked-with-the-practical-and-overstocked-with-the-trendy Tel-Twelve Mall. "Wish we'd have thought of shopping before we left Florida." They'd jointly decided on framed copies of their promotion board photos—the most personal things they could imagine.

"It *sounded* better in Florida than it does now. I haven't given *real* Christmas gifts since…let's see…I flew home from Coronado in '80: last time I was *here* at Christmas. And, my nightie's *fine*, babe: thanks. But…*how*?"

"I asked Donna to find something *appropriate*."

"Well, it is *that*, and *she's* probably about my size." *Now I've gotta figure out what to give HIM.* "I forgot how crazy retail can get this time of

196

year." She had to semi-shout, dodging another child dashing between kiosks. They puzzled at the Teddy Ruxpin displays crowding the Cabbage Patch Kids, gazed at the many displays of video cameras and VCRs, and rejected the this-was-what-I-found-at-the-last-minute trinkets in the gift shops. "I put my name in a jar for a free diving lesson…right over *there*." *Got us here.*

"What about the twins? Want to do something for *them*?"

"'*Want*-to' versus '*know*-what-the-*hell*-to' is the problem."

"Somehow, I think, my dear," he answered, holding up her hand and her ring, "I believe *this* is sufficient for everyone at *your* place. Probably the best I *could* have done for Ma. And *Charlie*, surprisingly enough." He gripped her hand tightly. "Is *this* what *you* want?"

"*Absolutely*. You?"

"I want *us*, honey, and *us* means *you*."

***

"Hey, you two," Howard called out as they entered the Mueller's Southfield condominium. "Shopping ain't what it used to be?"

"If I never do *that* again it'll be too soon," JJ mumbled. Barbara prepared little sausages for a Christmas Eve party; Howard washed dishes; the kids listened to the television in the living room while they picked up and cleaned.

The Mueller condo was a 2,500 square-foot detached cookie-cutter house—with a maintenance agreement—built into a hill. The entry hall/mudroom on the "street" side with an adjacent powder room opened onto the main floor great room that filled half the upper level, from the sunken living/dining room with a huge fireplace and picture windows, to the kitchen with its long island and small two-bench booth, to the hall leading to the master suite and den. The lower level was where the two-car garage butted the storage space, the kid's rooms and the second full bath.

After carrying Ann's bag downstairs (she was staying *there* Christmas Eve), JJ looked around the great room at the pictures on the walls. Ann's First Communion—he saw her in her dress after that; her Confirmation—*and* that. Wedding pictures—her brothers, her parents (both occasions), other pictures of a *lot* of people he didn't know…and *his* 6th Grade school picture. *Huh.*

Ann started helping Barbara while JJ helped Howard put dishes away. "Barbara," Ann muttered, "need some advice."

Glancing at Howard and JJ, she shifted towards Ann. "Shoot."

"What does 'messing around' mean to teenagers these days?"

Barbara didn't miss a beat. "If they *talk* about it, second base: but *not* bare skin. If they *whisper*, everything from the hips up. Why?" She looked back at her children, looking stern briefly. "*Girl* talk?"

"Guy. Alex and JJ."

"Hmm," Barbara arched an eyebrow. "Alex isn't usually *that* open." She looked back at the kids again, watching Alex clean a mirror. "I *didn't think* he'd got *that* far with Brianna: Eh, maybe, but she's a smart girl. Jenna's not *there* yet: no steady or serious guys that I *know* of. OK?"

"OK. Just checking. Meant more as I recall."

"It did when *I*..." She spotted the ring and took hold of Ann's hand. "And, what's *this*?"

I wanted...something more formal. "Johnny gave it to me this morning; it's his dad's wedding band."

"Let *me* see." Howard rushed over. "Oh, *right* hand: engaged-to-be-engaged! I'm so happy for you! And on Christmas Eve!"

"Slow *down*, everybody!" JJ was startled at the commotion but pumped Howard's hand as Barbara hugged. "This is a *promise*."

"Yes, yes, *we* know," Howard beamed. "Barb, *you* did a promise with Nate, didn't you?"

"Yeah, sort of. Before I went to 'Nam he gave *me* a little ring, but I didn't give *him* one. Maybe I *should* have."

"Let me see!" Jenna grabbed Ann's hand while Howard and Barbara hugged. "Cool! *I* get to be a bridesmaid! *You* can be an usher, Alex."

Alex studied the ring. "Doesn't it go on the other hand?"

"It means something different on the left hand," Barbara explained. "On the *right*..."

"Depends on *where* you are," JJ interrupted. "In Germany, women wear their *wedding* rings on their right hands, and I've seen..."

"*Shh*...just...*shh*." Ann covered his mouth with her hand, smiled and kissed him. "History lessons later." Howard vanished briefly, returning to give something to Ann. "And here's *yours*," she announced, placing Howard's old band on JJ's hand. "I've got *you* marked too, buster."

***

Chaos and joy, anticipation and disappointment, surprise and routine.
Leigh stepped off the jetway at Detroit Metro Airport and practically into her father's arms. "So *good* to see you," Ed murmured, passing her off to her mother. Ed had a cavernous voice likened to Boris Karloff.

"We need to talk with Ben," Cathy whispered quickly.

As always, road construction around the airport delayed getting out, but soon the concrete canyons of I-75 North were like welcoming walls. "Same as ever," Leigh mused.

"Not a *lot* different," Ed agreed. "They're tearing up the Southfield

198

expressway again next year, like *that's* new. Are you up for the Dietz's tonight?"

"Sure. Did you pass that message for me, Mom? Am I to meet the new sons-in-law?"

"I *did* and you're *supposed* to," Cathy answered. "Monica told me that *we* should do something in their temple sooner than later. Dinner *tomorrow* is with the Mueller's and the Parkinson's at River Hills"

"Huh," Leigh sighed. "More than the *Army* wanted. And, I haven't seen *Ann* in an age." Leigh thought it quaint that Mike felt obliged to tell his family about their pledge, but had no idea that their casual (*she* thought) promise would be so important to the Dietz's. When she informed her superiors of it, her commander blinked briefly and congratulated her, but nothing *official* was done other than that a memo to that effect was placed in both her dossier and her 201-file.

The Taylors enjoyed a large roast turkey in the palatial dining room of the Dietz's, and Leigh got to meet the sons-in-law. Sara—one of the few women ordained as a rabbi in America—gave a blessing for Mike and Leigh's future union in English and Hebrew.

After the feast, Leigh, Cathy and Ben repaired to Ben's small office on the first floor of their huge home. "The long and the short, Leigh, is that there's something not good happening in the Newhouse organization," Ben sighed. "There's been a change in management that has brought an unsavory character into more power than he *should* have."

"Who," Leigh asked.

"Joe Dryden is now their property management executive, which has income and a nebulous scope. And there seems to be a new sort of business that the Newhouse's are into, one involving whole neighborhoods, doing minimal improvements to a few buildings, then selling them all again." He shook his head. "In Detroit…doesn't make much sense. That and *his* well-known grudge for John Elrath. The more I learn about that man Dryden the less *sense* he makes…and the fact that his responsibilities are so ill-defined is more than a little troubling."

That evening, as Leigh listened to the quiet-yet-lustful lullaby from her parent's bedroom, she knew she was home. At the same time…*why is Dryden still so pissed at Blue-Eyes?*

Christmas Day

Why do I dream of a red bathtub? What the hell's that about?

By the little Christmas tree in the living room, Stella asked, "how long does it take to get those boots *that* shiny," gazing at his promotion photo.

"A *while*, Ma." Charlie had given Stella a new watch; she gave *him* a new golf bag. Stella gave JJ a small box that contained two rings: his grandmother's 3/4 carat diamond, and his mother's 1/3rd karat. "We're a ways from *that*, Ma."

"Your father saw it *then;* I see it *now*." She smiled brightly. "Her mother and I *shouldn't* have…," and she fell silent.

JJ smiled, winked and nodded. "We figured *that* out, Ma." He pecked her cheek. "Merry Christmas."

***

Waking up with a teenager…long time since I did that.

"I thought sailors wore bell bottoms." Jenna studied Ann's picture in the wreckage of the Christmas gift frenzy.

"I do *sometimes*," Ann explained, "bells and jumper are my *service dress* uniform. The promotion board wants to see *this* one: *summer dress mess* with skirt."

"Why is it called a 'dress-mess?'"

"Dress *mess* is more formal than *service* dress. Just different costumes with different names for different occasions."

"Why the skirt, then?"

"Ask *them*. Maybe they like legs."

There were cufflinks for Howard, and pearls for Barbara and Jenna. Jenna also got a CD player; Alex got an Apple II computer and several neckties.

"*This* was your mother's jewelry," Howard handed Ann a polished wooden box. "I'm sure she wants *you* to have it." Inside were her engagement ring, wedding band, and other pieces.

"I've *really* got no place to keep them," she protested. "In the barracks…"

"You can keep here what you can't stow safely there."

Ann shrugged. "*Very* well."

***

After cleaning up the wreckage of a continental breakfast, Stella dealt three-handed gin. Charlie fiddled with the big knob for the TV antenna rotor control until the picture was suddenly clear. "Got it," he declared. "Damn sunspots." He picked up his hand and turned off the sound. "Nothing interesting until the basketball scores start."

Make more stuff up, Charlie. "Not used to *this* game," JJ lamented, turning up the king of hearts.

"Don't play cards much in the service," Charlie asked, picking up and discarding the five of diamonds.

"Different games," JJ answered, picking it up and discarding the nine of hearts. "Similar, but different. More rummy and tonk, *lots* more poker and double pinochle."

"Games like *mine*," Stella asked, picking up and discarding the seven of clubs.

"We'll play *your* game sometimes," JJ mused, picking up the seven and discarding the jack of diamonds. "One version adds two sets of three and a run of five."

"Huh," Stella muttered, watching Charlie pick up the jack. "There are other versions I've heard of."

"Many, many versions of gin," Charlie mumbled, discarding the two of hearts. "There's whole books about it."

"True," JJ conceded, picking up the two. "And the name of *this* game is…gin!" Charlie had 33 points; Stella 47.

Charlie's deal. "So, JJ, been meaning to ask: how much do you *make* in the Army now?" He turned up the ace of spades. "*Ooh*, bad luck."

"I clear about ten thousand a year, with room and board paid for," JJ offered, watching Stella pick up the ace and discard the seven of hearts. "Not a bad living."

"You're in the *barracks* down there," Stella mumbled as Charlie picked a card off the deck and discarded the five of diamonds. "Don't they *have* housing?"

"Housing in Key West is *always* short, and costs *more* than the $400-a-month they pay for allowances." He thought for a moment, picked up the five and discarded the king of spades, watching Charlie pick it up. "*Might* have something first of the year.

"What about Ann," Charlie mumbled, discarding the ace of clubs. "Is *she* in the barracks?"

"Yep. Same problem." He picked off the deck and discarded the jack of hearts.

"You should go in together," Stella murmured, picking up the jack. "I'm going to knock with five."

JJ waited for the explosion of outrage from Charlie for such an *indecent* suggestion—that two *unmarried* people should live together—but there was nothing as the deck passed to Stella. "Eleven," Charlie sighed, glancing at the basketball scores. "Might be more economical. Does the Army object to such things?"

"Only when it interferes with duty," JJ answered guardedly, adding, "Fifteen. Just so you folks know, Ann and I will be moving out *probably* this weekend: we don't want to be a bother."

"OK," Stella sighed as Charlie changed the channel and tried to outmaneuver the sunspots with the antenna once more.

JJ stood up, thanking the *wonder* of his mother's game. "Dinner in a couple hours? *I* need a shower."

***

As the kids spent the morning setting up the computer and listening to the CD player, the grownups shared coffee. "So, Key West," Barbara smiled, pouring at the kitchen island. "I went there on my *first* honeymoon: still *waiting* for my *second*." She exchanged glances with Howard. "Not a lot to do but fish, swim and get loaded."

"That's about it. When I'm not working for the Navy, I'm working on school and getting *ready* to work for the Navy. Study while doing laundry; read while shining shoes; fill in answer grids while on watch. Social life…as you said, not a lot to do there but drink, fish and swim. There's tourist traps like Pirate's Alley and...."

"How did you run into JJ without a social life?"

"By accident, in the mess. If you'd told me we'd meet the day before it happened, I wouldn't have believed it: *I barely* believed it the day *after*."

"There's a fort," Barbara went on. "*We* went there."

"Fort Zach. *I* went there once. JJ's been there a few times."

"He's still a history buff?" Howard stirred sugar into his coffee.

"Not a buff: a scholar."

"What's the difference?" Barbara winked at Howard.

"A *buff* knows how many bullets a soldier carried: a *scholar* knows why he carried *that* many; how that figure was arrived at; how it drove tactics."

"*Oh*," Barbara, visibly impressed, smiled. "There *is* a difference."

"Does *that* bother you, Ann?" Howard fixed his gaze on his coffee cup. "*That* distinction, his devotion to detail? I'm assuming it's *not* yours."

"It isn't, no; but no, it's OK. John's studious and serious, but he's also warm and sweet, and generous with his time and attention. He's never *had* many girlfriends, so any '*us*' is new to him."

Howard looked curious. "How many *boyfriends* have *you* had? Not *that* many."

"You *knew* about Cable, right?" They nodded. "Before *him*, Don, followed by Rick in Panama City." *Not Roger...let them make the leap.* "*They* were it...and oh, well, *Sam* and a few prom dates."

"How long did *they* last?" Barbara was curious, not accusing.

"Cable was four years; Don four *months*; Rick...*six* or eight months. Sam was...3rd Grade to graduation. Prom dates were just *that*. JJ and I have been in touch since just after Labor Day, but..."

"If we add the time before *that*," Howard frowned, "thirteen years and three months."

"*Fifteen* years, Dad. Last time I talked to him was 6 September 1970: a day short of *fifteen* years before we saw each other again. I can't *remember* when we first met."

"*I* can," Howard said. "You were fifteen *days* old, and he was *seven* days old. Your mother took you over to the Elrath's and put you in the crib with him. You both slept through it."

"No *wonder* I'm so comfortable with him," *I said that out loud?* Everyone thought *that* was funny.

"I *hope* you don't mind about the kids," Howard sighed at length. "Barb's ex can be a real piece of work."

"No, Dad. It's fine. You can't kick 'em to the curb."

"I suspect you'd rather spend more time with *him*," Barbara smiled.

"We have different plans for our time up here, but, yeah, together is good, too. We want to take all you guys to dinner at least once."

"That would be nice: we accept," Howard beamed.

"Pop; Barbara; I have to tell you something…else." *First, this.* "John's *not* gonna stay out there for three weeks: he's going to find a room in a few days. *I'm* staying with him."

Howard shrugged "OK, honey. I can't *stop* you."

THAT was easier than… "Dad, you *know*…"

"You're a grown woman, Claudia Ann. We have *no* illusions about *that*."

THIS will be… Ann gazed at Alex and Jenna, engrossed in a computer game. *Just give me a few minutes of deafness, kids.* "There's one *more* thing…"

***

"What *is* this, now," Cathy reached for her glasses to see what was in the shadow box that Leigh had given her parents for Christmas.

"The replica CID badge and credentials I got when I graduated," Leigh explained. "Just been knocking around my place for years; I'm not even supposed to keep it *displayed*, they tell me."

"*Very* handsome, honey," Ed nodded. "How long will you be in Missouri, again?"

"The practicum is for three *cycles*: they want me to train other female CID agents in using *feminine* wiles." Leigh shrugged. "Training future Mata Hari's."

"But you say *they* think you're good at it…" Cathy started.

"That's…relative," Leigh grinned sadly. "My arrest record isn't as impressive as my confession/conviction record. I'm better at getting them to talk than I am at busting 'em."

"Confessions, though, save everyone a lot of time." Cathy declared.

"*Not* in a court-martial. We have to go through the *same* motions if they confess or not. Plea bargaining just fixes the sentence."

"Well, that's something, at least," Cathy sighed, smoothing her robe.

"So, dinner at two?"

"Yes," Ed answered, picking at his own robe, "that's what the message said."

"Then, *I* shall get into the shower," Cathy declared, standing and letting her robe fall. "*Anyone* care to *join* me?"

"*Right* behind you," Ed stood, letting *his* fall as well.

"Pass," Leigh sighed, averting her eyes. *What is Christmas without naked parents in the living room? At least they're...leaving the bathroom door open? ARGH!*

Where's my earplugs when I need them?

* * *

"I don't *see* it," Jenna sighed. "The *dress* is OK, but that little diamond is lost in *that* neckline. You *don't* wear jewelry well." Resplendent in a maroon velvet dress, she sat behind Ann on their bed as they got ready to go to dinner.

"I don't wear it *at all*," Ann agreed, feeling like a great weight had been lifted from her shoulders. "Clashes with dungarees; gets caught in wetsuit zippers. The little silver balls the Navy allows for earrings don't *look* right. I haven't *worn* earrings in *years*."

Jenna sorted through the jewelry box, handing Ann a heavy gold link chain. "Try this. Simple, elegant. Distracts from the fact you're not wearing nylons, not that you *need* them. Beautiful legs."

"Thanks. *You* look pretty. Do you think JJ will like *this* look?"

Jenna hid a smile. "I think *he* likes *you* in *anything*. Or *nothing*."

"*You're* right about *that*."

Suddenly Jenna was very serious. "We don't know each other, Ann, but I think he really likes you."

Think like a teenager. "He *says* he does."

"Then why don't you get married?"

Did THE KIDS hear...? "Not that *easy*. Getting married would make our future *un*clear, not clear. We'll be separated when our services decide to reassign *either* of us, *married* or not."

"So, you *want* to, but you *can't*." Jenna grinned widely. "I get *that*. But, do *you*, you *know*...?"

No... "*That's not* something *you* should ask anyone."

"But we talk about it *all the time* at school. *Everybody* knows who's *doing it* and with *who*. Besides, you're my *sister*. *Sisters* tell each other *everything*."

"John and I have an *adult* relationship, OK? Do *you* tell *your* friends about *your*...?"

"But I *don't*," Jenna pouted. "Not yet."

204

Nope: hasn't changed. Ann patted Jenna's arm. "Don't *try* to grow up too fast, Jenna. You need to set a *limit*—a line neither of you *dare* cross no matter how hot your passion gets, 'cause beyond *that line* are serious, life-changing, grownup consequences, OK? C'mon: time for dinner."

****

This place still looks like a plantation house.

JJ smiled when he saw the pillared façade of the old River Hills clubhouse, still looking like an antebellum movie set, despite the snow piles, shovels and rock salt bins.

"I'm *so* sorry, John," Barbara whispered as Howard offered his hand when they met in the lobby: one look at Ann and he knew why.

"Merry Christmas, Cloud," he whispered as they embraced.

"And a Merry to *you*, Johnny. We'll talk later. And here's...*hey*, you! *C'mere*, girl!" Ann leaned for an embrace with Leigh in a civilian pantsuit. Ed and Cathy, following her, shared some whispered conversation, stopped at the coat check and shook hands with everyone.

JJ smiled broadly. "*Hi*, Green-Eyes! *Twice* in *one* year!" He embraced her gently but smacked her offered lips. *Second girl, Ma.* "Everyone, this is Leigh Taylor, my friend in the MPs, and *her* parents Cathy and...excuse me, sir, but *we've* never met..."

Friends and family engaged in idle conversation as they came and went between their big round table and the lavish buffet line. As Cathy and Ed were getting food, Leigh watched her mother speak—briefly—with a man she didn't recognize. "Who was *that*, Mom," she asked when they sat down.

"*That's* Harry," Cathy sighed, side-glancing at Ed, "*friend* of..."

"...*ours*," Ed finished. "He and his *wife* sponsored our membership."

"Ah," Leigh smiled. "Have I ever...?"

"*No*," Cathy replied quickly, "*you* haven't met him."

JJ, between Leigh and Cathy, watched, trying *not* to see.

"*That's* his wife," Leigh asked, watching Harry and a woman sit at the other end of the dining room.

"No: Harry's a *widower*," Ed declared, cutting his ham. "Eunice died in...'68, Cath?"

"Just before *you* left," Cathy answered absently, forking in some beef. "*Terrible* shock."

"Terrible indeed," Ed agreed, "and *you* stayed in touch." He looked at his wife with odd eyes.

"*You* were *gone*, dear," Cathy declared, "and *he* was *not*."

Ann, between Cathy and Ed, felt Cathy's leg reach towards Ed. Cathy winked at Ann ever-so-slowly before she retracted the limb.

205

Ed grinned widely. "But we had *fun* when I got *back…*"

"We surely *did*, Eddie," Cathy smiled, puckered lightly, "and *wait* till I get you *home*."

JJ and Ann locked eyes before they glanced at Leigh, who tried but failed to keep from grinning.

Holiday dinners with Charlie Parkinson often ended poorly, but *this* Christmas, Charlie seemed to be on his best behavior. How much of that was attributable to the presence of the Taylor's and Mueller's was impossible to know.

Leigh's trained eye told her that Charlie was very wary around her father. She also sensed that the mysterious Harry was *more* than just a "friend" who she *may* have "consoled" while Ed was away.

God bless us, every one…

***

"Oh *GOD*, I'm glad *that's* done." JJ drove the Fury, unwilling to jam his six-foot-two-and-arthritic frame into the back seat of Charlie's Cadillac.

"Did he *ask…*?"

"No: he just made the leap, though I helped him *make* it by telling him I'm moving out with *you*."

"Yeah. People fill in the blanks pretty quickly if they *think* they know stuff that they really don't. It's why I have to question everything."

She leaned on him. "I don't know Barbara that well, but I *want* to. I'm getting to know Jenna. Good kid."

"Alex seems to be, too. If I took him with me to Kurt's about your car tomorrow, would that be OK?"

"I think he'd love just being around other men. His father doesn't do much with him."

"That's what he says, *and* why I want to do it."

And you would make a great big brother.

Thursday

"Morning all," JJ mumbled, pouring coffee. "You purloined my keys, honey?" Stumbling into the family room after *another* bathtub dream, he found Stella and Charlie with Ann, sharing coffee and crullers from the Danish bakery in nearby Keego Harbor.

"Morning," came the chorus; Ann looked up, smiled and nodded.

"When did you change the carpet up there," He winced at the bright sunlight, his head buzzing.

"Last spring," Charlie replied. "That leak in the ceiling…"

"Yeah, I *saw* that was fixed. The *glue* gives me a headache, even in the other room." JJ browsed through his stack of mail; glasses perched on his nose—he'd last got a bundle from his mother in November. His bank statement was the only thing that really interested him. "Ma, thanks for depositing my royalties, but I think I'll handle it from here on out."

"OK," Stella sighed. "You're welcome. When did you get glasses?"

Charlie read the paper. "Going to electronic deposits?"

"Uncle Sam's *making* us; we got our last paper checks last payday." JJ muttered, passing Ann his statement absently. *And I've got to talk to Eddie.* "I'll get the Institute to change where the checks go. Glasses...couple years ago."

Why did you...just over a year's pay...show me this in front of your parents? "Nice chunk of change, buddy." Charlie looked up momentarily.

"What do *you* have planned for today, JJ?" Charlie seemed casually—almost *politely*—interested.

"Kurt's got Ann's car in his custom shop; need to talk about it."

"What's wrong with it?"

"Age. '60 Rambler."

"Oh. Ann, do *you* have plans?"

"I'm going shopping with my sister."

"Eh. Well, you two have a good day. I have to go to work myself." He put his paper down. "Ed Taylor. How well do you know him?"

"I *don't*," Ann mused. "I met him once or twice years ago."

"*I* never met him before," JJ admitted. "And tonight, folks—*like* we said—*don't* expect us for dinner unless we *tell you*."

"You two have a good day."

***

"Morning, sunshine," Donna sat up and stretched, her old-threadbare-and-*too*-small Blondie Boopadoop t-shirt clinging to her.

Her hair IS straighter than THAT Blondie's. "Morning, Blondie. Start the coffee." Leigh was bunking with Donna to give her parents a gift of privacy for their amorous enterprises.

"*Good* idea." Donna swung out of bed, stretching to her full 6 feet before performing a cartwheel. "*Dojo* awaits."

"Just...*after* coffee. By the way," Leigh pulled an envelope out of her purse, "this is for *you*, from Ann Mueller. Important?"

Donna took it gingerly. "*Girl* stuff," she mumbled with a small smile. "I wrote her a few weeks ago; guess *this* is her answer. She's sweet on Cutie-Pie Johnny?"

"You *could* say that," Leigh smiled, stepping into her *gi* trousers. "They *look* serious."

"Good for them. I still want a kiss New Year's; haven't done *that* since

'73. I don't have a shift until New Year's Night."

"Good: we can hang out, maybe do *something* about...*this*." Leigh looked around while getting dressed. The Hammerfest home always looked like it had some work-in-progress...because there *always was* a work-in-progress somewhere in the house. Donna's suite—a combination bedroom, workroom, kitchenette, and bathroom—was scattered with sketches and clothes in one stage or another and sharing space with her medical textbooks: she was *always* in school.

"This...*what*," Donna was genuinely puzzled, pulling *her* pants on.

"This...oh, *never mind*," Leigh closed her *gi* coat over her t-shirt. "Maybe the *downstairs*?" Her father Evan's workroom—ostensibly a dining room—sported table-to-ceiling stacks of circuit boards and project boxes. They kept the living room more-or-less for *that* purpose, but seeing as it was filled with the hundreds of volumes moved to accommodate Donna's suite, it *looked* more like a library.

"This *isn't* a *barracks*, honey," Donna declared. "You need to resist the urge to clean and organize every day, especially around *here*."

***

"The Mercury Theater," JJ mused. "Dad and I watched the Indy 500 there in '65 in simulcast, when Jim Clark won."

"Four years before I was *born*," Alex grinned. "Boy, you're *old*."

Thanks, kid. "Got ten years on a *rock*." JJ drove the streets with familiar-sounding names, looking for landmark buildings in the neighborhoods; for businesses that just weren't there anymore. He was sad to see the deterioration of Detroit and her suburbs, the city that once had the highest standard of living of any metro area in the world, but was now a dirty and shabby shell of her formerly muscular self.

"Hey, kid," Kurt Parkinson greeted JJ and Alex with a jovial smile when they entered the shop. "How's the Army treating you? Looks like they feed you well enough." Kurt was a large man tending to fat who only vaguely resembled his father. He had brown hair like Charlie with less gray, longer arms, and was taller: six-feet-four. Kurt was, unlike Charlie, one of the most amiable men JJ ever knew.

"Alex, this is my stepbrother Kurt Parkinson; Kurt, my friend Alex Savio."

"Any friend of JJ's is a friend of mine." Kurt motioned to two chairs in front of his desk in a cluttered office. Papers and folders covered the room-filling faux-wood metal desk and the credenza behind it, making it hard to figure out how *any* work got done. "Now, about that old Rebel?"

"Yeah." JJ cocked a thumb to Alex. "His *sister's* car."

Kurt nodded. "Otis looked at it."

"Otis? He's still here?" JJ remembered Otis as a large black man who seemed old *then*, who used to tell about driving trucks in Europe during WWII.

"*Can't* get rid of him," Kurt answered. "He manages the collector car side two or three days a week."

"So, what did Otis say?"

"It's a *classic*: the top-end, four-barrel V-8 with electronic fuel injection *and* less rust than cars twenty years younger. It belongs in a museum or somebody's collection, *not* on the road. A hundred bucks in parts *should* get it running: rotor, condenser, points, plugs, belts, injector kits. *Maybe* a coil; can't know without the rest. If we *can* get it running, it's worth a lot to the right buyer. I wasn't about to do the work without the owner's OK."

"You got the parts?" JJ knew the constant tussle of the auto parts trade: can't get *this*, got too many of *that*…

"Can *have* 'em quick enough."

JJ turned. "Alex: what do *you* think?"

The boy, surprised and proud at being asked, gazed back and forth between the men. "You can't hurt it if you *try* to fix it and you *can't*, right?"

"Probably not."

"Let's try, then."

Kurt stood up. "Let's go up to parts."

✱✱✱

"Ah, you were my *father's* pupils, yes," the dusky man smiled. He was the current *sensei* at the strip-mall *dojo* where they learned as teenagers. "We earned our brown belts together."

"*Hai*," Leigh answered. "May we join you for your drills?"

"We would be *honored* to have two of our black belts join us," the *sensei* bowed, waving his arm to the room full of under-18 boys. "In the back, please. Class, remember: *I* am teaching *up here*, our *guests* are here to *work*." He cleared his throat. "Yeah, they're *women, gakusei*—one has earned a *dan* in Korea: my *compliments*. But *you* are here for *karate*, not to *girl-watch*. *Hajime!* Get in *line*, boys! *ICHI! NE!* Fists *up*, there! *SAN…!*"

✱✱✱

"So, JJ," Kendra Ashton exclaimed, bussing JJ's cheek, "you don't *call*, you don't *write*. What've you been doing?" Kendra was a buxom and brassy blonde who was a worker bee when JJ worked there but was now the parts department manager.

"Keeping the world safe for women and kids. Kendra, meet my friend

Alex. You still married to that…?"

"Cop? No, he got killed a couple years ago. Got me a fireman now." She smiled at an entranced Alex. "And what's your story, Alex?"

"When I'm not in school I play video games, ma'am," Alex grinned.

"Oh, don't 'ma'am' *me*, child: call me Kendra like all my friends do." As Alex went on a tour with Kurt, Kendra pointedly asked, "who's the kid?"

"Friend's stepbrother. He got dumped at his mother's just before Christmas."

"Sounds familiar." She dropped her voice. "Special friend?"

"Extra special."

"About *time*, boy."

My own time, thanks.

Two hours later Otis revved up the Rebel's big 327 cubic inch V-8's celebration of Detroit's power-gone-by.

JJ and Alex were talking about lunch by the time Kurt gave Alex an envelope. "Here's our formal offer. Take it to your sister and *advise* her that she should take the money and get a *new* car; I'll get her a deal at one of my dealerships."

"Hey, Kurt," JJ asked as they got ready to leave, "know any good places to stay around here? I'm not going to tempt fate for three weeks out at Birch Lake."

"Sure: one *just* opened up."

* * *

"Flapjacks, Dad," Donna asked her father, Evan. Leigh liked the bespectacled engineer whose clipped speech, thinning hair and pleasant manner—when he was *sober*—put her in mind of a mild Dickensian schoolmaster.

"Sure," Evan declared, sitting at the kitchen island just before noon. Leigh had sometimes helped Donna with Evan when he fell off the wagon twice a year—marked by the anniversaries of the loss of an infant daughter and his wife.

"Evan," Leigh sighed, "how have you been doing, if you don't mind my asking. You still in AA…?"

"Oh, I'm a *regular* Friend of Bill W, trying to cut out at least one drunk a year. I've got a meeting this afternoon."

"Working?"

"Two years running I've eliminated my spring bender; this year, no *fall* bender either; I got my first *365-day* chip last month. But you've only really *beat* booze when you're dead."

"Donna's proud of you."

"I *am*," Donna smiled. "*One* day at a time. Dad."

"Frankly, one *hour* at a time," he sighed, looking out at the snow-covered pool just beyond the kitchen's French doors "I know Donna's *relieved*. I've put her through a lot."

"You've put *yourself* through a lot."

"Yes, I have. And I have to ask your *forgiveness* for what I put *you* through when *you* were helping Donna."

"Eighth Step?" He nodded. "Just *don't* make us *do it* anymore, Evan."

"I shall try. Donna, dear, how was your, um *not*-date last night? You just broke up with a guy, honey, and I don't want you to fall into your usual pattern…"

"*DAD*," Donna answered sharply. "My *usual pattern* is I spend as much time with Nick as I can after some *other* guy breaks my heart." She glared. "What's *wrong* with *that*?"

"Then why not spend it *all* with him," Leigh glared. "He's a *good* guy…"

"Because…" Donna started, then whispered, "he wants too much from me."

"Too much what? Affection and companionship? When you run to Nick after a break-up, isn't that *just* what you're after, and *just* what he gives you?"

Donna sighed, made a face. "Maybe. Ann said we should know what we want from *each other* before we…"

"Good advice. *Do* you?"

Donna made a face. "I *think* so." She patted Leigh's leg as the doorbell rang. Puzzled, Donna went to the door. Evan, a cautious and careful man, followed his daughter.

"Leigh," Donna called moments later, "*you* have a visitor."

***

"Anita sent me," Ann told the ample woman in her fifties with graying hair. "My friend's sister-in-law. I was *hoping*…" Half expecting a small-ish boutique, she and Jenna were surprised that Milady's Closet in Royal Oak was a large stand-alone building. They stood on a luxurious carpet, surrounded by elegant *real* Victorian furniture and multi-colored wicker mannequins dressed in a variety of outfits. A customer taller than Ann and another about her size disinterestedly browsed the racks.

"Oh, *you* must be *Ann*: I'm Anita's partner, Hillary Maxwell. *We've* been *expecting* you. Please, *come* this way. Coffee? Tea? Cocoa? We can send out for *anything*…" They were led to another room with overstuffed chairs, mirrors covering two walls, a changing room bigger than Ann's barracks room, and refreshments in a small alcove. "This is where we serve our *special* guests. Now, *how* may we *help* a size sixteen long?"

"At minimum, I'm looking for warmer clothes and a replacement for my body shaper," Ann explained, and for the next two hours and more she was measured, feted, primped and flattered. She was shown a long line bra and girdle pair that just didn't feel right, but she *did* like a lighter, longer body shaper. She loved a line of bras that didn't squeeze her, a basic black dress that fit better than Anita's, heavier jeans that fit *really* well, dress pants and a jacket that seemed to be made for her, and a couple of sweaters that Jenna liked.

Taking a break from dressing and undressing every few minutes, Jenna muttered, "Your breasts don't move, and it's *not* just your bra."

"They *do*, just not *much*. My job is *very* physical, so I work out. If *you* work out, you *may* stay firm, but it's really a genetic lottery. My mother was blessed with firm breasts: *Your* mom, sort of."

Jenna looked away. "But you're *gorgeous*."

"*You're* no slouch, either. Just eat right and exercise, stay away from drugs, and for God's sake don't get anything pierced but your ears." She started sampling pantyhose. She usually wore stockings because of her long inseam, and the first trials proved why.

"You don't *need* nylons," Jenna told her. "Your skin's natural."

"Not for shaping, but my uniform skirts *require* hose."

"Can you wear your uniform to the party? At dinner yesterday, JJ looked so…"

"He said it was the only appropriate attire he has that still fits. But…" *She wants to show off her big sister; why not?* "OK; I'll find some hose, and I need a uniform blouse that fits right. What did *you* have in mind for your party? That dress you wore yesterday was pretty."

"Yeah, but, it's not…"

Not for attracting boys and making girls jealous. "A *party* dress."

"Yeah. Mom likes dorky, stupid stuff that makes me look twelve."

"Let's see what we can do *here*."

***

Half-expecting either Ann or JJ, Leigh bounced into the living room from the kitchen and was stunned to see, instead, Sid Jackwell. He was a tall, slender man with a full head of fine, fair hair and delicate-looking features except for some *very* hard, *very* dark eyes. His long arms ended in overlarge hands that seemed to want to drag on the ground. He was one of those people who, once seen, cannot be forgotten.

"Leigh," Sid greeted her with a commandingly quiet voice. "Glad to see you're well."

"Sid. You're in the security business now?"

"Yes." He glanced at Donna. "I want to *personally* assure you that my association with the Newhouse organization has been over for years. At one time, Randy wanted *me* dead: he may still."

He was never like Randy's other goons. "You could have sent a letter for *that*, Sid. Tell me what I *need* to know."

He nodded slightly and smiled. "I always liked your spirit. On your wedding night, Dave Harriman, Joe Dryden and I were outside your motel room. We heard screaming and yelling just before you stormed out of the room wearing only a blouse. I stopped you from going over the rail while Joe and Dave went into the room."

"Got an *eyeful*, did you, Sid?" *Cop a feel, too?*

"I *liked* you too much to *look*, Leigh." He shifted on his feet uncomfortably. "I dashed into the room and grabbed the *first* pants I could find. *That* was the last time I saw Randy."

"That explains why I woke up in Randy's underwear." She glanced at Donna, who, with arms crossed, smiled wryly. "Go on."

"Randy's jaw was shattered; his arm was all twisted around in a way I didn't think possible. Joe was trying to get him calmed down; Dave was frantic, didn't know *what* to do."

Sounds right. Dave is a follower; Joe, a leader. "How did I get back home?" *If all* <u>three</u> *guys were in the room, who was outside with me? A woman I sort of knew…who?*

"Then Joe started yelling to get you back inside while he got instructions from Mr. Newhouse on the phone. I went out and grabbed at you again and you socked me a good one in the head. Dave *tried* for your legs; you kicked him in the cojones so hard he passed out. You didn't deserve what I *knew* was coming, so I managed to give you a little sleeper hold, took you to *your* place and handed you to your dad."

Leigh and Donna looked at each other, surprised. "Thanks for that." *Why didn't Dad…but would he know Sid?*

"You're welcome. When Randy left the hospital, Joe swore he would get you back or kill you. *We* fought: he broke my collarbone; I broke *his* nose, his left thumb and his right foot." He smiled. "My arm's never been quite the same since." He sighed deeply, a sad sound. "Joe's gotten uglier, and higher in the organization."

"That's what Ben said."

He nodded. "Ladies; sir; I must take my leave of you. I wanted you to personally assure you that you have nothing to fear from *me* or mine." He handed each of them a business card that read *S. Jackwell; Organizational Readiness*, with a toll-free phone number. "If you need anything, please don't hesitate to call."

"Ann Mueller is in town, you know."

"Yes; so is John Elrath. The Newhouse organization knows as well; but *I'm* not sure just *how* or *why,* except that Joe has a *very* old score to settle with *him.*"

***

When a younger clerk appeared, Ann cocked her head towards Jenna. "How about a party dress for my sister? Not-*quite*-age-appropriate?"

The clerk sized up Jenna at a glance. "Size 6 in a women's; 30C or 32B?"

"Um, yeah."

"Red-to-brown or green?"

"Red; *not* green."

"Let's see."

It only took three tries to find a rust-red satin side-split dress with a tight bodice that showed *just* a hint of shaped cleavage, a deep-vee support bra, and a full slip to match. Jenna beamed until she looked at the price tag. "Oh, *no.* This is…"

"Consider it a Christmas present," Ann smiled. When they went to check out an hour later—round collared blouses, stockings and a dozen other bags and boxes in hand—the bill was about a third of what Ann expected. "Family pricing," was scrawled on the top of the ticket.

"If *you* don't mind, Jenna," Ann asked when they got in the car, "I need to make another stop just down the street here. Old friend of mine; old employer and instructor, if he's still *there*…"

***

When they returned to the condo, Barbara glared sternly at Jenna, then at Ann, as Jenna modeled her new dress. "Turn around," she ordered. Jenna became more stressed by the moment.

Try to do a favor and…

Suddenly Barbara had Jenna gathered in her arms, blubbering about her baby growing up. "It's *perfect* on her," she managed. "Where did you *find* it?"

"We went to JJ's sister-in-law's store for *my* needs, *but,* while we were *there*…"

"I'd have *never* thought of *that.* Wait until—no, we'll keep it here. Your father doesn't need to see it. If *he* just…"

"Barbara, we'll just keep it *our* secret. I've never met Jenna's father, but…"

"Pray you never *have* to. We'll talk about *him* later. Are you free for lunch tomorrow? I have a ladies' association meeting, and I'd *love* for you to come. Just friends—professional women."

Ann smiled, inwardly groaning at the prospect of a hen party, though

214

"professional women" didn't sound *that* bad.

JJ and Alex soon arrived and Alex gave his big sister the envelope with great pride and ceremony. *Oh. My. God.* She read it *once*, then a *second* time, then a *third* just to be sure. "John, this is …." She handed him the offer, shaking her head.

He whistled. "Well, Kurt *says* it's rare. They didn't make that many of 'em—*he'd* never *seen* one—and the body's in great shape."

"But *ten thousand dollars*?"

Barbara looked, blinked hard and muttered something about "boys and their toys."

Maybe he's doing a favor for his little brother's friend. "He's in touch with serious collectors."

"*Woah*; that's more than *I* paid for it," Howard told her. "It's up to *you*, honey. I gave *you* the title: it's *yours* to do with as you please."

"Here," Ann handed JJ a heavy bag, "*late* Christmas present."

JJ looked in the bag at two *very* large books. "*Oh*," he grinned widely, "Bowditch's *American Practical Navigator*; wow!"

"I got them from my old dive instructor; little surprised he's still *there*." She pecked his cheek. "I'll make a *real* sailor out of you yet."

***

"Looks different from this angle."

"*Everything* does, babe."

They drove into the new Brookfield Institutions that afternoon. The new gated security off Woodward—replacing the little guard shack off Lone Pine that had been manned only on nights and weekends—took some getting used to, but the institution had to change with the times. New roads confused him slightly, and Moby Pool—more accurately, Moby *Concrete Pond,* where he walked with Clare—was gone.

But other landmarks were unchanged. He pointed to a trough of rocks running down a hill. "There's the Slide. It's a flowing stream from spring to fall, but in winter it's just glare ice. Looks like they've put the kibosh on *that*, though."

"On *what*?"

"Some people banged themselves up going down it when I was here so they stretched a fence across it. Over there's the Chinese Dog Ramp. A quarter mile long, five landings and a hundred-foot rise. In cross-country, we had to go up that thing three times a month."

"Lotta work."

"Thought I'd die."

"Why do you call it the Chinese Dog Ramp?"

"That sculpture up on top of the slope: somebody thought it looked like a Chinese dog. It *does* from *here*, but it's really a frog. Here's the Art Institute. I saw *Fritz the Cat* there."

"That X-rated cartoon?"

"Yeah. I went with…who? Can't remember now." They drove down a long, steep and narrow hill that cut over to Faculty Row, rolling to a stop at the end of the row of connected houses. "This is their new place. They were six doors down until Clare moved out. Remember: they know *of* you, not *about* you." He led her up a few concrete steps, then kicked the toe of each shoe twice on the last step before he knocked on the door. "There was a time when I didn't knock."

The face that greeted them at the door was a bespectacled older gentleman in a flannel shirt and loose-knit sweater. Dave DeHaven greeted him quietly, shook his hand with formal ceremony, spoke in clipped cadences. "JJ, how are you? Come on in. Claudia: pleased to meet you."

Ann followed JJ into a tiny, overheated entry hall that split four ways: to the small kitchen, to the back door ten feet away, to a narrow staircase upstairs, and to the living room. There sat a large woman with florid skin and dark, wiry hair, dressed in a floral kaftan, beaming brightly at JJ as he kissed her cheek, and extending her hand to Ann.

"You're Claudia," Marie DeHaven smiled. "I'm *so* pleased to meet you."

"Glad to meet you," Ann smiled sincerely. JJ led Ann to a love seat against the outside wall in front of a bay window. He felt at ease since the layout of their new, smaller place wasn't much different from the one where he'd spent so much time as a boy. The furniture hadn't changed—small, sturdy, but worn with age—and it *felt* like home.

"I have a date to see Karen Saturday," JJ began.

"Oh, *good*," Marie answered. "I know she's eager to see you. Claudia, JJ said you're from around here, too."

"Bloomfield Hills born and raised," Ann smiled. "Over by Round Lake." *I should say "I go by Ann" but…*

Conversation floated for several minutes while Ann looked around the room. There were pictures of Dave and Marie, several of two young women—including wedding pictures—she presumed were Karen and Clare. Both had JJ in a dress uniform off to the side. "Had to drag him *that* close," Marie sighed.

"I've *always* had to drag him into pictures," she answered absently. "And he's known my family since we were in diapers."

"Really," Dave grinned. "That long?"

"Our parents were old friends," JJ added. "Since before the war."

"Oh," Marie smiled. "I see."

Probably more than you're letting on. "Just one of them things.

Thousand-to-one coincidence that we'd meet in Key West." JJ shrugged. "But it happened."

"I see. Promise rings, too?"

"Yes," Ann held out her hand. "I have *his* father's ring; he has *my* father's ring. Christmas Eve."

"How romantic," Dave grinned. "Do you plan on getting married while you're in the service?"

"Bad timing, as *you* know," JJ sighed.

"Yep," Dave nodded.

Marie agreed. "Hasn't changed any?"

"It has *not*." JJ explained: "Marie was an Army nurse; Dave was a Navy landing craft coxswain. They met in England during the war. *Neither* service was happy about them getting married."

"Oh, *you* were in the Navy?" Ann brightened. "Anchors aweigh!"

Dave smiled. "I haven't even *thought* of that in forty years."

"I *could have* resigned," Marie sighed. "but Dave was in for the duration and I wanted to serve. I stayed in England while he drove around Europe. Would you like a drink of something? Father, an old-fashioned, please. Beer, JJ? Claudia?"

"Fine, for both of us." Ann nodded. "I don't want to delay your dinner."

"Oh, no," Marie answered, "we usually just go up to the faculty lounge."

"Never *been* there," JJ frowned truthfully. The valedictorians were invited for their last meal in the fabled Brookfield Faculty Lounge before commencement, but with a 3.14 GPA, JJ was *not* among them. Of 125 young men in the Class of '73 only three were below a 3.0 GPA.

"Well, you can come with," Dave announced, returning with bottles of beer. "We bring guests once in a while."

"As long as it doesn't cost *you* anything," JJ grinned. "I don't want to put you out."

"Don't worry about it," Dave replied, with an air of finality. Ann suddenly realized where JJ's faultless generosity came from, and that the DeHavens *would* probably be buying *their* meals. But JJ remained silent, nodding politely.

JJ smiled at Marie. "How *is* Clare these days? I've *tried* to call her; I just get a recording. I haven't heard from her in two years."

"Oh," Marie lamented, "I *told* her to write to you. Surprised the recording still works."

Dave seemed to brace himself. "She's in a hospice in Redford."

"Uterine cancer, dear," Marie sighed.

Karen said it nearly killed Marie…and it DOES run in families. "Oh." JJ closed his eyes tightly. Ann reached for his hand; he squeezed…*hard*.

"What's her prognosis, Marie?" Ann's voice was barely a whisper.

"*Better*," Marie murmured. "She's *hopeful*. We saw her yesterday."

"More hopeful than she's *been*," Dave agreed.

"I'll go out there," JJ rasped. "Want to come with?"

"*No*, dear," Marie smiled with a loving look. "*You* need to see her alone." Then to Ann, "if *Claudia* doesn't mind."

Ann smiled. "I've heard enough about her *not* to be frightened. Besides," she patted JJ's knee, "he can't afford the gas to get back to Florida without me." JJ grinned bitterly, and squeezed harder.

"So, how's *your* mother, JJ," Marie asked. "Is she still out on the lake?"

"She's OK. Don't *ask* about her husband."

"No, we won't." Marie glanced at Dave, who, for the first time since JJ knew him, looked like he wanted to say something he was holding back. "*Will* we, Father?"

"Marie, I *have* to. He has a *right* to know." They glared at each other, silently communicating the way that old and intimate friends do.

"What good would it do *now*," Marie murmured.

"It is the *truth*, Mother. *His* truth." Dave had a stern aspect to his eyes that JJ had rarely seen. "The first semester you were here, *John…*"

That name was surprising because Dave called him *JJ* from the instant they met. When he was caught sneaking in after curfew after a late night out, Dave naturally called him by the more formal *John*—as parents will do to get their charge's undivided attention.

"…your *stepfather* met with the dean and I about the Thanksgiving holiday." Dave looked distinctly uncomfortable; Marie gazed out the window. "He said 'how much to keep him *here*?' And Dean Crossley asked '*why* would we need to do that?' Your stepfather said, 'name your price.'"

THAT'S what Uncle Andy got so mad about at Lois's wedding: he was trying to get rid of me on THEM.

"Archie Crossley was a reasonable and generous man, and the school always tries to accommodate student situations in every way, but you lived only a stone's throw away. Archie said 'Nothing at all:' you weren't the *only* one as you know. Then your stepfather said 'how about Christmas?' We were *stunned*. Archie told him that the school only kept students who lived on another continent over the long holidays—and *they* go to friend's homes. Your stepfather pulled out a wad of cash and started laying hundred-dollar bills on the table."

Dave stopped, as if the memory was painful. "I just said you could stay with us. He put his money back in his pocket and left without another word. I never saw him again until your graduation, though he *did* have the *courtesy* to *call* to make sure *someone* would take you in for *every* holiday.

And, ah, when he asked about the summer break, I merely said that *that* was impossible because the Lions used the school for spring practice."

I wish I felt more about this than I do. Not at all surprised about Charlie. But, Clare... JJ sighed, "I thought it was *something* like that, Dave. But just knowing…" he shrugged, "but it changes nothing. Thanks for telling me." He smiled warmly. "I fell in love with your family that first Christmas. I love you all still."

"And we love *you*, JJ," Marie mumbled absently. "Of all the boys and girls we've watched grow into men and women in these institutions for thirty-eight years, *you* were the one we grew the fondest of."

"Why else would you have put up with your Friday's Child?"

Dave chuckled, Marie laughed, smiled sincerely. "Claudia, if you *ever* find yourself angry at him for just being himself, remember *we* helped make our *Friday's Child* that way."

"And I thank *you* for keeping him safe." Ann got up and bussed Dave on the cheek. "Now, please, *before* you protest, there's a steakhouse at Lahser and Maple—where that pancake house was—that I've wanted to try. Please, as *my* guest, come with us. And, please, call me *Ann*."

The DeHaven's were gracious during the delightful meal. Though outwardly congenial, there was a part of JJ that was crushed, heartbroken, and distraught over Clare.

And he felt like a shit-heel for it because he had *finally* found his Cloud.

Friday

Lazy morning…
Mother and son watched a gentle snowfall through the big picture window in the family room, sipping coffee while Ann got ready for her luncheon. Before he got up, Ann had filched his keys and got fresh-from-the-oven cinnamon bread. He was planning a quiet day catching up with homework and laundry…and being there for whatever creation his mother prepared. *If it's meatloaf with chocolate cereal inside, I'll move out tomorrow.*

Stella cocked her head and frowned slightly, listening to Charlie clomping into the kitchen, clearing his throat, coughing. He stomped heavily into the family room, poured coffee, added a slug of something brown from a decanter and sat at the big round table, staring at JJ. "Johnny-cake," he slurred, drooling a little, "*this* place is sold. We're moving at the end of January."

Here it comes. Just hope it all falls on me.
Stella looked startled. "Charlie, *please* don't…"

"*I'm* talking, Stella," he growled. "I paid for this asshole to go to one of the best prep schools in the country, and he goes off and wastes it by sucking up more of *my* tax dollars in the Army, then has the *gall* to *not* even *be here* for *dinner*!"

"They *said*," Stella began…

Charlie cut her off with a snarl, his voice rising in volume. "I've paid *your* way since your balls dropped, you little pissant. Now, you *freeloader*, I want your shit *out* of here before you *crawl* back to the Army or it *all* goes out. And I want that *WHORE* of yours *out of MY HOUSE TODAY!* DO YOU HEAR ME?"

As he spat out the last words, Stella shot him an evil glance. *"CHARLIE!"*

That's it. He had been waiting for Bad Charlie since his mother said he could stay there…then he heard Ann coming down the stairs. *Get done before Cloud hears it.* He glanced at Stella with the grim determination of a fighter about to hit above his weight. *This is gonna hurt both of us, Ma.*

Once before this morning—JJ was not quite sixteen and had just come home from Wolverine—there was a moment when Charlie looked into JJ's eyes and saw that *one part* of him that he could not break, bend, or dictate to…and he fell nearly silent. *This* morning, Charlie *once again* saw *that one part—and he fell silent once again.*

"Charlie," JJ managed, "I *appreciate* everything you've done for my family. And I *know* you'll take care of my mother. I'll take from this house that which is *mine*, and that Ma wants to *give* me."

He glanced at Ann as she appeared from the kitchen. "Ann, bag and baggage: we're *leaving*."

"Bag and baggage, aye," she answered, turning on her heel.

JJ smiled malevolently; his voice quiet. "And if you *ever* call anyone *I* *know* a filthy name like *that* again, I shall *rip* off your head and *shit* down your neck. Do *you* hear *me*?"

He followed Ann up the back stairs, unconcerned about a response. "Make it quick. If he argues with you, ignore him. If he interferes, deck him." He looked deep into her eyes. "This needed to happen, honey. I'm just sorry that Ma…"

She put her hand over his mouth. *"Shh.* Let's just *shove off."* Downstairs they heard loud arguing before Charlie roared *"BULLSHIT,"* slamming a door behind him. Moments later, his Cadillac skidded out of the garage and down the driveway, banged into the Fury, and sped away.

Silence filled the old house. JJ looked out the back window at the Fury. *Right rear taillight torn off, but the bumper's still on. Jerkball.*

He met Ann, handing her his keys. "Load yours up and get the car started. I'll be out directly."

But baggage was easy; "stuff" was *not*. He took a long look around his room, wanting to salvage a few trinkets—worthless to anyone else—to remind him of what had once been a home. There were treasured books—including those bequeathed to him by Mike's grandfather—and pictures of his family in a cigar box. There was a stereo—but *Charlie* bought that. There was a Smith-Corona typewriter Stella gave him for his 15th birthday—battered but working. *Need* it he did not—he had replaced it long ago—but *want* it he did, because it was *his*. There was a wedge of pink quartz the size of a football that a grandfather had found; a large bronze plaque of Abraham Lincoln that his father had given him; a hardwood paperweight he'd made for his dad; his Order of the Arrow certificate and other Boy Scout memorabilia. He had no idea *where* he'd keep everything, but he stuffed it all into his big kit bags to save it from Charlie's malevolent paws.

He lugged his bags down and out to the car. "A little longer, honey, 'cause I *ain't* coming back."

Stella stood at the big picture window looking out on the lake when they returned. "He *knows* he's gone too far," she sniffed. "That's what he *always* does when he goes too far: he just leaves." She looked at him, teary-eyed. "He'll apologize later, but for *now*…" She knitted her brows as she moved around the room, gazing at pictures. "Here," she handed him a chased-silver-framed photo of her parents—his Nana Burgess and the grandfather he never knew. "And take *these*," she handed him a silver creamer and sugar bowl on an engraved tray. "They were an anniversary gift to Mom and Pop." She took down two of his grandmother's paintings of Round Lake.

From the dining room, Stella handed Ann a box of etched crystal plates and stemware—a wedding present from Stella's parents. She followed that with a 12-place coin-sterling flatware set engraved with an "E" in an oak chest. This was followed by an armload of photo albums that she gave JJ. Finally, she scooped six decks of cards out of a family room cabinet drawer. "When in doubt, lead with a queen, Johnny."

Lead with strength, but not too much. "Ruff the trump first, Ma." He took the painting that had always been in *his* room—Nana Burgess's faithful copy of Fredric Remington's *The Emigrants*—down from the family room wall. "If he objects, he can come and get it."

Ann, after hauling the last of the cargo to the car, came back in the family room just as JJ was saying "take care, Ma. Don't let him…"

"Don't worry about *me*, dear," Stella answered with a grin. "He won't hurt *me*."

"Stella, send anything else to my place." Ann gave Stella a slip of paper with the address. "*Please*," she hugged her, "*please* stay safe. Call Dad anytime."

She held Ann at arm's length. "Take care of yourselves. I *guarantee* you Charlie will apologize even if I have to *persuade* him."

They drove away, stopping the Fury at the intersection of Long Lake Road and Middle Belt, JJ gripping the steering wheel so hard his hands hurt. "Any idea where the post office is out here?"

"Negative."

"I *think* I remember." He drove around the lake, even though just doubling back would have been half as far. He quickly filled out the top of a change-of-address card but balked at the bottom. "Can I…if I knew *what* it was, I'd…will *you*…?"

She filled in her Southfield address as "new."

* * *

"A mean drunk in a three-piece suit is still just a mean drunk," Howard shrugged, "and, a bully's a bully." They were in the living room in JJ's new home-of-the-moment, with all his worldly goods (save those in Florida) still in the Fury. Ann and Barbara had gone to their luncheon.

"*Why* do I let him do it, Howard? Really? Why?"

The older man grinned. "You don't *allow* it: he does it on *purpose*. It's what bullies do. It's how *he* gets control—by making you *lose* yours. But it sounds like *you didn't*. When I met Charlie on Sunday, I thought him outgoing, convivial. Monday, well, *felt* different."

"He was sizing you up. He doesn't see eye-to-eye with anyone but himself. Even his *sons* don't like him. *I* get along with *them*, but…"

"Maybe he's jealous of your relationship with them."

"*There's* a thought." *And Julia…*

"He didn't treat you well when you were younger, either?"

"He didn't want me around, so he farmed me out and took Ma all over the world as an excuse. I got a 'roomer and boarder' speech from him about every other week when I lived there, told me I wasn't *producing* to *his* requirements."

"Producing *what*?"

"Grades; book reports; work, even. Every time I thought I was getting in his good graces, he started yelling about something else. I was at Brookfield seven miles away because he just didn't want me around. For all the pretense of us living in *that* neighborhood when Dad died—*before* Charlie—we *had* to have been broke that first winter. More than once I heard Mom on the phone borrowing money so we could eat that first few weeks. She *said* it was between bank stops, but…"

"She called us—me—sometimes."

"Oh. Then…*something* happened just before Christmas, and…all that stopped. Maybe *poverty* drove *her* to Charlie. Wish I understood *her* better; wish she understood *me* better."

Howard cleared his throat theatrically. "If I *might*, Johnny: your mother barely *knows* you, and *you* don't really know *her*. Add it up: between the time you left for Wolverine and the time you enlisted, you saw each other a total of *maybe* six months, and *you* were working much of it. And…fifteen to eighteen is a pretty important block of time in a guy's life. And since you enlisted…maybe a *month* out of every *year*?"

"That's…*true*. Never thought of it that way."

"I've known your mother since 1935, and I can tell you that she's a *lot* harder to *get* than a lot of people. She's…*very* complicated."

"Huh." It struck him that he *had* to say something to Howard, even if incongruous now. "I was *so* happy to see Claudia that afternoon. I probably ruined her dress."

"The dress survived. She's always been important to you, son."

Son? "I *want* to marry your daughter, Dr. Mueller, but let's not get ahead of ourselves."

Howard grinned. "Term of endearment, John." He glanced at a clock. "Well, let's get that loot out of your car. Stow it here with Ann's."

"I appreciate it. I should get my light fixed, too." *Take it up NOW.* "Ah, sir: Ann and I…"

"Are *adults*. John: I can't think of either of you in any other way."

***

"Never been here before," Howard declared as the Fury pulled up to the Northwestern Inn and Suites, a *big* deluxe business center hotel just off Northwestern Highway a few miles up Telegraph Road from the Mueller condo.

"Brand new," JJ grunted, getting out. Once inside, he glanced briefly at the directory—it boasted an indoor pool and a restaurant/bar—and registered for a double queen/kitchenette suite—complete with separate sitting room with a gas fireplace—that included breakfast and a happy-hour/appetizer buffet in an exquisite atrium in the core of the hotel.

"Huh: New Year's Gala," Howard muttered, reading the big poster in the lobby. "Barb keeps *wanting* a honeymoon…"

"Think *that'll* fill the bill," JJ smirked. "A hotel three miles from home with her teenagers in the next rooms? You *romantic* devil, you…"

Howard sniffed, "*I'll* manage *my* wife: *you* manage…Oh, *don't* you laugh, Johnny." He sighed. "*Our* lives are run by *un*manageable women: she'd *like* it, nonetheless." Howard smiled at the clerk. "Is your three-bedroom penthouse available New Year's?"

JJ took a picture of Tiger Stadium at Michigan and Trumbull off the suite's wall and hung the Remington copy in its place.

Wherever that painting is will be home.

***

"Barbara, can you use this crystal?" JJ held the box open after the ladies had returned. "You're not *supposed* to store it like this…"

"Something my mother might have had." She held an etched glass goblet in the light.

"I can't use it in the barracks."

"I suppose not. I'll find a place for it." Barbara wiped away a tear quickly. "Never had the chance to get my mom's. She passed when I was stationed in Germany; my sisters-in-law took it all."

JJ opened the silver chest. "Any takers? Would look funny next to my mess kit."

"Engraved with an *E*: Edwards: my maiden name." Barbara bussed JJ's temple gently. "We could be kin."

Howard wrapped his arms around Barbara. "The kids should be home soon, and *we* have to think about supper."

"Hotel's got a restaurant," JJ shrugged. "Come on with *us*."

After a leisurely and pleasant dinner, the kids swam in the pool while the grownups investigated some of Stella's albums, with their decades-old imagery of Howard and the elder Claudia, Stella and JJ's dad Jake.

"Howard," JJ mused, downing a third shot of schnapps, "you ever been on a firing squad?"

"For a funeral? No. You?"

"Yup. I think I am again."

One of the albums, though, was *Charlie's*, and in it was a copy of a memo from something called NP Management, dated 1967:

Re: Future Plans
   Met woman with convenient name and daughter at Albany convention. Approached; interested. More later.

***

"Yeah, babe…c'mon…here's the…" he collapsed onto the "…bed." She pulled his sweat pants down.

"Eddie," he mumbled, "Eddie…"

"I'm *not* him, babe, *or* her. A little *help* with the sweatshirt, babe…thanks, but…no, the *briefs* can…OK, take 'em off, too. I'll…" He started to shiver as she got ready. "Cold, babe? I'll warm you up."

"Eddie," he sobbed, *"poor Eddie!"*

She held him in bed until he was quiet.

So…who's Eddie?

Saturday

Where…what? Bathtub again? Eddie's in it? Huh?

He woke up hard, dimly wondering how he got in bed. He remembered seeing part of *The Right Stuff*, but it was hazy. His sweats were off and…*where's Ann?*

He found her in the kitchenette, reading. "Morning, Johnny. How did you sleep?"

He sat, cold and dazed. "Morning, Cloud: OK. You manhandled me into bed?"

"*Woman*-handled, thank you. *You* passed out drunk."

Schnapps: love the stuff too much. "First time in a *long* time." They held hands on the table, sipping coffee. "Gonna pay for it for a few days." He cleared his throat. "You're *sure* you don't want me along today?"

Pay for it…how? "Dad says she only knows *him* about every third visit. What did the DeHaven's mean by Friday's Child?"

"I used to show up at their place on Friday nights." He looked out into the atrium, where breakfast was being served. "Lunch with Karen; meeting Leigh, too…this morning."

"Just make sure you're ready for the party tonight."

"*Not* a problem." He sighed. "Karen and I were out for drinks once and I *tried* to make a pass at her. She told me: 'I love you as a friend, John, but that's all. Sorry.' Nicest push-off *I* ever got. Kissed me goodnight, too."

"A memory to share." She paused. "Who's Eddie?"

"Wolverine roommate. Why?"

"You were crying about him last night. 'Poor Eddie' you said over and over again."

"You sure you want to know?"

She inhaled deeply. "Uh-huh."

"He was a skinny little guy, glasses and all. One night two guys sat on me while four guys sodomized him." He blinked. "Anything else?"

OH… "What *you* want to tell me."

"I told the authorities what happened, and their friends *tried* to get me to change my story for the rest of sophomore year. I didn't. Now I get nightmares…*sometimes*."

You were right, Sandy; unspeakable.

***

"Adam Block, Mr. Elrath: I work for the Dietz firm." They shook hands, smiled politely. Leigh and JJ had been in their booth at the Ram's Horn family restaurant just long enough to get coffee before a solid, bald man slid silently into the seat next to Leigh.

You move like guys who kill in the dark, pal. "What do you *do* for the

Dietz firm?"

"Diverse services."

Leigh smiled, "JJ: I told you I busted Jay Pardon in Korea. He called you 'the toughest bastard I ever knew.' Why would *he* say *that*?"

"You *really* want to know?" She nodded, slowly; Adam was impassive. "He and his buddy Herman Jimenez held my roommate down while four other guys cornholed him. I ratted out those guys and *the four* left, but Jay and Herman became my roommates. I didn't sleep more than four hours at a stretch until I got home because I wouldn't take it all back."

She smiled wanly. "Pardon shanked a guard in the federal prison at Marion last year. He'll get the needle."

I should feel SOMETHING. "Ain't Karma a *bitch.*"

"It *is.*"

Adam gave a slight smile. "Sir; there are plots afoot, plots with some very bad people. Herman Jimenez *may* be one of those people."

He didn't flinch when I... "You *know* Wolverine?"

Adam smiled, the kind of smile that could reassure or frighten, depending on the eyes: *his* were warmly bright. "I know Wolverine Military Academy *was once* a good accredited private high school that was foundering in the late '50s until a new owner bailed them out. From what we can *tell...*"

"Who's *we*?"

"My organization. We were asked to investigate Wolverine by the Dietz firm. To continue, their marketing and business model changed. They kept the magazine ads your family probably saw, but they started placing brochures in every police station, court lobby, and juvenile counseling center in the Western world. 'Parents/guardians of at-risk young men,' the tagline read, and added 'ask about our Second Century Fund.' It appears that families with money can send their little monsters to Wolverine to save them from...justice. Our guess is that about one in five boys at Wolverine when *you* were there were 'at-risk young men.' Jimenez was outmaneuvering the Florida authorities who wanted to ask him about some gang-related Liberty City murders. Pardon was at Wolverine instead of spending six years at a reform school for burglary, assault and a few other things. Their keepers paid into the Second Century Fund."

"Yeah: Jay was a Second Century kid. Didn't know if Herman was, though. Any idea how *much* they paid?"

"Average seems to be three times the annual tuition."

"Who's Wolverine's owner?"

"We haven't found the cheese at the end of *that* maze yet, sir."

"You can call me JJ."

Adam frowned enigmatically. "Wolverine has become a hobby for my organization, Mr. Elrath. Knowing what *you* endured in that place—we have some witness accounts—*we'll* just call *you* 'sir.'"

Somebody gives two shits about that place? "Adam: thank you for the information. Now, can you please excuse us?" Adam stood and departed as quietly as he came. "So, Green-Eyes: What are *you* doing New Year's?"

He can shift gears like that? That must have been what's preserved his sanity. "Something with Donna, probably: *she* thinks you're *cute*. What are *you* offering, Blue-Eyes? Not making out in your *room*, not with *Ann* there..." *Mike gets <u>that</u>, but Ann...*

"No, but our hotel has a soiree; I can get you a *room*..."

"*Donna* knows that place: I'll let you know. But, um, I need a favor tomorrow, from *both* of you, while you're *there*..."

***

The well-kept grounds around the weathered Kirkbride Plan brick pile that was the main Pontiac State Hospital building were covered in a sheet of untouched white snow, marked here and there with stands of birch trees gleaming in the brilliant, cold sun. Walkways, driveways, and parking lots were well-shoveled and salted. Even the benches were cleared, for many of the inmates for Eastern Michigan's premier mental hospital were allowed out on the grounds from time to time. Built in 1878, it was one of nearly three-score such facilities in the US—a design intended to facilitate the recovery of mental patients.

The corridors were wide and long, the ceilings high and vaulted, and smelled of wax and old paint. Ann tried to recall the last time she saw her mother. "Was I here before?"

"No," Howard answered. "*She's* only been here a couple of years."

They walked for what seemed like miles before they reached Claudia's room. She was loosely strapped in an armchair, gazing out the window at the building's other wing on the other side of a ditch.

"Claudia," Howard murmured, so as not to startle her: Claudia didn't acknowledge him. "Claudia, it's Howard. Claudia Ann is here."

He touched her shoulder ever-so-lightly; she gave a start as if she'd been shocked, whipped her head around and grimaced at Howard before she noticed Ann. "Hi, Mom."

Claudia stared at Ann for many moments, then glanced up at Howard. "Scram. We'll call for you." She began to tremble all over, slightly. "Turn my chair, will you?"

Ann rolled the chair around away from the window. Claudia gazed at her as if she were seeing a newborn child, blinking and tearing. Claudia's hair was snow-white; the skin on her face sagged; her eyes clouded.

"How are *you*, Mom?" Ann wiped a tear away from her mother's face.

Claudia made an odd sound that could have been a chuckle. "As well as can be expected." She looked away, then back at Ann. "What day is it? What date?"

"Saturday the 28th of December, 1985."

A mist seemed to fall over Claudia's face before she made the sound again. "The last date *I* remember clearly was in the spring. Howard came with George." She looked away again. "It's days like *this* that are the worst. I can remember things but I know I'll lose them again." She regarded Ann for a long time. "You still in the Navy?"

"Yeah, Mom."

"And you're wearing a ring."

There's still something in there. "Yes. Johnny Elrath and I made a promise to each other."

"Johnny…"

"Elrath, Mom. He's my best friend."

Claudia started tearing again. "I always liked Johnny. You were too young, and he was too…" She faded.

"We're older now, Mom."

"There was a time when the four of us…" Claudia paused, looked around, and back at Ann. "Ask your father about Stella and Jake. We loved them so."

"I will Mom."

"You should…" Claudia's eyes glazed over, and her trembling returned but passed. "Just a few more minutes, dear." Claudia reached for Ann's hands with her cold and frail ones. "Your father blames himself for this." She looked around the room. "But this is just…bad…luck." She drew Ann closer. "Your father's a good man," she managed with a visible effort. "OK?"

"OK, Mom."

"OK, honey. Send your father in before I lose it. And Claudia?"

"Yeah, Mom?"

"Don't *ever* come back. *Please*."

***

"How long has it been? Eight, ten years?" Karen and JJ exchanged quick kisses before sitting in a booth with a digeridoo on the wall. The restaurant in Troy was a mock Down-Under saloon-eatery chain. While he found chains to be creepily similar in decor, he preferred them because the menu was always similar no matter where he went.

"Clare's wedding in '79, so *six*. How *is* that husband of yours, anyway? Two kids, too."

"*Three* babies," she corrected. "Jim's fine, says hi." She fingered his

228

ring after they ordered. "So, what's *this* about? Are wedding bells to ring soon? Do I have to find a dress in a hurry?"

"Claudia. It's a promise ring." When he first met her, she was a wispy size 6, but *that* was fourteen years and three kids before.

"*Your* Claudia? You *found* her?" She swept back her light brown hair with a practiced gesture, smoothing her skirt at the same time.

"We found each other. She's in the Navy; goes by Ann now."

"I'm *so* happy for you. You're living in a little grass shack on the beach?"

"Ah, no. We're *not* sharing quarters…"

"Why not?"

"Well, we, ah…"

"You're *chaste*? Oh, *sweetie*, the way *you* talked about *her*…"

"We *have* slept in the same bed, made out, but sex? Our separation—inevitable—would hurt too much if we went that far." *Change the subject.* "So, how *is* Clare? Your folks seem hopeful."

"She'll *never* be the same."

"I asked her to come with me in '82, but you guys wouldn't approve."

She smiled while filling her chest with air: Karen had a certain look that was exotic, erotic and ironic all at once. "She *believed* that, but Mom and Dad *prayed* for you two to get together. Why do you think I *called* you? *You* were the only person who could—or *would*—give her what she needed then."

"What *she needed*?"

"Grown-up-and-sweaty *passion*, sweetie."

What? "*You knew* we'd…"

"*We* were desperate to get her back. *You* were what she needed."

"You *set us up*?"

"Didn't take much, did it?" She winked. "John, you *loved* her without restraint. She loved *you*, but her heart was torn between *you* and *us*. Tina's death changed all that; I don't think she cared much about *what* we thought anymore. But only *you* could pull her out of her pit." She patted his hand. "Can't thank you enough for that."

"Pit?"

"Depression. She's been treated for it since junior high. You don't know *all* our family secrets."

"Why does it suddenly start to feel like rape?"

"For a *week*? With Mom calling every day? Besides, *she* had to seduce *you*."

He squinted. "You *knew* that?"

"Not many secrets between *these* sisters, sweetie."

"Not even that pass I made on *you*?"

She smiled. "She knows *we* went out while she was at school. She didn't ask about what *happened*." She blinked. "Brother/lover-I-never-had, you hold a unique place in my family. We *all* love you; if you'd been around in that summer of '78 *I'd* have been tussling with *Clare* over *you*. And our *thing* in '74? I used to wonder…" She smiled; her secret smile meant only for him. "A *unique* place, sweetie."

I guess.

***

"So: who *are* you and *what* are your intentions with *my* baby sister?" Dr. George Mueller, MD, was bigger than his father and had lighter hair, but was still not a large man.

"*Almost* convincing, George," JJ smiled, shaking his hand. "Haven't seen you since, what, '67?" JJ hadn't seen *his* whole family—Elrath's *and* Parkinson's—together in the same place since Lois's wedding in 1970, and *that* didn't end well, but *this* family gathering seemed…tame.

"Sounds right. So, Brenda's up in Midland? I should call her. Claudia tells me you jump out of perfectly good airplanes." Here there were Mueller's and Savio's, Cresto's (George's wife Holly's parents) and Bell's (Jim's wife Carol's mother and brother) smiling and laughing together as if they wanted to be in the same place at the same time, and *no one* was waiting for an explosion of temper.

"Once in a while. *Landing* in an Air Force plane is a *lot* riskier than jumping out of one."

"I *should* resent that, but I don't fly."

"Hard to insult you, then. I hear you're a doctor of some kind."

"Sports medicine. Part orthopedics, part physical medicine."

"Huh. I see both regularly. I hurt myself a few years back."

"I *thought* you walked funny."

"They say I don't pronate."

"That'd do it. What happened?"

JJ told about his accident. "Bothers me more as I age."

"It *would*. Military doctors are primarily interested in your duty effectiveness, *not* your long-term health. I won't talk shop, but I'll have a look at you. My office is in Livonia: Call and I'll wedge you in."

Been bent so long now I've lost track of doctors. JJ excused himself and sat down in the kitchen's breakfast nook, which was quieter than the condo's living room. Because his hearing had been damaged by years of loud noise, multiple voices were sometimes irritating.

He watched Ann laughing with Jim and his mother-in-law Annette Bell before Barbara sat down in the nook across from him. "JJ, your stepfather called this morning looking for you. Howard said you weren't here. It sounded like he *expected* you to be here; called Howard a liar. If there's anything I can't stand, it's arrogance like that."

Good to know someone else sees through Charlie. "Prospective stepmother-in-law, where have you *been* all my life?" They exchanged embraces briefly, JJ trembling. *I want this too.*

Ann drifted into the kitchen with Carol, a smallish brunette with a bright face, whose grey eyes reminded him of Kristin's. "Remember me," Carol asked, extending her hand. "I interviewed you in Grenada, and in '73 for the Birmingham *Eccentric*."

"Oh, *yeah*. We talked out on the dock. Grenada's kinda fuzzy: sorry."

"I burned my feet on that dock. You weren't eighteen yet when I got that assignment, so I had to ask your mom for permission to interview you. She said 'no publicity is required.' Never will forget that."

"Ma…wait: did you go out to the house?"

"Yes. She had to sign a release. Why?"

"There was an older man there? Loose jowls?"

"Um, yeah: He was about as friendly as a porcupine. You said he was your stepfather by the time we *did* talk, and you were on your way to the Army, so…*there*, that one." She pointed to the living room wall where Howard had just hung a framed newspaper clipping. "I dug *that* out of my files."

He wandered over to the wall, gazing at the yellowing paper, his Order of the Arrow photo, and the headline: "Top Scout to Join Army."

…less than one in a thousand Boy Scouts is awarded the Order of the Arrow…a 1973 graduate of Brookfield Academy…to join the Army…

Ann was at his elbow. "Wow, you're *famous*."

"It's more a fraternity than an award."

"This one, too," Carol added as Howard hung another framed cutting next to the first. "Bloomfield Man Wins Silver Star in Grenada," the Detroit *News* headline read:

Staff Sergeant John "JJ" Elrath, a 1973 graduate of Brookfield School…a member of the famous Rangers…awarded America's third highest honor…for valor in the face of the enemy…led a small group of Rangers in holding off Cuban reinforcements… Detroit Scout Council Troop 1006's most-famous alumnus grew up in Bloomfield Hills…

"I got a byline for *that*; page three above the fold," Carol smiled, "We used my interview and material from the *Eccentric* piece. I got the interview because I was the only Detroit reporter there. You got me my *first* national coverage. When my stringer went to talk to your mom about it, she said she didn't have anything to add."

"Not if Charlie was around."

"Hey, hero," a soft voice behind them said. "Long time no see."

They all turned to see Debbie Ford, whose head barely came up to Ann's chin. JJ didn't recognize her—having not *seen* her since 6th Grade—but Ann leaned for an embrace.

"Girl, *good* to see you," Ann gushed. "Been since '83, yeah? And Bob! *Twice* in *one year*!" She had encountered Bob when she was home briefly in between the Far East and Florida just that January.

"I *still* don't dance, Ann, as much as Deb wants me to." Ann's escort at Jim's wedding had grown to nearly Ann's height and was still a round-faced, blue-eyed blonde.

Debbie sighed, "we're setting a date, Ann. You going to be available?"

"*Could* be. When are you thinking?"

Debbie made a small face. "Second week in January."

"Small, then?"

"*Fast*, then," Debbie blushed.

OH! "You're *pregnant?*"

"*Probably*. I haven't *tried* one of those home tests…"

"I hear they can be messy." *Mirrors and chemicals and not getting enough pee in the right place…*

"Yeah; too much like work. I see the doctor Monday."

Bob, in the meantime, spoke with JJ. "Deb says you're in Army intelligence? I'm an interrogator; joined the Reserves to help pay for school."

"Ah. I've done some Reserve support. You guys are just as good as we are, but you don't get much live work and you've got more women in *your* outfits than we do."

"That's us. We know *what* to do, we just don't do it *for real* very much, and our tents are co-ed in the winter."

"What's your language?" All Army interrogators were required to have some fluency in a foreign language: profanity didn't count.

"German. Our Active component advisor wants me to go over to the counterintelligence side."

"I don't know much about *that* side of the business; I can get you in touch with someone who *is* a camouflage inspector, though. What do you do for a living?"

"Technical writer: I write operator manuals."

"Ah: Like the Holy Hand Grenade of Antioch?"

"I've got that old Monty Python bit hanging over my desk as an example of how *not* to write instructions. It's a *living*…"

"All right, everyone," Howard rapped a counter for attention, and kids were flushed out of their warrens. "Most of you've *heard* of John Elrath, Claudia Ann's friend since they were in diapers and a neighbor for many years. Well, he's made his way back into *her* life, and now, *ours*; and *now* he wants to *stay*. So, raise your glasses, please: John Elrath, *welcome* to our *home*, our *hearth*, and our *hearts*. May your stay be *long* and *joyful*."

John Elrath!

JJ had no idea *how* to respond, so he merely raised his glass of pop and squeezed Ann's hand, mouthed "thank you" as…*his new family toasted him.*

Dad gave that toast to Holly and Carol. "Now you're *ours*, babe. *All* ours." Ann laid her head on his shoulder.

"When Dad said you were bringing Claudia up from Florida," Jim told JJ a few minutes later, "my *first* thought was 'who?' Then I remembered you from the neighborhood." Jim was shorter and more easy-going than George and shared their father's bonhomie.

"Ann said the Marines wouldn't have you. How come?"

"Flat feet. They *were* making exemptions, but I didn't make the cut." He shrugged. "Just as well. Wouldn't have married Carol if I had. How's Lois these days? I had *such* a crush on her."

"*Everybody* had a crush on Lois. Smart, beautiful, self-important; what's *not* to crush on?"

"I asked her to a dance once, and she just laughed."

"That's *Lo*, all right."

George hung a framed copy of an article on Ann that appeared in the Detroit papers, written by a wire service reporter in Baltimore. "We kept this hanging on our wall for the longest time," Holly said. "I've got more copies. When *you* want a copy, Ann, you can have one to hang on your own wall."

"Bloomfield Woman First Navy Diver," the Detroit *Free Press* headline said. The article began:

Claudia Mueller, a 1973 grad of Bloomfield Hills Central High School, is the first woman in the world to be a rated naval diver.

It went on about diver training (which came from the Navy), her military record (ditto), and a line about her record-setting swimming in high school (from *Sports Illustrated*).

"I got scooped on *that*," Carol moaned. "My sister-in-law; did I catch heat for *that*. But *we* should talk sometime: I need a *new* story line…"

"How about: 'Woman Diver and Army Ranger Hail from Detroit,'" JJ offered. "Don't have to mention that we…now *there's* a thought. Grew up together, lost each other, found again. Romantic, anyway. What?" Ann looked at him strangely. "OK, *pragmatically*, honey: right *now*—even if we *were* married—our services will separate us without thinking. We *need* to change that. If the powers-that-are were to see a well-written piece..."

"Or *two*." Carol looked interested. "A classmate of mine's in Miami, always looking for women-in-uniform stories. If I start *here*, with the *Free Press*, then she *continues* the theme in the Miami *Herald*, that *might* get some attention because the wire services *always* pick up themes that appear in two different papers." She grinned at JJ. "I read your book. Pretty impressive, for an amateur." She suddenly lit up. "There! *That's it*!" She grabbed each of them by the arm. "'Lady Diver and Soldier-Scholar.' *That's* the hook. And the angle is separation-by-service. When can we talk?"

JJ gazed at Ann. "Well? Do we want to talk about *us* on the record?"

"I will if you will. Name a date and time, Carol: We'll be available."

***

"I need to figure out what all I'm gonna do in two and a half weeks." JJ flopped onto the suite's sofa, trying to concentrate.

Ann sat in the small armchair, searching through the cable TV directory. "I want to get together with Uncle Allan and Aunt Margaret some time: didn't have time at the party. And I need to get my dress mess uniform dry-cleaned. Any idea what their turnaround is?"

He looked in the courtesy brochure. "Says...a business day. Allan is your *father's* brother; Margaret is your *mother's* sister? And they're married to each other?"

"I didn't know it was weird until high school; thought it was convenient."

"Not sure how weird it is. My uncles are cousins married to sisters— my aunts. My Uncle Murph married his first wife's sister after she died."

She laid her head back on the chair, listening to him but trying not to pay attention. "I need some *serious* downtime. Been going non-stop since last Friday. Johnny, let's just do *nothing* tomorrow, OK? We need to do laundry and unwind."

He laid out on the sofa, silent until he heaved a mighty sigh. "A few nights running I've had a dream about a red bathtub. Couldn't figure out why until...A guy I marched punishment tours with; talked to once in a while—Jason Samson. He marched tours because he talked to me—often. Christmas morning 1970 I found him in his bathtub, arms slashed open; water drained out; bathtub red from his blood." He closed his eyes tight. "That's what happened to my friends at Wolverine, but I don't know if he did it himself or it was done *to* him." He opened his eyes to her face next to his as she knelt on the floor, her eyes welling with tears. "I *don't* want that to happen to you."

Sandy…OH! "Sorry."

"Don't be *sorry*, honey. It's just some shit that happened to me." He gripped her hands powerfully.

Remember those classes on PTSD, and what Wendy said. "OK." She surprised herself with a cheery-yet-sultry response, holding his hands, smiling as brightly as she could. "Downtime tomorrow?"

"Sure."

And they kissed on it.

Sunday

"Morning, Johnny" She woke when he kissed her forehead. "You OK?"

"Morning, Cloud: I'm fine. Coffee?"

"You gotta ask?" Her belly protested painfully as she joined him in the kitchenette. "*Ugh.* Want to *see* the bends?" She opened the big, fuzzy bathrobe she got at Anita's and pulled her nightie up to look. A slight blue patch on her lower abdomen was barely visible. "Don't see it *that* way much."

"How can you tell the difference between the bends and anything else?" He gazed at her exposed anatomy, concentrating on the patch of mottled blue and trying *not* to see her more exciting parts.

"These patches. The bends come on all at once—they *are* gas bubbles. Other pains are usually more gradual." She covered up and tilted his book up. "Hornblower?"

"Bolitho. Same period or thereabouts, but the stories are richer. I think I hear housekeeping next door. Breakfast?"

"Sure." They went down to the breakfast buffet, finding seats in a quiet corner along the outer wall from which they could see their 2nd Level door.

"Somebody put some thought into this place. Kinda nice down here." He looked around the basketball-court-sized atrium; at its glass roof above the five terraced decks of guest suites and penthouses. Dotting the big space were movable ponds and fountains, terraced planters, and seating areas broken up by real-plant arbors and real stone walls. "Why would a fountain be running in the dead of winter?"

"Cleans and humidifies the air. Keeps the plants from drying out."

"Where did *you* learn *that*?"

"I took an elective in hospitality management. Why?"

"Habit. Know your source."

"Yeah. So, nothing scheduled for today," she mumbled somewhat later, stirring a passable fruit compote.

"Nope," he replied, slathering peanut butter on an English muffin.

"You said you'd slap me if *I* said 'schedule' again this trip."

"I *did*." She leaned towards him, winking. "Go ahead."

He tapped her chin with a finger. "That'll do."

***

With their dress uniforms ready for dry-cleaning and their laundry underway, she turned the TV on while he sat at the desk and started a list of what he *needed* to do and another of what he *wanted* to do. Before long he was moving sticky notes around on two separate pads. "Need a computer that can make spreadsheets."

"Ask Alex. He knows about those."

"Gotta go to the bank…"

"Let's hang back until business gets started again first of the year."

"Gonna talk to Mike's dad tomorrow."

"Why?"

"Need him to…Cloud?"

"Huh?"

"Want to be my beneficiary?"

"Your insurance? It *should* be your mom, John; as long as *she* lives and we're *not* what we're *not*."

"I suppose. And I want to call Jenny and Sarah. The alumni directory says Jenny's in real estate. I want to see if she can get the selling price of the house out of curiosity. I just want to catch up with Sarah."

"Something you're *not* telling me?" She put her mock-cross face on.

"You know everything, honey. Skinny-dipping, touchy-feely with Jenny. Sarah was just a friend."

He went back to his lists while she allowed herself to become engrossed with *Tightrope. Always liked Eastwood. Knows how to act despite only having one character in him.* The phone rang; she answered it, speaking briefly until she turned and made a face. *Charlie…*

He picked up the phone on the desk. His expression after he hung up matched his mood: a confusing mix of relief and frustration, anger and sadness. "I'm going to guess Ma got *this* number from your dad."

"Is *that* OK?"

He shrugged. "I'm not hiding. His apology; about a sincere as he *ever* gets." He got up and poured more coffee. "I don't want Ma to have to choose between him and me. I *shouldn't* win that contest." His face turned dark. "She doesn't *need me* anymore."

"She *needs you* to be happy, Johnny. As long as you *are*, she's OK, regardless of Charlie's opinion of *me*."

"You *heard* that?"

"I heard *enough. We'll* be OK, babe."

"I know because *you're* here." He grinned his half-grin. "If *you* can tolerate *my* family. *I* barely can, but *you'd* have to…"

"Strive for neutrality, like you said about step-families."

"Yeah. Last night, with *your* family, was…"

"*Our* family, babe. Scary?"

"Not scary—*alien*. I never thought anyone would *want* me like *that*, and I'm *not* even…Marry me."

"What, *now*?"

"We'll know when."

"I'm still thinking about the *first* time you asked."

"On *that* note," he grinned, "*I'm* going to call *another* girl."

"If *you're* going to be *that* way, *I'm* going swimming."

He looked up Jenny's number in the alumni directory. They chatted for several minutes before he hung up to see Ann in her swimsuit and her mock-cross face. "Dear heart, huh?"

"Oh; sorry."

She bussed his forehead. "Just skinny-dipping in the dark. No need for an apology. Join me for PT."

Just then, the phone rang and he answered. "Leigh and Donna will be here about 1500."

***

"Ann, it's none of *my* business, but, what's your condition?"

"*Female* condition?" He nodded; she shrugged. "Uterine malformation and irregular periods. A lot of what I talked about with Dad and Barbara was that medicine wasn't sure that I could even *conceive*. When I miscarried…"

"Something of a miracle in the first place."

"*Very* much, but I…."

And the phone rang. "OK, send them up." He smiled. "They're *here*."

"Three gals and one guy in a hotel room," she grinned. "*What* fun."

"I *only* have eyes for *you*, Cloud." He smiled benignly as he opened the door and sat with her.

"*Hey*, guys," Donna grinned minutes later, taking her coat off, "long time no see."

"Yeah," JJ smiled, watching her, "a few years. Thanks for…"

Donna smiled warmly. "*Glad* to do it. It fits, Ann?"

"Fits *well*," Ann declared. "*Hi*, Donna."

"*Hi*, Ann. *No* volleyball today."

Leigh grinned as Ann chuckled: "So: can we *change*?"

"Sure." They came out of the bedroom in a few minutes, Leigh in a *perfectly* respectable Speedo; Donna in a *way*-too-small, faded and threadbare Blondie Boopadoop t-shirt *barely* over a *WAY*-too-small bikini top and *not*-covering-enough G-string bottom that didn't match.

"Back later," Leigh called on their way out the door.

***

Clutching beach towels against the chill, Leigh and Donna made their way to the mostly-empty pool. Splashing like tourists, they watched two men, not together, at the glass wall outside the pool area. One, with dark hair and eyes, tried to look interested in the kids in the shallow end. The other, shorter and wearing a blaze-orange hunting coat, didn't bother with others but concentrated on *not* looking at them.

The girls swam to the deep end of the pool, hanging on the wall and kicking up water. "Blondie, distract the dark one while I chat up the smaller guy."

"Think *this* outfit's distracting?"

"Looks uncomfortable."

"*Naked* would be *more* comfortable: this G-string is *up* my…On your go…"

"OK: go!" Donna swiftly pulled herself out, whipped off her t-shirt, and smiled at her swarthy target, gliding to the door with swaying hips.

Perfect. Leigh pulled out and walked swiftly to *her* target, who was enthralled with Donna's performance, as were three wide-eyed teenage boys and an open-mouthed gentleman in the pool area.

It IS cold out here! "Hey," Leigh purred at the hunter. "Sid or Joe: who are *you* with?"

He quickly switched his gaze to Leigh. "Wha…*lady*, I'm…I…"

Leigh wore *her* smile, crossing her arms and lifting her chest *just* enough. "*Do* you *work* for *Sid* or *Joe*? Simple *question*." Leigh wasn't as tall or as well-endowed as Donna; her glowing green eyes over her sweet smile and her ability to *look* better-endowed at will were *her* interrogation tools. She could barely see Donna's encounter with the other guy in a double reflection off the glass. *Wonder what he's thinking?*

"I…I work for…for Block Associates, miss. I…uh…I'm *not*…"

"That's fine, pal." She turned to look at Donna, who had her guy laughing while she jiggled and tossed her wet hair, her hands on her hips, legs apart. "Any idea about *him*?"

"He's an employee of the Newhouse organization."

"Thanks." She winked slowly. "I'll make sure *Adam* gets a good report."

***

"What class is *that* for," she asked absently as he was filling in a class grid.

"America before the Revolution. I actually read the books for this one." He gazed at her in his jeans and her Navy sweatshirt as she was folding paper into animal shapes. "I admire..." And there was a knock on the door: Ann let them in, their hair damp.

"Thanks, guys," Leigh grinned, slightly out of breath. "Needed to know *who's* watching."

"We got *really* close," Donna smiled, drying her hair, "found out some things."

"Too bad JJ *missed* that," Ann grinned.

"Replay, *Cutie-Pie*," Donna laughed, flapping her towel open.

"*Ah...*" he stuttered while Ann and Leigh smiled benignly.

"I'm gonna retire this *damn* thing once and for *all*," Donna plucked at her bra. "Hasn't fit since I was a B-cup."

"When was *that*," Ann grinned.

"Um...5th Grade? My 12th birthday I got a *C*-cup suit; September, '66."

"You were a Big Girl, too, eh?"

"You *know* it. We're forming a club," Donna smiled as she headed into the bathroom.

"Really had to do it fast, guys" Leigh sighed. "No time for explanations and Donna's *always* ready to bait guys."

"What did you find out," JJ asked.

"Adam's outfit's *and* Randy's are watching us. I'm going to bet Newhouse also has someone embedded *here*."

Ann glanced at Leigh sidelong. "Your *parents* divorced before, no?"

Leigh smiled. "They never went through with it." They chatted for a while until Donna came out of the bathroom, back in sweatshirt and jeans as Leigh went into the shower.

"Thanks for this, guys," Donna smiled. "The best way we could think of..." She glanced benignly at JJ. "Sorry about the flashing."

Too small to cover your... "My eyes aren't that fast," he blushed.

Donna waved her lashes skillfully. "I *saw* your *eyes*, Cutie-Pie."

Ann smiled. "Yeah: *my* bullshit detector just went off, too. You're a *guy*, pal. We'd think there was something wrong if you *didn't* react." She stood up to flex her hip. "How's *your* dad, Donna?" Ann had heard disturbing rumors of Donna's father in school, but she *tried* not to pay attention.

"Dad's good. He just got a patent on something he called a cellular packet network. He says with *it* they can make a truly portable wireless phone that can connect to *any* similar network without needing a wired-phone base."

"Sounds Dick Tracy to me," Ann snuffed.

"Greek to *this* nurse-practitioner, too. I try to get by just knowing how to check the oil in my car. *Your* mom? Leigh said she was committed?"

"Still *is*. She has good days and bad."

"Thanks for your letter. Just about what *I* was thinking."

"Thanks for the heads-up on Joe," JJ sighed. "I'd heard stuff from Leigh and Mike's dad, but…*hey*, Leigh. What about dinner? Toothpick chow at happy hour, the restaurant or…?" They were still chatting when JJ answered the phone. "Huh. The kids brought pizza."

"*Kids*?" Leigh was puzzled.

"Alex and Jenna."

They brought two large pizzas, a 6-pack of soda and another of beer. They had the new *1984* on the TV while they ate. "My earliest memory," Alex announced, "was a TV news show about the end of Vietnam. Were *you* there?"

"We missed *that* by a few years," JJ answered, "but *I* got sent there by mistake."

"Really," Ann exclaimed. "How did *that* happen?"

He told the story in as few words as he could, trying to keep a straight face about the silliest set of orders he'd ever followed—or *heard* of.

"Amazing," Leigh shook her head. "And entirely credible."

"That's the scary part," JJ agreed, watching John Hurt's Winston Smith peel back the title page of the *Newspeak Dictionary*. "The Army can screw up so monumentally that it blinds us to what good they can do."

"So, *why* do you stay in?" Jenna looked interested.

"Mine is a fantastic, physically and mentally demanding job," Ann answered. "And I'm the first of my kind. I'm doing it so *you* can follow if you want."

"Well," Jenna smiled, thoughtful, "I think, sometimes, I *might* join the Navy. but, diver?" She shook her head. "No, not for me. I never liked Jacques Cousteau. I *might* want to be a nurse like Mom."

"I wouldn't trade *my* gig for the world," Leigh grinned, distractedly drawing with JJ's colored pencils. "Fun, travel, adventure; interesting work, and orders for Bum Fuque, Egypt just around the corner."

"There's *that*," JJ glanced at Ann. "We go where we're sent."

"And *that's* hard," Ann agreed. "Death of *many* love affairs."

They were quiet until Donna poked Alex with her foot. "Know what they mean?"

"Sort of." He stared at her, captivated. "They can't be together long."

"Worse than *that*," Jenna mumbled. "They *can't*…"

"*That* depends on the people," Leigh sighed. "Mike and I have what's considered a healthy, *adult* relationship, even though we don't see each other very often." She glanced at Ann, who shrugged. "Every couple handles *that* differently. Mike and I have known each other since 7th

Grade. We fell in love by mail over the course of *another* six years. But *JJ* and I met in church in 8ᵗʰ Grade." She smiled. "He and I *have always had* a different *kind* of love: *first* base, *never* second."

"Without *sex*," Jenna smiled.

"Right. Mike and I are *apart* more than we're *together*. We *love* when we're together, and we write—call sometimes—when we're apart."

Ann inhaled deeply. "John and I are happy, but it *will* hurt when we're separated—and we certainly *will* be."

JJ smiled. "We have *now*, and that *has* to be enough."

"No matter what *we* do," Leigh sighed, drawing, "being in the military post-Vietnam is hard: trying to have a normal *sex* life—let alone a *social* life or a life *out* of uniform—ain't easy. I showed my ID in a convenience store to buy beer once and some guy spat on me when I turned around. He ran away laughing about how he always wanted to do that to some warmonger—and I'm just a military cop."

JJ added, "I sometimes get the feeling that the services did what the country told them to do in Southeast Asia, but because it didn't end in a victory parade, people want to charge us for confetti storage."

"There's a lot of misperception about us," Ann mused. "All the chiefs I know were in Vietnam at one time or another, plus most of the officers over lieutenant. Can't see *any* difference between them and any others."

"I've been around Vietnam vets all through my service," Leigh agreed. "and not *once* has any of them *ever* gone psycho like they do in the movies. I see stories about mutinies, officers getting murdered by their troops— and a few of those *did* happen—and about officers and NCOs going armed against their own people. I've never seen *most* of that, but civilians don't believe me."

Alex mumbled. "So, what we see on TV…"

"Mostly bullshit," Leigh replied. "There are a few accurate portrayals, but for the most part, bullshit."

"The media are *not* interested in houses that aren't on fire," Donna interjected. "If they told the *truth* about vets it wouldn't play to the psycho-murderer model. So, they make them out to be what *sells*: crazy villains. And it *does sell*." She sighed. "And *I* get to clean up the mess in the VA."

"*You* work at the VA?" Ann was surprised.

"Allen Park NP ward sixteen hours a month: VA footed part of the bill for my training. Now I work with drunks and junkies in *two* different places; at least for the next year when *that* obligation's done."

"Still," Leigh smiled, "we have whatever time we make for ourselves. *You* have interesting eyes." She handed Alex a slip of paper that bore an elegant study of his face in grey. She handed Jenna a drawing of her profile in red and pink. "*Quite* stunning, Jenna. Your face is *beautiful*. Johnny," she grinned, handing him a study of his eyes in blue. "I've drawn *your* eyes *so* often…and Ann," she passed her a brown-line detail of her eyes in a heart-shape. "I remember the *first* time I drew you in 9th Grade."

Incredible. "Didn't know you were still doing this," Ann smiled.

"Some people like my work," Leigh shrugged.

"Yeah, like *Korea*," Donna smirked. "One of her paintings was in their national gallery for a while."

"Really," JJ wondered.

"Yeah. A pastel-and-watercolor I called *Korea at Dawn*. It's in a mess hall at Camp Casey now. My art helps me stay sane."

***

After their guests left—and all but Alex pecked his cheek—JJ felt an awkward silence. Ann smiled. "You and Leigh are *that* close?"

"We helped each other through some *very* rough times in '69 and '70. Without Green-Eyes I'd have *never* made it." He looked up at her. "And I *told* you about…"

"Yeah: before *our* time. And Donna? *Cutie-Pie*?"

"I met her at the Dietz's. She's *something* else."

"You have more friends than you thought."

"Yeah. Not sure what *I* did to *deserve* it."

"Family loves you if you *think* you deserve it or not. You only have to love them back. *Friends* love *you* because you to love *them*."

He turned the TV off. "Tired."

He shivered between the cool sheets until he felt them flap up and *she* slid in; her long flannel nightie with long sleeves…gone. "Hi, Johnny."

"Hi, Cloud." He could hear her breathing, her heartbeat strong and steady; see her bright eyes and bare shoulder.

"You're right: We have *now*." She pulled up against him. *"Shh*: just…*shh. Just hold me." Hold me and don't let me go until we… and THAT'S his… OOH! RIGHT place! OH! WOW!* She held him tighter, breathing fast and shallow before she thrust her hips forward and cocked a leg over him, shuddering with a small choking sound from deep in her throat.

HOLY…OH!! He met her thrust with his, vibrating. *AH!!*

They were still, breathing shallow…savoring *that* moment.

"Cloud, did *you*…?"

"Yup. So did *you*."

"Uh-huh. You OK?" *You're naked and in my arms. What could be wrong?*

"I'm *wonderful*, babe, except for your elbow in my ribs."

He shifted. "And the *mess*. Sorry, but I *wasn't in*…?"

Sex is mostly in the mind. "You were *close,* but sex *is* messy. You *felt* different in a Speedo." *And we WERE twelve.* She moved his hand to her breast as she shifted her hips slightly. "Now you've felt me up *for real.*" *And your hand is COLD!*

OH! Move like THAT again and I might have another accident. "Thought second base came *before* the home run."

"*Not* a homer, babe."

"A line drive to center field. Regrets?"

"Oh, *no,* babe; of *course* not; expecting *it.* I just...I *usually last* more than a few seconds."

"Me too, but we've been working up to *this* for half our lives."

She giggled and arched her back. "Fifteen *years* of foreplay. But oh, *you* are *worth it.*"

"Yeah? I'm *that* good?"

"You are for *me.* I see your face when I go deeper than eight fathoms— fifty feet."

"Me?"

"Since I first went that deep, yeah: '70 or '71."

"You do *that* often?"

"Not lately. Now all I *want* to have to do is roll over to see you."

"For the next few weeks you *can.*"

She reached for him. "Babe; if we...?"

He gently squeezed her breast. "We'll *always* have each other, no matter *where* we are."

"Yeah. And *maybe,* someday, when we cuddle like *this*...we'll figure out where our arms are supposed to go *and* have a towel handy."

Monday

"Morning, Cloud." He touched her cheek with a thumb.

"Morning, Johnny." She slid her hand sensuously down his back and they touched lips softly before she slapped his backside. "All hands on deck, you *lubber*; full speed ahead."

***

She had never driven in that part of Detroit, where the Motor City auto industry tried to hold itself up with "value-added" rustproofing services, bump shops and customizing services. She remembered dimly going to a movie at the legendary Mercury Theater on Shaeffer Avenue as a child, but couldn't remember much else about it. She parked Barbara's car on a big concrete apron in front of a building; one wall contained several incongruous red bricks in no particular pattern. Under the sign that read "Kurt's Kustom Kar and Koach" was the nearest door—the parts department—where a dark-skinned woman with *Kendra* embroidered on her shirt greeted her. "Can I *help* you, ma'am?"

An NCO's first reflex is to snap "*don't* call me 'ma'am;' I *work* for a living" …but thought better of it. "I'm looking for Kurt Parkinson? I'm Ann…"

"Oh, *you're* JJ's friend," Kendra cried. "*So* pleased to meet you: I'm Kendra Ashton. I'll get Kurt." She picked up the phone and pushed a button: "Kurt, please come to the parts department; you have a customer waiting. Kurt; parts." Off the phone, she gushed. "That boy *needs* domesticating, that's for sure."

After a few minutes—mechanics came and went, glancing at her with curiosity—Kurt came through a green steel door. "Ann? *Good* to meet you. Come this way." He led her past several salesmen on the phone, filling out paperwork. "Monday's *always* busy," Kurt murmured. "Like everybody decides to get something done to their rigs on the weekend and calls Monday." In his office, he gestured to a chair. "So, what can I…?"

"I'm accepting your offer," she started. "*Never knew* the Rebel was worth…"

He smiled. "I know a collector with more money than sense and a warehouse in Dearborn *full* of '60s Detroit big iron. He'll pay a *lot* for a running Rebel."

"*I* don't have a bank here. If you *can*, I could use *some* cash…"

"I'll give you *all* cash: for the collector side, *that's* good business."

WOW! "That's a *lot* of greenbacks," she frowned.

He smiled. "OK. Because you *are* who you *are*, I'll do $5,000 in cash and a cashier's check for the balance."

"That's…*better*."

"*Geez, you* drive a hard bargain. OK: $3,000 in cash and a cashier's check?"

"I can live with that," she smiled. "Should I come back?"

"No, no; I can get the check in about an hour. Let me show you around." They went around the shop…unusual for Ann that she could watch people working metal without wearing safety glasses. The shop had the usual array of equipment, from arc welders to disintegrators. Kurt pointed out his pride-and-joy: a new frame-straightener jig they had just built. "I can put *any* frame into shape with *this*."

"Fifty-ton bottle jacks," she mused. "We push decks and bulkheads with those. We've got 200-tonners for hulls; they need a dolly to move."

"*Really*," Kurt gasped. "I didn't know *what* you do: JJ just said diver."

"Storekeeper; hull tech; diver; in *about* that order," she smiled. "That's what *my* week's like. *Diver's* more memorable."

"Yeah. You should come out to the house, have dinner, meet the wife."

I can do this. "How about Saturday?"

"Um…Mary's got a party…Sunday?"

"Ah, we're at your brother's. Monday?"

"I'll make *that* work with the boss." They wandered around the shop and parts areas, discussing metalworking in general. Kurt showed her the corner of the shop where JJ had set up his little workshop, once again used for storing odds and ends. "He could do about anything we needed."

"Huh. You do trucks *and* cars here?"

"Anything with wheels, engine or not. I get farm equipment in here sometimes. I've got a guy who used to build trailers, can weld like nobody's business. Just got a new TIG rig for trailer bodies." He looked at her warmly. "I'm glad JJ found a home in the Army after…my father *isn't* one of *our* favorite people."

Tell me about it. "*We've* met; *I* wasn't impressed, either."

He grinned. "And, seeing JJ the other day: I'm *so* glad he found *you*."

So are we.

***

This place reeks of wealth.

"Welcome to Dietz, O'Bannon and Associates. How may I help you?" The receptionist was about his age, dark hair and eyes; pretty and very conservatively dressed, with an unattractive telephone headset clamped on her head.

"JJ Elrath to see Ben Dietz." The office was airy, spread out on the ground level with hardwood paneling and solid wood furniture, and filled with natural light from all four walls. Though the law firm occupied three floors of the building, the brothers Dietz stayed on the ground floor.

She looked in a book; spoke into her headset. "He'll be right with you." Seating was provided by plush leather chairs—*not* the typical waiting-room/lobby fare—along one wall, facing a gallery of paintings of Detroit in years gone by. *Either they don't get crowded, or…*

Soon a large, swarthy man strode into the lobby, extending his hand. "John: *good* to see you," Ben smiled genuinely. "Come on back. Monica is looking forward to seeing you again. Where are you staying?"

"The Northwestern down on Telegraph."

"Yes: know it well."

"I'm trying to set something up to see Kurt sooner than later."

"Your brother, yes. We *still* don't know the Parkinson's well…" Ben led the way into a small conference room. "So, what can I do for you?"

"My mother's been handling *some* of my affairs, but she's getting on in years…" After he'd laid out his needs, he passed Eddie's business card and his publisher's details. "Eddie Evans is my money guy. If you can work with *him*…”

“Certainly. I *know* Eddie’s *father:* he retired last year, but I’ve never done business with his son.”

“I’m going to see Eddie Thursday. Hold off until Friday?”

“As you wish. You *must* promise to come out to the house soon.”

***

“What do nurse-managers do?” In exchange for using her car, Ann bought Barbara lunch.

“Scheduling and budgeting, mostly,” Barbara sighed, sipping coffee. “Paper-shuffling; *endless* meetings; computer-fighting.” They sat in a window booth at Eileen’s; a fashionable cafe with small servings, high-on-the-wall planters and European posters not far from Barbara’s hospital on Woodward Avenue.

“Sounds like *my* job these days, without the budgeting.”

“You use computers too?”

“More all the time. My duties involve *tons* of paperwork that’s *all* getting computerized; my storekeeper job floats on them now.”

“The higher you go, hey?”

“Pretty much.”

“How high do you want to go, Ann?”

“I’d be happy if my next promotion—to Chief Petty Officer—were my last,” *I said that out loud?* “I intend to stay in the Navy for at least twenty years, not *necessarily* as a diver.”

“You can do that? Change jobs?”

“*Diver* is less a *job* than a way of *doing* a job. I’m a Jill-of-all-trades with duties *way* beyond swimming. Most of *my* diving-time is spent in maintenance, planning and management, reports, surveys. Otherwise I’m counting O-rings, trading this stuff for those things—the Navy *runs* on bartering—and shuffling paper like you. I weld or plumb something occasionally, but mostly I supervise others doing it. I *could* just say ‘I don’t want to dive anymore’ without too much trouble. I’d still be in the dive community—*probably*—just not *diving*.”

“To change the subject completely,” Barbara looked out the window. “I want to thank you both for the time you’re spending with Jenna and Alex. Nate’s girlfriends—they’re usually younger than *you* are—don’t want to be associated with teenagers, especially poor Alex. My ex-husband prefers *younger* women, as I discovered…you get the idea.”

“Uh-huh.”

“But they *really* like you two.” Barbara smiled pleasantly. “I do too.”

“Well, *we* like *you* guys too. JJ’s family just doesn’t *work*.” She shrugged. “A lot of baggage there.”

"Yeah." Barbara made a face and sipped more coffee. "Charlie called late Friday night demanding to talk to JJ. Howard said he wasn't there. He called Howard a liar and hung up."

"Friday? They called *us* Sunday. We figured they got the number from you guys."

"Howard gave Stella your number when *she* called Sunday morning. Was *that* a mistake?"

"No. He doesn't want to lose track of her. Don't tell him about Friday, please. That'd just make it worse."

"I told him Saturday night."

"How did he take it?"

"He called me his prospective stepmother-in-law and asked where I'd been all his life." She winced. "He was on emotional overload."

"Yeah. He isn't used to family gatherings where blood isn't spilled. We have dinner with his parents Sunday after next, and I'm dreading it."

"Not at *their* place? The woman is hopeless in the kitchen."

"No, we're hosting at Fox and Hounds. We planned it on the way up here."

"Huh." Barbara sipped her coffee. "Some road trip, hey?"

"Yeah. Never had one like *that*."

There was a very loud silence for several moments before… "Ann, you and I *both* know that JJ's *not*…"

"Yeah. I let the cat out of *that* bag when I wrote you, didn't I?"

"That, and our little talk Christmas. Unless you two did the deed the instant you met in September, you probably wouldn't have noticed a miscarriage in October; and by your *letter*…."

"Did *Dad*…?"

"Howard hasn't done *that* math: He'll tell *me* if he does." She signaled for a coffee refill. "When you wrote me, you needed to talk, and it's *my* job to listen. What matters is that JJ was willing to step up. *NOT* saying he *wasn't* the father *was* his idea, yeah? Uh-huh. Integrity aside, there's the courage to do what's *needed,* regardless of consequences, and your Johnny has *that* in spades. You don't get a Silver Star for sitting in the rear with the gear."

"Look, I…" Ann began, but Barbara stopped her.

"I *know*. I've *been* there. Went nuts over a *great* guy who turned out to be not-so-great. Only I *married* mine." Barbara sipped coffee, forked in some of her lunch, and touched Ann's hand. "You two are good together: I can see that; Howard has *said* that. You have a great future together. And it doesn't matter to me that *he* wasn't the father and I doubt it matters to Howard. If he starts asking, I'll just head him off with 'because the *real* father is an *asshole*.' True, yeah? *No* sweat, buddy."

***

"So, in the end," Jenna concluded, "IBM and Tandy will outlast everything except maybe Apple, and Tandy only because Radio Shack is everywhere." She was holding forth on the state-of-the-art for personal computers when Barbara and Ann returned to the condo, and the phone was ringing.

"Uh-huh," JJ muttered. "Typewriter it shall have to be, for now, anyway."

"So," Ann touched JJ's shoulder, "what was *your* day like?"

"I met with Ben, talked about legal stuff. How about your day?"

"Went out to meet Kurt—he gave me some cash and a check and we have dinner with them next Monday. Had lunch with…"

"Kids, I need to tell you something," Barbara interrupted. "Your father and Chrissy are sick. They ate *something* and…"

"Sick? How sick?" Jenna panicked.

"*Very* sick. They…"

"Where *are* they, Barbara?" JJ's tone was flat.

"Barbados. The clinic there…"

"I *may* be able to help."

Barbara, puzzled, gave JJ her notes. "It's what I've got."

"My phone book is at the hotel. You want to hang out here, honey?"

Jenna cried; Alex stoically stared out a window, trying to comfort her. "I'll hang out here."

***

"I *have* to go in, Ann." They sat in Barbara's car in the hotel parking lot, engine idling; it was near-midnight.

"He'll overload."

"Maybe. We *both* know PTSD when we see it. He needs *help*, Ann."

"It's not *all* the same, Barbara. Better called a *spectrum* than just a *disorder*."

"We both *know* that, but *we* need to address *his*."

"Very well."

Ann and Barbara entered the suite while JJ was wrapped in his sweats watching TV. He was startled when Barbara wrapped her arms around him and started to cry.

"Thank you *so* much, John. Thank you," she whispered over and again. "The kids were *so* happy, thank you, thank you." Stiff and uncertain, he gradually responded by holding her, silently but warmly. It was several minutes before Barbara let go, wiping her eyes. "I haven't cared so much about *that* sonofabitch since the kids were born," she sniffed, trying to laugh. "Oh, I must be a *sight*."

"You're *fine*, Barb," JJ murmured, "just fine."

"Oh, you're *such* a schmoozer, JJ," Barbara giggled. "And a good man. Tell me, please, what *is* CloudWays?"

"Eh, a little outfit I know." *No sense in denying it.* "Just glad they could help. But I'd appreciate it if you just left *me* out…"

Ann nuzzled his neck. "*Why*, babe? The kids want to *adopt* you!"

"Did *you*…?"

"No, John," Barbara interjected, "Ann said *not* to." She put a hand on his cheek. "Please let *us*, or tell them yourself."

"I can't Barb," he replied flatly. "I just *can't*." He shrugged. "The world is full of people who want to be thanked for doing what they're *supposed* to do. I can't ask *that* from anyone, and I can't *expect* it, either. Not even from you."

"*Shh*," Ann covered his mouth. "Just…*shh*." *I have to think.* "Let's go have a drink."

New Year's Eve

The bar was closing when they got there. Barbara had been quiet before she sighed, "JJ, *when* did you decide that what *you* do has so little value?"

"Not sure what you're asking, Barb. It has value to the *kids*, to *you*…"

"Yes, but why does it have so little value to *you*?"

"Its value to *me* is being able to help the people I care about."

"You're not the hero of your own story," Ann announced, suddenly brightening.

"Making a few phone calls is *not* heroic. Falling on a grenade; running into a burning building; *that's* heroic. Being in the right place, at the right time, with the right resources is just *serendipity*. But if I can't shut you down, let's just leave it at 'thanks.'"

***

"Morning, Cloud." The morning came bright and cold. He gazed over at Ann, her back to him in her own bed.

"Morning, Johnny." He crawled in behind her, warm in her nightie.

"Mad at me?"

She took his hand from her hip and pressed it to her breast. "No, babe. Frustrated." She rolled over. "Letting us be grateful *isn't* an entitlement."

"It *feels* like one."

"Well, it *isn't*. *We* need it: *us* mere mortals who receive the gifts of you Olympians. *We* need to burn some laurel leaves in your honor once in a while. Just because *Charlie*…"

"Wait…that "Star Trek" rerun the other night…?"

She smiled and kissed him. "Come on. *You* have a guest coming in a few hours."

***

"JJ, *so* good to see you," Sarah Simonetti *nee* Silverman gushed. "Been since *before* graduation, no?"

"Yeah. *You* haven't changed a bit." The vibrant woman he embraced *hadn't* changed, nor had she put on an ounce of weight (it seemed) since they last met. Her brown hair was shorter and not quite so lustrous, but there was still fire in her bright brown eyes.

"*Stop* schmoozing, big guy. I follow *your* exploits with wonder, told everyone you were my pal."

"What 'exploits'?"

"Your *medal*, hero. I read about it in the morning paper just after our son was born and got my husband up out of a dead sleep to show him. Then I went out and bought your book."

"Oh, *you* were the one…"

"Come on! They could barely keep it in stock." She reached into her purse. "Sign mine?"

For Sarah, My Sweetheart—JJ Elrath, Dec. '85. "There. Now, did you *read* it?"

"Twice. Your bio of Robert E. Lee as an inspirational icon and strategic dunce was the best of the book."

"If you like *that*, read Connelly's *Marble Man*. Um…" he sighed, "Clare's in a hospice…"

She gasped. "*Where?* What's her…?" They chatted until the hotel's crew wanted to move *their* two chairs to get ready for the New Year's gala.

"Let's go upstairs; you can *meet* Claudia, finally." He knocked on the door a few minutes later. "Honey?"

"Yeah, come on," Ann called from the desk. "Just doing…oh, hi. You *must* be Sarah; I go by Ann nowadays. Would you like coffee?"

"Sarah Simonetti. *You're* the *one this* dreamboat looked for in *my* eyes all the time. Coffee…fine, yes. Need to stay awake for the New Year's gala."

"New Year's a big thing by you?"

"Big thing for the school. All the schools in the bishopric send their kids to St. Stan's for New Year's. I'm *still* filling the balloons for it…"

"Huh. As it *happens*…"

***

Male Caucasian, five-eight, 180, athletic build, hard brown eyes, probably blonde hair if he didn't shave his head, 40 to 50…

"I've been eyeballed by pros, Miss Leigh, and you're one of 'em." She had slipped into MP-mode and was startled when Adam smiled at her as he approached her booth. The Bollywood Grill was decorated as a homage to the big production numbers of subcontinent films, but they maintained an American family-restaurant menu with Indian-like named items on the menu, like Bombay broiled pork chops and New Delhi roast beef.

"If there's no one else around, can you please *just* call me Leigh? 'Miss' makes me feel like I'm on a plantation." Adam had called her *Miss Leigh* since she first rode in a Dietz limousine in 8th Grade.

He took a seat across from her in the booth. "It's what the *firm* allows." The waitresses of all races were dressed in only slightly ridiculous sari-like uniforms, thankfully without the sashes.

"Which firm? The number I *called*…"

"Is a part of Dietz, O'Bannon & Associates. Block Associates is one of the 'associates.'" He perused the menu. "The sandwiches here are pretty good."

Huh. Don't see liverwurst on rye often. "You come here a lot?"

"We use this place often."

"Sunday night I identified your watch…"

"Yes; my compliments on that. Ricky's usually not caught out, But Miss *Donna*," he grinned, "Ricky says we should hire her." Curious, Leigh ordered the liverwurst and onion on light rye; Adam the beef tongue. "We're going to brush Newhouse back this evening."

"What do they *really* want, Adam?"

"You, back in the fold…we *think*. As long as you're in the Army, they can't expect much in that regard, but with you getting closer to Mr. Mike, they're getting desperate."

"My friend JJ: what are they interested in with him?"

"I believe their interest in Mr. Elrath is personal to Joe Dryden. If it comes…*nuts*." Adam stood up. "He's *early*." She looked around swiftly.

She hadn't seen Randy Newhouse in thirteen years but recognized his arrogant swagger, perpetual sneer behind his amber glasses, and the impossible-to-train cowlick, even under his broad-brimmed hat. Adam took a guarded stance, glancing back and forth between his people and Randy's. Randy stopped next to Leigh, *indirectly* glancing at Adam.

"Can I speak to *my wife* alone, please," Randy mumbled.

Leigh nodded, "it's what we're here for, Adam." Adam stepped across the room, watching Randy as he sat down.

"You're as beautiful as ever, honey. Come home with me."

Something's wrong with your eyes. "Randy, my home is in Georgia right now. Technically I was *never* your wife."

"*We'll* fix that," Randy grinned breezily. "Nothing that lawyers and money can't get anyone out of. That annulment? *Easy* to void. We can get you *out* of the Army…"

"But why would you *want* to, Randy? I don't *love* you: I haven't even *liked* you since our wedding night. What the hell do you want with *me*?"

He waved a hand. "To keep your *family* alive, sweetheart, and to give *you* some peace. Oh, you can have your big yid on the side if you want: I don't care. But we *need* you *here*, with *us*."

"Are you *threatening* my family, Randy?" She flicked her gaze at Adam. "Because, if you *are*, I can make our wedding night look like *play time*...."

"Not *me*, Leigh. It's not *me*. It was *never* me...or *about* me." He sighed, and looked at her somewhat pathetically, if indirectly. "Look: I *tried*, OK? This is moving *WAY* beyond...Hell, I never *could* control it." He sighed again. "Just think about it, OK? You want all the legal stuff and the not-so-legal stuff to end, come back home."

"Just tell me *why*, Randy. Tell me why my friends and I seem to be under surveillance, why Adam thinks someone wants people dead."

"Not for what you *know*, doll, but for what you *don't* know. You've told people about our son, how he *ain't* yours. But *ignorance* of the facts will get people you *don't know* hurt...*bad*. We need you *here* to keep you—and *them*—safe."

"Way *not* to answer, Randy. And what about John Elrath? What have you got against *him*?"

He suddenly looked genuinely puzzled before he asked, "Who?"

Randy doesn't ever look puzzled.

✳✳✳

"Miserable damn thing. I *hate* it."

"*It*...what?"

"Garter belt...may not...no, don't *need* it, really, even if the regs...."

"Don't *wear* it. My battle scarf without shirt and tie is *way* out of the regulations."

"You *still* think a tie is a haberdasher's conspiracy?"

"Yeah. Besides, I'll *never* find a long-sleeve button-down shirt that fits right."

"So, what are *you* suggesting *I* do?"

"It's not a military function; you're not gonna get gigged for being out-of-uniform. Who'd complain if you didn't wear *any* stockings?"

"*You* wouldn't complain if I didn't wear *anything* at all."

"Only because you're unattractive in *that* shade of blue."

She threw a stocking at him. "When was the last time *you* shaved *your* legs?"

"Never. Isn't there a pantsuit version of the dress blues?"

"These aren't *dress blues*; winter dress mess. Yeah, but *they* fit me worse than the skirt." *And I didn't bring them…*

He watched her fidgeting. "Just take the damn thing off."

He's right again, damnit. She gave him a look; he left the bedroom. "Let's go," she declared moments later, pulling her coat on. "Is there some significance to that scarf color?"

"Military Intelligence light-blue—my branch. I *could* wear green for special operations."

"Huh. *That* color matches your eyes."

***

A testosterone-and-estrogen-fueled blast moderated by holy water.

"Never been to a Catholic school dance before," JJ smiled over a cup of punch. St. Stanislaus School in Wixom held the annual New Year's party for northwest Detroit-area Catholic schools in their vast triple gymnasium every year.

"CYO dances were a lot like this. Look," Ann nodded towards Jenna, chatting up a boy just a little taller than she was, and was surrounded by others. "She's a success. You see Sarah?" The ratio of adults to kids at the party was somewhere in the vicinity of 1:15. There were four priests, a couple of monks, a half-dozen nuns in habits, and a score of teachers and staff in attendance. The rest were parents, adult siblings, and a couple of maintenance staff.

"Over by the balloons." Sarah—who taught 6th Grade—was still inflating and making balloon shapes. "Have you seen…? *There* he is." Alex, on the other side of the room, stood in a corner, alone with his hands in his pockets. The band—a four-piece combo with a vocalist on a raised dais on the far side of the gym—played mostly slow dances not loud enough to hurt anyone's ears. "No Brianna?"

"Can't say. But I'll get *him* noticed." She handed him her cup and walked around the edge of the dance floor, drawing glares from the girls and gazes from the boys. She was the tallest woman—nearly the tallest *person*—in the room, and so distinctive in her uniform that everyone couldn't help but notice. She stopped in front of Alex, held out her hand, and led him to the dance floor.

"Never seen it better done." The voice behind JJ belonged to a large man in monk's robes. "Charles Kowalski," he said, extending his hand. "And you are?" Though *she* didn't dance well, even *her* uncertain steps were better than Alex's.

JJ introduced himself. "She's Alex's big sister." Meanwhile, the nuns were vigilant about *all* dancers leaving room between them for the Holy Ghost.

"Lovely girl, too," Charles beamed, shifting his bright eyes to JJ.

253

"Monks were *men* first: we can *appreciate* pretty women." He watched them for several more moments. "What's your outfit? I did my time with the 26th Marines."

"75th Infantry."

They watched the dancers for several more moments. "After Khe Sanh I left the Corps with shrapnel in both legs and my life dedicated to God."

When the music ended, Ann hugged her brother and kissed his cheek so her barely-there lipstick could *just* be seen. It took two minutes for three girls to come around, and another two before a half-dozen boys did. She stayed with Alex until they started giggling…and laughing.

"Worked," he mused, handing her cup back. He introduced her to Brother Charles, who was soon called away.

Soon Jenna came. "Alex has like three friends at school, and *none* of them are here."

"He should have more soon." They heard a gale of laughter from his direction. "What happened to Brianna?" Ann watched Alex chat with a pretty blonde.

"There." Jenna pointed to a tall, pretty brunette in a white flowered dress, talking to a couple of other girls. "She's the closest Alex *has* to a girlfriend."

"Do you know her?"

"Homeroom."

"Introduce me." Jenna hooked JJ's arm and led him off.

What? Ann watched perplexed as JJ had no trouble convincing Brianna to dance. A moment later someone was plucking at Ann's arm.

"Care to dance?" An older gentleman smiled. "Your escort is being kind to my granddaughter; Thought I'd return the favor. Not that *you* would need help."

"I don't dance well," she protested.

"You dance at least as well as I," he breezily told her as they took their turns on the floor. "Allow me to introduce myself: Captain Albert Hardstone, US Navy, Retired. They *taught* dance at Annapolis when I was there. You're having a spot of liberty?"

"I needed a break from the tropics. Thought I'd try the Arctic."

"Divers always had a sense of humor." Polite applause broke out as the band stopped and announced a break. "I never thought I'd *meet* a woman diver, let alone *dance* with one."

When JJ led Brianna off the floor and she wandered off, he was ambushed by Ann and her dance partner. After introductions, Ann chided him. "*You* can *dance*?"

"Just as well as Fred."

"Astaire?"

"No, Flintstone. Did I step on her feet? These jump boots…"

"Don't think so…Look." Alex and Brianna found each other.

"I thank you, young man," Albert announced, shaking JJ's hand. "My granddaughter is painfully shy. Her parents are on some getaway, so she's with me this evening."

"Alex and Jenna aren't where *they* expected to be, either," Ann told him, "but now they're where they *want* to be."

In a few minutes, Sarah plucked at JJ's sleeve. "Mind if I borrow him, Ann?" The song wasn't long, but he felt clumsy in Sarah's arms. "*Relax,* big guy: It's *just* a dance."

"Yeah, sorry. Just…we *never…*"

"We were friends who climbed trees, kissed a couple times and saw *Fritz the Cat.*"

"That was *you?*"

"You *sweetly* apologized for the animated sex and I flashed you."

"Oh, *yeah*: *Wanted* to see *under* those bloomers."

"Too late now. Those big boots of yours are *not* made for dancing, pal…"

An hour later the ball drop warning was sounded. The nuns scattered on the dance floor; another circulated among the adults, whispering "restraint, please."

The appointed moment (2200/10 PM) came, and the strains of *Auld Lang Syne* reverberated. Alex managed a peck from the blonde and *more* from Brianna. Jenna hugged two of her friends; a tall boy in a bow tie got a kiss. JJ got a smack from a woman who was kissing everyone, a hug from some other woman he hadn't met, and both from Sarah. Ann got a hug from Albert and a peck from some other rather dashing fellow.

✳✳✳

As they drove away, the kids were lit up as though it was Christmas all over again; Jenna full of gossip. *No one* believed that the beautiful Amazon dancing with that nerdy Alex was his *sister*. And Brianna with that Green Beret (his Ranger *black* beret was stuck under a jacket epaulet)? *Talk* of the party. Though Alex wasn't as bubbly, he *was* more verbal than usual, asking about the boys Jenna danced with, and… "who were you making out with in the hall?"

"*Making out with* in the *hall?*" Ann half-turned in the seat. "Really?"

"Billy Reidy. I lost a bet."

"You *lost?* What would you have gotten if you'd *won?*"

"He'd do my chemistry homework for a week."

"What was the bet?"

"I bet him Alex wouldn't dance with Brianna tonight. Sorry, Alex. I just didn't think you'd…"

"That's OK. *I* didn't think I would either. Then Ann…why did everyone want to be friends with me just because I danced with you?"

"If somebody popular likes someone who isn't, people want to know why."

"And why would *Billy* care?" JJ found it curious.

"They're cousins. Billy pushed Brianna to come because Brianna likes you."

"Brianna *likes me*? We…*she*…oh!" Nobody could wipe *that* smile off Alex's face.

***

"Do me a favor, babe: *try* to mingle tonight?" The lavish buffet at the Northwestern covered ten tables and included everything from egg salad to caviar, hot dogs to lobster tails, plain lettuce to truffles. Ticket-holding revelers and key-holding guests could climb the stairs to the upper levels (except Five, which required a room key to access) and sample exotic dishes like sushi and tempura chicken and even fugu above the main party.

"I'll try, if the noise isn't too…noisy." *Mingling* was never JJ's strong suit, but he pushed himself into it because, for the first time in a *long* time, he *wanted* to fit in.

"*There* they are," Ann nodded at Leigh and Donna at about 11:30. "That's *Nick*… *some*body…Paulson. Haven't seen *him* since graduation. He hung out with Leigh's friends."

"You *all* weren't…"

"No. The social world at Central was complicated."

I'll bet. "I'll help Nick with their luggage." Doing that gave JJ an opportunity to get away from the noise and crowds that rattled his nerves, if only for a few minutes. He'd never met darkly handsome Nick.

"You know Donna well?" Nick's voice seemed small for a lawyer.

"Not *well*. You?"

Nick shrugged. "Better; longer."

Meanwhile, Ann and Donna sampled the fare in the atrium. "So: Nick. *He's*…?"

"Yeah. The kind of *beautiful* guy you need after a breakup, or if you just want a good cry on a willing shoulder, or when you're not with anyone else. He's *always* there."

Her Sam? "He's too good-looking to be a doormat, girl."

Donna made a face at Leigh; who shrugged resignedly. "*You* told me that, too." She glanced at the 2nd Level where Nick and JJ leaned on a rail and chatted. "*Should* I make love with my doormat?" She smiled up at him; he waved. "We both *have rooms* here…"

"Remember what I said," Ann glanced up with her, "be *sure* you want the same things *before* you…"

"Yeah," Leigh sighed, "and that you need to *stay* friends *after*. Why do you think he's always available when you need him? He's waiting for *you:* take the hint."

"Yeah, I *get it*," Donna sighed, wiped a quick tear. "We *don't* want to end up alone; we *care* for each other; we *don't* just want a quickie. So…doormat no more, Nick. But after *that*, my *dear* freind…we'll *have* to figure it out."

Three…two…one…

1986

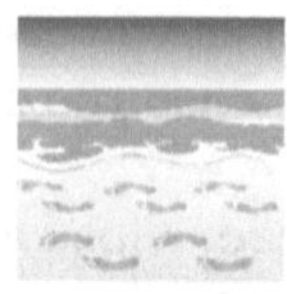

January

New Year's Day

Happy New Year!

As the balloons dropped in a corner, Jenna swapped hugs and smooches with a handsome boy she'd been flirting with on the 2nd Level; Howard and Barbara were locked in a passionate honeymoon-like embrace in their 5th Level penthouse room, having got the kids a room of their *own* for the night; Alex hugged and kissed a *beautiful*, older (must have been all of twenty) girl he had met only minutes before on the 3rd Level; JJ kissed Ann deeply near the pool door; minutes later, Donna *and* Leigh intercepted him—one at a time—as Nick, much to *everyone's* surprise, was in a lip-lock with Ann for *a while*.

Should old acquaintance be forgot…?

***

As they turned out the lights that night, JJ mumbled, "You know Nick *that* well?"

"Hardly at all. *That* was a mid-kiss conspiracy." *HELLUVA kisser, too.*

"Huh?"

"You kiss someone because everyone *else* is kissing everyone *else*, then think: *'let's* play along.' Mid-kiss conspiracy."

"Huh. Leigh and I *kinda* did that in Grenada."

"She told me that she just wanted to see the brass squirm." She crawled into his bed. "*She* told me about Fort Gordon, too." She kissed his chin. "*You're* her Blue-Eyes."

"She's *my* Green-Eyes." She rested her head on his shoulder. "Jealous?"

"Of Leigh? No. *Donna,* maybe…*you two* were going at it."

"*That* was mostly *her* idea."

"*You* didn't resist. And you call yourself a *wallflower*." She pecked his cheek and crawled into her own bed. "Let's get some shuteye."

***

Where's my...

She awoke alone in a room, naked and feeling a little clammy under a heavy quilt. Her memory was out of sequence: she remembered kissing JJ (*Mm, boy!*) and Nick (*WOW what a kisser HE is*); getting *in* this room. She remembered struggling out of her sweater, but *not* hanging it neatly over a hanger in the closet. *Did I drink THAT much? HOW many shots? Six, maybe...seven? Who took my stuff off...Donna; Ann...some GUY?*

"Ugh," she groaned, glancing at the window, glaring sunlight beaming through. "Wish *Mike* was here." She shook her head briskly to get the cobwebs out when the phone rang. "Hello?"

"Hi, *oytzer*," Mike replied. "Your *mom* said you'd be *there*."

"Hi, honey. How goes it?"

"Good. See you in a few minutes."

"What? Where *are* you?"

"*Just* got in town, on my way to you."

"You're *here*?"

"That's affirm. See you suddenly."

***

Oh, how happy I am!

The sun wasn't quite up when she opened her warm brown eyes to his irresistible baby-blues. They made quiet, gentle love as the sun rose, *knowing* that they would *always* be together, one way or another.

***

There was a gentle knock on her door; she opened it slightly, staying behind it. They wrapped themselves around each other in passion as soon as he walked in. "Nice surprise," she smiled.

"Even *bigger* surprise as soon as I—OK, *we*—get *my* clothes off..."

"The bed's in *there*."

"And *we're* in *here*."

"So chain the door; housekeeping's on the way."

***

"Ann, let's talk about getting..." The champagne-and-bloody-Mary full-menu brunch buffet was in full swing when they got to it mid-morning. Howard and Barbara were just getting plates; the kids were swimming.

She stared *at* him, not *seeing* him. *Does sex change my mind?* "No."

"Oh," he pouted. "You're *not* interested?"

"I was asking myself if *making* love *changes*...I told myself 'no.'" She swallowed. "Tideline, my love. We *haven't*...because, *after*, separation will hurt. It *will*, but…I *need to* make *us* work, together *or* apart. But neither of us can still *perform* like teenagers anymore."

Just don't get used to it. "*We* can, honey. I *didn't*…as a teenager."

"*Sounds* like a *personal* problem. John, if we're going to be sharing quarters, expenses *and* laundry bags: what are *we* paying for *this* place?"

"About $40 a day plus local phone calls."

"For *this*?"

"I got *this* from Kurt. Howard used it to get their penthouse; I used it to get Leigh's and Donna's rooms." The plastic card he handed her read:

Owner Discount. Ten days at Owner Rates; Remainder of Stay at Family Pricing (Subject to Availability).

"*Wow*. Kurt *owns* this place?"

"This one and a couple others. He's done well."

"I'll have to thank him for it."

"If we're *sharing* our fortunes, *you* need to be aware of my investments."

He NEVER talks about money; he makes the same as I do. "*What are* you talking about?"

"Eddie…"

***

"Hey, Donna," JJ smiled, stretching his back in the pool. "I see you have *perfectly* acceptable swimwear as well."

"I *do*, thank you, even if *you'd* just as soon have me naked." she grinned demurely, adjusting a shoulder strap of her tankini at the edge of the pool. "And a happy new year to *you*, again."

He watched Nick walk into the pool. *Somebody got lucky.* "And a happy to *you*, too, again. Good night?"

"Great," she sighed. "I wanted to see *your* dreamy blue eyes up close again; once *wasn't* enough. Where's Ann?"

JJ smiled. "Getting ready for 11 o'clock Mass." Just then Leigh and Mike walked into the pool area. "Well, I'll be *dipped* in *shit*. When did *you* get here, brother?"

"I landed at 7 this morning," Mike declared. "Was delayed in Chicago, else I would have been here yesterday afternoon. Hi, Blondie," he sighed, leaning for a hug.

"You *said* you'd be here yesterday," Donna pouted, "I was all ready for the big surprise and *you* never made it."

"Yeah; blame American Airlines. Listen: Leigh and her family are being introduced at our temple Saturday…"

"Really," Leigh made a surprised smile. "You were going to tell *me* when?"

"Right *now, oytzer*. But afterwards there's a *very little* party at *my* place. We want you *all* to come."

"Don't know that *we* had anything planned..." JJ mused. "Pencil us in."

"Sure," Donna exclaimed. "Nick and I will come to *both*..." She glanced at Nick. "*Won't* we?"

Nick shrugged. "I haven't *been* to temple for decades," he sighed. "As good an excuse as *any*..."

"Now, if you'll *excuse* me," JJ declared, pulling himself out of the pool, "*I* have another *social* obligation to fulfill..."

***

"*Whew*! Haven't done *that* for a while." Barbara, filling a two-piece *very* attractively for a woman of 46, plopped down next to Ann's chaise after having swum some *very* impressive laps after Mass. "How's JJ doing?"

"Good." Ann cleared her throat. "We *are* getting quarters together."

Barbara grinned. "Does the *Navy* have objections? *Thinking* about cohabitating with men was illegal for us. *Men* did it all the time, but *us* delicate flowers—*never*."

Hope I get this right the first time. "They won't think *that* highly of my just shacking up, but they can't *stop* me. We accept that our services will likely separate us in the next year or so, but we *want* to be together." She made a face. "Did *that* sound right?"

"Sounded pretty *damn* right to me," Barbara yawned and stretched distractingly, gazing at Howard and the kids playing horseshoes. "So: Galliano shots in our jacuzzi? I'll *chain* the door for an hour."

"Warm?"

"Can *boil* eggs."

"Let's go."

***

"How was *your* new year's, JJ?" Stella dealt three seven-card hands methodically in the weak sunshine through the big picture windows.

"Great, Ma," JJ murmured, picking up his hand. "Saw Leigh; *she* says hi." He picked off the deck and discarded the ten of hearts. *Returning that album didn't make much fuss...*

"Who," Charlie intoned, picking up the ten and discarding the nine of hearts.

"You're not keeping high hearts, Charlie," Stella mumbled. "Leigh Taylor: you met her and her family at Christmas dinner." She picked off the deck and discarded the five of diamonds.

261

"Oh, I keep forgetting you count cards better than I," Charlie lamented. "That young woman that Ann knew, too?" He watched JJ pick up the five and discard the seven of clubs.

"Yep," JJ agreed, watching Charlie pick up the seven and discarded the six of spades.

"I *knew* Ed Taylor," Charlie sighed casually, watching Stella pick off the deck. "In real estate?" She discarded the king of clubs.

"Yeah." JJ guarded his hand. *He KNEW Leigh's dad?* He picked off the deck and discarded the ace of hearts.

Charlie picked up the ace. "Yep. The name of *this* game is GIN!" Stella had 32 points; JJ 43. "We did business when I was in real estate," he continued as JJ dealt.

"Before Ellie died?" Stella picked up the hand JJ dealt and discarded the five of clubs.

"Yep. I sold out to Newhouse. Huh." Charlie picked off the deck and discarded the ten of diamonds.

"Newhouse," JJ cleared he throat, picking off the deck and discarding the five of diamonds. "Their sign is on *this* place, too." *What else AREN'T you saying, Charlie?*

"Yep," Charlie agreed. "Threw 'em a bone," picking up the five and discarding the five of clubs.

"Tomorrow," JJ perused his hand, "I'm seeing Eddie Evans."

"Who?"

"Eddie Evans, that friend of mine from Wolverine." Utter silence fell: The cards, the wind off the lake, even the radiator, which had been knocking all afternoon, fell silent. "He's with Evans and Towne."

"*What for?*" Charlie stared coldly with his who-do-you-think-you-are smirk.

"Investment advice." Charlie's face fell as if it were wet plaster, and for the rest of the afternoon he said *nothing* of substance.

Well, well, Charlie. Now I KNOW what cards you're keeping.

***

"Am I boring you?" They sat at a small table left over from the New Year's bash just outside their suite as JJ sipped schnapps—a Christmas gift from Howard.

"A little," Ann admitted, pink and wrapped in her big fuzzy robe, unaccustomed to the liqueur but feeling warm for the first time in days. "You have *your* studies and your projects; I have *mine*. You've had your visits; I've had mine, and they sometimes overlap. I'm a *little* concerned about your antisocial tendencies." *And the ghosts that haunt you...*

"Not so much *antisocial* as *non-social*. I just don't *connect* well."

"Johnny, you *know* it's PTSD, right? You get the same classes I do."

"Comes in *many* flavors, honey. Apropos of nothing, what *did* Deb say?"

We'll take it up later. "Oh; the rabbit lived."

"She disappointed?"

"More like *relieved*. They're setting a date anyway; they're coming by for lunch Friday."

Thursday

"Morning, Cloud." It was snowing when he awoke, gentle flakes floating by the window.

"Morning, Johnny." She got up to move her sore hip. He reached out for her flannel-covered leg; she arched her spine while he caressed her thigh. "No time, babe," she murmured, gently stopping his hand. *Feels SO nice...*

"Mm." *Tideline, Elrath, tideline.*

"So, bank, and broker. And you want *me* along because...?"

"The bank account will be for our *joint* bills: you *and* me, kid. *And*, I want *you* to meet Eddie."

***

"Why are we *here*" she asked. "Why not the one a block from the hotel?" The parking garage under the National Bank of Detroit building between Woodward and Griswold was half-full. Snow wafted in as they hustled through the door.

"Not all *branches* are correspondent banks" he answered. "The most *portable* is the 'main branch,' as the bankers call it."

The elevator brought them to a vast and opulent lobby, busy with customers. Before they got into a not-short line, she saw... "JJ: that redhead over there: it's *Sam*."

"No shit? Want to wait in line?"

"Not if I don't *have* to." Ann called out before she saw the nameplate: "Sam Potts."

He turned his cool brown eyes up; his round face and expressive mouth broke into joy. "*Ann!* Of all the...where...? And, you *can't* be..."

"Hiya, Sam," JJ smiled. "Been a while."

"Well, *Christ* you two, come along with me." Sam led them from the granite-tiled, brass-and-glass teller area across the carpeted personal banker area to a small conference room, where he stopped for a quick hug. "You *found* each other again."

"Yeah, in Key West," Ann agreed. "A few months ago."

"What were *you* doing down there?"

"Still in the Navy, Sam."

"You too, Johnny?"

"No; Army."

"*That's* right; I *saw* that. Well, you here for a while?"

"Another couple of weeks. You, ah, *run* this place?"

"I'm a glorified, overpaid teller with the title of 'personal banker.' Keeps me off the streets; pays the alimony."

"Alimony?" She was surprised. "To *who*?"

"Rachel Kemp."

"Came in senior year?" She dimly recalled a spindly blonde/brunette.

"Yeah. We got married in '78, and she ditched me in '81."

"Sorry, Sam."

"Eh, water, bridge, long time gone. You're *still* in the Army, Johnny?"

"Yeah. Paper shuffler ..."

Sam looked thoughtful. "No, you're *more* than that. *You* got a medal in Grenada."

"So did a bunch of other guys."

"Oh, OK. So, *you* have business." They opened a new joint account for his royalties and moved his old balance into it, ordered checks, deposit slips and two of those new cash cards for it. The Navy Credit Union had a cash machine where they could make deposits, and there were a couple others in Key West. Once *she* was a bank customer, Ann turned some of Kurt's cash into traveler's checks.

"Sam, can I link a regular bank account to an investment account?"

"Um," Sam stumbled. "There's no *good* way to do *that*, Johnny. What *kind* of investment account?"

"Most of *my* money's over at Evans and Towne, but I can't write *checks* on..."

Sam turned pale. "*Evans* and *Towne*? *Really*? *You* have...?"

"Yeah; buddy of mine's doing me a favor."

"*Oh*." Sam blinked and seemed weak. "Some favor. I can look into it." He sighed, "too bad about Nyquist, huh?"

"Bill? What about him?" Ann was more interested than JJ.

Sam looked surprised. "Thought *you'd* know. He got killed in that Cambodian thing."

"That *Mayaguez* mess? He was a *Marine*?"

"Air Force. Said he was inspired by *your* example, Johnny."

"How?"

"He saw an article on you in the *Eccentric*. No idea *why* he would have remembered *you* after all that time."

"We should get together while we're up here," Ann suggested. "Dinner, drinks, something."

"Sure. I'll bring Darla."

"Darla Templeton? Bottle-blonde cheerleader…?" *First-class bitch?*

"Yeah, *that* one. But *she's* found religion."

"Darla Templeton," JJ mused. "Got a *brother*, Ed?"

"Yeah. He's a Wayne County deputy now."

"Huh. He was Lois's friend in '68, took me to Alban's while my dad was laid out. I've liked ham-and-swiss-on-light-rye ever since."

"Small world."

***

"JJ Elrath for Eddie Evans."

"One moment." The receptionist—a small, older woman with big glasses—spoke into her headset. "Mr. Evans will join you."

A black-suited usher appeared out of the wall behind the receptionist, announcing, "*Mr.* Elrath: *come* with *me*, please." His voice was as *distressingly* deep as Lurch's.

There was something Ann found disquieting about the offices of Evans, Shadsworth, Morgan, and Towne in the Penobscot Building just a block from the bank. The two-story entry foyer leading to the airy lobby was like something out of a movie, with its opulent furnishings on sculpted carpeting, and large oil paintings on the walls. *Just what IS this place? That sign "Private Capital Management" on the wall sounds strange.*

They were led to a small conference room with a big picture window overlooking a wooded roof garden across the street, gleaming in the sunlight after the night's ice storm. As soon as they entered the elegantly furnished wood-paneled room, a small man with thin hair in a tailored suit came through a hidden door. JJ reached out his hand. "Eddie, how *are* ya? Let me introduce Ann Mueller. Ann: Eddie Evans." She shook hands with Eddie, who was surprisingly strong.

"Ann, I'm *so* pleased to meet you." Eddie's voice was smooth, comforting. "Please, both of you, sit. Would you *like* anything? Coffee, tea, something stronger? JJ said *you* would be a part of his financial review, Ann, and I *can't* refuse *him* anything, so…"

"*My* first question is—*you* own this place?"

"My *family* is the majority partner in the firm. I'm the managing partner since my father retired."

"Eddie manages what I left behind from when I worked for Kurt," JJ added, "*and* a little more." He was perfectly relaxed, matter-of-fact. "Maybe coffee, Eddie: black."

Eddie pressed a button in the tabletop. "Coffee black, please Margaret," he spoke into the air.

"What's meant by 'private capital management?'"

Eddie smiled. "You can't just walk in off the street and open an account here: we only deal with referrals. Our *affluent* clients expect more *personal* service than most banks *can* or *will* provide. Let's start, shall we?" Eddie produced two binders from a valise and handed one to each of them. "I'll let you study the summary while we wait."

Ann read the first page carefully. *From $16,100 to over $1.2 million in seven years. WHAT the...?*

"So, Eddie," JJ smiled as the coffee arrived. "How have *you* been? Haven't seen you since, what, '82?"

"*More* than fair. I got married last year."

"Well, great; congratulations. Who's the lucky girl?

"I've known Maryann forever. She..."

"John Jacob," she interrupted, "how did *you make over* a million dollars?"

"Ask *him*."

She glared at Eddie as she fanned through the binder. "I don't see *how* legit investments can perform like this."

Eddie made a slight, calming, spread-fingered gesture with one hand and produced his own binder from the valise. "They *can't,* and they *don't*. On page three...yes, there. Right at the top, there's a line that says 'Outside contributions.' That's where *most* of the account comes from."

"What 'outside contributions?'"

"Page nine. 'Outside contributions breakdown.' You see $400 a year in bonds—that's his Q-bonds. Then you see cash—other money he sends us. Then the *next* line is labeled 'Settlement.' *That's* from the lawsuit."

"What I told you about yesterday, honey," JJ added.

"And the next line is 'Director's Salary,'" Eddie continued. "That's been the *next* most significant contribution: $120,000 since 1979."

"'Director' of *what*?" She knew a *little* about managing a business from her college classes, and knew that $20,000 a year for an absent director was *a lot*.

"CloudWays."

Answers that. "How, *exactly*, does CloudWays work? You gave Wendy a business card, but you *called* someone Monday, didn't you?"

Eddie sipped his coffee. "Invoking specific *names* gets the wheels rolling for—how shall I say it—*concierge* and emergency services. The operators have 24-hour availability to find the required resources. The billing to *most users* is nominal: $150." Eddie set his coffee down. "It was a need we wanted to fill."

"Eddie," JJ murmured. "Add Mueller to that list."

Like I need...eh, maybe. She flipped through the pages. "Here. 'CloudWays Disbursements: $2,421.' What's that?"

"My end of Wendy's trip," JJ answered. "*I* kick in a few bucks."

Why does THAT not surprise me?

"CloudWays is a non-profit," Eddie added. "Most of what *we* pay for is fuel and other non-deductibles. Those performing services usually *donate* their time; the equipment owners let us *lease* for a deduction."

The rest of the meeting was something of a blur for her. JJ was taking out fractions of the annual increase, leaving most of it to grow the portfolio. *He agreed to let me contribute to this trip…like he's going to argue?*

When Eddie finished, she flipped to the last page. "OK, here. 'Projected Net Worth, 1993.' That's given regular contributions and growth?"

"Yes, exactly. Up to his planned retirement from the Army."

"That means the outside contributions are going to keep coming at $20,000 a year?"

"Yes. The directorship is for *his* lifetime. The settlement was what my *family* agreed on, but *I* regarded it as insufficient, so *I* tacked on the directorship of CloudWays. It's the least *I* could do."

He needs his Army pay like I need a third foot. "Can you manage a few thousand of *my* bucks?"

"Honey," JJ murmured. "Hold on. Eddie: joint access to my side?"

Eddie breathed deep. "Limited, *unless* you're married. Precedent, you know. But yes, Ann, I *can*…"

JJ held her chin. "Let's say $10,000 a year without my express say-so, Eddie."

Doubles my Navy pay. "John, no. We're *not*…"

"And another name on my phone card?"

"Phone card: certainly. I *can* arrange *joint* access to your account *with a limit.* We can do *that* just how *you* do it: A credit card with the bill coming here. I'll just need Ann…to…" Eddie quietly left them alone.

* * *

"OK, Sergeant Big Bucks," she started as they drove out of the parking garage. "Let's *hear* it. You *told* me about the lawsuit, but…details, please."

"When I was deposed in '72 and '73, I just told everybody *what I saw* those guys do to Eddie. The suit was settled in '74, but…" he stopped. "Before I went to Germany in '76, I told Eddie and his family about what happened to me *after;* nobody asked me *that* before. Because I told the authorities *who* I saw that night…"

"Leigh and Mike told me *some*, John." She swallowed hard. "I needed to know the *source* of your nightmares, babe."

My best friends. "OK." He was quiet, maneuvering through the unplowed side streets. "The inmates ran *that* asylum; probably still do. I think *that's* why the family gave me that money: for what happened *after*. But I'm left with a pile of money, a dodgy back, sensitivity to cold, and nightmares once in a while…but *never* when *you're* in my bed.

"The entitlement gene missed *me* like it missed my dad. If they'd given me that money right after Wolverine, I'd have *given* it away. But by '79 I realized that I was so busted up that I might just *need* that money to live on if the Army doesn't let me stay in and I can't make myself a living."

"I'm *sorry*, babe…" She concentrated on the treacherous Northwestern Highway traffic and the icy-mud-covered road—Michigan used *sand*, not *salt*, in the winter.

He had a sudden thought; unbidden. "*Where* did the money come from for the girls' weddings? I *saw* those bills; they weren't cheap. *Was* Charlie paying for them, finally?"

"Probably," she answered, "but now *you're* probably the richest sergeant in the Army."

He chuckled. "And *you* have access to it, too, making you…"

"The richest petty officer in the *Navy*." She smiled. "But it *ain't my money*, honey."

"It *could* be *if*…"

"*Don't*, John. Not *now*." She gazed at him as he watched the roadway, quiet except for the sand and ice grinding under the tires. "Tell me about CloudWays."

"*Not* named for you: it was already a going concern when we took it over. Eddie's *father's* mother got sick when *he* was overseas, and there was no way he could get back to see her before she passed. He wanted to make sure that *less* of *that* kind of thing happened, and so do I: Ma *did* get sick while I was in Germany. According to Eddie, his dad looked for a solution until he found that someone *else* had started a firm that could do what he wanted.

"CloudWays moves about one service member a month for a Red Cross-verified family emergency. Door-to-door, *from* anywhere in the world *to* anywhere, any time of the day or night. *Most* of what they do is medical transport—organs for transplant; sick people for special care; specialists wherever they're needed." He sighed. "I'm going to say this *once*, Claudia Ann Mueller, love of my life: I've come to feel safer in *your* embrace than I can *remember* feeling in my mother's. You *want* me, Cloud? I'm *yours*. Forever and ever amen."

What's left to keep us apart? Little things—just my career in the Navy and his with the Army. "Please, not *now*, babe."

"I'm a patient man, honey."

***

"Johnny; you don't drink much. Knowing what I do about *you*, I sometimes wonder why." Leigh and Mike joined Ann and JJ at the hotel's happy hour.

"Leigh, I admit there *have been* moments when I thought that an escape of some kind was preferable," JJ grinned widely. "I tried *a lot* of things after Wolverine—the standard gamut of dope and pills you can get almost anywhere." The atrium was more-or-less back to where it had been before the New Year's party, with errant balloons hiding in corners and a few renegade tables and chairs stuck on upper levels. "Nothing actually worked for me because the scars and the memories were still there when it wore off. Then there's Charlie: a *fine* example of the efficacy of inebriants to dull one's feelings. But, from time to time, I drink too much peppermint schnapps." He sighed, downing his second shot. "I have little pouches in my mind where I put everything. March around in circles long enough and you'd do it, too. You guys occupy a *very special* pouch."

"Hey, Leigh," Ann grinned sadly, breaking a long silence, "do *you* remember Bill Nyquist?"

"Your junior prom date? He was at that Christmas dance, too, yeah?"

"Ah," Mike added, "9th Grade: he had a talent for metalworking."

"Yeah, that was him," Ann smiled. "He joined the Air Force and was killed in '75; that *Mayaguez* thing."

"*Damn*," Mike groaned. "I worked intercepts on that mess."

"*I* propose a toast," JJ announced, "to the *memory* of Bill Nyquist; junior prom date, metalworker, fellow veteran, and one of the last casualties of that most-misunderstood Cold War struggle to find the limits of Soviet power: the American adventure in Southeast Asia."

Bill Nyquist!

The three paratroopers sang the last, funeral verse and chorus of "Blood Upon the Risers" while Ann hummed along:

Gory, gory what a helluva way to die!
Gory, gory what a helluva way to die!
Gory, gory what a helluva way to die!
And he ain't gonna jump no more!

From behind the bar, an older man joined in, reverberating mournfully in the atrium.

Friday

"Morning Johnny. Know what I want to do today?" She pulled her covers around her.

"Morning, Cloud. No, what?"

"Get warm and stay naked."

"My money's corrupting you."

"Please. I haven't spent a nickel of your money…directly. I haven't been *really* warm for more than a few hours for two weeks, and I need to air out."

"*Our* money, my dear. Wouldn't Bob be shocked?"

"*He's* wanted to see me naked since we met."

"How about we *all* get naked in here. Think Debbie would be up for that?"

"*She'd* lust for *you*. Maybe I *should* get dressed for a few hours."

"*And* I need shaving cream, toothpaste and sticky notes."

"While *you're* out, can you get me a box of tampons? Don't need 'em *now*, but probably *soon*…"

"Sure. What kind?"

***

"So, Deb," Ann whispered, "what happened?" They met for the Friday lunch buffet in the atrium that catered to the business crowd.

"Thought I *was*, but I'm *not*," Debbie shrugged. "Are you free next Saturday?" The buffet featured five different kinds of salads, the usual bread and cold cuts, tenderloin tips in a rich gravy and JJ's favorite: egg salad and caviar sandwiches.

"Think so."

"Stand up for me?"

"*Proud* to."

"Adams and Big Beaver. 9:00."

"Really," JJ was stunned. "You a *member*?"

"Yeah. Since '71."

"Huh. My father and grandmother were eulogized there, my sister Lois was married there. I haven't been there regularly since '70. Small world."

"Yeah. Did you *know* the Taylors? Leigh's our age."

"Leigh Taylor? Sure. Saw her last night…"

"Oh, she's *here*? We need *her*, too."

"Listen, JJ," Bob mumbled as the ladies went far afield, "this is kind of last-minute. Deb's got Ann and a friend from work and my sister…"

"Carol?"

"Yeah. I've got Deb's brother and Ann's brother Jim. Can you balance my side of the aisle?"

"Sure." He looked curious. "Why the rush?"

"We've been engaged twice now," Bob offered. "The first time we broke it off because we just couldn't bring ourselves to set a date. The second time was at Thanksgiving, and we just said 'we do it by New Year's or break up for good.' Then Deb heard Ann was coming up—now, Leigh." He watched Deb for a moment, smiling. "The earliest Saturday we could book the church was 11 January. So…"

JJ was suddenly distracted by a familiar face. "*Jenny*," he called, "over here!" Jenny hurried through the crowd, embracing JJ as he stood up. "Hey, sweetheart," JJ whispered. "*So* good to see you." Her hair a little thinner, but she had the same bright face and Rubenesque build.

"John, babe, *WOW*!" She pulled away, holding his arms. "Look at you! War hero and famous author! My husband is jealous."

"Jenny *Jacobs?*" Jenny hugged Ann and Debbie, who were surprised to see their old grade-school classmate again.

"Hi, I'm Jenny Kent," she extended a hand to Bob. "*They* know my maiden name. Good thing I stop in here for lunch on Fridays, hey?"

"Yeah, sure," JJ said. "You here alone?"

"With some people I work with," who she waved away. "I got what you asked for, Johnny." She scribbled *Ask 799; Sale 750* on a cocktail napkin. "About what you'd expect." She smiled broadly. "Gotta give Newhouse their due: they do well on high-end properties. *Then*…" She suddenly looked sad.

"Then, what?"

"They show up on *our* doorsteps offering to cross-sell our listings, then calculate commissions on the *brokered* price instead of the *listing* price: half of what we'd *usually* get and *not* what everybody *else* does, but it's better than zero and faster. We stay alive, but barely. They cut their fees on residential properties to nearly nothing and make money in commercial. That, and they can bury us in signs."

"Yours is a family owned firm, right?"

"Yeah. Mom and Dad were both realtors. Now my brothers and I run it. We're starting a whole new venture with Ed Taylor out of New York. We're becoming Jacobs/Taylor, give Newhouse a run for their money."

"Leigh's father," JJ mumbled. "She *talked* about that."

"Glad I'm not in real estate," Debbie mumbled. "Jen, *come* to my wedding?"

"Wow! When?"

"Next Saturday."

"Sure."

As the ladies chatted, JJ whispered to Bob. "Reception?"

"Ideas?"

"How many?"

"Both sides, about sixty, maybe."

"I can get you a good price here. After?"

"Can't afford a real honeymoon right now."

"Weekend here, then? Like I said…"

"Appreciate it." Bob looked at Debbie, bright and cheery. He smiled. "*How* much?"

"Cheap: consider it a wedding present. It's for Ann, too."

"Uh-huh." Bob looked dubious. "Why? *We* just met."

"It's what buddies are for."

***

"Jenny's a little taller and a little blonder," Ann sighed at dinner. "But she packs her weight well. Good to see her again."

"Yeah. Says she plays tennis and basketball couple times a week. Still swimming, too."

"Still skinny-dipping?"

"*That* she didn't say." He shifted uncomfortably. "Her husband has had trouble coming back from the war. I want to stay in touch."

"He's older?"

"Five years. I've been dealing with nervous vets for years."

"Me, too. We do what's needed, Johnny."

Saturday

"Morning, Johnny." She blinked herself awake in the dull sun, watching his back stretches.

"Morning, Cloud." He kissed her ear before he pulled his sweats on. "Want to call Tom." He twisted his neck painfully. "Laundry; laps; that thing with Mike and Leigh." He glanced at her with a small smile. "Laps, maybe."

"*Maybe.*"

He called Florida after they started laundry; she went down to the pool. After several minutes he hung up and scratched some notes as housekeeping was knocking on their door. After their workouts, he relayed what Tom had said: three apartments in the same building just coming on the market.

"Wow. Why so cheap?" She stood in water up to her armpits, glistening and breathing deep—the one time of day when she felt physically fit and not slightly beat up.

"Not *that* attractive. Partly furnished; no view to speak off; off the strip; no pool nor washer but a laundromat next door. Tom said we can pay him back the deposit." He hung on the pool wall, breathing hard. "It'll

272

be ours when we get back."

"*Tideline*, babe—*most* of the time." She sauntered toward him.

"Hu-huh. Apparently, he and Kristin are spending a *great* deal of time together."

"And how's Tom with that?" She stood in front of him and ran her hands down his sides, resting on his bony hips. *Good luck, Kristin.*

"He *has* spoken to her father." He reached for her waist. *Be happy, Tom.*

"What? How?" She pressed closer to him.

"Telephone; Christmas. He took both Kristin *and* Betty out for New Year's. They double-teamed him at midnight."

Startling...no, knowing them. "You mean a *threesome*?" She drove her hips into his. *Fascinating; erotic.*

"Who knows? With him—or *them*—in one of the lowers and us in the upper? *Might* be fun." He slid his hands up and down her back.

"Yeah. And a deli in front?" She pressed her chest against his.

"Yeah, where we got our late supper." He locked his hands behind her.

"Sounds...fabulous. What about the *other* lower?" Their faces were inches apart. "Housekeeping done with the room?"

He looked up at the reflection in the atrium wall. "Looks like it. *Wendy's* expressed an interest."

"Oh. Then *how about* we do *some*thing about..." she gently rocked her hips, "...*that*?"

***

Leigh, Ed and Cathy lit out of Adam's limousine amid smiling strangers, who all seemed to know what they were there for. The Dietz's met them just inside the door and walked them into the crowded sanctuary, where the second pew in the center was miraculously clear.

As they filed in, Mike took care to see that *he* was first in, and Ben took care to ensure *he* was last. Leigh thought it odd, but having never been to a Jewish service didn't know any different. Many more faces smiled and nodded. Donna winked broadly.

The service began with Hebrew that sounded lyrical—the only word Leigh *barely* understood was *Israel*—that the congregation responded to by standing up. The next words Leigh understood was when the rabbi smiled at the Taylors and said, "today, our reading will be in English."

There followed a familiar-*sounding* Old Testament reading, and an amusing sort-of sermon about hangovers being God's way of admonishing overindulgence. Then, the rabbi stepped into the sanctuary and raised his hand towards Mike. "Michael Dietz, *please* introduce us."

Mike touched Leigh's elbow and stood up. "This is my Gentile friend,

Leigh Elizabeth Taylor."

Leigh smiled and stood, trying *not* to feel like a prize cow. "*This* is my mother, Catherine Ingle Taylor, and my father, Edward Addison Taylor." Cathy and Ed smiled beatifically, nodding.

The rabbi smiled and clapped his hands together softly as the congregation nodded appreciatively. He then gestured to Donna, who stood. "This is *my* friend, Dominic Michael Paulson, who is of our faith." Nick stood unsteadily as the congregation smiled and the rabbi applauded.

As a member of the congregation sang *Kaddish* to end the service, Leigh suddenly felt as if she belonged, but was mildly surprised, that Donna introduced Nick. *Never one for half-measures, Blondie.*

***

There was homework to be done at the Northwestern; there was a bizarre film version of *Lord of the Rings*; there was *Enemy Mine*. After she came back from confession (once a month) Ann placed a phone call to Florida. She hung up, slightly stunned. JJ, reading for his meteorology course, looked up. "Problem?"

"No. Betty's *seen* that place: small bedrooms but big main rooms: kitchen and living room in all three units are undivided." She paused, smiled broadly. "So were *those three* at New Year's."

"Huh. So, they…"

"Apparently. *You* ever do that?"

"Me? I was lucky to have *one* at a time. You?"

"Never even came *close*."

***

"Hi, Monica," JJ grinned when she answered the double front door of the Dietz home. She looked like a female version of Mike in a pantsuit, with steel-gray eyes, pale, ruddy skin and thick brown hair.

"Oh, *hello*, John," Monica burbled, embracing him lightly; Mike's parents *never* called him JJ. "Come in, please. Michael's probably in the kitchen." She extended her hand to Ann. "I'm Monica Dietz."

"Ann Mueller. Forgive him for his lack of manners…"

"Now *wait* a minute! I just hadn't…"

"Never mind," Monica smiled. "You're *welcome*. Please; refreshments are in the dining room; the party's all over the lower level."

"We'll be visiting my brother Monday…"

"Oh, the *Parkinson's*; yes," Monica answered. "We *still* don't know them well. I *should* make more effort." In Bloomfield Hills, neighbors for years might barely know each other unless something *else*—usually church or school—joined them.

"I *love* your home, Mrs. Dietz," Ann enthused. "So…*big!*"

"Oh, *please* call me Monica. Come, let me *show* you the place." Though JJ had been in the 4,500-square-foot neo-Classical revival home, he still marveled at the round foyer with its curved stairway; at the living room's limestone fireplace that took up an entire wall floor-to-ceiling—its façade turning the corner onto an adjoining wall; at the dining room big enough for an infantry platoon to chow down; at the commercial-sized kitchen; at the library bigger than Ann's condo living room; at the five bedroom suites upstairs taking up as much space as the first floor of Ann's billets. "Ann: Michael tells me *you're* in the Navy: His uncle Mordechai was in the Navy during the war. What do *you* do for them?"

"I'm a diver, among other things," Ann answered.

"Oh, *that* sounds exciting! I know John does something in intelligence in the Army, like Michael. I worked with the USO during the war."

"Oh, thank you for serving. You know, the USO is mostly absent now…" JJ had always thought Monica was a delightful woman. At the same time, he admired the easy way Ann made friends: JJ usually made new friends only after old ones were out of his life.

Then he heard Monica say "…such a delightful story, Ann. John, you should write a book about how you found Ann again."

"I *should*," he smiled. "If I were any good at writing that sort of thing."

"I *read* your book," Monica smiled. "Not the sort of thing I *usually* read, but you *have* a way with words. *You* can probably write anything."

Mike appeared, offering canapes, bussing Ann on the cheek. "Glad you came, brother," he mumbled. "Our *closest* friends and family…"

"Hey, Donna," Ann smiled, "Who's…"

"Hi, guys," Donna grinned. "These are Mike's sisters, Sara and Kiera."

"Pleased to meet you," JJ grinned, "only Kiera and I *met*…"

"New Year's '73," Kiera declared. "He's one great kisser, too."

"The Parkinson's are *your* family, aren't they, JJ" Donna asked. "Because I *just* saw Jo and her dad come home."

Jo? "Huh," JJ frowned, "haven't *seen* my niece for…"

"So, this was a *what?*" Cathy plied Monica with questions in the kitchen.

"Introduction," Ben answered. "We don't use *shidduch*—Jewish matchmaking—so we *bakenen*—introduce to *honor* the traditional ways." He smiled. "And Donna introduced *her* friend because he's not of our community. It's *proper* that this be *done*, whether a woman does it or not."

"And we started doing *that* here in Detroit," Sara explained. "No reason women can't make their own matches."

"*I* did," Leigh smiled.

"Fascinating," Ed intoned. "My foster family was lapsed Jews."

"Didn't know *that*, Dad," Leigh frowned. "You don't talk about your youth."

"Not a lot to say, honey," Ed replied. "Rural Albany, scrimping just to stay alive. First time I saw a bill larger than a ten was 1939, when I got a job delivering milk. They died in a fire when you were little."

"I remember *that*," Leigh frowned. "You were sad for *weeks*."

"Well, Mike," Cathy asked, gazing sternly at Mike, "does she *belong* to you now?"

Having just walked into the kitchen, Mike seemed confused. "Um, no, *ma'am*…"

"What's with the 'ma'am?' Shouldn't *we* be on better terms than *that*?"

"Well, ah, Cathy, I…"

"And shouldn't *you* be asking *me* for something?"

Mom, don't: Please? "Honey; Mom's just being…"

"*Ahem*," Ben interrupted with a grin. "Forgive my son's *forwardness*, Mrs. Taylor. Would Michael be *acceptable* to *you* and *Mr.* Taylor as a suitor for your daughter?"

"*Well*," Cathy grinned. "About time someone asked *me*. I'm not *sure*, *Mr.* Dietz; *what* are his *prospects?*"

"*Mom; Ben*," Leigh groaned, "*we're right here!* Sandy: just *ask* Mom and Dad if we can go out."

"I, well, I…OK: Cathy; Ed: may I have your permission to call upon your daughter?"

Ed glanced bemusedly at Cathy, who stood, hands on hips, frowning sternly at Mike, who looked like he wanted to run away. She inhaled deeply, filling her chest expansively against her tailored suit, an odd expression on her face. "The *call-upon* cow left the milking parlor *years* ago." She walked carefully-yet-saucily towards him, placing both her hands against his cheeks. "Hurt her, and I'll flay you alive," she whispered, kissing him gently. "You'll get *used* to me, boy."

✳✳✳

"Fabulous marinara," Leigh exclaimed. "they used real wine." They were relaxing in the Dietz's big basement after the party.

JJ mumbled. "I can't tell."

"You don't *like* food much, do you, brother," Mike asked. "Mama put out her *very best* veal recipe first time we fed you, and you said it was 'good.'"

"Sorry, brother, but my taste buds are dead. My mom's cooking would be refused by starving African villages."

"Fact," Ann agreed. "Stella's culinary skills are so bad the Borgias wanted to hire her."

"Not a nice thing to say about your boyfriend's mother," Leigh smiled.

"OK, Leigh," JJ chuckled. "I'll give you an example. Ma was making some casserole—can't remember *what* was in it—and the cap came off the pepper shaker and dumped into it. She scraped off what she *thought* was too much and stuck it in the oven. It was so bad the dog turned his nose up at it." He smiled. "True story. She can't taste sour milk, and can barely smell bad meat."

"No wonder you're so skinny," Mike chuckled. "Undernourished."

"If I hadn't gone to boarding schools starting at fifteen, ptomaine was in my future."

***

They sat in the kitchenette's booth, sipping her chilled wine when he, without ceremony or warning, pulled two composition books out of his backpack. "My letters to you. Last one was after our first weekend."

She smiled and stared at the battered books before she reached in *her* book bag and pulled out two big envelopes. "Mine to *you*. There's four. One, just after Don shipped out; one when Dad got married. One when I left San Diego and Cable; the last…after I miscarried. I had to say some things that I couldn't just *say* face-to-face. Not then." She smiled. "Just read them, babe."

They spent the next hour perusing—not *quite* reading—each other's lives on paper. She scanned as far as August 1985:

…Key West is a desolate-yet-colorful place. It would be so much better if I knew where you were, if I could touch you, hold you. My heart seems incomplete without you, even if I see you in my dreams …

She cocked her head. "I want to go to Mass with *our* family tomorrow. Brunch after. Want to come?"

"If you don't mind a lapsed Protestant, sure."

"I've never held it against you, and I *don't* want to convert you. Mom couldn't convert Dad: not sure she tried."

He nodded, with her last letter's words in his head:

…Your love and friendship mean more to me now than I could ever have imagined…holding YOU in my arms was the only thing that saved me tonight.

***

"Thanks for today, *oytzer*. It's important that my people know *of* you before we go much further."

"How *much* further?"

"*Any* further."

277

"Do they expect me to convert?"

"What's important to any Jewish community is that you lead a good life."

"Is sex outside marriage part of a good life?"

"Rabbi Swarovski had a lesson in Hebrew school: if two people are kind to each other, their love cannot be a sin."

"I'll *remember* that."

Sunday

"Morning, Johnny." Roused by his sheet-wrestling as sunlight filled the room, she wrapped a bare arm around him absently.

"Morning Cloud." He shivered as they touched lips gently. "I *love* you, Cloud."

"I love *you*, Johnny. Nine o'clock Mass."

***

"I'm surprised you *don't* know my family," Ann smiled, shaking Charlie Junior's hand that afternoon. His hair was thinning; his spare frame was at least half a head taller than his father's.

"So you said," his wife Dorothy answered, bussing JJ on the cheek: They lived in the evening shadow of the Mueller condo. Like Julia, Dorothy had a pretty, oval face and a terrific figure, even in her Oakland County Sheriff's uniform.

"Beer for everyone but Dot? Red *or* white, dear?"

"Rosé, Chuck," Dorothy tried an exasperated face. "He *knows* what I want; he's just being *Chuck*. Look around while I get out of my monkey suit." The layout of the Parkinson place was like the Mueller's: an entry hall that led to the kitchen/dining room or the sunken living room; a short hall to the master bedroom and den. Like the Mueller's, the walls were lined with photos. There were Brenda's and Lois's wedding photos, and Will's and Kurt's and their own. And there was Julia's graduation from the FBI Academy, another of her wedding. There was also Charlie and Stella's "family" wedding photo, with fourteen-year-old JJ twisting to get out of the shot.

"You were trying too hard to get out of that picture," Ann mumbled, standing next to him, gazing at a framed Washington *Times* wire-service version of Carol's article that hung near a corner.

"Julia sent *that* to us." Charlie was behind them. "I got a Silver Star myself."

JJ took the proffered beer. "Korea, yeah?"

"Pork Chop at the end: A week that *seemed* longer."

"Anything like the movie?" Ann was curious, having just seen it a few afternoons before.

"No. Even the book was fudged."

"See any Chinese?"

"Too many." He was quiet. "Alive *and* dead."

"Julia says you guys met in Florida?" Dorothy emerged in a casual pantsuit.

"We ran into each other there, but we grew up together," Ann smiled. "My dad says JJ was barely a week old, and I was barely two weeks when they put us in the same crib. We've slept together since we were in diapers." She caught JJ stifling a chuckle. Realizing what she'd said, she chortled herself. Suddenly he burst out laughing before they all did.

"Could *not* have timed *that* better with a script," Charlie managed. Dorothy grimaced to hide a grin. "I *thought* it sounded odd. Anita said you were old friends."

"Our parents were in high school together," JJ went on. "We were neighbors on Round Lake until '67."

Charlie added, "Jules said something about a chance meeting?"

Ann told of their reunion. "Then the Navy fell on me like a stock anchor."

Dorothy looked surprised. "For a *kiss*?"

"Professionalism's at stake," JJ explained. "Since we're in different services *but* the same pay grade, there's less concern about *us* than there would be otherwise."

"But I've got three years' in-grade on *him*, so I *really* outrank him." Ann gave a slow wink.

"She's *always* been in command of my heart," JJ smiled.

"*Good* one," Charlie smiled as the ladies rolled their eyes and groaned.

As afternoon turned to evening and Charlie's dinner turned to dessert and aperitifs, the conversation turned to families. "Your mother's a lovely woman, JJ" Dorothy grinned. "But that *mess* you and Jules were in, when was that? 1970?"

"Yeah. *You* guys know, but—short version for Ann: We'd been swimming, and I was in my bathroom with the door closed; Julia was out in my bedroom. I hear a scream and open the door, and she's trying to cover herself and growling at the old man *in my room*. He grabs *my* throat and starts accusing *me* of…you get it. Julia said he'd done *something* like that before, with her and her cousins."

"Ugh," Charlie grunted. "Only time I had reason to curse your mom."

"Julia's gotten over it."

"Only with JJ's help," Dorothy smiled, downing her crème de menthe. "And I never thanked you for *that*, JJ."

"Yeah," Charlie added. "At first, I…"

"What *help?*"

"You asked her out. Not *once*, but *often*." Dorothy looked like she was giving testimony.

"We didn't *care* about your relationship-by-marriage—*that* was just technical," Charlie admitted. "She hadn't *started* dating yet that first time. She was *interested* but..."

"Terrified," Dorothy finished. "More than once she told me 'no boy would *ever* be interested in me.' Sad because she's always been a beautiful girl."

"But all *I* did—and it terrified *me*—was ask her out for pizza and a movie," JJ muttered.

Dorothy smiled. "She couldn't *sleep* the night you called her. I told her to go run around the block. Probably the most exercise she got all that summer. Right then *I* thought you were the greatest sixteen-year-old boy in the world. I had just made the Sherriff's Department, and Julia seemed destined for spinsterhood..."

"Come *on*," Charlie blurted in disbelief. "At *sixteen?*"

"*Oh* yeah," Ann nodded. "Sixteen is make-or-break for a girl's social life. If it's dead *then*, it *often will* be because you just give up."

"Right," Dorothy agreed, "and I could *see* Julia giving up. If you *hadn't* called, she'd probably *still* be living with us."

"After that first date," Charlie added, returning with another beer for Ann. "The old bastard called me, said 'I *know* this little pervert has assaulted my granddaughter. Get her to a doctor immediately.'"

"I *saw* that," JJ grinned.

"Yeah. I looked at Julia—floating and bubbly like I hadn't seen her before—I just laughed and hung up."

"And the old man was *flabbergasted*," JJ chuckled.

All evening, Ann thought Dorothy looked somehow familiar. "Dorothy, how *are* your brothers these days?"

"They're...how do *you*..." Dorothy stopped, smiled. "Oh, *my*. Your *hair* was longer."

"It *was* you, in Pontiac..." She explained their chance meeting years before outside her mother's care facility. "I was so sad my parents were divorcing, but Dorothy..."

"I was just going on shift, and Ann was crying about a block from the station. I offered a tissue, told her about *my* parent's last *interlude*. But JJ: I gather you and Charlie Senior are not on good terms...?"

"We've *never* really been on *good* terms, but I'm starting to worry about losing track of Ma if the old man feels like cutting me off."

"Would it be OK if *I* looked in on her from time to time? She's, what, 62 now?"

"Sixty-three this month."

"And he's…seventy…seven?" Dorothy glanced at Charlie. "Seventy-eight in September? The Sheriff's Senior and Family Task Force will keep tabs on them, OK?"

"I'd appreciate it. And, Dorothy: I want to thank you again for our little chat when Nana Burgess died, the one about step-families."

"Oh, *that*," Dorothy smiled. "I've been in *two* of 'em; I've figured out how to live with them. *Strive for neutrality* is how *I* survived."

"Still, Dot, I was fourteen, scared, didn't know shit from Shinola. You at least put me on the right *path*."

"Well, John, you paid *us* back by saving Julia."

As they were getting ready to leave, Charlie smiled at JJ. "Brenda's wedding: Jules got home at the crack of dawn *looking* like she'd been swimming. You know *anything* about *that*?"

"It was *SO* muggy we went into the lake in our underwear."

Brother eyed brother suspiciously. "Yeah? Underwear?"

OK; we TOOK IT OFF; we were sixteen; she was GORGEOUS. "Yeah?"

Charlie grinned. "Uh-huh. That's what *she* said. Not sure *we* believed *her* at the time, either."

"Charlie," Ann offered with a smile. "I have it on *good* authority that your brother, at *that* time, had *not* yet…"

"Cloud? Please? He doesn't need to know *all* the details."

"Just the *important* ones, babe."

* * *

"How long will he be gone for, Mom?" The two women walked back to the parking structure after Ed boarded the last Detroit-New York flight of the day.

"End of January, then he's here for six weeks, then off again for a month." Cathy stopped. "In June he'll sell out to his New York partners, and Jacobs/Taylor *should* be launched and he'll be *here* most of the time."

"Must be wearing on both of you."

"Like you and Mike. How often do *you* see *him*?"

"Maybe every three months for a long weekend as long as we're in proximity. We write or call or both every week."

They were quiet again until they got to California Circle. "Leigh, I'm going to say this once and never again: Grab what happiness you can *while* you can. Marry Mike and lead separate lives together if you *have* to, but go for it."

"OK, Mom."

"I *mean* it, honey. Your father and I—our separations are wearing *us* out. He's selling out in New York because he wants to be *here*. And *my* job: they want to bump me up."

"Great, Mom! To what?"

"The prosecutor's office. More money; more responsibility."

They were quiet again until they sat at the kitchen island. "Just…keep doing what you love, honey. And keep loving *who* you want."

"OK, Mom. You too."

Monday

"Morning, Johnny." She crawled into his bed and kissed his ear softly.

"Morning, Cloud." The sky was broodingly dark when they woke up, and with the temperature fluttering around freezing it was threatening more sleet and snow.

"Remember my appointment today. Because I *shouldn't* get pregnant, we need an IUD until *you...*"

"…Get a vasectomy, yeah." While the services provided basic health care, they did *not* provide birth control.

"I *hate* to ask, babe, but…I don't know what the exam and tests and all that are going to *cost*. I have *some* cash now, but…"

It's OUR responsibility now. "Take the Visa card; Eddie put you on the account. Yours should be in the mail when we get back. I've *got* to finish that meteorology class this morning and get it in the mail. PT?"

"Let's get to the pool before the kids do."

***

"Beer, please," Ann mumbled at the bartender of The Rock Station—the Clawson version of Dinky's. The hard-nosed woman moved slowly.

"Boilermaker with rye, Mickey," Sid announced a few minutes later, plopping on a stool not far away. Guitars interspersed with posters of '60s and '70s rock bands hung forlornly on the walls. He dropped the shot in the beer mug, waited a moment and downed it.

She watched the doors out of the corner of her eyes, waited a few minutes, got up and went to the rest room. After a few moments she walked past Sid and out the front door, started the Fury and waited.

"Hi, Sid," she smiled as he got in with her ten minutes later. "Been a while."

"Hello, Claudia," he grinned, his hands deep in his pockets. "Glad you called." He looked around. "I want to congratulate you on your achievement in the Navy. I always admired you."

"Thanks; we've known each other since 1st Grade, so that's a *lot* of admiration. But *you've* moved up in the world, too. Your own business?"

"The Newhouses of the world keep me busy." He shivered. "I was only with Johnny Elrath in 4th and 5th Grades. Looks like he's got it together."

"Yes, he *does*. What can you tell me about any threats to Johnny or Leigh?"

"I'm afraid Johnny's in Joe Dryden's sights. Leigh; persistently a matter of Newhouse interest."

"Johnny's because of some junior high thing, Leigh says. But what are they *after* with Leigh, Sid? There's *no way* she had that kid."

"*I* believe that it's *not* Leigh's ex-husband that's pushing this program. I *know* Dryden's up to his neck in it, but he doesn't have the juice to do it on his own. To create this kind of fuss over a fifteen-year-old boy who's never met his supposed mother…something *else* is going on. Can't quite figure out just what."

"But…*why* does *Joe* want *so* much to say *Leigh's* the kid's mom?"

"We *don't* know."

***

"Mary, this is Ann," JJ grinned as Ann extended her hand.

"*Finally* putting a face to the name," Mary answered with a gentle smile. She had thinning and graying auburn hair, and was struggling with weight after seven children.

"And *Jo*? Haven't see *you* for an age." She smiled thinly but said nothing, sitting on the sofa. Josephine—the older twin by twenty minutes—was fair like her father and rail-thin. There was a time when Jo and her *sister* Mary were openly contemptuous of JJ. He had no idea why since they had exchanged perhaps three words—ever: *They* preferred to sneer at him. Kurt came into the living room with drinks and appetizers. "So, how's the rest of the brood, Mary," JJ asked.

Mary grinned. "Mary is OK, last we knew; that was last summer. She doesn't *communicate* a great deal."

She went on about the five boys JJ barely knew before Jo mumbled, "*I'm* doing OK, JJ. Better than I *was*."

"She moved back in last month," Kurt sighed.

"Just *say* it, Dad: I took too many pills," Jo added thinly, glancing at JJ. "You never knew *why* we hated you."

"You don't *have* to do this now, Jo," Mary intoned. "*They* just got here…"

"Yeah, Mom, *I* have to." She looked into JJ's eyes for the first time he could remember. "I read your book."

"Like it?"

"I was determined *not* to, but you *seem* to know what you're talking about, so yeah."

"A lot of people say that."

"Know anything about firearms?" Kurt interrupted, gazing curiously at JJ.

"In my line of work, you know a *little* about a *lot*."

Kurt led them into a corner of the dining room where a gun cabinet sat with several long guns inside. Kurt pulled one out and handed it to JJ. "This one?"

"Huh: M97 Remington 12-gage trench gun. Genuine?"

"Mary's father brought it back from France in '18. We take it out once in a while." He pulled out a pistol and handed it to Ann. "Her mother's."

"A .45," Ann mumbled.

"Nope," JJ answered. "Nine-millimeter Browning Hi-Power. Mary's *mother's*?"

"She grew up in a rough neighborhood. Just got *this* one," Kurt pulled out a bigger shotgun. "They call *this* a road-blocker: 10-gauge magnum semi-auto. One round of #4 shot is like firing a *box* of .25 ACP. With a tube extension…fires five rounds in three seconds: destroy a car front end *that* fast."

The evening progressed with talk about families, military service, the price of gas and the pernicious effects of prolonged vacations. Jo added a phrase here and there. As Kurt and Mary were cleaning up from dinner, Jo swilled her coffee, then glanced pointedly at Ann. "My sister and I didn't associate with *real* people in school. We hung out with the wrong ones. *I wanted* to hang out with *you*."

"*Me*," Ann answered, surprised.

"Yeah, especially after you won that race. I thought it was *great*: Mary said it was another concession to the patriarchy."

JJ answered, "you didn't give people a chance, Jo. Gynocentrism was a dead end."

"Like *any* cult, it's an end in itself. It can't adapt, can't tolerate any resistance or serious examination." Ann, having heard of the movement, didn't recall anything positive about it.

"My sister *still* can't see that, but *I* did even *then*," Jo agreed. "Recipe for extinction, but I followed *her* lead since we were thirteen…can't say *why* now. Mary's on her fifth relationship in two years. She keeps pushing people away with her slogans. She tried switching for a while, but even the gynes she *agrees* with can't stand her philosophical intensity. Guys only get *one* thing from her."

"What does she *offer*?"

Jo smiled sadly. "She's like: 'I'll talk *my* politics, copulate *my* way, scream of *your* violation of *me* when I tire of you and call it a relationship.'"

"Pretty empty for guys."

"Not much better for gynes—oh, hell, *women. I've* been that way. I'm twenty-nine and lonely: tired of it. So, I took too many pills." She suddenly smiled, a beautiful look on a *very* pretty, round-faced girl with light blue eyes like her father. "You and Julia hit it off."

"We had fun as kids," JJ shrugged. "When did *you* last see *her*?"

"Um…that engagement party at *your* place, and that *awful* cabin with Gramps Charlie." Kurt and Mary returned to the living room, sitting curiously with their daughter. "He *saw* the three of us while we were changing. The *letch* just stood outside the window watching us getting dressed for I don't *know* how long."

"*That* can be life-changing," Ann grimaced.

"Then *you* were in *his* house. Mary made a leap of logic, figured *you* were just like *him*, and I did too. Sorry."

JJ muttered, "you know Donna Hammerfest, lives…?"

"Just across the way, yeah. She's helping me."

"Jo's an outpatient at Beaumont now," Kurt added. "Donna's *quite* the young woman."

Ann smiled. "I've known *her* since junior high; not *well*, but I know she's a good gal."

"And the Dietz's want to know *you* better, Kurt," JJ mumbled. "*You* should break the social inertia and knock on their door. *You* should reach out." The Parkinson's were Catholics whose children were younger than the Dietz's kids. Contacts between the families were thus casual and brief.

"Well," Mary sighed, "I *can* use *you* as an excuse…"

When the evening ended, Ann and JJ exchanged hugs with Kurt and Mary before Jo got off the sofa, wrapped herself around JJ, and peck his cheek. "I'm sorry, JJ. Write me, OK?" When she embraced Ann on the way out, JJ thought he'd entered an unreal, twilight world.

Tuesday

"Morning, Cloud. See anything you like?"

"Morning, Johnny. Just Northwestern Highway." She stared out the bedroom window—ice in sheets clinging to the glass. The sun refused to peek out from behind the gray cloud deck, yet the day was bright. "Want to talk about what we're telling Carol?"

He breathed deeply, the suffused light making her look angelic in her long nightie. "Sure."

"What we *feel*…what we *think*…others in our same situation."

"Honey, if we want our *services* to listen…"

***

"First, your careers, achievements, and plans." Carol started, "then, your relationship: how it *started*, how it *grew*…" The breakfast crowd in the atrium was breaking up.

"The *important* thing, Carol," he interrupted, "is that we're *still* just *people*. Uncle Sam gives us everything we *need* to do our *jobs*, but he *doesn't* provide us with a lot of emotional nourishment. Changing lovers every time we change stations ain't an answer for everyone. We've *all* had short-term lovers and one-night stands, but it gets to a point where we don't *want* that anymore, and we don't *want* to quit the service, either."

Ann continued, "what *we* want is a chance to choose our life partners the same way as everyone else does, and just a *little* consideration as to how we *might* stay together."

"Not *quite* what my editor wants to see." Carol scribbled notes.

"We'll give you anything you need," Ann replied, "but Uncle Sam has spent *beaucoup* bucks getting us the training *and* experience we need to manage our jobs and people; we *know* that. But, there's *plenty* of mid-career people who have in-service lovers they're *not* supposed to have but that they'd *like* to keep. But they *also* know they're just Sixty-Day Wonders…"

"What's *that*," Carol perked up.

"Sixty-Day Wonders…" Ann started.

"Or Sixty-Day Janes; or Joes," he finished. "In-service lovers we could lose any time, and we *all* know it."

"How many, you think?" Carol asked.

"*Without* naming names," Ann mused, "at least *three* other couples that *we* know personally; that means, probably *scores* of them. Then there's the *other* thing: If I *wanted* children, I'd have two options: get out or get married. If my partner's a civilian he can tag along anywhere, but if he's *this* big ape here," she smiled, "*that* gets dicey because no one's figured out how two-service couples—let alone two-*different*-service couples *with children*— would work, and *that* issue's just over the horizon."

He shrugged. "If the military wants to keep its middle managers—us— to keep the machine running, it's going to have to make some adjustments as to how it treats us *off*-duty. *You* know the old saw: 'If *we want* you to have a wife/husband, we'll *issue* you one.'" He grinned sadly. "You *can't* put men and women together in the same outfits 24/7 and expect *that* to still work."

"*Or* be funny," Ann agreed. "Congress mandates gender equality— more all the time—but DOD just says 'gender equality, aye' without thinking what it *means*. They can't issue an emotional—or *hormonal*— shut-off switch for the thousands of young adults they need to add *all the time* to replace the old salts. To make their services work, they *also* need to mandate *relationship* equality with civilians."

"Relationship…equality…with…civilians," Carol scribbled. "OK, what about promotions? Would your relationship affect *that*?"

They talked until nearly noon, Carol scribbling all the while, before Ann and JJ realized they had another appointment to keep.

***

"Room 120," he told the Deglove Hospice desk clerk.

She called and smiled. "She's expecting you." He kissed Ann's forehead in the well-appointed lobby and walked down the well-lit, quiet, hospital-like hall lined with pastoral murals, thickly padded floors, and light wells between doors. The last time JJ was in *any* kind of a care facility was 1969, the last time he saw Gramma Burgess in a 16-bed Medicare-only room: it was *nothing* like this.

Dressed in a floral kaftan and jeans with her mane of thick and wiry DeHaven hair held under a kerchief, Clare waited outside her door. She smiled and embraced him, kissing him lightly on the lips. She barely came up to his chin, but her eyes…very much like Ann's, sparkled with her own fire.

"Ware, I want to say how sorry I am…" They sat on a loveseat in her 14x10 room, hand-in-hand.

"Stop." She smiled. "*You* didn't have anything to do with it. I knew I wasn't well when last I saw you, but I didn't know how bad I *was*." She looked away. "You're the only one still calls me *Ware*."

"I'll stop…"

"*Don't you dare.*"

"How do you *feel*?" An aide knocked on the door softly, asking if they wanted anything. Water for her, coffee for him.

"*Most* days, like today, I feel pretty good. *Some* days, I'm great. Some days—tired. I've been having more great days than tired." She gazed out the window at a stand of birch covered in ice, glistening in a shaft of sunlight.

"What are the doctors telling you?"

"Wait and see. We think the last round of chemo got it."

"Work?"

"I've got tenure, so the job's not a problem. Just 40% salary on long-term disability. I had to let everything else go—Karen picks up my mail at the apartment. *This* place…" She looked around. "My health insurance will cover up to two years here."

"Then what?"

"I either get better or—I've got another year to figure *that* out." She nudged him. "How about *you*? How's your back?"

"Aging. Karen says you…"

She kissed his hand. "Trust *me*, John. *Please*. I'm improving."

"You *look* good, like your *Modern Teen* cover…"

"Oh, God, I always *hated* that picture. Looks like I just came from the dentist, my face is all puffy." Her '72 magazine cover had her hair in a scarf, gazing—beautifully—with her dimpled grin, catching the fire of her eyes perfectly. It was *that* image of her that he always remembered.

She gazed out the window as he glanced around the cream-colored room at hand-drawn pictures from Karen's children; a poster board painting dotted with notes from her school adorned a closet door; a painting from Karen's easel brightened a dark corner; cards and pictures brightened every level surface. "Jenny Jacobs and Sarah Silverman say hi."

She giggled, a gratifying sound in that antiseptic place. "*God*, how'd you see *them*? How are *they*?"

"Fine. Jenny looked into a real estate matter for me. I just saw Sarah New Year's." He paused, squeezed her hand. "Why *didn't* your family want you to come with me?"

She sighed, squeezed back. "They would have been overjoyed." She made her stern listen-to-me face. "Sorry I misread them."

"Is there *anything* you need?" He kissed the side of her head.

"I need to know that my almost-would-have-been-forever-love is OK." She kissed his cheek and fingered his ring. "*Her*?"

"I *wrote*…"

"I *just* haven't had it in me to write back, Johnny; sorry. Does she know I used to wear your pants?"

"*She* wears them now."

She made her incredible face. "*No*."

"Yep. She doesn't have to roll the legs up like *you* did."

She squeezed. "She's taller?"

"Six feet one. She's out in the lobby."

"Of *course*, she is," as she laid her head on his shoulder. They were quiet for several minutes before she once again held his face in her hands, kissed him gently, and whispered, "I will *always* love you, Johnny. I *lied*."

"When?"

"When I said my family wouldn't approve of us…that *wasn't* the reason I didn't go: At that point I didn't *care*. It was because you were *still looking* for the girl in the window—the girl of your dreams you *kept* looking for in my eyes—and I *couldn't* take the chance that you'd *find* her someday and leave me alone."

I NEVER could have left you. "It's *OK*, Ware." *Not even for Cloud.*
But you make heartbreaking sense.

Smiling, Ann greeted her rival for his affections with trepidation, Clare insisted on sharing the loveseat with her as the three of them laughed about JJ's foibles and quirks…and he had a sudden *Deja-vu: It's what I saw before I hit the ground: the two women I love the most laughing together.* It was all he could do to keep from tearing up.

Clare suddenly turned serious. "John, can you excuse us for a few minutes. *Just* girl talk. Nothing *you* need to hear."

Puzzled, he left. Equally mystified, Ann waited before Clare spoke. "That New Year's was the *only* time *I've* ever seen him afraid of *anything* but his nightmares."

Of course, you know about Wolverine. "When I suffered a miscarriage back in October, he was willing to *say* it was his, even though it wasn't, because the *asshole* who…" She sighed. "Hard to beat *that* for raw guts."

"That's our Johnny: always ready to step into the shit to save someone." She sighed and smiled. "*I* can't be to *him* what *you've always* been: the girl of his dreams." She started crying; Ann stretched an arm around her. "Sorry," she sniffed. "Didn't expect to *do* that."

"It's OK. He makes *me* do that sometimes."

"He *can*, can't he?" Clare giggled; wiped her eyes. "If you didn't already know, John has the most generous heart of any man *ever*. I cried in bed with him practically naked, and he never…" She looked into Ann's eyes. "*I* had to grope *him*."

Rival? No; you were there for him when I wasn't, and he needed someone like you…or me. "Thank you for saving his heart." She kissed Clare's temple.

"His heart has *always* been yours, Ann. I just *borrowed* it for a while."

* * *

"Clare looks…" *How do I say "your old girlfriend I just met looks good?"*

"Yeah." *Emaciated.* "Thanks for being her friend."

"We have to share friends, too." *Even former lovers, as appropriate.* "I'm sorry about her illness."

She NEEDS to know. "Thanks, but," He smiled, sadly. "Before I say what I need to say, understand that I *love* you, truly, deeply, and forever. I *always* will. *You* were with me for all my punishment tours at Wolverine; every beating and humiliation. Then, Christmas '71: I was at the DeHaven's and I woke them up with a nightmare. She came to my room; held me in the dark; waited until I could sleep again. After that, I saw both of you in my *better* dreams. But Clare was *physically there* when you *weren't*, and she reminded me *so much* of *you*. She always *said* I'd find the girl of my dreams someday; she always *knew that* was *not* her…it was always *you*. Before September, you were my *other* brown-eyed girl; now,

289

you're my *only* brown-eyed girl."

Um... "Did she ever *say* that she loved you?"

"I *felt* it more than I heard it. She'd say 'I *love* you, buddy,' or some such, but she never came out with 'I love you, John." He inhaled deeply. "I had dreams about the *two* of you; *not* erotic…laughing together; made this morning feel like *Deja vu*. And those dreams made—*make*—me *so* happy. And I saw the *three* of you playing Ma's game just before I hit the ground."

"We were all three with you?"

"The three women I care most for, yes. I didn't *want* to die busted up on some Georgia sand pile; then you said 'you're *mine*, Johnny'…and I didn't." He gazed at her. "Believe me when I say that *you* are the *only* woman I want to spend my life with. Clare was…my *dream* of *you*."

She smiled. *NOW* "I believe you. *I* had a weird dream not long ago…saw a woman I *knew* was her…funny."

I keep dreaming of that red bathtub. "Huh. Think *Carol* got it this morning?"

"We'll know when we see the articles."

"What will the *Navy* make of those articles?"

"Same thing the *Army* will: confusion, slight panic, another commission to study the problem for another few years, nebulous changes in policy. What will *we* make of them?"

Friday

"Morning Johnny." They awoke to the gentle tapping of ice pellets on the window, warm and safe in each other's arms.

"Morning, Cloud. Can I say *once* more how much I love you?"

"*Absolute*ly," she smiled, straddling him, closing her eyes in utter joy.

***

"I have *Dad's* stature," Debbie chattered about her dress—her mother's re-cut by Donna's skilled hand—as they sat in the sauna at *Spa Nouveau Toi*, a tony establishment with valet parking in the heart of Birmingham that was *never* so *gauche* as to advertise: A tasteful, small sign on the building was all it needed because if you lived *there*, knowledge of *it* was part of your DNA.

"He was smaller?" Ann knew little of Debbie's background other than she moved into the neighborhood with her mother just before 3rd Grade.

"He barely came up to Mom's chin. I hardly ever saw him after 2nd Grade; the divorce was *so* mean." They *had* discussed a bachelorette party before Debbie declared she'd rather just get her hair done and relax.

"What do you *do* at the hospital, anyway?" Leigh poured water on the rocks.

"Physical therapy," Debbie replied. "Clinic and bedside. Keeps me fit."

"Not like karate would," Donna smiled.

"You *know* I tried that, Blondie; I lack the discipline. Preferred swimming."

"We're thankful for that," Ann murmured. "Best breast-stroke ever."

"State champs in '70," Debbie sighed. "Great medley squad."

"We were all rooting for you, Ann," Carol joined in.

"Indeed," sunny Annette Bell added. "Most *remarkable* swimming."

"*Oh*, how we applauded," Lizzie Ford, a tall and thin woman with reddish hair, added. "I did some swimming myself an age ago. *Nothing* like you girls, but…"

They talked and primped into the evening, and all the while Ann kept hearing Clare in her head: *his heart has always been yours.*

***

"Not sure if *we* ever met," JJ frowned. The Fox-Trot was a "gentleman's club" in Dearborn where the cabaret license allowed their dancers to take off more than was permitted in most other "clubs" in the suburbs.

"Probably not," spindly, brick-top George answered lightly. "I lived with Dad. Long and acrimonious divorce story I won't bore you with. I didn't see my sister between the time Mom moved out in '63 and when Dad died in '74." The scantily-clad not-all-*that*-young women on the dais were good-looking but not *that* attractive.

The private dance—on the stage, of course—for the groom was announced, and an attractive redhead affecting a Cossack costume with a stage name of Valentinovna appeared from behind the curtains. With Barry White's "My Everything" playing, she only had eyes—and smiles— for Bob. She strutted her *barely*-covered stuff as well, as *tastefully* and as *brazenly* as JJ had ever seen. *I've seen exotic dancers from here to Denmark, but this one's special.*

Later, as the guys were trooping out, JJ saw the redhead serving drinks behind the bar. Mike muttered something to her in Russian; she smiled widely and gave a reply as they left. "What was *that*," JJ wondered.

"I just told her that her talents were wasted slinging booze. She says dancing pays better but isn't as steady: she gets a lot for *her* act."

"I'll vouch for *that*," George sighed. "That *one song* cost me a hundred bucks."

"Lot more than she could *ever* get in a G-string…"

***

"If *we* ever get married, render me unconscious if I want to go to even *this* much effort."

"That's affirmative."

"And if you repeat *that* to anyone, I'll brain you."

"Check."

"Or if we *ever* get…married."

"That's affirm."

That's…yeah…affirmative.

***

"What did you tell your parents about your bunking out this weekend?" They listened to the night sounds of a hotel going to sleep.

"The truth: I got a room here to make the logistics of tomorrow easier and, well, the party *could* run late."

"You *didn't tell* them *I* was *staying* with you, *did* you?"

"Did *you* tell *Cathy?*"

"Mom *doesn't* think we're chaste."

"Pops doesn't, either; Mama doesn't *want* to think about it."

She reached for him in the dark. "Let's baptize these sheets, *zeeskeit*."

Saturday

"Morning, Cloud. You're beautiful like that." He watched her at the window in the clear and bright dawn sunlight.

"Morning, Johnny. I *feel* beautiful. Haircut; manicure; sauna to clean my skin. Feel like a *woman* again." She opened the curtains, gazing at the little woodlot dotted with the construction debris.

"You need *primping* to feel like a woman?"

"Sometimes. Storekeeper, welder, plumber… don't feel very *feminine*. But," she grinned, stripping off her nightie and his covers before climbing on top of him, "*this* feels better when I *feel* beautiful."

***

"*Hi*, Sandy," she purred into her pillow.

"Hi, *oytzer*," he breathed, flat on his back. "Happy now?"

"I *am*; *you* sure *acted* happy just now."

"I *was*; I *am*. *Always* happy to be with you."

"I can *see* that…and *often*. Swim before breakfast?"

"Just…let me catch my breath from *your last* workout."

***

"Just hope the furnace gets us through another winter." Pastor Lou Beckham—an older gentleman who JJ didn't know with wispy grey hair and a mottled, bulbous nose—glanced at the thermostat.

"If it's original to the building—1966," JJ murmured, "it's on its last legs. My grandmother donated it."

Pastor Lou regarded him curiously, studying his uniform with casually-practiced care. "Your *grandmother*?"

You served, somewhere. "You'll find her signature—Helen Burgess—on the church charter."

Pastor Lou smiled broadly and said nothing more.

The most memorable moment of the ceremony for JJ was Debbie's sudden, glowing joy when Pastor Lou loudly intoned: "I now pronounce you husband and wife." She was so radiant he doubted if she heard the "let no man put asunder" part.

***

A large floral arrangement was delivered to the reception. "So, they *do* care*," George mumbled, studying the card: *The Ford Family*.

"They, *who*," Bob asked, admiring the three-by-four-foot table decoration.

"I called Cousin Charlotte last Friday, told the receptionist that Deb was getting hitched. They made the connection."

"*What* connection," Debbie wondered.

"We're *cousins* to the firm, Deb," George looked to Annette, who nodded with a grin. "Dad was a sonofabitch to *everyone*, not just Mom, but they remember *us*, anyway."

After the glasses rang for the umpteenth time as the dishes were cleared—and Bob pecked Debbie again—Bob stood up. "My friends—old *and* new—we want to thank you all for coming on such short notice. And I want to thank Debbie for *finally* agreeing to do this. Thanks, honey: I'll get you that honeymoon soon."

"And of course," George rose, "we toast the happy couple: May your future be as bright as you feel today. Deb and Bob!"

Deb and Bob!

From time to time, JJ saw…*he looks familiar…that big guy in the white jacket.*

As a Central High classmate's three-piece combo played for Bob and Debbie, Ann muttered, "at least they can finish *one* dance," and explained to a tableful of Fords and Bells how Debbie and Bob met at Jim's wedding…and their quick exit to the cloakroom during their first dance.

"I *never* heard that version," Annette grinned. "Carol got married and suddenly Bob was sweet on a girl from another school *I* didn't meet for a year."

"Me neither," Liz smiled. "Deb went to a party with Ann and came back over-the-moon about a boy that I'd never *heard* of."

"No cloakroom here." JJ grinned mischievously, standing up. "Care to dance, my dear?" He held out his hand to Ann, formally.

"You *know* I can't dance, babe; New Year's notwithstanding."

"And you think I *can*?" They giggled their way through their *very first* dance together, to Joe Cocker's "Up Where We Belong."

"You're right: We *don't* dance, but it's an excuse to hold you in public."

"*Of course*, I'm right, and good thinking. Your jump boots…just keep them moving. Who are you looking for…or *at*?"

"Don't know; guy in a white uniform looks…familiar. Who's that guy in the suit over there, keeps looking at you?"

"Sid. An old friend; known him only a few years *less* than I've known you. He's watching *all* of us; he's in the security field."

The friends laughed and talked in the atrium long after the families left. Mike and JJ sang the rarely-heard bridge and third verse of "Rangers in the Night," crooning *nothing* like Sinatra:

Rangers in the night! We're out here scared and tired and
Waiting for the light! We need love too, but we're here!
Fighting for the right! Crawling out of sight!
Lonely, cold and hungry, dirty
We're still out here; doing our duty!

Never in the light! We're all alone here
Friends are out of sight! We had girls once, but no more!
Waiting just to fight! We're Rangers in the night!

And, once again, *sans* the "*scooby-dooby-do…*," blessedly.

***

"*That* could have happened with us. *They* were fifteen years apart, too." They were watching *The Natural* and she was suddenly struck by the "lady in white."

"You getting pregnant before I left home?"

"Yeah." *If you'd been at senior prom, I'd have given it up…but I would have lost that baby, too.*

"I dunno, honey. You may not have *liked* me then. I was pretty angry."

"Why?"

"Because I had to leave *Brookfield* and go *home*, only, Birch Lake didn't *feel* like 'home.' *You've* always felt *so* much like home."

She got up, tapped up the thermostat, and got into his bed. "Ask me again, babe."

He stared at the TV and clutched her shoulders. "*Please* marry me, Claudia."

And *what*, dear reader, do *you* think she said?

***

"JJ looks good; not as *haunted*."

"Yeah. You knew them both in school and never made the connection?"

"Nope. Blue-Eyes and I were never close *like that*, and Ann didn't talk about boys."

"She's a great gal."

"Really? You know this how?"

"We've *talked*; written a couple times; mostly about JJ..."

"Oh yeah? *Two-timing* me with my *friends*? The *kind* of *talk*...?" She grabbed him under the sheets.

"*No!* The *other* kind!"

Sunday

"My Adonis in the morning light," she awoke gently and moaned, stretching, luxuriating in the warmth of the bed and the sight of him standing at the window, naked in all his beat-up glory with the bright sun beaming through the sheer curtains.

"And Venus back at ya."

"How do *you* know," she swung out of bed. "I could have turned into a Medusa."

"If you *were* a Medusa, I'd already be doomed." He gloried in the feel of her arms around him. "Didn't *I* see you reading Bullfinch?"

"Uh-huh," she kissed his ear. "For my world literature class." They stood before the window, looking out on the small park behind the hotel through the half-frosted glass.

"Did you *mean* it, Claudia?"

"Yes, John. Just a question of when and how."

"Do we announce it?"

"Maybe. Let's see what the evening brings."

***

"Ya know," JJ announced as they entered Fox and Hounds from the courtyard, "I can't remember the *first* time I was here. But the last time...Karen's reception in October '79."

"I was here for Dad and Barbara's wedding on 30 July '75," Ann answered, glad that her dress slacks were effective against the biting cold.

JJ pulled Will's parka closer to him. "The day Hoffa went AWOL?"

"Yeah, stole all our thunder," Howard replied. "He disappeared from the Red Fox over on Telegraph and Maple. Didn't know anything about it until later."

Barbara mumbled, "I was here for a hospital function maybe three years ago." Like so much of the Detroit area, the place had seen better days. At one time it *had* been "where the elite meet to eat" (as the placard above the main dining room door read) in the northwest suburbs. That was *before* the riot of '67, the drug wars that followed, the STRESS squad and nearly two thousand homicides between '69 and '70—*before* Detroit's downward spiral began.

They sat around a table at the bar that overlooked the sunken main dining room with its aging red-and-gold wallpaper: clean but showing its age, though the sconce lights probably hadn't been polished in years. The whole place had an air of something out of the 1940s, which may have been the last time it was updated.

Charlie and Stella arrived just as the second round of drinks did. Sitting near the bar wasn't palatable to Charlie, so they moved to a table near the edge of the dining room, a quiet alcove out of traffic. Not that there was a great deal of that: even at the dinner hour on a Sunday, the dining room wasn't even a quarter-full.

"Well, *Johnny-cake*; how's your vacation been," Charlie asked just after the main course dishes were taken away. He hadn't said much for most of the meal. He *seemed* sober—he'd only had one highball—but JJ was wary. *Has the feel of a preacher at a stag party—out-of-place. And he did just use his favorite ranting nickname.*

"More relaxing than I had anticipated," JJ answered, the belittling *Johnny-cake* stinging—as Charlie meant it to. "Just being able to see you folks and old friends have been..."

"How *is* that place you're at?" Charlie interrupted anyone who wasn't uttering words of *his* interest: *he* wasn't *interested* in JJs well-being.

"Gorgeous, actually," Ann replied. "The room is comfortable, amenities are great, happy hour give us a chance to unwind..."

"Expensive, isn't it?" Charlie didn't even look at Ann, staring at JJ.

"Not *that* bad. We got a..."

"Howard," Charlie shifted his gaze without even a blink. "I have a *truck*-full of *Johnny-cake's* junk. I can arrange for it..."

"Charlie," Stella admonished him, "we can talk about *that* later."

"There *is* no *later*." Charlie glared at her, snapping out his words quickly. "*Don't* interrupt me." He turned his gaze to JJ. "Do you think I don't know what you're up to? The bank *told* me you *took* your mother's money. You'll be arrested and charged with theft if you don't return it tomorrow morning." His voice raised an octave. "Now, you *thief*. I said I'd come and eat. But you will *do* as I *say* or you will *go* to *jail*." He turned to Howard with steely hatred. "Forget it. I'm throwing that *trash* away. *Anything* that reminds me of this little bullshit artist gets pitched." He looked at JJ again. "Put that money back, or you will go to jail. Try to contact *us* again, and I'll *KILL YOU!*" With that, Charlie stood up from the table—loudly clattering the remaining glasses—shouted "come *on*," at Stella, and stomped away.

Barbara was stunned; Ann not *quite* as much; JJ disgusted; Howard showed a mixture of clinical interest and slight embarrassment.

But Stella *rolled* her *eyes…drummed* her *fingers* lightly…and *didn't budge*.

"*Stella,*" Charlie roared, halfway to the door, "we're *leaving*. Come *on!*"

She *didn't budge*, smiling slightly at Howard.

"*STELLA,*" Charlie screamed like an elderly Stanley in a bad nursing home production of *A Streetcar Named Desire*. "*GODDAMNIT NOW!*"

"*I* want to visit with my son and my friends." She calmly switched her gaze to Charlie as he stomped back to the table.

Charlie, vibrating with rage, pointed at JJ. "*THIS* bullshit little thief? I've paid *his* way since *before* his balls dropped. I've paid…"

"*No*, Charlie, *you* have *not. For the last time, YOU HAVE NOT!*" Stella's voice was barely above a whisper, but it was *that* look-here-you-dumbass whisper. "It was *Jake's* money." If she put her mind to it, Stella could have made lasting world peace with *that* whisper.

Estelle Rosalie Burgess Elrath Parkinson was neither a demonstrative nor an assertive woman—*most* of the time. *But*, on the rare occasions when she *was*, mountains crumbled, politicians became interested in public policy, seas parted, talk show hosts grew a conscience, planets spun out of orbit, and bullies great and small fell instantly silent.

JJ switched his gaze to Stella. "What's *that*, Mom?"

Howard nodded, smiling benignly. "*I've* been the trustee for Jake's estate. *I* set up that 17th Airborne Division Memorial Scholarship Fund as a blind. After we paid the mortgage on the house, paid off the cars and the business debts and settled with the IRS, there was still plenty left. It paid for Lois's and Brenda's college *and* their weddings, *and* for JJ's schools. *Jake's* money—JJ's *father—not* yours, Charlie. He gave *me* that responsibility because he knew…"

"He knew I'd just spend it all in the first month," Stella finished, blushing.

"You *lying BASTARD*," Charlie shouted at Howard. "*You…*"

And he charged us rent to live under our own roof? "Different light on much of *my* life," JJ muttered as he stood up.

"You just would have spent it on *yourself*, Charlie," Stella glared. "I knew *that* from the beginning. That's why I never *told* you about that. But *I* needed security, and *you* are *it*." She glanced at Howard. "I was *so* hurt,

Howard, the will…cut *me* out completely until the kids turned 21. I was desperate…finally called…But like you and he *both* said, the kids *had* to be taken care of."

JJ inhaled deeply, smiled bitterly and breathed, "*now*, Charlie, I believe *you* were *leaving?*"

"*YOU SONOFABITCH!*" Charlie roared at JJ and lunged forward, swinging a fist.

JJ caught the low-speed haymaker calmly, easily. "Now, *Charlie,*" he smiled, as he might to an errant child. "That's *quite* enough. *You* are neither frightening *or* impressive."

Charlie glared at JJ with savage malice, struggling to free his fist. "*YOU…!*" But suddenly, Charlie caught a glimpse of that solid, immovable part of JJ's soul that he *could not* frighten or bully; that part that was beaten and bullied and frozen and marched and isolated into him at Wolverine. "*You,*" Charlie hissed over and over, "*you…*" as he slowly lowered his fist.

"Now, Charlie, *calm down,*" JJ grinned without humor. "If *you* want to go, Charlie, *we'll* get Mom home. *Understand*, Charlie?"

Ann stared at JJ, his face an impassive-if-grinning mask. *I've seen livelier statues…*

Stella stood slowly, facing Charlie, speaking in her tone that could stop time itself. "*Charles,*" she intoned, straitening his tie, "*I'm* going to visit with *my friends* and *my son. They'll* bring me home. And *you DO choose to GET in your CAR* and *GO NOW…Charles. GO…NOW…CHARLES!*"

Without another word, grimace or gesture, Charlie straightened his coat and left. A long stillness followed as the world of the Fox and Hounds slowly reset itself to its staid Sunday-dinner-normal.

"Mom, you OK?"

Stella glanced at her son. "I'm fine, John. I'm just fine." She sighed, brushed back a stray lock of hair, and smiled at him. "I met a *fine* young man recently, John. I'd like to get to know him, if I may. So, Debbie Ford got married yesterday, Ann? Lovely little blonde girl, remember her well. I have a card…" She reached for her purse.

"She'll be *thrilled,* Stella," Ann grinned, surprised.

Suddenly more animated than JJ had seen her since his father was alive, Stella exploded with a torrent of words as if a dam had burst. "And your friend Jenny? I remember *her*; good that you get together with your old friends. Howard, I'm *so* sorry about Claudia. I want to see her sometime. Please, let me…Oh, let's have lunch, Barbara, Ann. Just us girls. My treat. You're still up here for another week, Ann? We need to…"

"Mom…Mom, *slow down,* OK? We can…"

"Stella, slow down, dear. Slow *down.*"

Stella stopped, glanced at Howard, sipped her water slowly, breathed deeply. "He's like an *albatross*, Howard: a *drunken albatross*. He's a good provider. John, I'm sorry that he *never* liked you. I *let* him keep you away. But I missed *so* much, seeing *you* become…this *fine* young man I see here."

"Mom, *please*," Ann murmured, a hand on her shoulder. "John and I have an announcement…"

When JJ and Ann took Stella home, Charlie's silhouette was in the living room window. He met Stella in the family room, stared wordlessly at them while they hugged Stella goodnight. He glared at JJ even as Stella informed him of his engagement to Ann, patted his arm and left the room.

***

"I'll have to send her a note, Johnny. Give me her address in the morning?" Debbie *was* thrilled that Stella remembered her at all, and was moved by the enclosed check.

"Sure. Just make it sooner than later, because they're moving."

"Tuesday. I'll make sure of it."

They said their goodbyes and went to their separate rooms: The Bells in the Honeymoon Suite up on the 5th Level; Ann and JJ to their own 2nd Level place after declining the Bell's offer to share their jacuzzi.

Weary, a few minutes later they were stripping off their more formal attire for sweats, as the closing credits rolled, why *Valley Girl* was ever made into a film, and pouring their champagne—a gift from the hotel staff, celebrating their engagement—into the supplied flutes.

"Waste of Cage's talent," Ann declared.

"I don't know," JJ protested. "The story…"

"…is barely *there*. *You* like the legs and cleavage."

"True, but…"

"Never mind: I'm going to bed."

They lay on their separate beds watching a dubbed French mystery film before JJ murmured, "I think Mom will be OK."

"I think you mom's *been* OK, babe. We'll sound her out at lunch Tuesday; Dad will call; your sister-in-law will look in. She'll be fine. And she wants to get to know *you*."

"So she says. I *need* to know her, too. But *no* comments on her cooking."

"No culinary criticism, aye." They were quiet for a few moments before she pulled her nightie off and slipped into his bed. "*Shh*. Just…*shh*." She nestled her head on his shoulder. "I'm *so* happy right now."

"Glad I could help." *Is this what happy feels like? Been so long…Did I see Herman…where did I… power of suggestion…gotta be.*

"I said *shh.*" After several minutes she stretched her arm across his chest. "Know why we're still together, future husband?"

"We were buddies first, everything else after, future wife."

"Correct."

"A friend will help dig a ditch."

"A buddy will help dig a grave."

What's that smell...gas?

Moments later they heard and *felt* a *WHOOSH* as a fireball burst into their suite.

Turn the page...to

The Safe Tree: Friendship Triumphs